"Einstein may have said something once about science and religion, but The X-Files *was able to show us what could not be said.* The X-Files and Philosophy *beautifully clarifies the issues of scientific knowledge and religious belief in a way that appreciates pop culture and it shows us important truths (no matter how Out There those truths are)."*

—CHRISTINE A. JAMES, Valdosta State University

"A huge part of the intrigue of The X-Files*—just as with life—involves grappling with our notions of what we know, what we believe, and how we come to such conclusions. The stories recounted in* The X-Files *tease these issues out like no other show in history and, now,* The X-Files and Philosophy *helps us to delve deeper."*

—JACK BOWEN, author of *If You Can Read This: The Philosophy of Bumper Stickers*

"Is the truth really *Out There? This conspiracy of X-philes would have you at least wanting to believe that answers to some millennia-old questions are still worth trying to decipher. Are the answers supernatural, scientific, spooky? Depends on how you ask the question and go about finding the answer, but there's some sage advice here for starting your own X-File investigation into whether science or faith is the way to go, what types of things exist, why we should fear some things and trust others, and how, even if we find the truth, we might have a hard time believing it."*

—JASON T. EBERL, Semler Endowed Chair for Medical Ethics, College of Osteopathic Medicine, Marian University

"There are persistent, unresolved mysteries that affect our daily lives, but these are often marginalized or even ignored. Luckily, there are those among us who dedicate their careers and talents to investigating such mysteries. No—not just special agents like Mulder and Scully, but the philosophers Robert Arp has rounded up for this volume. Any further similarities between the two groups have mostly to do with the fact that members of both typically have windowless offices."

—TUOMAS W. MANNINEN, Senior Lecturer in Philosophy, Arizona State University

"Millions of television viewers have been gripped by The X-Files, *many of them wanting to believe along with Mulder in the existence of conspiracy theories, paranormal activity, and monsters.* The X-Files and Philosophy *takes up in deft, engaging, and Scully-like fashion the epistemological, scientific, and ethical issues raised by this modern sci-fi classic."*

—CARRIE-ANN BIONDI, Associate Professor of Philosophy, Marymount Manhattan College

"The X-Files *trades in creature-features, conspiracy theories, and pan-governmental secrets.* The X-Files and Philosophy *brings us just what we've all been waiting for: new insights into the deeper lessons we can take from Mulder, Scully, Skinner, and the rest. Be careful, or you may find yourself rethinking everything."*

—RORY E. KRAFT, JR., Assistant Professor of Philosophy, York College of Pennsylvania

"Which one are you? You know what I mean. Are you a Scully or a Mulder? Or do you just have a single, favorite episode that struck 'Home' with its surreal, can't-pull-your-eyes-away-from-the-TV-screen storyline? In this collection of hard-hitting philosophical investigations, you'll find that it doesn't matter. What will matter is that you'll have to swear an oath to never, ever reveal the Truth about what you will soon learn. For you . . . The Truth won't be Out There anymore."

—JOHN V. KARAVITIS, CPA, MBA, and popular writer

"Once upon a time there was a guy with the improbable name of Fox Mulder. He started out life happily enough, as these things go. He and Dana Scully feared the possibilities, but they both looked for the truth. Here in your hands is the Truth itself, in a book that ranks right up there with getting a pony and learning how to braid your own hair."

—JOE STEIFF, Professor of Cinema Art and Science, Columbia College Chicago

"What is truth and why is it Out There? Is Scully or Mulder the real skeptic? You'll probably be left with more questions at the end than you had going in—but that's a familiar feeling for any X-Files *fan."*

—RONDA BOWEN, consultant ghost writer and truth finder

The X-Files and Philosophy

Popular Culture and Philosophy® Series Editor: George A. Reisch

Volume 1 *Seinfeld and Philosophy: A Book about Everything and Nothing* (2000)

Volume 2 *The Simpsons and Philosophy: The D'oh! of Homer* (2001)

Volume 3 *The Matrix and Philosophy: Welcome to the Desert of the Real* (2002)

Volume 4 *Buffy the Vampire Slayer and Philosophy: Fear and Trembling in Sunnydale* (2003)

Volume 9 *Harry Potter and Philosophy: If Aristotle Ran Hogwarts* (2004)

Volume 12 *Star Wars and Philosophy: More Powerful than You Can Possibly Imagine* (2005)

Volume 13 *Superheroes and Philosophy: Truth, Justice, and the Socratic Way* (2005)

Volume 17 *Bob Dylan and Philosophy: I'rs Alright Ma (I'm Only Thinking)* (2006)

Volume 19 *Monty Python and Philosophy: Nudge Nudge, Think Think!* (2006)

Volume 30 *Pink Floyd and Philosophy: Careful with that Axiom, Eugene!* (2007)

Volume 35 *Star Trek and Philosophy: The Wrath of Kant* (2008)

Volume 36 *The Legend of Zelda and Philosophy: I Link Therefore I Am* (2008)

Volume 42 *Supervillains and Philosophy: Sometimes Evil Is Its Own Reward* (2009)

Volume 45 *World of Warcraft and Philosophy: Wrath of the Philosopher King* (2009) Edited by Luke Cuddy and John Nordlinger

Volume 49 *Zombies, Vampires, and Philosophy: New Life for the Undead* (2010) Edited by Richard Greene and K. Silem Mohammad

Volume 51 *Soccer and Philosophy: Beautiful Thoughts on the Beautiful Game* (2010) Edited by Ted Richards

olume 53 *Martial Arts and Philosophy: Beating and Nothingness* (2010) Edited by Graham Priest and Damon Young

Volume 54 *The Onion and Philosophy: Fake News Story True, Alleges Indignant Area Professor* (2010) Edited by Sharon M. Kaye

Volume 55 *Doctor Who and Philosophy: Bigger on the Inside* (2010) Edited by Courtland Lewis and Paula Smithka

Volume 57 *Rush and Philosophy: Heart and Mind United* (2011) Edited by Jim Berti and Durrell Bowman

Volume 58 *Dexter and Philosophy: Mind over Spatter* (2011) Edited by Richard Greene, George A. Reisch, and Rachel Robison-Greene

Volume 60 *SpongeBob SquarePants and Philosophy: Soaking Up Secrets Under the Sea!* (2011) Edited by Joseph J. Foy

Volume 61 *Sherlock Holmes and Philosophy: The Footprints of a Gigantic Mind* (2011) Edited by Josef Steiff

Volume 64 *The Rolling Stones and Philosophy: It's Just a Thought Away* (2012) Edited by Luke Dick and George A. Reisch

Volume 67 *Breaking Bad and Philosophy: Badder Living through Chemistry* (2012) Edited by David R. Koepsell and Robert Arp

Volume 68 *The Walking Dead and Philosophy: Zombie Apocalypse Now* (2012) Edited by Wayne Yuen

Volume 69 *Curb Your Enthusiasm and Philosophy: Awaken the Social Assassin Within* (2012) Edited by Mark Ralkowski

Volume 71 *The Catcher in the Rye and Philosophy: A Book for Bastards, Morons, and Madmen* (2012) Edited by Keith Dromm and Heather Salter

Volume 73 *The Wire and Philosophy: This America, Man* (2013) Edited by David Bzdak, Joanna Crosby, and Seth Vannatta

Volume 74 *Planet of the Apes and Philosophy: Great Apes Think Alike* (2013) Edited by John Huss

Volume 75 *Psych and Philosophy: Some Dark Juju-Magumbo* (2013) Edited by Robert Arp

Volume 79 *Frankenstein and Philosophy: The Shocking Truth* (2013) Edited by Nicolas Michaud

Volume 80 *Ender's Game and Philosophy: Genocide Is Child's Play* (2013) Edited by D.E. Wittkower and Lucinda Rush

Volume 82 *Jurassic Park and Philosophy: The Truth Is Terrifying* (2014) Edited by Nicolas Michaud

Volume 83 *The Devil and Philosophy: The Nature of His Game* (2014) Edited by Robert Arp

Volume 85 *Homeland and Philosophy: For Your Minds Only* (2014) Edited by Robert Arp

Volume 87 *Adventure Time and Philosophy: The Handbook for Heroes* (2015) Edited by Nicolas Michaud

Volume 88 *Justified and Philosophy: Shoot First, Think Later* (2015) Edited by Rod Carveth and Robert Arp

Volume 89 *Steve Jobs and Philosophy: For Those Who Think Different* (2015) Edited by Shawn E. Klein

Volume 90 *Dracula and Philosophy: Dying to Know* (2015) Edited by Nicolas Michaud and Janelle Pötzsch

Volume 91 *It's Always Sunny and Philosophy: The Gang Gets Analyzed* (2015) Edited by Roger Hunt and Robert Arp

Volume 92 *Orange Is the New Black and Philosophy: Last Exit from Litchfield* (2015) Edited by Richard Greene and Rachel Robison-Greene

Volume 93 *More Doctor Who and Philosophy: Regeneration Time* (2015) Edited by Courtland Lewis and Paula Smithka

Volume 94 *Divergent and Philosophy: The Factions of Life* (2016) Edited by Courtland Lewis

Volume 95 *Downton Abbey and Philosophy: Thinking in That Manor* (2016) Edited by Adam Barkman and Robert Arp

Volume 96 *Hannibal Lecter and Philosophy: The Heart of the Matter* (2016) Edited by Joseph Westfall

Volume 97 *The Ultimate Walking Dead and Philosophy: Hungry for More* (2016) Edited by Wayne Yuen

Volume 98 *The Princess Bride and Philosophy: Inconceivable!* (2016) Edited by Richard Greene and Rachel Robison-Greene

Volume 99 *Louis C.K. and Philosophy: You Don't Get to Be Bored* (2016) Edited by Mark Ralkowski

Volume 100 *Batman, Superman, and Philosophy: Badass or Boyscout?* (2016) Edited by Nicolas Michaud

Volume 101 *Discworld and Philosophy: Reality Is Not What It Seems* (2016) Edited by Nicolas Michaud

Volume 102 *Orphan Black and Philosophy: Grand Theft DNA* (2016) Edited by Richard Greene and Rachel Robison-Greene

Volume 103 *David Bowie and Philosophy: Rebel Rebel* (2016) Edited by Theodore G. Ammon

Volume 104 *Red Rising and Philosophy: Break the Chains!* (2016) Edited by Courtland Lewis and Kevin McCain

Volume 105 *The Ultimate Game of Thrones and Philosophy: You Think or Die* (2017) Edited by Eric J. Silverman and Robert Arp

Volume 106 *Peanuts and Philosophy: You're a Wise Man, Charlie Brown!* (2017 Edited by Richard Greene and Rachel Robison-Greene

Volume 107 *Deadpool and Philosophy: My Common Sense Is Tingling* (2017) Edited by Nicolas Michaud

Volume 109 *The X-Files and Philosophy The Truth Is In Here* (2017) Edited by Robert Arp

In Preparation:

Hamilton and Philosophy: (2017) Edited by Aaron Rabinowitz and Robert Arp

Mr. Robot and Philosophy (2017) Edited by Richard Greene and Rachel Robison-Greene

The Man in the High Castle and Philosophy (2017) Edited by Bruce Krajewski and Joshua Heter

Jimi Hendrix and Philosophy (2017) Edited by Theodore G. Ammon

The Americans and Philosophy (2017) Edited by Robert Arp and Kevin Guilfoy

American Horror Story and Philosophy (2017) Edited by Richard Greene and Rachel Robison-Greene

Iron Man versus Captain America and Philosophy (2017) Edited by Nicolas Michaud

Stephen King's Dark Tower and Philosophy (2018) Edited by Nicolas Michaud and Jacob Thomas May

Amy Schumer and Philosophy (2018) Edited by Charlene Elsby and Rob Luzecky

Twin Peaks and Philosophy (2018) Edited by Richard Greene and Rachel Robison-Greene

For full details of all Popular Culture and Philosophy® books, visit www.opencourtbooks.com.

Popular Culture and Philosophy®

The X-Files and Philosophy

The Truth Is In Here

Edited by
ROBERT ARP

OPEN COURT
Chicago

Volume 108 in the series, Popular Culture and Philosophy®, edited by George A. Reisch

To find out more about Open Court books, visit our website at www.opencourtbooks.com.

Open Court Publishing Company is a division of Carus Publishing Company, dba Cricket Media.

First printing 2017

Printed and bound in the United States of America.

The X-Files and Philosophy: The Truth Is In Here

ISBN: 978-0-8126-9958-6

Library of Congress Control Number: 2016963350

This book is also available as an e-book.

Contents

X-Philes and X-Philosophy

The first episode I saw of *The X-Files* was "Home" from Season Four, and I was utterly mesmerized. It was the cleverest, coolest, and *creepiest* thing I had ever seen on Fox. I started renting older seasons on VHS (I know, I know . . . this was twenty years ago). I was in my first year of grad school at the time, studying for the PhD in philosophy, and after watching a dozen or so episodes, I remember thinking, "Wow. A show with a scientific skeptic who has to deal with a conspiracy theorist who believes in the existence of aliens and the paranormal." I was hooked. The Greek word φιλέω (*phileó*) means "love" or "affection" while σοφός (*sophos*) means "wisdom," so I'm not only a lover of wisdom as a philosopher, but I'm a lover of *The X-Files* as an X-Phile.

I thought it was funny when Mulder would put forward the obviously crazy hypothesis for some event or occurrence, and Scully would respond with some more common-sense, scientifically grounded explanation, *and it was Mulder who turned out to be right every time!* I remember reading somewhere that a scientific-oriented person enjoys science fiction, the paranormal, ghost stories, and magic precisely because these things appear to defy scientific explanation, and the scientific-oriented person wants to know what's *really* going on.

That's certainly true for me. *The X-Files* made me want to dig deeper and find explanations for UFOs, near-death experiences, crop circles, vampire stories, and the Abominable Snowman. I know that people can be gullible, or mistaken, or want to believe something that really isn't the case—myself included, at times—and that there are other people who take advantage of these gullible or simple-minded souls to sell souvenirs, or provide "therapy," comfort, or even closure for them. I found out that people believe some really strange and stupid stuff.

For example, remember that guy John Edward who had a show on the Sci-Fi Channel from 1999 to 2004 called *Crossing Over with John Edward*? He claimed to be a psychic who talked to the dead, but really what was going on was a combination of hot reading (he gathered information about some person, and that person didn't know that Edward knew the information) and cold reading (he used generalized questions, comments, and suggestions, read body language, and reinforced what a person said in a "fast-talking" way to make it look as if he was talking to the person's dead relative). He would stand in front of an audience and "communicate" with a dead person related to someone in the audience. He was a phlebotomist and dance instructor by profession and trade, for Christ's sake! There's a funny-as-hell SNL skit with Will Farrell playing Edward that you've got to see, the beginning of which goes something like this:

EDWARD: Welcome to *Crossing Over* . . . Okay. I'm sensing that someone over on this side of the room has a name that starts with an F.

FRAN: Oh. My name's Fran.

EDWARD: Hi Fran. Did you have someone who passed away recently?

FRAN: Yes, I did, but it was two years ago, really.

EDWARD: It was a man, right?

FRAN: No.

EDWARD: Okay. It was a woman, right?

FRAN: Why, yes! Wow! You're good!

EDWARD: Her name started with a J, right?

FRAN: No.

EDWARD: Okay. Her name had a J in it, right?

FRAN: No.

EDWARD: Okay. Her name started with an L, right?

FRAN: No.

EDWARD: An M?

FRAN: No.

EDWARD: Okay. It started with either T, B, C, or G.

FRAN: No, no, no, and no. It started with an S . . .

> **Edward:** [*interrupting*] It started with an S, right?
> **Fran:** Why, yes! You're amazing!

South Park lampooned Edward in the "The Biggest Douche in the Universe" from the sixth season—another must-see piece of television.

And you've heard of crop circles, right? Not only have we been able to simulate those in a few hours by stepping on crops with a few boards and rope—kind of like cross-country skiing—but we've actually interviewed several of the drunk guys who do this regularly in the middle of the night all over the world (Doug Bower and Dave Chorley being two of the most well-known pranksters from the late 1980s), and they have shown us how they do it with a few boards, some rope, a little geometric knowledge, and *lots* of liquor.

And check this out. *Coast to Coast AM with George Noory* is a radio program featuring topics in conspiracy theory and the paranormal that airs on XM satellite radio as well as on terrestrial radio stations in the middle of the night. On January 5th, 2016 the topic was cryptozoology, a pseudoscience concerned with the supposed existence of cryptids, mysterious and elusive creatures like Bigfoot, the Loch Ness Monster, and Chupacabra that have been or would be featured in a "Monster of the Week" *X-Files* episode. I happened to be listening for a few minutes, and a caller noted something like the following:

> That there is no hard evidence of these cryptids is baffling because they exist. There are too many accounts of these creatures for them not to exist. One of these days, someone will find a carcass. They have to.

There are a few things to note about this piece of poor reasoning. First, the caller seems to see the value of "hard evidence" and one can only assume that the carcass he mentions would be an instance of that evidence. Yet, he has not appealed to that hard evidence in order to justify the existence of cryptids. What he has appealed to, however, is known as one of the most unreliable forms of evidence: witness testimony. "There are too many accounts of these creatures for them not to exist," he claims. Crack open any law school textbook dealing with courtroom evidence and you will see references to hundreds of studies that have been performed in the last fifty years showing how people will claim to have witnessed events that did not occur or see objects that do not exist. There's even a phenomenon known as a *mass* or *collective hallucination* whereby *several* people claim to see something that really does not exist—like the Virgin Mary at places like the Zeitoun district of Cairo, Egypt, in the late 1960s or at Lourdes in France in 1858. What the caller has committed is a form of the informal fallacy known as *appeal to the people*, *appeal to the masses*, or in Latin *argumentum ad populum*, which looks like this:

Premise: Several people claim X is true, or is the case.

Conclusion: Therefore, X *is* true, or *is* the case.

The caller fallaciously concludes that cryptids exist because "There are too many accounts of these creatures for them not to exist," when what he really should do is suspend judgment until someone finds a carcass. (BTW, that suspension is going to be indefinite, because there ain't no such thing as a cryptid!)

Just about the time I was watching *The X-Files* in grad school, I started doing work in philosophy of science and philosophy of biology. As *philosophers*, we're all trained to be critical thinkers offering arguments complete with conclusions that actually follow from premises and premises that are supported by evidence that any rational person can come to see. As *philosophers of science*, we're all kind of in agreement with the basic methodology and truths of science, and we see places where philosophy can help clarify ideas in science.

One of the first things a philosopher of science learns is how to define science and demarcate it from other disciplines—this is called the *demarcation problem*. One obvious way science is distinct from all other disciplines has to do with the use of the scientific method of forming a hypothesis and testing it with publicly observable evidence over and over, if possible. We're all pretty much familiar with the scientific method, as it comes up in several of the science classes we take when we're kids.

Referring back to our crazy *Coast to Coast* caller, a carcass would be a good start as a piece of evidence, then one could hypothesize that some Bigfoot-ish, ape-like creatures inhabit a certain area. However, cryptozoologists *have* hypothesized the existence of Bigfoot-ish, ape-like creatures, but have never found authentic evidence of them—Big Footprints, for example, have been shown to be produced by casts. Besides, we discover new species of animals on a daily basis all over the world, so even if it turned out that there are Bigfoot-ish, ape-like creatures in communities hanging out in the woods, there certainly wouldn't be anything spooky, supernatural, or other-worldly about it. Also, it's likely that the furry walking creature that's lumbering along in the famous Patterson-Gimlin video is just some dude dressed up to look like Sasquatch.

In fact, almost all of the classic pictures and videos of cryptids either 1. have perfectly rational, common-sense explanations—what looked like the Loch Ness Monster across the lake from a distance really was a small boat creating a wake, for example—or 2. have images of things that have been fabricated by some prankster—again, the guy who made a plastic dinosaur-looking head, propped it up on a small toy submarine in Loch Ness, and took a famous picture of it in the late 1930s (Christian Spurling) came forward eventually to reveal the hoax in 1993 just before he died.

I guess that I completely agree with Doggett when he claims in the episode "Invocation" from Season Eight: "You know, these words—'anomalous,' 'supernatural,' 'paranormal'—they propound to explain something by not explaining it. That's lazy!" Scientific research and explanation requires hard work, but the payoff is worth it. Relatively rare medical conditions like porphyria (which causes skin lesions, especially when exposed to sunlight), hypertrichosis (which causes excessive hair growth all over your body), sleeping sickness (which causes violent convulsions, lesions, and eventually a coma-like state), and necrosis (cell death that often manifests itself in black patches on the skin) that are reported in the scientific community, for example, do a sensible job of explaining the origin of folklore concerning "monsters" such as vampires, werewolves, and zombies.

So far here, I've been doing a bit of critical thinking about cryptids, werewolves, vampires, and other legendary creatures, and you'll find more philosophizing about such beings—as well as the demarcation problem—in the pages of this book. There are numerous philosophical themes that arise when you consider the entire body of *X-Files* stories. In other words, there's a lot of X-Philosophy to *The X-Files*. "Biogenesis" is concerned with the universe in eternal flux, "Providence" ponders purpose, and "Essence" speculates about the definition and nature of life, while "Ghost in the Machine" and "Jose Chung's *From Outer Space*" consider what counts as conscious existence and experience. The philosophical topic of freedom versus determinism is the focus of "Clyde Bruckman's Final Repose"—speaking of which, consider the depth of Skinner's claim from the Season Six episode "S.R. 819":

> Every minute of every day we choose. Who we are. Who we forgive. Who we defend and protect. To choose a side or to walk the line. To play the middle. To straddle the fence between what is and what should be. This was the course I chose. Trying to find the delicate balance of interests that can never exist. Choosing by not choosing.

But there's much more X-Philosophy, if you're an X-Phile: the major dilemma in "Wetwired" is whether we're justified in killing an innocent person being used as a tool of harm; "Lazarus" and "One Breath" ask us to think seriously about near-death experiences; "Miracle Man" and "Humbug" present issues surrounding magical or incredible acts and the charlatans who exploit such supposed feats; "Gender Bender" takes on the hot-button topic of queer theory as well as the social pressures concerning identity and sexuality; "Fearful Symmetry" ventures into the philosophical realm of environmental ethics; "Eve" hits the controversy of cloning; heck, there's even an episode titled "Empedocles" which is aptly named after the fifth-century B.C.E. Greek philosopher (one of the very first philosophers in the history of Western philosophy, actually) who posited the forces of Love and Strife at work in a universe fundamentally composed of earth, air, fire, and water.

You'll find many of the above topics discussed as you continue to read.

Besides the nature of science, what counts as evidence, and the kinds of critical reflection that should occur when we're confronted with anything that smacks of the paranormal or supernatural, in this book there are serious discussions of the slogans I WANT TO BELIEVE and THE TRUTH IS OUT THERE. Can the desire for something to be true—the "want" to believe—actually make it true for someone? And what is truth anyway? Should we have "faith" in things non-scientific along the lines of the musing mystic Mulder? Or do we have a moral obligation to be skeptical scientists, like Scully?

I really do think we have a moral obligation to be skeptical scientists. Otherwise, we'll continue to think that *Monster Hunters*, *Ghost Hunters*, and *Ancient Aliens* feature really existing beings and legitimate science. Or, we'll continue to push teaching children the useless idea that some god created living things essentially as they appear to us today, and that species have not necessarily evolved by natural selection. Or, we'll continue to listen to idiot stars pontificate fallaciously about how vaccinations cause autism and that the entire body of psychiatry is unfounded. Or, like the poor souls who listen to *Coast to Coast* religiously, we may actually start to believe that we were abducted by aliens, the US Government has been fluoridating the water since the 1950s as part of a New World Order plot to pacify people, or that we met Chupacabra when we went to Peru to see Machu Picchu.

The X-Files is great story-telling. And there are some great philosophical topics found in and through those stories. Read this book; it contains well-written chapters put together by some really sharp folks. I love *The X-Files*! But it's *just* story-telling, people! In the real world, Spooky Mulder is very, very rarely right. But, I do love fantasizing that he *is* right and imagining what it would be like to meet Flukeman, The Great Mutato, or the Chinga doll—of course, any introduction would have to occur à la Hannibal Lecter in *The Silence of the Lambs* with these beings inside of a cell and me safely on the outside . . .

I

Mulder or Scully?

1
Why Scully Is Usually Wrong

STEVEN B. COWAN

We learn in the first episode of *The X-Files* ("Pilot") that FBI agents Fox Mulder and Dana Scully take very different stances toward the strange phenomena they investigate. The two have barely met when the following exchange takes place:

> **MULDER:** In most of my work, the laws of physics rarely seem to apply.
>
> **SCULLY:** What I find fantastic is any notion that there are any answers beyond the realm of science. The answers are there. You just have to know where to look.

Later in the same episode, when they are driving down a lonely road, the car engine suddenly stops and they are blinded by a flash of light. Afterward, though it seems that only a few seconds have passed, Mulder's watch tells them that over nine minutes have passed. He suggests they may have been abducted by aliens. Scully exclaims, "There's got to be an explanation! . . . Time can't just disappear. It's a universal invariant." To which Mulder replies sarcastically, "Not in this zip code."

Fans know that Scully's search for a scientific answer to the bizarre events that take place in each episode almost always fails. Most episodes follow a typical pattern. Something weird happens such as when Lauren Kyte's recently deceased boss, Harold Graves, seems to be responsible for several murders ("Shadows"). Mulder then offers some paranormal explanation. In this case, he believes that the murderer *is* Harold Graves—that is, his ghost! Scully, though, interjects a scientific explanation: Graves must have fabricated his death. "There's no such thing as ghosts or psychokinesis," she declares. However, Scully is almost invariably proven wrong. In this case, DNA evidence shows that Graves is truly dead and the viewers of the show are given unmistakable proof that Graves's ghost is the culprit.

Why is Scully usually wrong? What's the point the writers of *The X-Files* are making in continually debunking her scientific explanations in favor of Mulder's paranormal theories?

There's Got to Be an Explanation!

This, we could say, is Scully's motto. Why? What underlies her insistence that science is where we should look for answers? One plausible possibility is that Scully represents a widely-held view called *scientism*. This is the view that science (especially hard sciences like physics and chemistry) is the only or best source of knowledge. Other disciplines (such as philosophy, theology, history, psychology, and certainly things like astrology and UFOlogy) are merely sources of opinion. If other disciplines ever do provide us with knowledge, according to scientism, it's only when their conclusions are consistent with what science tells us.

That Scully may be an advocate of scientism is indicated in the quote from the pilot episode mentioned earlier: "What I find fantastic is any notion that there are any answers beyond the realm of science." Another indication is her blatant statements about the impossibility of supernatural explanations. For example, "Time can't just disappear" ("Pilot"); and "There's no such thing as ghosts or psychokinesis" ("Shadows").

Or take the case in which Mulder and Scully travel to Montana to investigate the killing of Joseph Goodensnake ("Shapes"). The man who shot him swears that he fired upon a ferocious animal. Leading up to the spot where Goodensnake's body lay, they discover a trail of footprints that are at first human but then change into an animal-like form. What's more, Goodensnake's canine teeth are especially elongated and he has a scar on his body from what looks like an attack by a wild animal. Mulder, of course, suspects that Goodensnake was a werewolf. But Scully exclaims, "No one can physically change into an animal!"

Perhaps the best evidence of Scully's scientism occurs at the end of "End Game." An alien bounty hunter has been sent to eliminate a race of alien-human hybrids created by the US government. When Mulder tracks the bounty hunter to an ice-bound US Navy submarine, Mulder is exposed to the alien's toxic blood that contains a retrovirus. Mulder is able to survive because extreme cold suppresses and eventually kills the retrovirus. Scully later finds him and is able to keep his body temperature low long enough to cure him. In her official report of the case, she narrates,

> Several aspect of this case remain unexplained, suggesting the possibility of paranormal phenomena. But I am convinced that to accept such conclusions is to abandon all hope of understanding the scientific events behind them. Many of the things I have seen have challenged my faith and my belief in an ordered universe. But this uncertainty has only strengthened my need to know, to understand, to apply reason to those things which seem to defy it. It was science that isolated the retrovirus Agent Mulder was exposed to, and science that allowed us to understand its behavior, and ultimately it was science that saved Agent Mulder's life.

Viewers of the show know that Scully's confidence in science is misplaced. In the fictional universe of *The X-Files*, there really are ghosts, werewolves, and alien bounty hunters. On the assumption that Scully is a scientism-ist, we may plausibly see the entire series, in part, as a critique of the notion that empirical science is the only source of knowledge. It may be that there are other sources of knowledge that put us in touch with realities that scientists as such cannot know.

The Truth Is Out There

In the world of *The X-Files*, there are many sources of knowledge besides science: astrology, faith, clairvoyance, intuition, even tea leaves. These sources are taken seriously even if how they work is mysterious. Clyde Bruckman, the clairvoyant, knows where the body of a murder victim is ("Clyde Bruckman's Final Repose"). Mulder asks how he knows this. Bruckman replies, "How should I know? . . . I just know."

Probably all of the alleged sources of knowledge featured in *The X-Files* are controversial. Yet what should not be controversial is that science is not the only source of knowledge. The reason is that scientism is self-defeating.

A viewpoint or statement is self-defeating when it contradicts itself. Take the statement, "I can't speak a word of English." The statement is proven false in the very uttering of it. Likewise, take the thesis of scientism: "Science is the only source of knowledge." This is clearly not a statement of science. Rather, it is a philosophical statement about science. Which means that, if scientism were true, we could not know that this statement is true!

Moreover, the practice of science presupposes knowledge from non-scientific sources. For example, science presupposes the existence of a world external to the human mind. It also presupposes the uniformity and orderliness of nature. It assumes the importance of honesty in reporting the results of scientific experiments. None of these things can be proven scientifically. And yet most of us, including scientists, think we are justified in believing them.

All of this tells us that there is truth to be found in other sources of knowledge than science.

The Only Scientific Explanation . . .

If Scully is not a scientismist, then she's certainly an advocate of *methodological naturalism*. This is a view not about potential sources of knowledge, but about the nature of science itself. The methodological naturalist insists that science must be conducted in a certain way. Specifically, in looking for causal explanations of phenomena, science by definition can only appeal to natural causes. In other words, according to methodological naturalism, a *scientific* explanation is a *natural* explanation. If someone theorizes that the cause of some phenomenon is a non-natural entity, as Mulder often does, then that person is not doing science.

Scully's methodological naturalism is explicit in "D.P.O." When Jack Hammond, a pizza delivery driver in Connerville, Oklahoma is found dead in his car, most indications are that he was struck by lightning. Agent Scully is inclined to concur but is mystified by the lack of any lightning contact points on the body as well as by the statistical improbability of this explanation. There are only about sixty lightning deaths in the US in any given year, but Jack's would be the fifth in Connerville in recent days. Given these anomalies, Scully expects that Mulder will propose some paranormal explanation. Surprisingly, he denies that he's reached any conclusions of that sort. But he admits, "I just don't think it's lightning." Frustrated, Scully responds, despite the anomalies, "The only possible scientific conclusion is that Jack Hammond was killed by lightning." Ghosts and aliens may be possible explanations for Jack's death, but only the lightning explanation would be a scientific one.

Her methodological naturalism surfaces also in her attempts to debunk Mulder's paranormal theories. On one occasion, Scully is enlisted by her former instructor and lover, Jack Willis, to help him apprehend a bank robber named Warren Dupre ("Lazarus"). Cornered by the agents, Dupre shoots Willis and he, in turn, is shot and killed by Scully. While EMTs work to save Willis's life, Dupre's corpse reacts to the jolts from the defibulators used on Willis. When "Willis" wakes up later in the hospital, it is Dupre's consciousness that inhabits his body. It doesn't take long for Mulder to notice "Willis's" subsequent out-of-character behavior and figure out what has happened.

Scully, however, thinks that "Willis's" odd behavior can be explained psychologically as due to the stress and trauma he's recently undergone. She declares, "I believe it's a long way from saying Jack's had a Near Death Experience to saying his body's been inhabited by Warren Dupre." But as evidence mounts that something is just not right with Willis, Mulder performs an experiment. It so happens that Willis and Scully have the same birthday. Given their past relationship, he'd be expected to know that. Yet Mulder gets Willis to sign a birthday card for Scully even though her (their) birthday is months away. Mulder confronts Scully:

MULDER: I'm not sure Willis is Willis. Can you at least accept the possibility that during his Near Death Experience some kind of psychic transference occurred?

SCULLY: Can't you accept the possibility that this isn't an X-File? . . . Just because someone forgets a birthday doesn't mean he's been possessed.

In the episode "E.B.E.," we see one of the most telling, and humorous, exchanges between Mulder and Scully. Soon after a night in which multiple UFO sightings are made near Reagan, Tennessee, the agents investigate the site where a weary truck driver reported having a "close encounter."

Scully: From the trucker's description, the shape he fired upon could conceivably have been a mountain lion."

Mulder: Conceivably.

Scully: The National Weather Service reported atmospheric conditions in this area that were possibly conducive to lightning.

Mulder: Possibly.

Scully: It is feasible the truck was struck by lightning, creating the electrical failure.

Mulder: It's feasible.

Scully: You know, there is a marsh over there. Those lights the driver saw may have been swamp gas.

Mulder: Swamp gas? . . . How could a dozen witnesses including a squad of police vehicles in three counties become hysterical over swamp gas? I've investigated multiple sightings before. . . . None had this much supporting evidence. Anecdotal data, exhaust residue, radiation levels five times the norm.

Scully: None of that evidence is conclusive. . . . Isn't it more plausible that an exhausted truck driver became swept up in the hysteria and fired upon hallucinations?

A tense conversation in "Born Again" concerning, by Mulder's reckoning, a case of reincarnation, sums up Scully's stance toward the paranormal. Mulder asks her, "Why is it so hard for you to believe even when all the evidence suggests extraordinary phenomena?" Scully gives a response that would be typical of a methodological naturalist: "Because sometimes looking for extreme possibilities makes you blind to the probable explanation right in front of you." The methodological naturalist (and the scientismist, too) insists on a natural explanation even when one is not available.

All of this suggests that *The X-Files* is partly aimed at undermining methodological naturalism. We may see this more clearly when we shift our focus from Scully to Mulder.

I Want to Believe

Fox Mulder is neither a scientismist nor a methodological naturalist. Concerning the latter, he would not necessarily see what he does, the investigations he makes, the conclusions he reaches, as *un*scientific. Rather, he would see himself as simply following the evidence where it leads. Scully, of course, would want to see herself that way too. What makes the difference between them then?

The difference is that Mulder is open to a wider range of possible explanations for the phenomena they investigate. For him, paranormal explanations can sometimes count as good *scientific* explanations. He has, therefore, what we may call an "open" philosophy of science. Scully, however, has a "closed" philosophy of science. Being a methodological naturalist, she limits the range of good scientific explanations to natural ones.

The problem with methodological naturalism is precisely what *The X-Files* continually shows us in its fictional universe. In that world, ghosts, aliens, demons, and God actually exist. Scully is usually wrong because she has adopted a scientific method that rules out such things and thus prevents her from finding the truth.

This is not to say that she's wrong to look for natural explanations. Even Mulder looks for natural explanations. Natural explanations are more common and generally more likely. Scully's mistake is in adopting a method that rules out everything but natural explanations. It's a method tailor-made in her universe to prevent her from discovering the truth on those occasions when the right explanation is *not* a natural one.

The lesson for us is clear. *What if* ghosts, aliens, demons, or God actually exist in our world, the real world? And what if, as in *The X-Files*, they sometimes left traces of their existence that we could observe? How could we know whether or not this is the case? Which philosophy of science—Scully's closed methodology or Mulder's open one—would be more appropriate for us to adopt? Which one would truly allow us to follow the evidence wherever it leads? The answer should be obvious.

Someone may object and insist that we should nevertheless follow methodological naturalism and limit science to natural explanations. The reason, they might say, is "because ghosts, werewolves, aliens, demons, and God don't exist! Nature (and natural causes) are all there is. So, our scientific methodology need not consider such possibilities." But this objection is circular. It assumes what it needs to prove, namely that supernatural or paranormal entities don't exist. But how can that be proved if we adopt a method that rules out such beings before any investigation even begins?

I Have Seen Things

Scully is usually wrong because she adheres to scientism or methodological naturalism or both. Yet, as fans of the show are aware, Scully's skepticism toward the paranormal wanes as the series progresses. By the eighth season, when Mulder is missing and Agent John Doggett takes his place, it is Scully who often proposes supernatural explanations and leads Doggett to the truth. Soon after they meet, Scully tells the skeptical Doggett:

> I have seen things that I cannot explain. I have observed phenomena that I cannot deny, and . . . as a scientist . . . it is a badge of honor not to dismiss these things because someone thinks they're BS. ("Within")

Scully eventually came around to Mulder's point of view because she experienced too many things that she could not explain naturally. Science is a real source of knowledge. And science usually finds natural explanations for phenomena because natural explanations are most often the right ones. But Mulder and Scully teach us that we should be open to other possibilities.

2
Trust No One . . . But Yourself

KYLE A. HAMMONDS

The two protagonists of *The X-Files* series seem to be characterized by certain defining qualities: one is a "skeptic" and the other a "believer." This is in the context of the characters deciding whether they believe in extraterrestrial aliens.

As the show proceeds, it pretty clearly takes a side on the whole skeptic-believer thing—the showrunners pretty clearly establish that aliens exist and the philosophy of skepticism is just kind of a bummer in the *X-Files* universe. Despite offering definitive answers about extraterrestrial beings in the context of the show, though, the journey of the characters and their struggles with belief bring up some quintessential questions on the nature of faith, reason, and persuasion that apply beyond the show.

Trust No One

The Pilot episode for *The X-Files* finds FBI agent Dana Scully being sent by bureau superiors to assess the validity of a special project that is being pursued by another agent. This project—the titular X-Files—is managed by an agent named Fox Mulder, who uses the project to investigate unexplained phenomena that are out of the bureau mainstream.

Upon their first meeting, Scully and Mulder experience a philosophical conflict that will define their relationship: a sharp difference in how each of them interprets case evidence. While Mulder is open to accepting anecdotal evidence and open to unconventional explanations of perplexing case findings, Scully—relying on her background as a medical doctor—will only accept answers that are scientifically viable.

"What I find fantastic," Scully remarks in the Pilot, "Is any notion that there are answers beyond the realm of science." And surely many of us experience the same sort of conflict in everyday life! Though we humans live in the same world, we are often divided over our explanations of experience and interpretations of what is reasonable. Matters of politics or religion are clear instances of human division stemming from dissimilar interpretations of similar evidence. Scully and Mulder's conflict is therefore an example of a tension that many of us live with: How can two people examine the same information and interpret it differently? And further, can commonly cited evidence such as anecdotes really be considered *reliable* evidence in making a case for the reasonability of our interpretations?

Examining *X-Files* characters with narrative theory holds insightful potential for understanding how similarly reasonable people, such as Scully and Mulder, may each interpret evidence differently while still both having good reasons for their conclusions. Ultimately, through the lens of narrative, it's clear that Scully and Mulder's unique life experiences frame the way they interpret information within the context of certain personal values. Both agents are subject to narrative structures (such as Scully's medical training or Mulder's memory of his sister's apparent alien abduction) that enable and constrain their individual worldviews in different ways.

Scully and Mulder's Narrative Reasoning

One way to find the truth out there on our topic is to look to rhetorician Walter R. Fisher and his philosophy of "good reasons." While Fisher's writing on rhetoric was largely completed well before *The X-Files* was begun, his work offers much insight into the common conflict that Scully and Mulder often exemplify: traditional rationality versus other means of knowing. By traditional rationality or, in Fisher's terms, the *rational-world paradigm*, Fisher meant a point of view that supposes all reasoning is based on deductive thinking. The sort of truth that was the concern of early empirical thinkers. These thinkers, whom some trace back as far as Aristotle, were primarily interested in verifying evidence using the senses. Such evidence, in this line of thought, should be repeatable and testable.

In Aristotle's view of rhetoric (in simplest form: the art of persuasion), rationality is key to verifying evidence. The rational argument known as the syllogism, employed by Aristotle and adopted by many later empiricists, requires deductive reasoning. To use an *X-Files* themed version of a classic, simple example: Scully is human and humans are mortal; therefore, Scully is mortal.

Scully and her scientific mind would readily uphold the conclusion that she is mortal because she and others may observe that she is of the human species and that no human has ever been recorded to live forever. Scully explains her experiences from the perspective of this rational-world paradigm. Those using this rational-world paradigm, such as Scully, argue that if a conclusion doesn't add up when using deductive reasoning, it is invalid.

Recognizing the prominence of the rational-world paradigm, Fisher explicitly wondered how so many seemingly reasonable people could disagree so profusely about how to understand the world around them. He wondered whether one camp was necessarily more reasonable than the other . . . or whether these groups were even really mutually exclusive. Fisher, among other rhetoricians, acknowledged that no matter what position someone takes on a subject, they usually follow some line of rationality—they use some form of logic. The difference, according to Fisher, is that the rational-world paradigm emphasizes rationality alone, while sometimes overlooking a primary role of experience: framing—what we learn from our past influences how we interpret the present and think about the future.

Accordingly, Fisher proposed a *narrative paradigm*—a point of view suggesting that experience is selected and arranged in memory (or "plotted") and that all human communication, also being selected and arranged, might be considered a part of narrative. The innovation of Fisher's paradigm proposal in 1984 was that all stories are guided by certain values in addition to following rationality. To Fisher, the combined elements of rationality and values (learned from previous life stories) account for differing interpretive standards among reasonable individuals.

He called a story's ability to make rational sense in the context of our experiences *coherence* and described how well a story fits within our value systems as *fidelity*. Specifically for Scully and Mulder, different backgrounds framed how they would interpret case evidence, each perceiving varying degrees of coherence and fidelity in explanations of case evidence. Fisher's theory is a particularly good fit when considering Scully and Mulder because it is grounded in principles of experience and story-telling—the elements of casework that our favorite FBI agents seem to disagree on.

Scully as Traditional Rhetorician

Setting up the dichotomy of the show in terms of narrative requires exploring how Scully and Mulder may each be emblematic of potentially opposing viewpoints. During their first joint work on a case, Scully and Mulder meet an array of seemingly fantastic occurrences. When the agents visit the site of a murder they have been assigned to investigate, they experience interference with their electronic devices, sudden changes in magnetic fields, and mysterious "loss of time" or memory loss ("Pilot").

Mulder immediately pairs these incidents with information from literature he had read on extra-terrestrial presences. Scully, however, reasons that she wants "the truth" and that "there has got to be an explanation" for the unlikely phenomena experienced by the agents. Scully's desire for *the* truth indicates her belief in a single, correct understanding of the events. Further, in order for Scully to believe that an understanding may qualify as being correct, it must conform to a certain type of explanation. Even though she calls for *an* explanation, she clearly—at least initially—rejects outright any explanations that do not match her understanding of truth, which, in her case, is scientific truth.

Scully is the epitome of a traditional rhetorician: a figure who strongly appeals to the rational logics usually associated with Western thinkers. At the end of the Pilot, Scully clearly reveals her strong adherence to the rational-world paradigm when she reports to her agency superiors that "Agent Mulder *believes* we are not alone." Scully, conversely, refuses to draw conclusions in her report on the case that has been investigated.

This seems to indicate that her conclusion is that the case is indeed *inconclusive* specifically due to the lack of available empirical evidence for her to examine. Mulder's conclusion that extra-terrestrials had been involved in the case is based on eye-witness accounts and oral reports: anecdotal evidence. Mulder's assertions are chalked up to mere beliefs, which can't be verified under Scully's rational-world point of view.

Mulder and Phenomenology

While agent Mulder certainly accepts the positive uses of medical science and its underlying philosophies, he also finds that science has limits. During the Pilot, Scully is asked by FBI administrators to describe what she knows about agent Mulder. She notes that Mulder's reputation is such that he is regarded as "the best analytical mind in the Bureau." He's also an Oxford-educated psychologist. While Mulder does not have the exact same scientific background as Scully, he is also no stranger to empirical methods and deductive reasoning. In defending himself to his partner, he admits, "I'm not crazy, Scully. I have the same doubts you do" ("Pilot").

But if Mulder is as skeptical as Scully of supernatural explanations for the phenomena he experiences in the field, why is he also so open to nontraditional conclusions regarding his work? Mulder, at least in part, falls into what is called a phenomenological point of view: he is interested in how the world is *experienced* . . . and some experiences have difficulty being explained using scientific reasoning.

Mulder himself had an experience that he has no scientific explanation for: he witnessed the abduction of his sister by extraterrestrial alien beings. According to Scully, Mulder's interest in unconventional cases and strange conclusions about these cases—no doubt brought on by his witnessing of an alien abduction—earned him the nickname "Spooky Mulder" in the FBI academy ("Pilot"). Also, according to Scully, Mulder's quirky interests have paid off in the past as he famously caught a dangerous criminal using his research on serial killers and the occult. Unconventional studies and unconventional thinking became an unexpected virtue for the FBI.

But was Mulder's success an outcome of luck or a result of his eccentric methods? Fisher's proposed narrative paradigm gives Mulder more credit than Scully does, by framing his valuing of ephemeral, untestable data as constituting a sort of reasoning. While the validity of this sort of reasoning is dependent on the values of the person evaluating Mulder, it may be worthwhile to remember that Mulder's interpretations often turn out to be reliable. The persuasive power of story–based evidence is not arbitrary.

Experience and Narrative

The show's major tagline—"I want to believe"—is apt for how Fisher describes the reasoning process. We reach conclusions based on whether something makes sense to us, whether that sense refers to our logics, our values, or both. Consider again how Scully and Mulder drew conclusions about their case at the end of the Pilot episode. Both agents, directly or through stories, experienced strange things: electrical disruptions, loss of time, and a wheel-chair-bound girl jumping up and running, to name a few.

Scully's experiences prior to working on the case established her scientific values. Even with the disruption of what her previous experiences would have led her to expect, Scully did not abandon her values because such stories wouldn't have "coherence." Therefore, she simply re-evaluated the evidence using logics conforming to her world view. Likewise, Mulder, perhaps overzealously desiring to uncover evidence of the supernatural, relies on his beliefs about extra-terrestrial involvement in his sister's abduction to cause him to consider unconventional explanations of case evidence. Further, he often refuses to ignore such considerations, whether they seem likely (under anyone's worldview) or not.

At this point, it may seem as if the narrative of the show positions Mulder as being an obviously more open-minded agent because of his willingness to accept more types of evidence than Scully. However, the through-line narrative of the *X-Files* is more complicated than that.

The camera reveals fantastic things to the audience—things that are sometimes not even known to the characters. While this may seem, on the surface, to confirm that the show advocates for Mulder's point of view, there is more to be considered. These direct audience revelations place viewers in the center of the conflict: providing story-based "evidence" to the audience in the vein of Mulder's worldview. However, this evidence is recorded and re-watchable, allowing the audience to ever confirm their suspicions about the fantastic events of the show, in the vein of Scully's point of view. Neither worldview is necessarily affirmed or denied in any meta-narrative sense.

Making Connections

Mulder best reveals his reasoning process when he proclaims, "We're trying to find a connection" ("Pilot"). This indicates that a connection has yet to be found. So the statement is future oriented: Mulder wishes to link future action or explanations to previous experiences. He wants to structure the past in such a way as to make sense of the present and predict the future. Patterns, predictability, and confidence in our ability to pursue goals is what makes us, as humans, willing and able to act. The value of narrative consciousness, then, seems at least two-fold: narrative provides a way to be reflexive about decision-making in the present and also a way to select reasonable and comfortable future goals or "plots."

To connect all the information from our own case: Fisher suggests ways to explain *how* Scully and Mulder examine similar evidence yet arrive at different conclusions, and *why* each, individually, has "good reasons" for his or her beliefs. While Scully has the historical weight of traditional rationality on her side, Mulder's unconventional belief in extra-terrestrial forces based on anecdotal evidence and stories may be considered reasonable—perhaps even reliable—when examined through the lens of Fisher's theory.

Fisher does not propose to provide a mechanism for uncovering "truth" when two value systems come into conflict. In fact, it is likely that he would find the very notion of more or less correct value systems to be a contradiction—values are necessarily subjective. How one might argue for the truthfulness of fact-based evidences is for other projects.

Fisher simply and profoundly reminds us that no individual or single value system has a monopoly on "good reasons." With lessons from Fisher in mind, it is clear that Scully and Mulder each operationalize a world view that is based on faith.

The truth is not only "out there" for each character, but also within, "in here."[1]

---

[1] I am incredibly grateful to Jay Allison and Karen Anderson-Lain for their feedback on this chapter.

3
Scientist versus Pseudoscientist

DANIEL MALLOY

Mulder and Scully: the believer and the skeptic. Only Mulder isn't a believer and Scully isn't a skeptic.

Mulder isn't a believer precisely because he wants to believe. If he were a believer, he wouldn't want to believe—he would believe. There's no sense in wanting what you already have.

And Scully isn't especially skeptical. On the one hand, she isn't a skeptic because she plainly believes it's possible to know things. Skeptics, at least philosophical skeptics, doubt whether we can know anything at all. On the other hand, in the course of her work with Mulder, Scully comes to believe some extraordinary things based on evidence that would not satisfy most popular skeptics and debunkers.

It's closer to the truth if we say that Scully is a scientist and Mulder is a pseudoscientist. The difference between them largely consists in what sort of evidence they'll accept to support a theory. Scully usually demands the sort of evidence we would call scientific: evidence that we can observe, test, and repeat as we need to. Mulder, on the other hand, is often satisfied with citing some combination of speculation, coincidence, rumors, and myths to support his theories.

Let's look at the justifications offered by Mulder and Scully for accepting or rejecting particular theories. This is really a way of thinking about one of the core problems in the philosophy of science: the demarcation problem. How can we tell the difference between science and non-science, or, more specifically, between science and pseudoscience?

You Can't Prove It's Not True

One of the mantras of pseudoscientists like Mulder brings us to one of the essential problems with pseudoscience, according to philosopher Karl Popper (1902–1994). The mantra is "you can't prove it's not true." Mulder may not say that as often as "Trust no one" or "The truth is out there" or "I want to believe," but it's still prevalent in his arsenal of catchphrases. According to pseudoscientists the world over, the inability to test a theory serves as evidence for that theory. Science, however, doesn't work that way. An untestable theory is not a theory.

A list of the explanations "Spooky" Mulder offers for various cases reads like a *Who's Who* of pseudoscience. Mulder is open to absolutely everything, from parapsychology and cryptozoology to astrology and alchemy to demonology and witchcraft. And that's not mentioning his pet theory of alien abduction. Some think that this kind of willingness to believe is a sign of open-mindedness. They're wrong. To be open-minded means to be willing to accept evidence before deciding whether to believe a particular thesis. "Spooky" Mulder is too eager to believe to be open-minded.

And, like a lot of people who want to believe, Mulder tends to overlook or dismiss or explain away contrary evidence. One answer to the demarcation problem identifies this trait as the essence of non-scientific, and particularly pseudoscientific, thinking. Proposed by Popper, the criterion of falsifiability holds that in order for a theory to be scientific, it must be falsifiable. That doesn't mean it needs to be false. It means that any scientific theory has to lay out the conditions that would render it false.

A theory that cannot possibly be proven false—an unfalsifiable theory—is not scientific. It is not scientific precisely because it explains too much. According to Popper, any scientific theory must generate predictions. Those predictions can either prove correct or not. If the predictions are so vague that whatever happens can be interpreted as confirming the prediction, then the prediction wasn't falsifiable, and hence the theory that generated it isn't scientific.

To take a classic example, consider the "predictions" generated by astrology. In "Syzygy," Mulder and Scully encounter a pair of teenage girls who are supposedly granted supernatural powers, including telekinesis, by a rare planetary alignment. Madame Zirinka tells the agents about this alignment, and how it will focus "all the energy of the cosmos" on anyone born on January 12th, 1979. Her other predictions are even less helpful and informative, "Things are going to fall out of the sky, disaster lies await" and "Relationships are going to suck." Look at these predictions in turn: "Things are going to fall out of the sky" could refer to almost anything, from rain to leaves to planet-killing comets. What things? Where? When? "Disaster lies await" is basically always true—any event, even achieving your lifelong dream, can be a disaster.

And finally, "Relationships are going to suck." Which relationships? Hell, I'd be satisfied with a *kind* of relationship: romantic? familial? friendly? collegial? Are my pets going to turn against me? And how are these unnamed relationships going to suck? Will there be fights, or some sort of distance or coldness, or miscommunications, or well-meaning but wrong-headed gestures? With so many kinds of relationships, and so many ways for them to suck, there's no way that Madame Zirinka's predictions won't come true. So they, and the astrological "hypotheses" they're based on, are unfalsifiable, and therefore unscientific.

The Absence of Evidence and the Evidence of Absence

It's commonly pointed out that Scully spends nine seasons and two movies repeating the same line: "There has to be an explanation for all of this." Frustratingly for those who sympathize with Scully, it seems that the more outlandish Mulder's theories are, the more likely they are to turn out to be true. Be it a theory about human mutations that resemble sharks ("Hungry"), or enable them to hibernate for decades at a time ("Squeeze"), or theories involving the existence of such supernatural entities as demons, succubi, and incubi (various, including "Avatar" and "Terms of Endearment"), all of Mulder's pseudoscientific speculations seem to be verified.

The important term here is "seems." Because one of the interesting wrinkles of Popper's falsification theory is that if it's correct, even a truly scientific theory can never be verified. The best we can say is that it hasn't been falsified—yet. In response to the pseudoscientist's mantra that "You can't prove it's not true," Popper replies that, in fact, we can't prove that any theory is true. All we can say is that it hasn't been proven false yet.

But when we do prove a theory false, as we have with many pseudoscientific theories including just about everything Mulder believes, we should just discard it, right? Let's move on to the next theory so we can make some progress! But that isn't how scientists actually operate. Scientists don't come up with a theory, test it, and if the test fails, abandon it. If an experiment yields negative results, then most often scientists adjust the theory in light of the results, rather than abandon it outright.

For example, when astronomers first observed Uranus in 1781, using existing models of gravity, they made predictions about its orbit around the sun. Those predictions, as it turned out, were wrong. Astronomers did not give up the theory of gravity, but instead developed new theories to explain the anomaly. Among those theories was the existence of an as-yet-undiscovered planet beyond Uranus, whose gravitational pull would cause the oddities in Uranus's orbit. That theory was proven correct when Neptune was discovered in 1846.

This example points to another difficulty for Popper. Popper's model of science is based on scientific investigations that take place in laboratories. That model of science involves designing experiments to test specific theories, or specific parts of theories. But much science does not take place in laboratories, and the kind of experiments Popper has in mind are impossible for many field sciences. Geologists, for example, can use computer models of volcanoes and faults to test their theories, but only actual eruptions and earthquakes can either confirm or falsify geological theories.

Normal and Revolutionary Science in the Bermuda Triangle

One of the core problems with Popper's view is that it identifies science with specific experiments—as though theorizing were not also part of science, or science was done in isolation from any broader context. In response to this weakness, philosophers and historians of science have offered solutions to the demarcation problem that encompass broader views of what science is, and what distinguishes it from pseudoscience.

Of these attempts at a broader criterion of demarcation, the most influential has been the approach proposed by Thomas S. Kuhn (1922–1996). In his *The Structure of Scientific Revolutions*, Kuhn argues that science is a collective, historical, and evolving endeavor. In the history of science, the institution repeatedly goes through two sorts of phases: phases of "normal science" punctuated by phases of "revolutionary science."

During all its phases, the purpose of science remains constant: to discover the truth about the world around us and how it works. The difference between the normal and revolutionary phases is in terms of what Kuhn calls "paradigms." Paradigms are frameworks for science: they establish what scientific problems are and how to go about solving them.

In normal science, the ruling paradigm is not challenged. Science is a kind of puzzle solving, attempting to resolve problems or refine answers within the paradigm. Revolutionary science occurs when a paradigm reaches a crisis point—that is, a point where the puzzles created by the paradigm can no longer be solved using the tools made available by that paradigm. During these revolutionary phases, scientists search for new paradigms. Once a new paradigm has been discovered and achieved sufficient acceptance, normal science resumes under this new paradigm.

For example, Newton's theory of gravity was the paradigm for astronomy and physics for about two centuries. During those two centuries many previously unsolvable (and unthinkable) puzzles were raised and answered. However, some problems arose that Newtonian physics couldn't resolve. Most famously, the planet Mercury doesn't behave the way it should according to Newtonian physics.

As with Uranus, there are anomalies in Mercury's orbit around the sun. And, as with Uranus, some proposed that these anomalies could be explained by the presence of an as-yet-unobserved planet, this one closer to the sun than Mercury. This postulated planet was dubbed Vulcan, but it was never found. Then, in the early twentieth century, the theory of relativity was proposed as a replacement for Newton's theories. Einstein's work successfully predicted all the same things that Newton's did, only with greater accuracy, and was able to resolve puzzles that Newtonian physics couldn't resolve—such as the anomalies in Mercury's orbit.

Or consider the case of mysterious disappearances at sea. Under one paradigm, it was thought that certain parts of the ocean were cursed by gods or inhabited by monsters, and that that caused ships to be lost. The so-called Bermuda Triangle was one such supposedly cursed place. Hence the importance of Mulder's location in "Triangle." He's boarded the reappeared Queen Anne, thought lost since 1939 in the Triangle. It's thought to have been destroyed by a German U-Boat, but Mulder and the Lone Gunmen know better: it was in the Triangle, so nothing as mundane as a torpedo will do to explain its disappearance.

This is all based on the idea that an exceptional number of ships disappear in the Bermuda Triangle. The problem is that that is simply not the case. Since the days of gods and monsters of the sea, a new paradigm has been introduced to the study of shipwrecks, one which includes context and statistics. It turns out that a ship is no more or less likely to go down in the Bermuda Triangle than it is anywhere else—it's just more likely that a ship will be in the Triangle than in many other parts of the ocean. The waters of the "Bermuda Triangle" are well-trafficked shipping lanes. A ship going down there is no more surprising than a car crashing on a busy highway.

The Crisis of Pseudoscience

If science is a collective enterprise that operates under these two modes, what is pseudoscience? Kuhn's theory does not provide a single answer. Broadly, we can say that pseudoscience is any supposedly scientific endeavor that falls outside of the current paradigm, but that's an inadequate response. In times of crisis, new paradigms are proposed. These proposals are part of science, but by definition they fall outside of the current paradigm.

On the other hand, we might say that pseudoscience is any supposedly scientific endeavor that still pursues a research program that was abandoned along with the paradigm that birthed it. Thus, pseudoscience is a kind of relic of an earlier paradigm. Prominent examples of pseudoscience certainly match this model: astrology and alchemy were, at one point, normal science. Then their respective paradigms shifted, and astrologers and alchemists were faced with the choice between adopting the new paradigms and becoming astronomers and chemists, respectively, or maintaining the old paradigms.

Unfortunately, not all pseudosciences fit this mold. While some pseudosciences are the still lingering ghosts of old paradigms, others are firmly based on misunderstandings of the current paradigm. For example, one current pseudoscientific theory is called "quantum consciousness." Espoused by self-help guru Deepak Chopra, the theory of "quantum consciousness" relies on widespread misunderstandings of certain aspects of quantum mechanics (the science of subatomic particles) to defend a particular spiritual view of the world and our place in it. There is no question that this and a variety of other "New Age" beliefs are pseudoscientific. At the same time, however, they are pseudoscience based on the current paradigm.

Or consider the idea of "genetic memory," espoused by Mulder in "Aubrey." In this episode, B.J. Morrow is, unbeknownst to her, the granddaughter of serial killer Harry Cokely. When she gets pregnant, her grandfather's memories surface, and she begins carrying out murders similar to his. Now, the idea of genetic memory is controversial to begin with, but even its supporters don't propose that memories of specific actions or events can be passed down genetically. Neither DNA nor the brain work like that. But, there's no doubt that this piece of pseudoscience is based in the present paradigm.

Unlike Popper's clear, bright line between science and pseudoscience, Kuhn's criteria establishes, at best, a shifting line between what is scientific and what is not. To illustrate, consider astrology again. According to Popper, astrology has always been, and is by its very nature, pseudoscience. By Kuhn's theory, on the other hand, astrology was at one point scientific and then, without any change in what astrology was, it suddenly wasn't science anymore.

So, Popper's definition of science is too narrow, in that it discounts endeavors that are plainly scientific, and Kuhn's definition is too broad, in that it is unable to discount endeavors that are plainly pseudoscientific.

Is the Truth Out There?

In light of the failures of Popper and Kuhn, as well as others who have tackled the demarcation problem, some have advocated abandoning the problem altogether. This abandonment takes many forms, but the most prominent comes from philosopher Paul Feyerabend (1924–1994). Strictly speaking, Feyerabend doesn't so much abandon the demarcation problem as attack its very basis. Feyerabend argues that the distinction between science and forms of non-science, including pseudoscience, is an artificial and unsustainable attempt to privilege certain forms of knowledge above others.

Feyerabend's approach, however, goes a step too far. While we sometimes elevate scientific knowledge above other forms of knowledge, the criticism falls apart when we examine its defense of pseudoscience closely. While there are certainly non-scientific ways of knowing and types of knowledge, those subjects classified as pseudoscience are not among them. Part of the problem with pseudoscience is precisely that it pretends to knowledge to which it has no claim.

Pseudoscience typically fails not only as science, but also as knowledge by fostering demonstrably false or highly improbable beliefs and (what's worse) actively dissuading people from seeking out the truth. Mulder is the chief example of this: his desire to find extraordinary and supernatural explanations for events often leads to a refusal to accept straightforward, mundane explanations, regardless of the evidence supporting them.

Rather that join Feyerabend's anarchistic attack on science, a better route is to acknowledge that science itself is not epistemically unified. That is, while we may treat science as a single, institutional whole, it is actually a family of more or less related disciplines. Each discipline, while aiming at truth, has its own distinct subject matter, methods, and standards. What qualifies as evidence in biology or zoology, for instance, would be far too shaky to support a conclusion in physics or mathematics. The methods employed to study the physics of subatomic particles are vastly separated from those used to investigate the processes of biological evolution.

So, instead of a single, do-or-die criterion like Popper's, or the loose, moving boundary advocated by Kuhn, perhaps a better approach would be to put forward what philosophers call a family resemblance concept of science. A family resemblance concept, as introduced by philosopher Ludwig Wittgenstein (1889–1951), acknowledges that some of our concepts encompass things that are loosely related to one another, in spite of the seeming impossibility of offering hard-and-fast rules about what is or is not an example of this concept.

It works like this: instead of coming up with a single criterion, or a set of criteria for what is or is not science, we acknowledge that there are certain traits that many (though not all) sciences share. Physics and chemistry, for instance, depend on experiments that can be conducted in laboratories under strictly controlled conditions. Geology and ecology depend on meticulous observations in the field. Psychology, sociology, and biology all depend on sophisticated statistical models. None of these traits is shared by all sciences, but with a bit of effort, we can come up with a list of characteristics that are common enough among various sciences to say that if a discipline lacks all of them, or if a discipline rejects them, it is not science.

Consider the established science of zoology and the closely related pseudoscience of cryptozoology. Cryptozoology is the "study" of cryptids, or animals alleged to exist in rumor, myth, and folklore. Mulder drags Scully along on hunts for such creatures in "The Jersey Devil" and "Quagmire." In both cases, Mulder, like a true cryptozoologist, is relying on evidence that isn't evidence—usually anecdotes from supposed witnesses. Scully, meanwhile, insists on proper evidence. If there is a giant dinosaur-like creature living in Heuvelmans Lake in Georgia, there should be physical evidence: prints, tracks, leavings, and carcasses. For the zoologist, the existence of "Big Blue" is easy to dismiss, because of the evidence that should be there but isn't. Unless Big Blue is immortal—itself an easily dismissed idea—there would have to be a breeding population of lake-dwelling, dinosaur-like creatures. In the face of the nothingness where there should be evidence, the zoologist concludes the creature doesn't exist.

Which is not to say that cryptozoologists don't occasionally get one right. A number of creatures formerly considered cryptids have been discovered to exist—including okapi, mountain gorillas, and komodo dragons. The point is not that the cryptozoologist isn't occasionally correct; the point is that the cryptozoologist is just guessing, and often cherry-picking anecdotal evidence to support his guess. Cryptozoology is a pseudoscience because it rejects the standards of evidence, and the types of evidence, that many sciences, including those to which it is closely related (zoology) accept.

Prophecies and Predictions

The aim of sciences of every variety is to better understand the world we live in. Such understanding can help us figure out our place in the world and, sometimes, how to improve it. Pseudosciences often have the same aim, but unfortunately due to the sloppy and often wishful thinking involved in them, they undermine themselves.

You need look no further than Fox Mulder to see how this happens: a once promising young FBI agent, Mulder's obsessions with all things pseudoscientific ended with him on the run—and almost no convictions (seriously, did Mulder and Scully ever actually arrest anyone?).

4
Science and the Fantastic

MARC W. COLE

MULDER: When convention and science offer us no answers, might we not finally turn to the fantastic as a plausibility?

SCULLY: . . . What I find fantastic is any notion there are answers beyond the realm of science. The answers are there. You just have to know where to look.

—"Pilot"

One of the central (and most beloved) subthemes in all of the show's numerous subplots is the distinction between "science" and the "fantastic." It's part of what makes the show so watchable. But I think Mulder and Scully get the distinction between science and the fantastic wrong.

One of the things *The X-Files* does so well is to blend the two: for example, cryogenics—a "proper" science—was responsible for the freezing of the head of Dr. Arthur Grable in the episode "Roland." What was "fantastic" was the level of control Arthur had over his brother Roland. Thus, you have the perfectly "ordinary" scientific process of freezing heads with the psychic ability of controlling brothers' actions (at least sometimes).

Psychic abilities are outside the norms and conventions of mainstream science, sure. But are they fantastic? Why not simply unusual? Scully and Mulder imply the mainstream is scientific. But perhaps they should say that the divide is between the nature of consciousness and will on the "fantastic" side, and, on the scientific side, phenomena that obey laws of nature, even if some laws are really weird. Let's take a look.

The Realm of Science

What should be included in the "realm of science? Stuff that fundamental physics deals with is safely in the realm of science. Also the show treats most of the special sciences, such as geology, meteorology, chemistry, and biology as "proper" sciences. Let's acknowledge that fundamental physics and the special sciences belong in Scully's "realm of science." These sciences differ wildly in terms of subject matter. For example biology is a whole different ball of wax than fundamental physics; a human cell, say, is a very different object of study than a quark. So what do all the sciences share that permit each of them to hold citizenship in the realm of science?

Each of them, in varying degrees, relies heavily on observation and experiment. Observation is obvious: if I want to know what's going down in a cell, I should look at it. Possibly compare observations with others in journals. Experiment is a bit more tricky to nail down. Ideally, experiments are controlled, and can be repeated in any lab, anywhere. It's tricky to nail down because each science employs different kinds of experiments. At any rate, experiments and observation aim at general knowledge of the observed.

Wherever water is observed it's a sure bet you'll find the chemical compound H_2O. Through experimentation, we know that adding baking soda to vinegar results in an unstable carbonic acid. Often, both observation and experiment are employed. For instance, a great deal of observation and experiment, has not revealed any exceptions to the laws of thermodynamics (leaving aside debates in quantum mechanics).

Scully tells Mulder that the answers are in the realm of science, but one just has to know where to look. In other words, observation, experiment, and what is already known from these will give us the tools to figure out what's "really" going on—either the tools to launch a scientific investigation or the tools to demonstrate a falsehood or hoax.

Mulder says that if science and convention fail us, we can look to the fantastic as a plausibility. This is a really strange claim. For one thing, if the realm of science has not *yet* found a way to explain something, it doesn't follow that they won't eventually, using the same methods as usual. No, if Mulder's claim is to be taken at face value, then the "fantastic" is a realm with objects of enquiry that cannot undergo the treatments of experiment and observation, or be subjected to the discovered body of knowledge derived from them. Mulder, in effect, introduces the realm of the fantastic (though he accepts Scully's false distinction).

The Realm of the Fantastic

The X-Files traditionally divides the realm of the fantastic into three categories: *the alien*, *the supernatural*, and *the monstrous*.

With regard to the alien, I refer to both Extraterrestrial Biological Entities (EBEs; see what I did there?) as well as their technologies. In the episode "Deep Throat," there's a scene where Mulder is watching for UFOs over a secret military installation. Eventually, balls of light are seen dancing erratically and with great speed over the darkened landscape. The speed, sharp angles, and extreme acceleration clearly defy *known* laws of physics. On the other side of this coin, intelligent EBEs themselves are generally thought to be exceedingly unlikely and *The X-Files* introduces two distinct alien races at war, with humanity caught in the middle. But unlikely does not necessarily mean beyond the sciences. Presumably, if there were such entities, they could be studied using the usual methods of biology and chemistry.

The X-Files also dabbles in the supernatural, for example in "Shadows." The spirit of Lauren Kyte's boss, Howard Graves, is avidly protecting her from dangerous people as well as trying to explain that he did not commit suicide. He was murdered. In one eerie scene a terrified Lauren is awoken by ghostly sounds in her bathroom. As she walks down the hall, we hear a man's voice, presumably Graves, pleading silently for his life to unknown assailants. Upon entering the bathroom, there is the macabre and uncanny sight of blood running swiftly out of invisible wrists, coloring the bathwater a rich, rich crimson. This also is an event that would indeed seem beyond what is known about the laws of the world learned through experiment and observation.

Finally, there is the monstrous. There's a wide variety of the monstrous: the failed experiments of the alien-human hybrid experiments (and also the alien-human hybrid of the Chupacabra from the episode "El Mundo Gira"); the "natural" mutants such as Guy Mann in "Mulder and Scully Meet the Were-Monster"; finally, there are the monstrous beings that are a mix between the natural mutants, and supernatural ones. For example, the lycanthropes in the episode "Shapes" or the zombies in "Millenium" . . . or vampires ("Bad Blood"). Natural mutants are not outside the realm of biology and can be studied in terms of biology, identifying and observing what has occurred at the cellular level as well as the bodily changes. This is also true of the alien-human hybrids, failed and successful, as well as the Chupacabra. (That episode applies an *X-Files* alien twist to the Mexican creature of folklore.) However, the lycanthropes from "Shapes" and "Tooms" are different. It does seem that their identity does feature supernatural properties, perhaps beyond the scope of what is known via the sciences.

Let's bring these points together. According to Mulder, the realm of the fantastic is beyond the reach of the realm of science on the following grounds. Certain alien technologies are beyond the scope of physics because they violate known laws of physics. From the supernatural element of the fantastic, we have phenomena that seemingly defy known laws of everything: just how can blood already spilt, spill again, into a bathtub from wrists that are non-corporeal? And finally, from some versions of the monstrous, such as "Tooms," we have unexplainable beings insofar as they are also somewhat supernatural.

Naturalizing the Fantastic

But those events are beyond observation and experiment. True, stuff like blood from incorporeal wrists, voodoo, and flying crafts that defy the known laws of physics are extremely rare events. Well, rare from the perspectives of most of us. I imagine such crafts are a commonplace thing among those aliens. Also, such phenomena are really, really weird. So between such things being really weird and exceptionally rare, we just say they don't exist, or aren't scientific, or involve superstition.

For Western civilization, there is also a historical bias against the supernatural. This bias goes back arguably about five hundred years, but it really took off with Hume, Kant, and the rise of empiricism. A favorite target of these thinkers and this movement was the supernatural, both in the religious sense and the ghostly-witchcraft-y sense. The combined effect of relative rarity, strangeness, and cultural bias leads us to the basement office of the FBI, where Mulder and Scully exchanged those words. What Mulder and Scully both miss is that observation and experimentation fail less often than the norms and conventions in science. Scientists don't "normally" or "conventionally" inquire into invisible bleeding wrists, say. But observation and experiment could help us get a handle on unusual phenomena, at least partially.

Let's provisionally offer green cards to the alien, monstrous, and ghostly citizens of Mulder and Scully's fantastic realm. These green cards shall at least temporally allow them to live in the realm of science. These green cards are provisional; if they do not do their part in this realm, they'll get deported straight back to the fantastic! (Notice the cultural bias I am assuming: inside the heart of each citizen of the fantastic is a citizen of science just waiting to be released . . . or some such bullshit.)

As to the alien, alien bodies easily fall neatly within the realms of at least biology and chemistry. What of crafts that defy the known laws of physics? Everything rests on the "known" laws. In the *X-Files* universe, these crafts are a thing. They causally interact with the observable universe. Moreover, whatever they are doing, whatever engine systems they possess, clearly some kind of laws were harnessed and systematized. Should we interpret them as quantum mechanical laws? I don't know. The point is that there is another "level" of physics at work. And the shadow government spends a lot of resources trying to reverse engineer it. So it looks like both elements of the alien can be offered permanent residence in the realm of science.

What of the monstrous? As I showed in the last section, many parts of the monstrous would fit comfortably in the realm of biology. For example, consider the curious case of Leonard Betts. Since there's nothing to indicate he is a supernatural entity, then all that would be required is to get him under the microscope, so to speak, and observe what's going on. In fact, this is the approach Scully took with Eddie Van Blundht, Sr. (Remember: the h is silent.) in the episode "Small Potatoes."

The monstrous also includes characters such as Holman Hardt and Gerry Schnauz. Recall, Hardt can control the weather . . . sort of. His emotional states cause various sorts of weather. Schnauz could somehow project how he intended to murder his victims onto camera film without realizing it. Both

Schnauz and Hardt provide exceedingly interesting cases to study; biology to be sure. But biology by itself would not likely explain the mechanics of getting mental imagery onto film, nor the causal link between Hardt's emotional states and the weather. There would have to be a blend of sciences working in tandem to solve these mysteries. Notice that this is true even though, as far as we know, these two are each one of a kind. You can't get a large sample group to study what would be true generally of such kinds of beings. But they nevertheless exist and can be subjected to empirical study. A big part of the monstrous then can also be given permanent residence.

And similarly for the so-called supernatural phenomena. Consider Tooms . . . or even Donald Pfaster. In the former case, we have an embodied incarnation of evil. In the latter we have some kind of demon monster or something. So let's take a look at the supernatural. What does "supernatural" mean? In its most straightforward sense, it refers to events or things "outside" or "above" nature.

Strictly speaking, this can't be exactly right. Kyte saw and heard her boss; everyone saw and heard Chester Bonaparte in "Fresh Bones." Even if they are "outside" nature, there is a causal link with nature. The blood in the bathtub is a rich, rich crimson; Chester speaks; incarnate evil eats livers and hibernates. The *effects*, then, of such entities can be studied using all the usual methods of observation, and, possibly, experimentation. But what of the causes? Are the causes—Howard Graves and Chester Bonaparte—likewise natural? They do have natural effects after all. Things get messy either way you answer.

Let's suppose you say "Yes, they are some kind of strange natural entities." Well, you've implied an astonishing consequence. Consciousness and choices are explainable and observable via observation and experimentation. But presumably, Graves and Bonaparte "chose" to reveal themselves in the manner they did. Are free choices explainable via the natural behaving in law-like fashion (even if it's a weird physics)?

But suppose you say "No, they are not natural entities." Now we have a possible problem with the known laws of thermodynamics. How? Suppose an angel (perhaps the Four-Faced Man from All Souls?) wants to push a glass of water off the table. The first law of thermodynamics is that energy can neither be created nor destroyed. So, the total energy in the universe remains the same regardless of what is going on. Returning to the angel, we have two unrelated forces in play: the angel's will and the motion of the water glass as it slides across, over, and down.

So then it seems that "will" caused the glass to fall, and if it did so, it had to introduce its own kind of energy to start a process. It appears that energy in the universe is added to. The problem arises if I decide to push the glass of water over the table too. Suppose I have a strange condition: glasses of water induce me to push them over. And suppose I too have a non-natural part; my will. It seems glass of water somehow interfaces with my non-natural will, inducing it to push. It seems energy goes out of the world, and to wherever my will is. And, like the angel, my will puts energy in the world when I move my limbs.

So we are at the sharp point of debates about consciousness, free will, and science. Can angels, will, and consciousness be explainable via laws of the world, even if these laws are from weird physics? Or not? If not, how do the observed phenomena square with known laws, such as thermodynamics? At any rate, many supernatural entities do not live well within the realm of science specifically on the grounds of will and consciousness. We should revoke their green cards and deport them right back to the fantastuc realm. And we, together with all conscious and willing creatures, alien and monstrous, should go with them.

The Beginning

Contrary to Mulder and Scully, the fantastic-scientific divide is better characterized with consciousness and will on the fantastic side and observable phenomena that follow nature's rules on the scientific side—even if some of nature's rules and structures turn out to be really weird.

Returning to Roland, it is of course interesting how, naturally speaking, Arthur was able to affect Roland's mind. But this is an empirical question. As it turns out, what is truly curious is whether Arthur's will and Roland's are natural or not.

One final question: if they are not, just how does Roland's physical condition affect his will, as it clearly does?[1]

---

[1] I would like to thank Jade Fletcher, Matthew Holmes, and Eric Eck for helpful discussion of the ideas in this chapter.

5
Mulder's Metaphysics

ELIZABETH F. COOKE

SCULLY: If you have any doubt about my qualifications or credentials . . .

MULDER: You're a medical doctor. You teach at the academy. You did your undergraduate degree in physics. (Mulder reads from her title page) "Einstein's Twins Paradox: A New Interpretation. Dana Scully's senior thesis." Now that's a credential, rewriting Einstein.

SCULLY: Did you bother to read it?

MULDER: I did. I liked it. It's just that in most of my work, the laws of physics rarely seem to apply.

—"Pilot"

Agent Fox Mulder's openness to believe in everything from aliens to government conspiracies, shape-shifters to super-soldiers, mind control to clairvoyance, and Jersey Devils to Moth Men, inevitably raises an important philosophical question. Just what kind of world does Mulder think we live in such that all of these things are real possibilities?

Generally most philosophers would find Mulder to hold a terribly confused metaphysics, neither entirely based in matter (physicalism), nor entirely based in mind or concepts (idealism). Sometimes Mulder firmly believes in outlandish physical possibilities, such as lake monsters, while other times he firmly believes in equally outlandish immaterial entities like ghosts, and at no point does Mulder seem driven to reconcile these dimensions of the world.

Materialism versus Idealism

Metaphysics is the branch of philosophy that studies the most general features of reality, while ontology is the branch of metaphysics that studies being (or existence). The central questions of ontology are, What is the fundamental nature of the universe? and What is most real?

One of the first answers to these questions was materialism (or physicalism): materialism is the view that what is most real is matter, while immaterial things like souls, God, free will, and even minds are illusions. Many ancient philosophers held materialist views: for example, Thales held that all reality was essentially water, Anaximander earth, air, fire, and water, and Democritus atoms.

These days many philosophers yield completely to physics to answer the metaphysical question of what is most real. They think reality is whatever physics ends up telling us matter really is, such as subatomic particles or empty space or vibrating strings. So, rocks and clouds and tables are real only insofar as they are reducible to the most basic and truly causally efficacious material stuff.

Often the motivation for this view is that contemporary science is doing such a great job of explaining things materialistically, that we no longer need explanations that appeal to funky, immaterial entities, like free will or God or spirits, that were never very good explanations in the first place. But materialists will allow *some* sciences like psychology to talk about seemingly immaterial things like beliefs, desires, and fears, because they think these mental states are reducible to neurophysiology which is in turn reducible to biology which is in turn reducible to chemistry which is ultimately reducible to the fundamental microphysical structure of reality. So, really, all our states of mind are just particles in motion.

Instead of atoms or bits of matter, idealist philosophers think the universe is made up immaterial stuff like ideas or thoughts or concepts. Idealists reject materialism and argue that immaterial things like minds and ideas are somehow prior to matter. In fact, idealists think materialists look at everything backwards: materialists try to explain everything in terms of matter. But you can't even begin to make sense of materialism or any other "ism," for that matter, without first understanding the reality of the mind thinking about these things.

Why think that a scientist is getting at the most basic parts of reality by studying matter, when his immaterial mind is what allows him to study whatever he studies in the first place? Science depends on minds more than matter because minds are doing the actual scientific thinking. So, idealists conclude that what is most real is not matter, but mind or concepts, and matter itself will just be one more concept among concepts. This is more or less the view of modern idealists like Berkeley and Kant and Hegel. But is it the view of Mulder? Or is he a materialist? Or is he something else?

Mulder's Metaphysics: Materialist or Idealist?

Mulder can seem like a materialist since many of the X-Files do have materialistic explanations. For example, Mulder uses materialist explanations for the Moth Men who evolved green skin camouflage for life in the Everglades in "Detour," and Big Blue the lake monster in "Quagmire," and the aggressive parasite in "Ice," and the Neanderthal-like woman in "Jersey Devil," and a man-like creature that comes out of hiding every thirty years to feed on human livers in "Tooms," and a teenager possessing a proboscis and an insatiable appetite for human brains in "Hungry."

While far-fetched, all these X-Files have explanations falling roughly within the parameters of evolutionary theory, a completely materialist theory. And let's face it, the material world does have some pretty weird stuff that doesn't qualify as immaterial or paranormal in any way. African frogs change sex spontaneously, elephants mourn their dead, time stops at the speed of light, and causality breaks down at the quantum mechanical level of reality. The material world can seem like an X-File!

So, is Mulder a materialist? Well, not exactly. Because there are also plenty of examples of Mulder believing in things falling far outside materialist explanations. For example, in "Shapes," Mulder investigates a case on a Native American reservation that resembles the very first X-File, a human who shape-shifts into an animal to attack other animals and humans.

An elder tribesman explains that the Manitou, an evil spirit, inhabits a person periodically to release its own savage energy causing the shape-shifting, and Mulder accepts this story. And in "Avatar" Mulder explains Agent Skinner's visitation from a ghostly woman as a succubus who warns him of danger. Then in "Calasari" a still-born brother returns to haunt his living twin, and Mulder ends up asking the grandmother's Romanian priests to perform rituals in order to subdue the spirit and free the child.

Mulder again uses immaterialist explanations in investigating a man who survives virtually countless near-death experiences simply because he is genuinely "lucky," the one man on Earth with almost perfect luck ("The Goldberg Variations"). Mulder also accepts the power of religious snake-handling ("Signs and Wonders"), and voodoo ("Theef"), and even genies ("Je Souhaite").

In these episodes, Mulder makes no attempt to bring these theories "down to Earth" with a more materialist explanation. There simply are no materialist explanations for things like shape-shifting, luck, voodoo, genies, and ghosts, in terms of electrons and quarks. Yet, Mulder is happy to accept such immaterial entities. So, Mulder can't be a materialist if he uses idealist explanations.

Is Mulder an idealist? While idealists do not typically take on the topics of ghosts and avatars, this is the metaphysical worldview that admits the reality of immaterial objects, like minds, ideas, and free will. But since Mulder uses both materialist and immaterialist explanations, we have to look at a third option, a metaphysics that combines these two views.

Mulder as Ontological Pluralist

Some philosophers say that we don't have to decide between either materialism or idealism. Instead they argue for ontological *pluralism* admitting that reality is made up of many different kinds of things. For example, there are particular beings, such as Bob Dylan and Socrates and Barack Obama, and there may also be things like the color red, the number two, and the ideal of justice, as well as things like the character Hamlet and the world of *Alice in Wonderland*, and weather systems and foreign policy and moral laws, and the way we eat lobster.

And all these different things can be real, but they may not fit into one neat ontological category like "material beings" or "immaterial beings," and may not fit into one neat scientific theory like quantum mechanics or relativity theory.

We may be stuck saying that the world is pluralistic, and, what's more, we may have to appeal to many different kinds of explanations in order to make sense of our very real and everyday complex world. This view has the difficulty of explaining how all these things interact, but most pluralists simply accept this problem rather than accepting the absurdity of the other two metaphysical worldviews that deny the existence of either material or immaterial things.

The history of pluralism is long and includes Aristotle who famously claimed that "being is said in many ways" and gave ten categories of being, as well as Descartes who argued that mind and matter are two distinct substances, neither of which is prior.

Now doesn't this sound like the view that Mulder holds? He doesn't try to fit the evidence into either a materialist or an idealist metaphysics, but he's willing to follow the evidence and let it suggest what explanation might be called for. Many different metaphysical possibilities are open to Mulder because he is not concerned about how they all reduce to one ontological stuff.

Viewers are used to thinking of Scully as the scientist and Mulder as not so scientific. But these days ontological pluralism comes with support from science as well. Philosophers like Nancy Cartwright in *The Dappled World* and John Dupré in *The Disorder of Things*, both members of the Stanford School of the Philosophy of Science, known for its pluralistic approach to metaphysics and science, have argued for scientific and ontological pluralism. These philosophers probably aren't going to buy into the existence of ghosts and the transmigration of souls, like Mulder, but they would probably agree with Mulder's insistence that the laws of physics don't apply as often as we would like to think.

After all, we appeal to many different successful sciences to explain our own complex reality. For example, we might appeal to social forces when talking about things like marriage and child rearing practices, and economic forces when talking about employment rates, and biological explanations when trying to understand reproductive patterns in insects, and psychological explanations when trying to explain the mind of a serial killer.

Not all (and perhaps none) of these explanations are reducible to physical explanations that refer to electrons and quarks. But that in no way prevents them from being *good* explanations. And for these philosophers like Dupré and Cartwright, good explanations are scientific explanations, explanations that help explain and predict and control, and we are simply kidding ourselves if we think that all good work in science is ultimately reducible to microphysics. The progress of science is just not going that way.

As Patrick Suppes, another member of the Stanford School of the Philosophy of Science, has argued, science has become increasingly complex over time, increasingly specialized, and increasingly pluralistic: in other words, we are getting farther and farther away from a view that one science can unify all the others. And the fact that there is not likely to be just one simple scientific theory to explain everything suggests that the world itself must really be made up of lots of different kinds of things.

This pluralistic and scientific ontology is precisely what Mulder holds, and it allows him to see things that others don't see. Very often a person's metaphysics more than evidence serves as her guide to choosing beliefs and theories to consider. This isn't a bad thing, unless her metaphysics is bad. For example, if someone is a materialist, she isn't going to entertain the possibilities of ghosts, telepathy, mind control, God, or angels. Her metaphysics prohibits her from even considering those things as possibilities.

Mulder's pluralist metaphysics allows him to entertain possibilities others do not, and this in turn allows him to do fantastic detective work, while Scully's too often reductionist and materialist philosophy shuts her off from different parts of reality for which there is good evidence. In other words, Scully's metaphysics often does the work of rejecting theories even before she considers the evidence.

But while Mulder's pluralistic metaphysics allows him to see possibilities, he has way more work to do in sifting through the evidence and trying to make good judgments among all the different possibilities. His more open metaphysics doesn't do the work of rejecting theories for him. And Mulder does reject plenty of theories, both mainstream scientific, and paranormal.

In "All Things" Mulder checks out a crop circle case in England only to learn that it is a hoax. In "Clyde Bruckman's Final Repose" Mulder rejects the phony celebrity psychic The Stupendous Yappi, but Mulder accepts this actual precognitive ability to see people's future deaths in the aptly-professioned life insurance salesman Clyde Bruckman (Peter Boyle). Mulder is also critical of Scully's sister Melissa (Melinda McGraw), who uses New Age techniques like crystals and theories about negative and positive energy in trying to communicate with Scully in her coma.

As Dupré argues, pluralism requires a set of virtues and good judgments rather than a simple, one-size-fits-all formula to decide which theories to accept. And this is just what Mulder has, namely, good judgment—amazingly good judgment. Mulder's metaphysics is so open that he has to do the work of looking at the facts rather than appealing to one neat worldview to "decide" for him. In other words, Mulder has to do the work of a real scientist.

From the "Pilot" episode onwards in *The X-Files*, we see Mulder's pluralistic metaphysics clash with Scully's unified metaphysics, and it is always Mulder's metaphysics that can handle the cases. The apparent choice between physicalism and idealism is really a false choice, and Mulder, like today's pluralist philosophers of science, actually holds the position of ontological pluralism.

There really are many different kinds of beings in the world, not just in world of the *X-Files*, but in our own world as well.[1]

[1] I am grateful to Jerold J. Abrams for helpful comments on an earlier draft.

II

Here Be Monsters

6
The Great Mutato and Biotechnology

RICHARD BILSKER

One of the more bizarre episodes of *The X-Files* is Season Five's "The Post-Modern Prometheus," which first aired November 30th, 1997.

Much of the episode is tongue-in-cheek. It takes place inside a comic book, *The Great Mutato*. The episode begins with a hand opening the color comic-book issue, but once the comic is open, the episode is in black-and-white. Much of the soundtrack is reminiscent of cheesy circus music. There are appearances by Jerry Springer and the "Jerry Springer Show" at the beginning and end of the episode.

Even though it was written and directed by the show's creator, Chris Carter, there are reasons to discount all or parts of the episode as non-canonical. In addition to taking place inside a comic book and in black-and-white, Mulder asks for a rewrite from the author, saying "This is all wrong, Scully. This not how the story is supposed to end." Yet there's a lot going on in this episode.

Frankenstein

First published anonymously in 1818 when the author was not yet twenty-one, *Frankenstein: Or, The Modern Prometheus* is one of the most enduring stories. Though movie versions of the story are more well-known, the original novel is drenched in philosophical ideas.

Shelley was the daughter of the feminist philosopher Mary Wollstonecraft and political philosopher William Godwin. Over the course of the novel, there are discussions of women's rights, the nature of education, and vegetarianism. Victor Frankenstein was the Modern Prometheus, according to the subtitle of Mary Shelley's *Frankenstein*. His transgression was to discover the secret of giving life to dead tissue and then to exploit this secret.

The original Prometheus was the Titan from Greek mythology who transgressed by giving fire to humans, when it was previously exclusive to the gods. The novel is a nested narrative taking place entirely in a series of letters from arctic explorer Robert Walton to his sister Margaret back in England. Walton is single-mindedly pushing ahead with his plans against the advice of his more experienced crew when his ice-locked ship is passed by a giant man on a sled.

Later they meet Victor Frankenstein who was in pursuit of the giant, who we learn was Victor's creation. Victor is rescued by Walton and tells his tale. In the middle of that story, Victor relates the creature's story as told to him. At the end of the story Victor dies, the creature talks to Walton and continues his journey across the ice, and Walton turns back.

The Golem

It is often pointed out that there are similarities in the Frankenstein story to the tale of the Golem in Jewish mysticism. The most famous Golem story tells us that Talmudic scholar Rabbi Judah Loew ben Bezalel of sixteenth-century Prague created a golem out of clay to protect the Jews of Prague's ghetto from antisemitism.

The word "golem" means something like "unshaped form" in Hebrew. In effect, then, this is treading on God's territory, as Adam was created in a similar way. In most versions of the story, the golem couldn't be controlled and went on a rampage until Rabbi Loew figured out how to stop him. Literary versions of the story include Gustav Meyrink's 1915 novel and an *X-Files* episode, "Kaddish" from Season Four, in which a golem is created in New York City to avenge a Jewish man killed in his shop by neo-Nazi thugs. Mulder and Scully learn the story of the golem in investigating the death as a hate crime.

Post-Modern Prometheus

The title of the episode is explained by Mulder when he refers to the scientist, Dr. Francis Pollidori, as the Post-Modern

Prometheus because of his work in genetic engineering. The transgression of the Post-Modern Prometheus (for more on post-modernism and *The X-Files*, see Dean Kowalski's *The Philosophy of the X-Files*) is to discover the secret of turning genes on and off and using it. In this case, getting fruit flies to grow legs out of their mouths. It is not until later on in the episode that it becomes clear that The Great Mutato (I will refer to him as Mutato, as he is given no other name in the episode or the credits, much like the creature in *Frankenstein*) is the result of an experiment Pollidori completed twenty-five years earlier.

John Polidori was the name of Lord Byron's physician at the time of the weekend in 1816 that Mary Shelley conceived *Frankenstein*. Polidori himself wrote a story, "The Vampire," which was published in 1819. There are other parallels to the *Frankenstein* story throughout the episode. Victor's bride in the novel was named Elizabeth and she died at the creature's hand on their wedding night. In the episode, Pollidori's wife is named Elizabeth. As in the novel, the creature can speak (not the case in some movie versions of the novel). More than once in the episode a character says or implies that Pollidori is the real monster of the story. The creature in *Frankenstein* is educated by watching the DeLacey family and reading old books (Goethe's *The Sorrows of Young Werther*, Milton's *Paradise Lost*, Volney's *Ruins*, and Plutarch's *Lives*) in an abandoned room.

Befitting the nearly two centuries that have passed, Mutato reports that he learned from "books, records, and home media centers." In particular, he becomes a fan of Cher because of her performance in the 1985 movie *Mask*, in which she is the loving mother of a boy with *craniodiaphyseal dysplasia* (a disfiguring genetic condition). He has an appearance similar to Mutato. In the novel, Victor ignores his family (is off for years at the university in Ingolstadt, actually) without returning home to visit. In the episode, Pollidori ignores his wife and her desire for a child. In fact, he leaves for a conference in Ingolstadt near the beginning of the episode. *X-Files* fans might note that the real University of Ingolstadt was founded in 1472 and closed in 1800. The novel, though published in 1818, was set in "17—," an unspecified year in the previous century. It was at Ingolstadt that in 1776, Adam Weisshaupt founded the Bavarian Illuminati, a group sometimes fictionalized as the great conspiracy behind *everything*.

What prompted Mulder's involvement in this episode is a letter he received from Sheineh Berkowitz. She wrote him after hearing his name mentioned on a broadcast of the *Jerry Springer Show*. We first see Mulder and Scully in the car on the way to Mrs. Berkowitz's house. Scully reads the letter out loud as Mulder drives. Mrs. Berkowitz claims she is pregnant after she had lost a few days while no one noticed. We actually see these events in the teaser before Mulder and Scully enter the episode. Mrs. Berkowitz describes a weird smell, found all her peanut butter had been eaten, and remembers seeing a deformed creature and hearing Cher. The kicker, though, is that Berkowitz had a tubal ligation. Scully finds a comic book in Mrs. Berkowitz's son Izzy's room. The comic, "The Great Mutato," depicts a creature like the one described by Mrs. Berkowitz. It was written by Izzy.

Scully is skeptical as usual and thinks it's all a hoax driven by the desire for Mrs. Berkowitz to appear on television as part of the "tabloid culture" or to promote the comic book. Mulder balks and chastises Scully for reducing Mrs. Berkowitz to a cultural stereotype. Izzy tells the agents that Mutato is real and can be lured into the open with peanut butter sandwiches. They try this, but Mutato escapes them and they meet Dr. Pollidori's father who directs them to Pollidori. We later discover that Pollidori's father had been trying to make a mate for Mutato, but since he was a farmer instead of a scientist, they didn't exactly work. It is implied that townspeople were laced with horse, chicken, pig, and goat DNA. Pollidori kills his father and blames Mutato. Mulder and Scully find Mutato, save him and arrest Dr. Pollidori. Near the end, Mulder asks for his rewrite.

What is wrong, though, with genetic engineering? Mulder is concerned with the implications of Pollidori's experiments for humans. Pollidori and Scully say that they would not be done on humans. Mulder wonders why do them at all, then? Scully talks about knowing about how we tick and where we come from. Mulder is skeptical.

One answer that's often given to the "What's wrong?" question when discussing genetically modified organisms (GMOs) or genetic engineering in general, is that it is unnatural. This answer is unsatisfying for reasons that can be found as early as an essay by John Stuart Mill published posthumously in 1874. In the essay, Mill argues that there are at least two senses of the word "nature." One sense is nature as all that is or all that happens. The other sense is all that happens without human interference.

So, something that is unnatural in the first sense would be something that couldn't be or couldn't happen, like something that violates the laws of physics. Something unnatural in the second sense would be something made or caused by humans, which is sometimes called artificial. Mill's primary concern in the essay is to point out why nature, or the natural, should not be used to ground moral judgment. Nature in the second sense in irrelevant.

Nature Doesn't Equal Goodness

Nature in the first sense cannot be equated with goodness. Mark Sagoff expands on Mill's idea and identifies four senses of the word "nature,' differentiating them in terms of what "nature" is opposed to:

- **All that obeys the laws of physics. This is opposed to the supernatural.**
- **What God made (the sacred). This is opposed to that which humans make for their own purposes (the profane).**
- **That which is independent of human involvement (also called "pristine"). This is opposed to the artificial.**
- **What is true to itself (authentic, honest, or trustworthy). This is opposed to the inauthentic (Sagoff also calls this "specious, illusory, superficial . . . the sophisticated, worldly, or contrived . . . deceptive and risky").**

Sagoff, writing primarily about the food industry, notes that the industry advertises its GMO products as natural in the last three senses, but wants to be regulated only in terms of the first sense—the only sense in which GMO foods are actually natural. As consumers, then we need to be wary of equivocating in how marketers use the word "natural." This does not inform us about what is wrong with GMOs, though.

Lisa Bergin has recently analyzed this issue by looking at transgenic creations. Transgenic organisms, sometimes called "frankenfoods," contain DNA from at least two different species. This would include putting flounder genes into tomatoes so that they can better resist the cold or putting jellyfish genes in potatoes so that they will be bioluminescent when they need water. There is a "yuck!" factor here, but is this a good enough reason to reject GMOs?

Bergin identifies the root of the issue as purity and argues that this is an untrustworthy measure. She points out that the history of a using purity in this way is not pretty. It has been used in racial identity schema such as the "one-drop" rule, it has been used to challenge interracial couples as well as transgender and intersex people. This "logic of purity" can be seen in many cultures, as Bergin notes the anthropologist Mary Douglas discussed in her book *Purity and Danger*. We like everything to fit in neat little boxes and do not like metaphysical categories transgressed—everything has to be one thing or another. Bergin tells us that this notion seems to be what was behind her own discomfort upon hearing of the jellyfish potato. Yet, her feminist, anti-racist philosophical orientation bristles at this once it is raised to the surface.

This logic of purity has a long history in the philosophies of the European traditions. Plato's metaphysical view that the *idea* (or form) of a material object is more real than the object (the idea is what is *really* real) is the root of the theory. These ideas are eternal and unchanging as opposed to things, which are temporary and changing. At the same time, Plato also believed that minds and bodies were radically distinct kinds of substances, a view reinforced two thousand years later by René Descartes. This dualism led to other kinds of binary oppositions: male-female (and masculine-feminine), reason-emotion, science-nature, and white-nonwhite. In each case, the left side of the pair was more highly valued than the right side.

Latina feminist Gloria Anzaldúa also challenged the logic of purity as she did not easily fit into these binary oppositions. She lived in the borderlands part of Texas that used to be part of Mexico. Her family did not move—the border did, so she is both American and Mexican, but accepted wholly by neither group. As a lesbian, she transgresses the masculine-feminine divide. In thinking about this, she draws upon what is known about the Nahua religion of the peoples of the Aztec regions. As Bergin notes, the goddess Coatlicue herself is full of opposites and "contains male and female elements, she is beautiful and horrible, she represents both life and death." Unlike Platonic views, Nahua philosophy does not believe knowledge can come from a mind divorced from the body and reality is not static and unchanging. On a Nahua reading, Bergin thinks, the jellyfish and the potato might not be as separable in the first place—in a certain sense collapsing the senses of "nature" we were exploring earlier.

Feet on Fruit Flies

What framework are we left with to evaluate fruit flies with feet growing out of their mouths and jellyfish potatoes? Bergin argues that opponents and proponents of biotechnology have both relied on a logic of purity in their arguments. She is especially concerned as agribusiness companies through marketing of genetically engineered seeds are leading toward plant monoculture and away from biodiversity. A similar question can be asked about Dr. Pollidori's fruit fly. What would be the consequences of its release into the environment?

In one scene in "The Post-Modern Prometheus," a hapless lab assistant asks Pollidori "What would you like me to do with these?" about a petri dish of insects. As he is asking, he removes the lid and they fly off. The lab assistant then mutters, "Never mind." I don't think we should be marching with torches and pitchforks into biotech labs, but clearly we need to be concerned about these issues in a global manner that focuses on more than money or on how grossed-out we feel. There is much promise in GMO food—increased crop yield, weather resistance, and longer shelf life—that could make it easier to feed a more heavily populated planet. There is also much peril—crops or animals running amok and wiping out native species—species that might be necessary for our survival.

7
Monstrous Fear

ANDREA ZANIN

It lurks under the bed or in the closet, behind the curtains—waiting, drooling . . . *wanting* . . . sometimes from a distance, with the bulbous-headed, locust-eyed curiosity of an advanced intelligence and other times; with the insatiable appetite of a gaping maw inhabited by the rotting flesh of eons past.

It is imaginatively relative but *it* is known by every person-once-child who ever vaulted into bed with Olympic medal ambition in an effort to avoid that which skulks beneath.

It is fear: raw, visceral and life-affirming—something innate, part of the condition we call 'being human' but it's also cultivated and embellished, like a good story or a great TV series.

German archaeologist Klaus Schmidt believed that the further society is from nature the more it finds itself inventing things of which to be afraid. *Things* like the beasts, bogeymen, and behemoths that infiltrate the X-Files and instigate Fox Mulder and Dana Scully's quest for truth.

Many of the anti-rational monsters and bizarre supernatural elements that accost the two agents, especially in the show's Monster of the Week episodes, are reminiscent of a by-gone time; a time when industry dug its techno-hooks into nature and revolutionized the operation of the Western world. The Industrial Revolution happened in two waves, starting in 1760-*ish,* progressing until around 1870. For one-hundred-odd years, machines and factories quashed hills and grasslands with the power of economy, divorcing man from the very substance that breathed him into being. Coinciding with the mechanization of the revolution was a reactionary philosophical movement of romantics, which raged contempt against the development of industry and man's ensuing split from the natural world.

The Romantics (who dominated literature from around 1800 to 1850), argued that the more detached man was from the natural world, the less virtuous he was likely to be (Klaus's theory, in retrospect); that the destruction of nature had a dehumanizing effect. Philosopher Jean-Jacques Rousseau (1712–1778) was one of the movement's greatest inspirations. Rousseau argued that man's detachment from the natural world was corruptive, and Romantic philosophy expanded on this thought by proposing that man's separation from nature resulted in a type of depravity. And *damn*!—if the number of streets, high rises, and shopping malls characterizing modern cities the world over is any indication of our depravation and lack of virtue, then we're screwed—every which way. It's hell for the lot of us unless, of course, we pack up and hit the countryside with repentant fervor, *pronto*!

When Rousseau wrote *Reveries of the Solitary Walker* (1783), he described a state of "perfect happiness which leaves no emptiness to be filled in the soul" as something inspired by "the shores of the stormy lake, or elsewhere, on the banks of a lovely river or a stream murmuring over the stones." It's a romantic vision; one that stands in opposition to the scientific rationalization of the Enlightenment era (*ahem* . . . Scully) and the ensuing industrial expansion that took place not long after Rousseau's death.

The Romantics preferred feeling to thought; emotion to reason; intuition to intellect. Nature was considered sublime, with healing properties. In his essay *Discourse on Inequality*, Rousseau argues that "uncorrupted morals" prevail in the "state of nature"; that civilization (synonymous with industrial development) fills man with unnatural wants and desires, and by default unnatural fears. Industrial development—new and unfathomable—threw the western world into an abyss of uncertainty, robbing man of a healthy fear of his natural enemies and as a result modern society has embraced the likelihood of the monsters born out of the Romantic Movement.

Prometheus and Peanut Butter

Much of the art and literature incited by the Romantics' response to industrialization mourned the loss of what they believed to be the authentic world, a theme most especially evident in Mary Shelley's epic text *Frankenstein* (1818), subtitled *The Modern Prometheus*. Sound familiar? Sure—because Frankenstein (in misconstrued form—as monster rather than man) is a pop-culture phenomenon, darkening the door of Halloween year after year. *And also* . . . because you're an über-*X-Files* fan and there's no freakin' way you don't remember "The Post-Modern Prometheus," where The Great Mutato prowls the land in black and white anonymity—wolfing down peanut butter and listening to Cher whilst drugging and impregnating local ladies in the hope of creating a 'bride'. It's weird and gross but the blame cannot fall entirely on poor Mutato—a product of science gone wrong.

The episode is a direct reference to Shelley's *Frankenstein*; The Great Mutato, like Frankenstein's monster, is the result of an experiment—man fiddling with nature. Each creature, man's creation, is the *un*natural aftermath of a greedy imagination, and in Dr. Frankenstein's case, the result of a malignant mind perverted by industry.

Shelley uses Frankenstein's monster to make a scathing comment on man's adulteration and obliteration of the natural world—articulating how destructive the thirst for knowledge can be; not only to the environment but to "the self." In "The Post-Modern Prometheus" Mulder questions Dr. Pollidori (who is likened to Victor Frankenstein) about a recent experiment that has rendered into existence a fly with legs protruding from its mouth, saying "Why would you do that?", to which Dr. Pollidori replies, "Because I can."

It is this unadulterated arrogance that Shelley despises in her novel, and Dr. Frankenstein, who usurps the role of creator, is punished; he is responsible for unleashing the monster on the world and thus, he must pay with his death, as well as that of his wife Elizabeth and the monster he electrified into life. Pollidori also pays for his crimes, exiting the episode in a police cruiser; on his way to jail, presumably. The respective stories allow for the purposeful assimilation of man and monster, marring the distinction between good and evil and in so doing, alluding to man's corruptive state.

The X-Files might draw much of its inspiration from the monsters and maniacs that lurked in the Romantic era but the show takes it about twelve steps further; citing all manner of natural perversion, from mutants, werewolves, and swamp creatures to killer worms, murderous mites, and man-sized insects.

In "The Jersey Devil," the "wild man myth" (that forms the crux of the episode) articulates a "Universal symbolic fear of our dual nature as humans—as creators of life and destroyers of it," and in many subsequent episodes, the outcome of tampering with nature is something that comes across as a seriously bad idea. Interfering with the natural order usually results in chaos and catastrophe, made obvious in some of the early Monster-of-the-Week episodes: in "The Eves" genetic meddling culminates in murder; the same happens in "Blood" when a town's residents are exposed to a pesticide containing LSDM (designed to provoke fear in insects); in "Darkness Falls" a swarm of prehistoric mites attack and kill a crew of tree-slaying loggers; there's more murder in "Sleepless," when a Vietnam veteran is subjected to 'sleep eradication'; and in "Shapes" a werewolf incites terror in nature herself. And we are never afforded the luxury of looking on with detached disdain. The Romantics would argue that these freaks of nature are the result of a world corrupted by man, and as part of the human race; we are under suspicion.

Smoke and Mirrors

The X-Files does not allow us to escape culpability. The show is not a passive exercise in entertainment; it not only includes us but *implicates* us—luring us in and then exploding truth all over our wide-eyed faces. Chris Carter's series cleverly translates fear through the lens of allegory; through the language of science fiction, laced with a hit of horror—making the reality of our insecurities more palatable, offering a safe platform for cathartic intervention.

Little green men; flying around in saucers hatching plots to take over the world . . . *and all that stuff.* The fantasy lures us in *and then* we realize that *The X-Files* is a whole lot more than a weird-looking-but-strangely-cute extraterrestrial stretching its finger toward the moon and asking to phone home. Carter's aliens are all about world domination, death, destruction, an alien baby or two and—true to genre—a government cover-up. Some scary shit, right? Yup, even for our musing mystic and skeptical scientist—six seasons in, walking up a dark staircase in "How the Ghosts Stole Christmas":

> **SCULLY:** These are tricks that the mind plays. They are ingrained clichés from a thousand different horror films. When we hear a sound, we get a chill, we, we—we see a shadow and we allow ourselves to imagine something that an otherwise rational person would discount out of hand . . .
>
> **MULDER:** Tell me you're not afraid.
>
> **SCULLY:** All right, I'm afraid. But it's an irrational fear.

The thought of being abducted by an alien and fondled under bright lights, or being swiped by a sewer monster and incubated with worm larvae, is frightening but only *sort of* because, like Scully, we 'logic' the scenarios into submission. Mulder might call it "misplaced anxiety," as suggested by his comment in "Irresistible":

> It's been said that fear of the unknown is an irrational response to the excesses of the imagination. But our fear of the everyday, of the lurking stranger and the sound of footfalls on the stairs, the fear of violent death and the primitive impulse to survive, are as frightening as any X-File, as real as the acceptance that it could happen to you.

The proverbial monster under the bed; literal, hideous and unscrupulous in its fear-invoking propensity—it's all smoke and mirrors; masking a "greater" truth. But what does this mean for Mulder and Scully, and the *X-Files* mythology—if monsters are indeed a manifestation of minds perverted by industry, as suggested by Rousseau and the Romantics?

Perhaps the point is not the monsters themselves but what they represent—our own degeneracy. *The X-Files* manipulates its monsters into a metaphor for the moral disintegration of mankind, as acknowledged by Scully in the show's pilot, "It's like all the horrible acts that humans are capable of gave birth to some kind of human monster."

As an allegory for the human condition, the proverbial monster, disfigured in face and form, offers insight into a fractured psyche, a broken world—a society that tells us it's much easier to believe in aliens and UFOs, than cold-blooded human monsters who could pray on the living to scavenge from the dead ("Irresistible"). An idea that comes up again in Season Five, "The Post-Modern Prometheus":

> Psychologists often speak of the denial of an unthinkable evil in a misplacement of shared fears; anxieties taking the form of a hideous monster for whom the most horrific human attributes to be ascribed. What we can't possibly imagine ourselves capable of, we can blame on an ogre, a hunchback or a lonely half-breed.

It's much easier to cry monster than to invert our gaze.

Introspection's a Bitch

Before we learn to rationalize it, fear has the power to infiltrate and debilitate; it's the thing that makes childhood both terrifying and terrific in equal measure. As time progresses, what was once literal morphs into something metaphoric; the monster drooling under the bed becomes the skeleton occupying space in the closet. More than the truth about life's inexplicable paranormal strangeness we begin to fear the truth about ourselves—about who we are, the choices we've made and the impurity of our perception—a point articulated by Danish philosopher Søren Kierkegaard when he said "everything that makes a person impure and his observation impure comes from within" (*Three Upbuilding Discourses*). So really, man is his own worst enemy. When we were five we wanted the monster to stay put and at thirty-five we beg the skeleton to do the same. We choose to "live in a darkness of our own making" ("Without") because "it's easier to believe the lie" ("Gethsemane"). The fact is; introspection's a bitch—we work hard to cover up the truth about our very human inadequacies; we've deluded ourselves into believing that our fear is irrational when, really, we're just directing it at the wrong thing. And we like it that way. Why let the cat out of the bag? Now *that* would be a *helluva* scary tale to tell!

Mulder calls fear the "oldest tool of power", going on to say that "if you're distracted by the fear of those around you, it keeps you from seeing the actions of those above" ("Blood") but bearing in mind the self-perpetuating nature of fear, this idea could be rephrased, reading something like, 'if you're distracted by fear of the *monsters* around you, it keeps you from seeing the monster within.' Rousseau implored his listeners:

> Peoples! Know that nature once wished to preserve you from science, as a mother snatches a dangerous firearm from the hands of her child; that all the secrets she hides from you are so many evils from which she keeps you, and the trouble you find in instructing yourselves is not the least of her benefits. Men are perverse; they would be worse still if they had the misfortune to be born learned. (*Rousseau: Stoic and Romantic*, p. 33)

He begged humankind to embrace the healing properties in nature but man set out to subdue the world anyway, to advance himself, his knowledge and power, and to protect his faculties by the use of reason; a fostered logic that protects us from the monsters that prowl the conscience of our souls. Mulder's ultimate realization is not the alien invasion cited for 2012 or even that he was "right" all along but, rather, the realization that "evil, true evil, is a collaboration of men" ("The Truth"). Would Rousseau agree? Insofar as man collaborating to destroy his only saving grace; defiling nature and forgoing its healing properties . . . *yes*—it'd be the Romantic view.

And this Mulder and Rousseau have in common. That's not to say that Mulder would blame an impending extraterrestrial apocalypse on the Industrial Revolution, well, not consciously at least. But he is a man who tries to perceive reality (his version) through subjective feeling or intuition, over and above his education—in an effort to participate in the subject of his knowledge instead of viewing it from the outside. Mulder understands through instinct and, in the end, so does Scully—who is confronted by a nightmare born from her deepest fears and is forced to face a truth that she can no longer deny; that we are blind to a world of beings travelling through time and space imaginable to us only as flights of fancy ("Emily"). Fear of the monster (and skeleton), is a fear of "What if?"; a fear of the unknown. And existing in opposition to all of this ambivalence is nature, which offers something real; something true and constant to hold on to but we've chosen a different path and even in truth, we find no solace, only fear of the possibilities ("Existence").

8
Five Ways of Being a Monster

DAVID FREEMAN

> **SCULLY:** You know, on the old mariners' maps, the cartographers would designate uncharted territories by writing "Here be monsters."
>
> **MULDER:** I've got a map of New York City just like that.
>
> —"Quagmire"

When Mulder and Scully (and their eventual successors, Doggett and Reyes) aren't busy unraveling the intricate government conspiracy to cover up the existence of extraterrestrial life, they spend most of their time chasing monsters.

For many fans, the "monster of the week" episodes are some of the most memorable, the most fun, and certainly some of the most terrifying. Let's face it, if you woke in the middle of the night to find yourself being rudely probed against your will, what would you rather find staring back at you—some little grey men . . . or Flukeman?

From the days when we hid under the covers as children while the bogeymen lay in wait under our beds and in our closets, we have an instinctive fear of and fascination for monsters (and, naturally, there's even an *X-Files* episode that plays with this childhood nightmare, entitled "Scary Monsters").

The Five Types of Monsters

The Latin root *monere* ("to warn") gave the Romans the word *monstrum*, meaning something that was unnatural or against the natural order of things. Eventually, this evolved into our word "monster." So the idea of monsters implies that there is a pattern to the way things are in the world and any deviation from what is expected is a sign that something is fundamentally *wrong*.

Declaring someone or something a monster is drawing a line between what's natural or normal and what's unnatural or abnormal. There's a kind of dichotomy at play, making value judgments about aspects of reality—if something is natural or normal, then it's good; if it's unnatural or abnormal, then it's bad. This is a way of categorizing our experience of the world to make sense of it.

So what does it mean for something to be a monster? There are different kinds of monsters, which range from those that seem closer to our normal experience of the world and those that seem beyond our wildest imaginations. The monsters of *The X-Files* generally fall into five overlapping categories:

1. **Human monsters**
2. **Mutants**
3. **Unknown Species**
4. **Cryptids**
5. **Supernatural Monsters**

Human Monsters

In real life, killers tend to have simple motivations for their crimes, like greed, revenge, or some serious Mommy issues. In *The X-Files*, people kill because their microwave told them to ("Blood"). Or their tattoo ("Never Again"). Or because they inadvertently became immortal and aren't particularly happy about it ("Tithonus"). Or because of reincarnation ("Born Again").

Sometimes, just like real life, it's because they're simply plain evil. In any case, human monsters are completely natural beings, even if they commit acts that most people would regard as abnormal or unnatural. They are born, they (usually) work and pay bills, they die (so long as they look Death in the eye, at least).

Many people might say that this is what makes human monsters the most terrifying of all. They're just like us, except for the homicidal part. No one likes to imagine that their quiet, mild-mannered neighbor next door who is always puttering around the garden is actually growing those beautiful roses to help mask the stench of the bodies buried underneath the lawn.

So we try to find some explanation to account for the behavior of human monsters—she's mentally ill, he was abused as a child, they were influenced by that awful cult. The really unsettling part is when we're unable to explain why someone would do unspeakably horrific things to another human being.

Hannah Arendt famously wrote of "the banality of evil" after witnessing the trial of Nazi war criminal Adolf Eichmann, who showed no remorse for his actions or hatred for his persecutors, maintaining that he had simply followed orders. By all accounts, he seemed to be a perfectly average guy, if a little under-achieving and lacking the ability to think for himself. He took his meaning in life from belonging to something—whether it was the Rotary Club or the Nazi Party made no difference to him. His actions made him a monster, yet he was completely human.

Mutants

Sometimes, nature goes a bit cray-cray. People or animals are born with features that aren't really supposed to be there. Any good medical encyclopedia will list pages and pages of possible variations in form or function. It might be a result of some genetic mutation or some kind of environmental contamination, like exposure to chemicals or nuclear radiation—a particularly popular theme in the second half of the twentieth century.

During the Cold War, people feared the after-effects of nuclear radiation possibly more than the threat of annihilation. Around the same time, thousands of infants were born with horrific deformities as a result of a drug called thalidomide that expectant mothers took to alleviate morning sickness. These fears of mutation were expressed in the many monster movies that came out in the 1950s and 1960s—*Godzilla*, *The Fly*, *Them!*, you get the idea. It's these longstanding cultural fears that *The X-Files* plays into with its many mutants.

Mulder and Scully come up against the likes of the notorious Flukeman ("The Host"), the liver-munching contortionist

Eugene Victor Tooms ("Squeeze" and "Tooms"), the fat-sucking Virgil Incanto ("2Shy") and—admit it, you've been waiting for this one—the Peacock family ("Home"). Pretty much the most infamous episode of all, this was the first to receive a viewer discretion warning and the Fox network considered it so disturbing that they refused to air it more than once.

The only thing scarier than a regular mutant is a whole *family* of incestuous, mutant serial killers. Oh yeah, and their totally creeptastic run-down house is full of sadistic booby traps. And this is one household where you really don't want to be brought home to meet Mother.

To be fair, not all mutants kill people. Some of them are just regular people with genetic or physical differences that make them outsiders to others, like Eddie Van Blundht ("Small Potatoes"), the Great Mutato ("The Post-Modern Prometheus"), and pretty much everyone in "Humbug" (well, except for Leonard—he was totes creepy).

Unknown Species

Scientists estimate that there are perhaps some eight million different species sharing this planet with us. And each year about ten thousand more are discovered. We're vastly outnumbered and not all of our neighbors are friendly. The oceans in particular are enormous, deep and largely unexplored.

Consider the quote from "Quagmire," way back at the beginning of this chapter. If you want to get technical, the correct phrase was "Hic sunt dracones" (Latin for "here are dragons") and there were only a couple of globes that actually featured it. But Scully's a scientist, not a historian, so I'll forgive her for misquoting. To her credit, however, there were indeed a huge number of maps and globes that featured artwork of sea monsters lurking off the shores of coastlines all over the world.

The notion of monsters had a huge influence on medieval cartography and travel narratives. The travel stories of Marco Polo and John Mandeville famously borrowed descriptions of the "monstrous races" from Pliny's *Natural History*. These were bizarre "species of men" that were thought to dwell beyond the boundaries of the known world, such as the Cynocephali, who had humanoid bodies with dog-like heads, or the Blemmyae, who were headless but had eyes in the middle of their shoulders. The monstrous races also appeared on the edges of maps, representing the limits of the known and the intrusion of the unknown—the "out there" where Mulder and Scully seek the truth.

It is this cultural legacy of coming to grips with unexplored places and creatures that *The X-Files* plays with when it shows us unknown monsters from the edges of evolution. If you ever find yourself in an *X-Files* episode, you should stay out of the water. But not because of sharks. More because the sea-water itself might suddenly grow tentacles ("Agua Mala") or start eating your flesh ("Medusa").

Though, really, you're not much safer on dry land either. When hiking through the Cascades, it's probably best to run if you see any glowing green mites in the woods ("Darkness Falls"). I would also recommend not touching any pulsating, pus-filled wounds you might see on wildlife ("F. Emasculata") and don't touch any 'shrooms either ("Field Trip"). And if you think running to the Arctic, far from civilization, will keep you safe, then you aren't who you are ("Ice"). Mulder and Scully teach us that no matter how much we might think we have tamed our world, nature has other plans.

Cryptids

Somewhere in between unknown species and monsters of folklore, we have the entire field of cryptozoology. There's no real scientific evidence for the existence of these creatures, but that doesn't stop many people from believing they might be out there somewhere, living in obscurity and occasionally appearing in tabloids. Cryptozoologists study reports of unusual animals and attempt to determine if the sighting was genuine.

Some cryptids (the official name for these kinds of creatures) are just regular animals that happen to be an abnormal size or located somewhere they wouldn't normally be found. Some of them were thought to be extinct, either recently or as many as millions of years ago. Others don't appear in the fossil record and don't seem to be related to any known species, even taking on mythical or paranormal characteristics. Many people dismiss cryptozoology as quackery but the fact remains that our planet is an enormous place and, just as there are thousands of new species discovered each year, it's theoretically possible that more unusual or rare species might exist.

One of the most famous cases of proven cryptids is the coelacanth, a species of fish from the late Cretaceous that was discovered alive and well off the coast of South Africa in the 1930s and later in Indonesia. Even the gorilla was once considered nothing more than a fantastic rumor in the days when Africa still represented the heart of darkness to Europeans.

The cryptids of *The X-Files* include the Loch Ness-inspired lake monster Big Blue ("Quagmire"), the chupacabra ("El Mundo Gira"), and the fictional Wanshang Dhole, modeled on reports of vicious mystery canines ("Alpha"). There's also the curious case of the Jersey Devil, featured in the episode of the same name but actually quite a bit different than the "real" cryptid. The actual Jersey Devil of cryptozoology is usually described as something like a flying kangaroo with a goat's head, horns, bat's wings and cloven hooves. Mulder's Jersey Devil has more in common with the mythic Wildman (or woman, in this case), a legendary figure dating back to the Middle Ages who was covered in hair and lived in the woods, rejecting all semblance of "civilized society."

Supernatural Monsters

Every culture in world history holds stories of monsters in its mythology and folklore, usually with some element of the supernatural involved. Prominent examples from *The X-Files* include: vampires ("3" and "Bad Blood"); werewolves ("Shapes"); tulpas ("Arcadia"); the Golem ("Kaddish"); ghosts ("Shadows" and "Excelsis Dei"); demons ("Terms of Endearment" and "Je Souhaite"); and whatever the hell that insect thing was in "Folie à Deux."

These monsters are completely unnatural by definition. They're usually considered to belong to some other kind of dimension or unearthly realm, yet are somehow able to interact with ours. If human monsters show us the horrors lurking behind the façade of everyday life, then supernatural monsters offer glimpses into worlds beyond our entire sense of reality.

At the same time, we're sometimes offered the opportunity to relate to these monsters on an almost human level. In "Terms of Endearment," Wayne Weinsider is outwardly a perfectly average neighbor, community member and loving husband who just wants to have a child with his wife. It just so happens that he keeps ending up with demon babies because he's not really human.

"Kaddish" puts a new spin on the legend of the Golem by turning it into a love story. In Jewish folklore, the Golem was a creature fashioned from mud and given life through mystical incantations in order to protect the Jews of medieval Prague from antisemitic attacks. In writer Howard Gordon's take on the legend, the Golem is formed as a woman's expression of love for her murdered fiancé. Yet even in these instances the monsters remain inherently inhuman. Wayne is unable to fulfill his wishes to be a father, forever trapped by the limitations of his demonic biology. Ariel Luria may have created a living being to replace her betrothed, but a soulless mound of dirt can never love her back.

The Meaning of Monsters

Monsters have been with us for thousands of years, across all cultures and in many different forms. They reflect and express the fears and anxieties of the times and places that created them. At their essence, monsters are the products of our attempts to confront the unknown and the uncomfortable, the sense that things can happen to us that we have no control over. The enemy may dwell in lands unknown, or in the house next door, or even within our own bodies. Much like the Fear Monster in "X-Cops," monstrosity is in the huge, glowing red eye of the beholder.

III

It's a Conspiracy

9
How to Be a Good Conspiracy Theorist

DIANE GALL

While the monster of the week might draw the viewers in, it's the promise of The Conspiracy being revealed that keeps them watching *The X-Files*. The secretive shadowy Conspiracy supposedly runs through most aspects of our lives and we don't even know it.

But it's just a TV show, right? There are real conspiracies, like Watergate and Iran-Contra, and there are conspiracy theories, like The New World Order being brought about by The Illuminati or the World Jewish Banking Conspiracy, and the 9/11 attacks being a "false flag" operation orchestrated by the US government itself . . . or maybe the Israelis.

There are somewhat more elaborate conspiracy theories too: for instance, the theory that ancient astronauts, in the past, programmed the DNA of our neurons so that these neurons can be made unstable by triggering the aggressions centers of the brains of people who live in areas of the world where evidence of these ancient astronauts is hidden.

How can we sort the real conspiracies from flights of fancy? It really does seem that we learn that governments and corporations across the world have been hiding important information from us, as Wikileaks and Edward Snowden have shown us. Much of this information is information that we think we should have been told about. Mulder relies on The Lone Gunmen time and again for that little piece of information that helps him solve whatever roadblock he's run into.

But what exactly is a conspiracy theory? What is the difference between a theory about a real conspiracy and one that turns out to be a fantasy?

I'm Not Advancing Any Conspiracy Theory Here, Scully

No one wants to be called a conspiracy theorist. It's an insult, a dismissal. Except for a few who proudly and defiantly label themselves that way, people who insist that Lee Harvey Oswald was a government patsy want to avoid the label. (Besides, we all know that the Cigarette Smoking Man was the actual lone gunman, and he wasn"t shooting from the grassy knoll.) If we are going to call these implausible theories "conspiracy theories," we should ask what exactly is a conspiracy theory? I mean, there really are conspiracies. Since the term "conspiracy theory" is so widely understood to be a derogatory, dismissive term, we should try to go with the flow. So, as British academics Jane Parrish and Martin Parker do, perhaps we should call the kinds of theories that we shouldn't take seriously "conspiracy theories" and the kinds of theories we should take seriously as "theories of conspiracy."

What's the difference between a conspiracy theory and a theory of conspiracy? Put very simply, conspiracy theories offer very implausible explanations involving secret plots to account for an event. Theories of conspiracy offer explanations involving secret plots that *are* plausible, even if they are improbable (or even turn out not to be true). The difference seems to depend on the implausibility of the explanation, but psychologist Jovan Byford argues that there is a pattern to the logic of conspiracy theories that can help us start to sort out the difference. In other words, it turns out that conspiracy theories look a lot alike.

Byford argues that conspiracy theories typically have several aspects. The conspiracy involves a number of powerful, yet unknown people operating in secret (for instance, a small group of men operating inside the US government but without the knowledge of their superiors). The conspiracy is a prime motivating force in historical events (for example, the assassination of JFK, or the 9/11 attack on the World Trade Center. The conspiracy has a detailed and comprehensive objective (for example, that the US government engineered the attacks on 9/11 in order to whip up fear and hostility that would justify the invasion of Iraq; a "false flag" operation).

Lastly, conspiracy theories are nearly always irrefutable. No matter how contradictory the available evidence is, or how much evidence to the contrary is produced, it can all be dismissed as "what they want you to think," evidence of just how powerful, clever, and manipulative the conspirators are, or that those who are trying to debunk the conspiracy theory are either patsies or fellow conspirators. The conspiracy theory mentality gets fed by taking evidence that would normally be thought to refute and making it into evidence that confirms the conspiracy theory.

The conspiracy theory is almost entirely immune to any possible evidence that it is not true. Theories of conspiracy, on the other hand, look like any other kind of legal case. That is, you can think of something, that if it were true, would show the theory of conspiracy not true. But exactly how does this all work? How do you go about deciding whether a conspiracy theory or theory of conspiracy is true?

No Matter How Paranoid You Are, You Aren't Paranoid Enough

In "Madam, I'm Adam," Adam Burgess finds that everything he knows about himself is wrong. He doesn't live where he thinks he does. A different couple lives in what he thinks is his house. He knows the neighbourhood and everyone who lives there, but no one has any recollection of him and there's no record he ever existed. He explains to Byers and Jimmy that he thinks that aliens have transported him to an alternate reality, on account of the blue goo that he's found in every crevice of his body. Byers immediately dismisses him as a kook, or perhaps mentally ill, and gets up to leave Adam to it. However, Jimmy notices an implant that looks like some kind of electoral connection port sticking out from the back of Adam's neck. This changes Byers's attitude.

So, we have been given two explanations for Adam's situation: he's been abducted by aliens or he's delusional. I'm sure that we could think of a few more possibilities. Adam could simply be lying. He could believe what he is suggesting, but be the butt of someone's elaborate practical joke. Notice what we are doing here. We are trying to account for Adam's experience with a series of (what we think are) possible explanations for how it happened. This process is called "argument to the best explanation."

An explanation is just an account for how or why an event happened. It's not an attempt to convince anyone that the event happened. But an event has potentially any number of possible reasons for coming to pass. When we select one, then argue that this is how the event come to happen, we're arguing that our explanation is the best (that is, the correct) account of how the event came about.

In "Madam, I'm Adam," it turned out that both of our initial explanations were incorrect. It turned out that Adam was the subject of a sophisticated psychiatric experimental treatment. But the Lone Gunmen only came to see that explanation as the best explanation because they pursued the story and discovered more evidence that pointed towards the explanations they eventually accepted. This is one of the methods of science: gather evidence that distinguishes better explanations from the explanations we should then reject.

It is easy to simply say "Gather evidence that separates good from bad explanations," but what exactly makes one of these explanations *better* than the other? What do we mean by *better*? Well, certainly one place to start is to ask "What makes one explanation more plausible than another"?

It's the Only Explanation that Makes Any Sense

What makes for plausibility? Well, reasonableness or probability are key features of whether an explanation is plausible. But what exactly, in the absence of conclusive evidence, makes for reasonableness? Frequently, we rely on our own intuition or gut feeling. If we wonder why our car won't start in the winter, we go almost effortlessly to suspecting the battery. We do not typically start with suspecting sabotage, for instance. Informal logicians wonder about this too. In trying to rely less on intuition and more on a systematic way of thinking, they have identified a checklist for good explanations.

- **Internal consistency: plausible explanations do not contradict themselves**
- **External consistency: more plausible explanations do not contradict the evidence**

Clearly, internally inconsistent explanations are poor. You aren't even sure what the explanation means when the theory contradicts itself. But when explanations contradict the evidence, there's room for tweaking the explanation or revisiting the evidence to make sure you've gotten it right the first time.

But lots of consistent explanations turn out to be false. So, what else can we rely on? There are five more features of explanations that figure in making an explanation a good explanation:

- **Testability: Better explanations must be able to be tested.**
- **Fruitfulness: Better explanations can account for events we haven't yet encountered.**
- **Scope: The more things that can be explained, the better the explanation.**
- **Simplicity: The fewer things that need to be assumed, the better the explanation.**
- **Conservatism: Better explanations are consistent with our other wider beliefs.**

The more of the items on the checklist that can be met, the more plausible the explanation. Notice though, that two of them conspire against us (so to speak). Some conspiracy theories are notorious for being able to explain everything from the French Revolution to the Stock Market Crash of 1929 to the election of Barack Obama. Yes, blaming everything on the Illuminati can seemingly explain this but at the cost of assuming that there is a multigenerational, international, and secret organisation that is orchestrating everything.

Scope is one thing, but a theory which attempts to explain literally every event in history explains none of them. Similarly, when you have a theory that attempts to explain literally everything, everything you later encounter can be described in terms of the conspiracy. Yes, the theory is fruitful, but it runs afoul of simplicity and conservatism.

The difference between supernatural agency or non-human agency type explanations and those that rely on secret plots involving money or power is important. Offering a political conspiracy theory (Microsoft is rigging the US presidential election primary selection process; after all, they are providing the software that does the ballot counting and they have contributed to some candidates and not to others) is one thing, but aliens or ghosts bearing the weight of the conspiracy theory is another.

None of what I have said should be taken to mean that we should just dismiss explanations that seem crazy to us or rely on shadowy organizations (though, I am pretty sure we need not bother with The Lizard Elite theories). Any number of theories of conspiracy have turned out to be correct: for example, the Tuskegee experiments, the Gulf of Tonkin incident, and secret CIA mind control experiments (MKULTRA). These three conspiracies involve both craziness (The government *deliberately* infected people to study them over decades?) and shadowy groups (The CIA. Need I say more?).

He Never Gave In, Never Gave Up, and Never Sold Out

If it's this easy to avoid being sucked in, though, why do we still seem to have so many conspiracy theories being floated by the likes of Alex Jones? Philosopher Quassim Cassam argues that it isn't so much that people who accept conspiracy theories fail to have enough of the right information, but that they interpret and react to that information differently than they should. Two people can see the same information but come to radically different conclusions about that information. In other words, what seems plausible to one person seems less so to another. How can we account for this?

Cassam suggests that we pay attention to habits of thinking. People who accept one conspiracy theory tend to accept more of them. This suggests that the conspiracy isn't just making a mistake in reasoning, but is proneness to making mistakes of reasoning. If making certain mistakes in reasoning becomes a habit then we would expect people with this habit to accept explanations as plausible when those theories really aren't plausible. Cassam calls these sorts of habits "intellectual vices."

These vices are just like the familiar vices gluttony and sloth, except that they refer not to our moral habits, but to our habits of thinking. These vices, along with our intellectual virtues, make up our intellectual character. Intellectual virtues are habits like care in thinking, believing only to the extent that the evidence allows, attention to detail, skepticism, honesty, and humility. The intellectual vices include carelessness in thinking, closed-mindedness to alternative explanations, idleness in seeking out contrary evidence, gullibility, insensitivity to counter-evidence, and prejudging the evidence. So, how do we become the kind of persons who don't fall for conspiracy theories? Developing a virtuous intellectual character would fit the bill nicely.

You might still be wondering how to go about becoming this intellectually virtuous person. Aristotle said that "the way to become habituated in virtue is to perform virtuous actions." We should exercise the critical thinking skills we have been taught and learn on our own. Our attitude should be skeptical of extraordinary explanation, but not so much so that we do not take it seriously unless we have reason to do so. We should be open-minded, but not so much so that our brains fall out. We'd be less likely to be taken in because we would ask the right questions and treat the answers we get with the right attitude. We would look at those answers and ask ourselves whether the explanations we get are simple and comport with what we already believe. But what we already believe would be testable and tested. What is needed then is relentless exercise of the intellectual virtues until we internalize them and they become habits. These habits will not guarantee that we are always right, but we will make fewer mistakes.

It is possible to deal with conspiracy theories rationally and reasonably. And though The Lone Gunmen stumble their way through their investigations, and sometimes get duped into getting caught trying to break into fake data vaults, they more frequently find the truth by constructing explanatory theories that are warranted by the evidence and then testing those theories by following the evidence. More so than that, the boys have a skeptical but realistic sense of what is plausible and what isn't. Doing as The Lone Gunmen do with a story is not the worst advice for someone who has good evidence that the truth is out there and wishes to discover it for themselves.

Or, perhaps that's just what *they* want us to believe.

10
They're Out to Get Us

WILLIAM RODRIGUEZ

Beginning in 1993, *The X-Files* became a social phenomenon by incorporating elements of science fiction, horror, political intrigue, and drama into a fully articulated conspiracy-laden mythology.

The Pilot episode, penned by Chris Carter, wowed us with a story of alien abduction, experiments on teenagers, and a conspiracy between an Oregon medical examiner and a sheriff. As the show progressed, the mythology became more nuanced, until it culminated in a not-so-well-received movie in 2008. "I want to believe" became a mantra for fans.

The X-Files has a very simple formula: conspiracy stories—referred to as the *mytharc*—alternated with stand-alone Monster-of-the-Week stories. In nine seasons, *The X-Files* produced 202 episodes. Seventy-two of these were conspiracy-related stories. The *mytharc* begins in the 1940s and centers on a government conspiracy to hide the existence of aliens, their colonization, and eventual take-over of the world.

A shadow government, known as "The Syndicate," has made a pact with alien colonizers, who intend to take over the planet using a virus, known as "black oil." A second group of aliens known as the faceless ones destroy the syndicate and force the hand of the first group of aliens. This causes them to dispatch Super Soldiers, who take over key positions in the government, consequently forcing Mulder and Scully to go into hiding.

This *mytharc* was abruptly and violently subverted in the first episode of Season Ten ("My Struggle"), when Tad O'Malley unmasked the "real" conspiracy. What we thought was an alien invasion was in fact the plan for world domination by a fascist and all too human cabal. The mythological element of alien experimentation and medical experimentation was also subverted in the next episode, "Founder's Mutation," where we discover that the genetic manipulation was conducted by an unscrupulous doctor working for the Department of Defense.

A cursory observation of the program's formula would lead us to the conclusion that the conspiracy stories were unconnected and secondary, but this conclusion was likewise subverted by the Season Ten episode "Mulder and Scully Meet the Were Monster." In this episode we learn of a reptilian species that exists in our midst. One member of the species is "transformed" after a bite from a psychopathic human killer. It's probably no coincidence that one of the most prominent alien conspiracy theories posits a belief of an alien reptilian species in our midst. It now seems that the Monster-of-the-Week stories were related to the conspiracy stories after all.

The X-Files originally aired at an important point in American history and politics. The program was preceded by a period of political turmoil and instability, which included Watergate, the Iran-Contra scandal, and the fall of the USSR. 1993, the year the program debuted, coincided with the Presidency of George Bush Senior. It was in 1991 that Bush made his infamous New World Order speech for the reform and the renewal of America.

Bush was speaking to Congress of a new political order where the USSR was no longer a threat to global peace and stability. What he promised was a future where American political, economic, and military interests would be unrivaled. It was a speech that celebrated the triumph of American military superiority over the "forces of evil and oppression," vis-à-vis Saddam Hussein. What conspiracy theorists heard was an Illuminati call to arms. Expressions of American exceptionalism were interpreted as a hidden agenda that promoted subterfuge, secrecy, and political machinations.

The X-Files came of age during the Clinton Presidency. This was the period that gave rise to economic globalization, the militia movement, the Ruby Ridge standoff, and the tragedy at the Branch Davidian compound. One of the most traumatic moments of our history, and what scholars believe to be the genesis of a new conspiracy mindset, was the terror attacks of September 11th, 2001. (Chris Carter maintained in an interview with Salon.com, that 9/11, and its effects on civil liberties, was the prime motivation for the *X-Files* revival.)

Finally, it should not surprise us to find that the resurrection of *The X-Files* has occurred during the Obama Presidency. For many, this was a period of political insecurity due to the challenge to American hegemony by terrorism, of economic insecurity because of the loss of production jobs due to a globalized workforce, xenophobic fears caused by the challenges of refugee immigration, and the widely-held belief in the government's illegitimacy promoted by Tea Party "birther" claims. *The X-Files*, as a conspiracy theory promoter, provides a sense of meaning to many people in times of crisis and change.

What's a Conspiracy?

The English psychologist Viren Swami has defined conspiracy theories as "lay beliefs that attribute the ultimate cause of an event, or the concealment of an event from public knowledge, to a secret, unlawful, and malevolent plot by multiple actors working together."

Even though conspiracy theories have existed throughout history, and in every culture in the world, a resurgence of this mindset has taken place due primarily to 9/11 and the proliferation of the world wide web and social media. Scholars believe that the declining influence of "traditional gatekeepers" of information—the mass media, publishers, and state officials—makes it easier to secure information that is more democratic and outside of the mainstream.

One of the challenges of the Internet is the enormous amount of information in the hands of the consumer. Recent incidents, such as the Boston Marathon Bombing, have produced huge amounts of data from news reports, CCTV feeds, spectator videos, blogs, and eyewitness accounts. This huge amount of information is bound to contain inconsistencies which can be seized upon to build a counter-narrative. A second problem concerns the rapidity in the promotion of conspiratorial ideas. Usually, within a period of two hours, conspiratorial ideas spread and embed themselves in social media as well as the social conversation.

Robert Brotherton presents six characteristics that inform the context of conspiracy theory. First, conspiracy theories are based on claims that are not verified, and are held to be indisputably true by those who subscribe to them. These claims lack evidential support and are not open to validation by the conspiracists.

In the episode "My Struggle," Tad O'Malley drones on about FEMA concentration camps, and the obesity crisis in America, in order to establish links to a broader conspiracy. The fact remains that the FEMA claim has been widely disproven, and that the obesity claim can never be substantiated, but these claims are held regardless.

Secondly, conspiracy theories are proposed in opposition to mainstream information for no apparent reason other than a contrarian justification. These interpretations are made in order to oppose more complex explanations for an event. For example, Mulder blindly affirms the mother of all alien conspiracy theories; the crash landing of an alien vehicle and the government's cover up at Roswell, New Mexico in July of 1947 ("My Struggle"). Historical facts, countless examinations of said facts, and an Air Force Report in 1997—not to mention the eyewitness account of Dr. O'Malley in the same episode—all challenge Mulder's assertion.

Mulder is right on two accounts: there was a crash, and it did involve nuclear power. There was even a cover up at Roswell, but it was not for the reason offered by alien conspiracy theorists. It was no secret that during the Second World War the Nazis were seeking a technological edge by developing weapons for their war effort. Allied pilots reported seeing strange flying vehicles, which they called "foo fighters," over the skies in the last years of the war. These weird vehicles, some cylindrical and other resembling flying wings, were the precursors of missiles and jet planes.

As the Cold War unfolded the US became obsessed with the USSR's attempts to create nuclear weapons. Roswell, New Mexico, was the location of the top-secret US nuclear program, and had in fact been the base where the two bombs dropped on Japan had been housed. On July 8th 1947 a crash in Roswell led to the dissemination of misinformation. The military explained the event as a weather balloon crash.

This was partially true, since a balloon had crashed. What was withheld from the public was that the military had been conducting a top-secret spying program called Project Mogul. A series of balloons had been positioned with microphones in order to detect a Russian nuclear explosion. What crashed at Roswell had been a balloon but it was not for gathering weather-related data. In the summer of 1949 the Soviets did explode a nuclear weapon and began the arms race. In the 1950s Hollywood exploited the fear of Soviet invasion and nuclear proliferation by creating science-fiction stories of alien contact and invasion. This became the genesis for many of the countless stories of UFO sightings and alien abductions.

Third, conspiracy theories are sensationalistic with national and international significance. Based on examination of the episode "Founder's Mutation," it's easier to wrap our minds around the belief that aliens manipulated the DNA of children in utero, rather than accepting the fact that they are the product of a megalomaniacal doctor in cahoots with the military.

The fourth assumption made by conspiracy theory adherents is that everything is part of an intentional plan. Every detail is said to be intentionally deceptive, consciously planned, meticulously manipulated, and perfectly carried out. They see no room or place for chance, accidents or unintended consequences.

Tad O'Malley maintains that the US government is manipulating gun-related crime in order to rescind the Second Amendment and confiscate weapons from the public. One of the most insidious contemporary conspiracy theories, featured immediately after the mass shooting at Sandy Hook Elementary, establishes that this was a "stage hoax" or a "crisis actor" conspiracy. This account suggests that there was no shooting, and that the government paid actors to play the part of grieving parents, all in an attempt to take away people's guns. Such a theory assumes that law enforcement, officers of the court, public school officials, families, and countless actors are conspiring, and that no one would ever tell the truth. The logistics necessary to orchestrate this incident and to keep it quiet, not to mention countless other shootings, boggles the mind. Yet it is viewed as gospel truth in many pro-gun conspiracy circles.

Finally, conspiracy theories depend on the belief that our government has malicious, cruel, and harmful intentions towards its citizenry. Once again Tad O'Malley alludes to the alleged 9/11 conspiracy. Although the 9/11 Truth Movement has offered a very detailed explanation of what happened on 9/11, and who the agents responsible for the events were, no serious attempts have been made to explain their motives—outside of the belief that the government conspired to create a perpetual state of war, in order to promote the interests of the military industrial complex. It is far easier to offer such a vague explanation than to provide a coherent account identifying the motives of the participants.

Selective Doubting

Explanations for belief in conspiracy theories have fallen into two broad categories: psychological and socio-political explanations. As a philosopher, I would add a third epistemic explanation.

Recent psychological research has demonstrated that belief in conspiracy theories is complicated and requires much more study. It is also important to note that as the American Enterprise Institute demonstrates in its 2013 study *Public Opinion on Conspiracy Theories*, adherents come from all walks of life; they cross all socio-economic, racial, generational, gender, class, and political categories. The most prominent "liberal" theories of conspiracy include the 9/11 truth movement, anti-vaxers, the surveillance state, and the belief in CIA-sponsored activities that undermine national health and promote the interests of the power elite. The most prominent "conservative" conspiracy theories include the belief that our government is conspiring with aliens to control its populace, the belief that global warming is a hoax, holocaust deniers, the government's attempt to undermine the Second Amendment, and the federal government's invasion of US states ("Jade Helm 15").

Conspiracists exhibit selective doubting. In other words, believers in conspiracy theories don't accept information that they deem incongruent with their worldview. Recent surveys suggest that due to postmillennial developments—such as economic and political Globalization, global terrorism, and an unresponsive political system that caters to small plutocratic elite—an ever-increasing number of people are espousing conspiracy theories in order to find meaning in the face of confusing events.

An examination of public attitudes about 9/11 sheds more light on the believers than on the event. 9/11 conspiracy beliefs are based on a cynical distrust of the political system, and are intended to present a challenge to structures of authority. People who hold these ideas reject the political establishment, deem the government undemocratic and not responsive to the needs and concerns of the people.

A second related conclusion is that people who hold conspiracist ideas tend to be disagreeable and suspicious of outsiders, people who are considered strangers. This is illustrated by the fact that people in America, who believe that their rights are being abridged by the government (such as ranchers who believe their animals can graze on public lands without restriction), are more likely to support harsh immigration measures and lax gun control measures.

Finally, researchers have concluded that exposure to conspiracy theories makes you more susceptible to other conspiracies. For example Tad's belief that our government is covering up its involvement in 9/11 goes hand in hand with the belief that the government is hiding the fact that extraterrestrials visited and crashed-landed in New Mexico. These ideas may be contradictory but are held to be both equally valid. Researchers recently uncovered the simultaneous conspiratorial belief that Bin Laden had been killed prior to the US raid in Pakistan in 2011, and that he survived the raid.

Paranoia and Pathology

The earliest theories of conspiracy, influenced by Richard Hofstadter's *The Paranoid Style in American Politics*, dismissed this behavior as the products of extreme paranoia, delusional thinking, and narcissistic pathologies. Recent research seems to be more, mixed with some theorists supporting these conclusions and others challenging them.

A number of researchers at the University of New Mexico established that in the case of the white supremacist movement, conspiracies serve to maintain or increase low self-esteem, are outlets for hostile impulses, represent high levels of anomie, distrust of authority, political cynicism, and exhibit a tendency toward authoritarianism or a willingness to follow authoritarian leaders.

A second group of theorists have challenged the pathology thesis, and have proposed in its place an explanation based on the Marxist conception of alienation. They argue that events like 9/11 are the products of systemic economic and political causes that have contributed to a sense of hopelessness or anomie. In an examination of Malaysian Jewish conspiracy theories, Viren Swami shows that these beliefs reflect displaced racist attitudes towards the Chinese minority in that country. Malaysia has no Jewish community and it appears that the Chinese, because of their ascending economic power, have been replaced with the "Jews." The Jews have also been synonymous with American hegemony in the Islamic imagination. Hostility towards the Jews is really a reaction to a new economic reality, globalized capitalism, at the expense of Malaysian sovereignty.

Other psychological explanations include cognitive biases. These include: *proportionality biases* (the belief that significant events must have significant causes), *attribution biases* (turning to dispositional explanations for events even when there are adequate situational explanations), *and confirmation biases* (the selective selection of explanations that accord with your beliefs), and *motivated skepticism* (the rejection and denigration of incompatible information based on the belief that they are right).

This selective skepticism creates what scholars call an echo chamber, a type of polarization where individuals only read sources, and associate with individuals, who confirm their beliefs and opinions. Researchers from Facebook, and a recent Italian study, have demonstrated that challenging and debunking conspiracy theories does not change the thinking of conspiracists. In fact sharing information with them causes them to cling to their beliefs more strongly, creating what has been called the "backfire effect," leading to more polarization and closing off avenues to debate.

In Season One's "Deep Throat," Deep Throat asks our protagonist pointedly, "Mr. Mulder, why are people like yourself who believe in the existence of extraterrestrial life on Earth, not dissuaded by all of the evidence to the contrary?" To which Mulder responds: "Because all of the evidence to the contrary is not entirely dissuasive."

Evidence? I Don't Need No Stinking Evidence

The political scientist Michael Barkun, in his book *A Culture of Conspiracy*, has presented a socio-political explanation for the appeal of conspiracy theories. Barkun establishes that conspiracy theories attempt to explain simply what a more nuanced mainstream analysis cannot, thereby providing a secret knowledge which the brainwashed masses have no access to. Based on this understanding, Barkun classifies conspiracy theories into three types:

1. **specific explanations for particular events** (9/11, the spread of AIDS in the black community as a CIA genocidal plot);
2. **systematic conspiracy theories believed to have as a goal the control of a particular region or the world** (the Jews, Freemasons, the Catholic Church); and
3. **Super-conspiracy theories or the construal of a meta theory that incorporates hierarchically all existing theories** (viral pandemics, banking crises, one world government). This seems to be the thinking of Tad O'Malley, and his real life inspiration, Alex Jones of infowars.com.

Epistemic Explanations of Conspiracy Theory

Philosophically speaking, we have identified two epistemic problems related to conspiracy theories. The first problem relates to the low priority that evidence is given by conspiracists. The evidential standard is quite low when compared to science. While science relies on verifiable, testable, and peer-reviewed evidence, conspiracy theory is dependent on conjecture, second hand accounts, and cynicism.

The evidence used by conspiracy theorists is primarily based on negative evidence, focusing on gaps or apparent ambiguities. The kind of evidence valued by conspiracy theorists is highly subjective since they often rely on eyewitness accounts. Recent research on eyewitness accounts in the criminal justice system shows how problematic this can be since memories fade, memories can be manipulated, or we may just have memory gaps due to missing the larger picture of an event.

The second problem is related to the echo chamber problem mentioned above; conspiracy theories tend to be self-insulating. This allows them to be resilient due to their insulation from questions and challenges. This also presents the problem of "cascading logic" which encourages conspiracists to include more and more participants in a conspiracy. For example, while Roswell was a military cover-up, conspiracists have included the US government, the media, and the United Nations.

Conclusions and Connections

The AEI Public Opinion in Conspiracy Theories study examined the belief in a government cover-up of an extraterrestrial encounter at Roswell, New Mexico, using polls taken at different time periods. In a June 1997 study 25 percent of those polled by Gallup believed the official USAF report on Roswell, and 64 percent of Americans did not. To the question of UFOs visiting Earth, a September 1996 Gallup poll reported 45 percent of the responses were yes, while a CNN/Time poll reported a 22 percent 'Yes' response—and 27 percent of the 'Yes' respondents watched *The X-Files*.

The most recent poll was taken in March of 2013 by Public Policy Polling. The study found that 21 percent of the respondents believed in the conspiracy, and 24 percent of them were men. To the question of a US government cover-up, the September 1996 Gallup poll reported 71 percent of the responses were yes, while a CNN/Time Poll reported a 27 percent 'Yes' response—33 percent of these 'Yes' respondents watched *The X-Files*. The same question was asked in a January 2000 CNN/Time poll and 49 percent responded 'Yes'.

The most interesting question was asked in a September 2013 Public Policy Poll: "Do you think the US government has secretly allowed aliens to take over our society in exchange for help with industrial technological advances, such as electric power and the microwave, or not?" Only 3 percent responded 'Yes', while 10 percent were not sure, women were 5 percent of the 'Yes' respondents, and 7 percent identified themselves as Republican. An examination of the polls shows that during the 1990s and at the turn of the millennium, a significant number of politically and economically disadvantaged people believed in this particular conspiracy. The influence of *The X-Files*, in the 1990s and beyond, as a provider of meaning in these hard times cannot be overlooked.

A Harmless Activity?

Some scholars believe that conspiracy theories are harmless and actually provide a practical social function. For many people, who consider themselves voiceless and outside of the value systems of the mainstream, conspiracy theories can provide an outlet. For others, who consider themselves politically and socially alienated, conspiracy theories can provide a forum for their concerns to be heard. Still others may feel conspiracy theories give them hope in circumstances that are beyond their control.

Fox Mulder exemplifies the mottos than have become mantras for the television show: *The truth is out there, Trust no one, I want to believe*. In the face of the tragedy of his sister's disappearance, Mulder appears to take solace in the hope that Samantha may be alive. Under the circumstances, Mulder needs an explanation for her disappearance. It is much easier to believe that she was abducted by aliens than to realize that she may have been victimized by a serial rapist/killer who broke into the sanctity of their home, and carelessly murdered her. If her disappearance can be explained by an alien abduction, then the government cannot be trusted because of its complicity in a cover-up.

On the other hand there are scholars who believe that conspiracy theories present one of the greatest threats to security in this technological age. Since conspiracy theories have been shown to impact beliefs, attitudes, and behavior, there are real-life examples of these negative attitudes. As illustrated by the cases of Malaysians and white Supremacists, negative attitudes towards minority groups can turn violent. Exposure to conspiracy theory can be detrimental to your political intentions and behavior as well. Studies indicate that the endorsement of conspiracy beliefs is associated with lower voter participation and less engagement in politics, and has contributed to increased feelings of political powerlessness.

A belief in conspiracy theories has also proved detrimental in public health debates. The belief that vaccines contribute to autism has contributed to many parents not vaccinating their children, which has caused a resurgence of preventable diseases, which has then contributed to a public health crisis in many communities. The belief in African American and Gay communities, that HIV/AIDS was created by our government for the purpose of genocide, has had negative consequences in disease prevention, public policy, and medical experimentation. Conspiracy theories have been shown to create mistrust of scientific findings. In the case of global warming or Climate Change, it has been used to block any meaningful legislation that would ameliorate the consequences of this climatic threat.

Finally, the greatest threat has to do with the coarsening of public discourse. As we pointed out, the efforts to correct conspiracy theories have had the opposite effect. Two conclusions can be drawn. First, these theories circulate within specifically truncated, isolated, and homogeneous ideological communities or echo chambers. Secondly, these echo chambers choose only to read information that feeds into their belief systems and are unlikely to associate with people who espouse different ideas. This creates a disincentive for constructive dialogue, and impedes constructive problem solving attempts.

The X-Files is just a television show that plays fast and loose with facts in order to entertain, thereby providing a sort of platform for conspiracy theories. Yet, at the same time, *The X-Files* also provides a vehicle for disenfranchised perspectives to be scrutinized, analyzed, and evaluated.

Chris Carter and his cohort know that the best way to entertain is to challenge conventional thinking. They may also be attempting to break through the echo chambers that threaten our most cherished liberal and scientific principles.

11
The Conspiracy Is Real

CHARLENE ELSBY AND ROB LUZECKY

As we sit in the basement of the FBI building, we flip through the newspaper clippings of strange events from across the nation and even around the world.

- **A woman in a Virginia bathroom dies from a bunch of bee stings (Season Four, "Zero Sum").**
- **In Idaho an officer stole a jeep and raced home for no reason (Season One, "Deep Throat").**
- **One night in Wisconsin a bunch of teenagers inexplicably took off all their clothes and wandered around the woods (Season Two, "Red Museum").**
- **A salvage ship turned up in San Diego with its entire crew suffering from radiation burns (Season Three, "Piper Maru").**

It seems that these events, which are separated by states, weeks, and years, cannot possibly be connected. Yet, we want to believe that they are all part of a massive globe-spanning conspiracy that has existed since at least World War II.

Before we can say whether or not this conspiracy is for good or evil, before we can say whether or not it exists, and whether or not we should be siding with Mulder or Cancer Man, we need to be able to identify what a conspiracy is. We need to identify its ontology.

The term "ontology" might seem as intimidating as an alien bounty hunter with a flame thrower, but, while there might be a great deal to fear in reality, figuring out the ontology of something is not something that should cause us to put down our flashlights. To figure out the ontology of something is essentially a two-step procedure. First, we identify the constituent parts of something, and then we figure out how these parts relate to one another. Once we have the parts and the relations figured out we will have determined whether or not the thing we are investigating actually exists, and then we can begin the processes of figuring out whether we should side with Mulder, or simply dismiss him as that spooky guy who has the cluttered office in the basement.

Figuring out the ontology of something physical like the FBI building is a rather easy affair. First, we would look to the things which must be there for it to exist as a physical structure. We recognize that there once was somebody, or a group of somebodies who drew up the plans for the building. Then we recognize that there was a team of workers who used a bunch of physical stuff to erect the building. Finally, we recognize that there are all sorts of agents, special agents, officers, and even moles who identify the building as their place of employment. In identifying these various parts and their relation to one another we have laid out the ontology of the physical structure we call the FBI building.

Figuring out the ontology of a conspiracy is a bit more difficult. Unlike the FBI building, a conspiracy is not located in any one place at any one time. Perhaps one of the most pernicious aspects of a conspiracy is that it cannot be linked with any one person or group of people. Sure, we would like to say that Cancer Man is part of the conspiracy, and perhaps we'd want to include all the members of the Syndicate, plus Krycek, but what about Skinner, and what about Fox's father and mother? Also, trying to prove the existence of a conspiracy by identifying it with a particular person's actions is not a very reliable way of proving that the conspiracy exists.

When Skinner closed down the X-Files, he might have been in on the conspiracy, or he may have been bowing to pressure from someone higher up, or he may have been trying to save Mulder's life. An additional problem with trying to define a conspiracy is that it might not even exist. The problem with a conspiracy is that there is very little by way of material evidence that it exists. If we want to be rigid materialists and simply identify the real with that which physically exists, then it would seem that anything non-material is just an illusion. Trying to isolate a conspiracy to particular people, particular actions, or physical existence is just as futile as the Russians attempts to contain the Black Oil (a.k.a. Purity).

The Need to Believe in Conspiracies

The Polish philosopher Roman Ingarden provided us with some very handy conceptual tools to determine the ontology of weird things like conspiracies. Starting with the literary work of art (or works of fiction), Ingarden set out to prove that there are things in existence whose existence is as an intentional object—these things exist as objects of consciousness—but that doesn't make them any less *real*. Conspiracies have very little by way of physical existence, but they are absolutely real, in the sense that we can identify their parts and how they partially determine our actions.

The first ontological part of something like a conspiracy is that there must be some sort of physical clue in existence. While there is no particular material thing we can point to and say, "That's a conspiracy!", it does require some kind of observable *thing*, something that points toward a more Muldery explanation of events. This clue might be the mysterious ash you find by a body (Season One, "Pilot"), or it might be a shadow in the water, but the conspiracy requires some material hint that things are not quite as they seem.

The next part of a conspiracy is that these material clues do not have a complete meaning. Those lights in the sky don't belong to any known aircraft. That hum cannot be identified as the sound made any by known insect. We know that we are dealing with a real conspiracy, and we are not simply spooky paranoids, when it is impossible to doubt that there is something more out there, the meanings of these things are completely impossible to pin down.

Were we to take these physical clues in isolation, there would yet be no sort of conspiracy. A conspiracy is not itself the weird hum, the mysterious ash, or the shadow in the water. We might claim, then, that the difference between a plain old physical thing and the physical aspect of a conspiracy is that the physical aspect of a conspiracy includes some additional properties—they can only be made sense of within a larger context.

While it isn't necessary to explain away the existence of a black oil under an old truck in a parking lot, put some black oil into people's eyes and suddenly we're all wondering how that happened.

In other words, the meanings of these physical things aren't completely given. When I put the tape mark X on the window, I don't know when exactly the Lone Gunmen will show up, or even if they will show up at all. Is the X an indication of a conspiracy then? If it is, then really what isn't? Well, it very well might be the case that the pieces of tape on the window are in fact part of the conspiracy, but to narrow things down a bit, and perhaps make the conspiracy a bit less all-encompassing, Ingarden pointed out that for a literary work of art to exist, it has to be *concretized* by the reader—the reader, when supplied with a text, must fill in the blanks of the represented situations the text describes. Likewise, for a conspiracy to exist, we have to play a part in filling-in the blank spaces. It is not enough for there to be weird things which happen; for these things to be part of a conspiracy, we have to get a bit spooky and invest these things with meaning.

When these things are invested with meaning, then the physical stuff of the conspiracy world takes on a different significance. Where Scully sees a weather balloon or a bit of swamp gas, Mulder sees evidence of human experimentation with alien technology. While the actual objects Scully and Mulder perceive are identical—lights in the sky—their meanings are completely different. We might be tempted, at this point, to simply dismiss the evidence. After all, its interpretation is completely subjective. *But we don't*, because we know Mulder is right (except, of course, for when he's wrong).

The difference between the Mulder interpretation and the Scully interpretation is usually a question of relations. Whereas for Scully the world is a bunch of unrelated phenomena whose existence can be explained away scientifically, Mulder is more likely to consider all of the evidence in its mutual relations; the relations between the phenomena, more than their physical characteristics, define what they are and point to someone responsible. It's not just swamp gas—it's alien tech, and *someone* is responsible for its existence.

These someones are mysterious actors in pursuit of a common goal; who they are, and what that goal is, that's more mysterious. Once we have determined what evidence is significant, and what it means when interpreted in light of our conspiracy, we can make lists of the *things we know*; these things are what's in the brown envelope (assuming we can trust its source).

We know, for instance, that

1. **Scully disappeared for a few days;**
2. **Scully had a microchip in her neck;**
3. **Scully got cancer;**
4. **Scully's cancer went away with the Cancer Man's treatment.**

We immediately begin to assume that these things are related in significant ways, and now what becomes significant is what's not said. The parts of the conspiracy we can't see are the ideas that

1. **Scully was abducted by either aliens or government agents or aliens in league with government agents;**
2. **These someones put the chip in her neck;**
3. **Scully's cancer was definitely related to the chip and the conspiracy, along with the miracle cure.**

The schematized aspects are the things that we fill in as we learn more and more about the conspiracy. Once the blanks are filled in, we try to create a full picture of the conspiracy, the "represented object." The "represented object", for Ingarden, is what defines a literary work of art as a literary work of art—there's a representation of some guy named Hamlet, and he lives in Denmark. In a conspiracy, our represented object might be what we have concluded about the involvement of the Cancer Man in Scully's cancer. It's the narrative we infer from all of the evidence we have which, when imbued with conspiracy-meaning and taken together, leads to a pretty solid representation of the actual events—the Cancer Man knew Mulder's father, possibly had an affair with his mother, and was definitely involved in his sister's abduction.

The Real Conspiracy

When we say the conspiracy is "real", there are a couple of possible things we could mean:

1. that there is a conspiracy, that the Smoking Man really is involved in nefarious schemes; and
2. that a "conspiracy" maintains some kind of real existence—it's a thing that exists in the world (as opposed to in the minds of the believers, the schemers, or in the little bits of material evidence that appear as breadcrumbs on the road to truth).

The literary work of art is real, according to Ingarden, not just in the actual book in which we read the text; nor is it simply in the minds of the people reading it. It is a stratified structure that involves all of

1. the material;
2. the meaning;
3. the schematized aspects; and
4. the represented objects.

The conspiracy is much the same. It is a complex entity that doesn't just pop out of existence when the Cigarette Smoking Man retires to write mystery novels, when Mulder has doubts, or when the evidence disappears from the secret warehouse in the Pentagon. The conspiracy can survive any of these events because it is a complex organism; it doesn't just die when one of its parts is destroyed or having a crisis of faith.

The other kind of "reality" in our conspiracy is an epistemological one, i.e., it has to do with what we know about it; part of what makes a conspiracy a conspiracy is the fact that we don't know exactly what's going on behind the scenes. We don't know, when we think we've hit upon the conspiracy, if that's the *real* conspiracy, or if we're getting closer or further away from the truth. We might think that the conspiracy is about the government working in league with the aliens to experiment upon the human race, when the *real* conspiracy is the government using the idea of aliens to distract us from their experiments on their own people. This is where the conspiracy differs from the literary work of art.

It's easy to say, for the literary work of art, that the real *Hamlet* is the one that takes place in Denmark and in which the ghost of Hamlet's father appears to him to warn him of Claudius's treachery. Some other *Hamlet*, which details the adventures of a cat named Hamlet who goes to wizarding school, is not the *real Hamlet*. In *The X-Files*, Scully and Mulder *really* work on the X-Files, solving supernatural mysteries and uncovering global conspiracies. What the Syndicate is *really* up to, we don't know.

To uncover the *real* conspiracy, we have to take the clues as given and determine if what we suppose happened *really* did. Did Mulder's father *really* consent to his daughter's abduction? Was she *really* abducted by aliens, or by the government? The real conspiracy is hidden under a web of lies and misinformation, perpetuated by people whose ultimate purpose is to deceive, inveigle, and obfuscate. And here, then, is the essential nature of the conspiracy's real existence: it is out there, never solely right here, but continuing to subsist from material clues, and the actions of those who are its founders and perpetrators, as well as the well as the actions of Mulder and Scully who are attempting to bring it to the light of day. As long as these exist and continue to exist in relation, the conspiracy is real, in the senses that it changes the lives of those who investigate it, and gives some perhaps unsettling truths to the more mysterious aspects of the world.

IV

Governments Do Bad Stuff

12
Dilemmas for Prisoners

DENNIS LOUGHREY

The X-Files has everything you could wish for.

There are monsters, adventures, romance, autopsies, and an ongoing investigation into the paranormal. Of particular attraction is a series within the series, dubbed the mytharc. Here are aliens and dazzling ships, as well as hidden preparations for the *larger plan*, the colonizing of Earth.

In uncovering its secrets, however, the story line sometimes lacks cohesion. Truth is elusive in *The X-Files*, and it can be difficult to tell the real from the unreal. Yet this somehow becomes part of the general ingenuity of the show, probably because *The X-Files* is not afraid to make fun of itself.

Apart from these attractions, there's something else. Think of it as the art of decision. Or as a technique of evaluating options and making choices. You can see it in the calm of the shadowy group known as the Syndicate. You can see it most clearly in everybody's favorite Syndicate member, the Cigarette Smoking Man. It's part of what makes *The X-Files* a frightening and very superior piece of popular culture. And it helps to make the mytharc worthy of its name.

What is it, exactly? *Strategy* is the word that helps explain it. A strategy, or strategic way of making choices. In its modern form, strategic decision-making was first studied in mid-twentieth century US military research. *The X-Files* takes up this research again, transmuting it into a series of remarkable stories.

Military Research

As the Cold War entered its expansionary phase, the RAND Corporation, with the involvement in the early days of Douglas Aircraft Company, conducted rational choice research on behalf of the US military. The military was particularly interested in learning how to obtain an edge over the old enemy, the Soviet Union.

The work at RAND led to the development of an interactive decision game. This was the strategic game that was later termed the Prisoner's Dilemma. It was closely studied for its applications. It provided the doctrine of nuclear deterrence in the arms race. It also provided material for Stanley Kubrick's movie, *Dr. Strangelove*.

Imagine that a crime has been committed, and that two suspects are being questioned in a police station. Let's say that they are you and I. We have each been placed in different interrogation cells. We are both rational and self-interested.

The officers invite each of us to rat on the other. They tell us the following. If neither of us rats on the other, then we will be given a one-year custodial sentence on the basis of a trumped-up charge. However, if both of us rat, we will both be convicted, and we will receive five years apiece.

But there's more. If one of us rats and the other does not, then the ratter will be released without charge, while the non-ratter will receive ten years. So, if you rat on me, and I refrain from ratting, you go free and I get ten years. Likewise, if I rat on you, and you refrain from ratting, I go free and you get ten years.

These payoffs are shown in the below diagram.

	You rat	**You don't rat**
I rat	5 for me, 5 for you	No prison for me, 10 for you
I don't rat	10 for me, no prison for you	1 for me, 1 for you

The numbers shown are years of imprisonment, and they are not exactly looking good.

Think Like a Rat

What should we choose? Our situation seems clear. It's in our combined interests not to rat. If we both refrain from ratting, then we'll both receive a minor sentence, one year apiece.

It's here that we get to something unexpected and strange about this game. Your thinking person can hardly help noticing that what they choose will depend on what they think the other person will choose. They also notice that the other person is probably noticing the same thing.

Consider the situation from my point of view. Assume that I think that you will not rat. Clearly, if this is what I think that your position will be, then I can achieve a better outcome by ratting on you. We can read off the numbers in the You-don't-rat column (the right-hand column in our diagram). I will receive one year if I too refrain from ratting (we receive one year each), and yet I'll go free by ratting (I go free, you serve ten years). My strategy, then, should be to take advantage of your refraining from ratting by ratting on you.

Now assume that you will rat. After all, if I can reason that I am better off ratting, then presumably you can do the same, and clearly I have a reason not to trust you. We can read off the numbers in the You-rat column (the left column). I will receive five years if I too rat (five for me, five for you), while if I refrain from ratting then I will receive ten years (ten for me, you go free). My strategy, then, should be to fight fire with fire by ratting on you.

What is agreeable about this strategy is that I do not need to know what you are going to choose. I do not need to rely on trust. Should you not rat, fine, I am better off ratting, and should you rat, I am still better off ratting. Either way, I do better. As they say in the jargon, ratting *dominates* co-operating.

Ditto from your point of view. You will be better off ratting on me whatever I do. So the Prisoner's Dilemma's tough-minded lesson is that, from the perspective of *each* person, ratting is better, no matter what the other does.

Yet the sad truth is that ratting leads to a terrible collective outcome. For, considered together, we would both be better off by not ratting. By not ratting, we would receive only one year apiece. But, incredibly, this is not what we should do.

John Nash's work is important. Nash was one of those who worked at RAND. He came up with the idea of the Nash equilibrium. A Nash equilibrium is attained when each player is making the very best choice that they can, and they cannot improve upon it. The interests of both players converge on this state. In the Prisoner's Dilemma, both players ratting is a Nash equilibrium.

Repeated Prisoner's Dilemmas are often studied. In these cases, you have to meet the same opponent time after time, meaning there is the opportunity for payback. These repeated cases are interesting from the point of view of *The X-Files*, because this is a TV *series*, and so if you rat in one episode, then there is a risk that your victim will come after you in the following episode. The Cigarette Smoking Man's way of managing this risk is to prevent repeated cases from occurring. He is the murderous type. Trusting no one means never leaving loose ends.

People in everyday life are probably a lot nicer than this, and more trusting. Rather, this is the way we could be, if we would like. A way to ensure that we would come out ahead in interactive decision situations. We could become rats. As David Lewis put it so well, ratting is "*rat*ional."

Relevance

These strange ideas from research for the military were taken up again by *The X-Files*. The stories of *The X-Files* exemplify the Prisoner's Dilemma's unexpected outcome, that ratters do better, even though, considered collectively, everyone is worse off.

The way of the ratter is brought to life by the characters who comprise the Syndicate, the shadowy secret government. These people lurk in dimly-lit corridors, clubs, and conference rooms. You have to admire the fact that, watching them, you *know* that they would not accept that ratting is anything other than entirely rational.

The most representative face of the Syndicate is the Cigarette Smoking Man, who operates according to very particular rules. In portraying the way that the Cigarette Smoking Man deliberates, *The X-Files* takes up again the investigations of Cold War research. A crucial part of the *X-Files* central mythos is a byproduct of a strategy of deliberation that was first worked on in mid-twentieth century US military research.

Masterfully portrayed by William B. Davis (himself once a student of philosophy), the Cigarette Smoking Man embodies the way of the rat, along with the associated strategy of distrusting others. He has the words "Trust No One" engraved on his cigarette lighter. To successfully carry out the mission at hand, he must trust no one.

Who can act as a counterpart to the Syndicate? The answer is the peerless duo, Mulder and Scully. Along with their deep chemistry, they pursue their investigations into the paranormal at the frontier zone between the known and the unknown. There are also the characters known as the Lone Gunmen. This resourceful trio take up and even extend, in their own inimitable geeky way, Mulder and Scully's truth-guided obsessiveness.

When acting in situations that involve other people, these characters mostly refrain from ratting. This co-operative policy, together with an emphasis on evidence gathering, and not being too suspicious of other people, and at least trying not to be untrusting, provide the main guide to the characters of Mulder and Scully and the Lone Gunmen.

The Rat Mentality

Many episodes of *The X-Files*, particularly those that comprise the mytharc set, are exceptionally successful in illustrating the more direct, no-holds-barred style of strategy in which the Syndicate specializes. To make things interesting, though, let's consider a few examples that are hard to interpret in this way.

Turn first to an occasion in which the Cigarette Smoking Man looks less than wholehearted in his actions. In the episode "Herrenvolk," he passes on the opportunity to kill Mulder's mother, providing a spectacularly unconvincing justification, when by his own lights he had reason to kill her. Yet, despite the Cigarette Smoking Man's backsliding, he keeps on going, living in accord with his mission, exercising a kind of pure will, a strange autonomy.

Throughout the episode "Musings of a Cigarette Smoking Man," the Cigarette Smoking Man leads a sort of double life, serving the Syndicate by day and writing science fiction by night. When he finally has a story accepted for publication, he attempts to abandon his life in the Syndicate, and to give himself over to his writing, even to stop smoking. Yet, when the editor changes the ending of his piece, he is filled with such extreme rage and disgust with life that he abruptly terminates his fling with the writerly life. He uses his feelings to attain strength of will, and he returns wholeheartedly to the ways of the Syndicate.

This episode contains overlapping stories about the Cigarette Smoking Man. It includes flashbacks of an origin story about how he became the Cigarette Smoking Man, plus a few personal career highlights, and some interesting US history that you don't learn at school. For example, that the Cigarette Smoking Man assassinated President Kennedy, and that he presided over a group of shadowy and definitely not good-natured nut cases, and argued the case for killing Martin Luther King, and that he then personally carried out that assassination. Some sources have these events as not actually canonical, but you get the picture. The Cigarette Smoking Man *could* have done these things. The episode shows how the Cigarette Smoking Man thinks. He makes certain that there will be no repeat case.

Finally, consider the wonderful episode "Jose Chung's *From Outer Space*," a story that is not graced by the Cigarette Smoking Man, and is not even part of the official mytharc. Yet it is smoothly insightful. Towards the end of the episode, Mulder approaches Chung, a science-fiction writer who is writing a book called *From Outer Space*. Chung's book mocks the investigative work that Mulder and Scully, along with a large number of amateur UFO researchers, undertake.

Mulder believes that the consequence of this book's being published will be that his and their activities will be held up to ridicule and stereotyped. Mulder believes that this is precisely what shadowy Syndicate figures want to achieve. Mulder asks Chung not to write the book, pointing out that Chung's publisher is a subsidiary of McDougall Kesler. This name sounds uncannily like the real-world McDonnell Douglas, formed in 1967 by a merger between McDonnell Aircraft and Douglas Aircraft, the latter being the entity that set up RAND.

No need to overstate the point, however. What really distinguishes this episode is a glimpse of the reach of organization and control that spreads beyond the Syndicate. Mulder tells Chung that he suspects "a covert agenda for your book on the part of the military, industrial, entertainment complex." This wider form of the organization supports the Syndicate's strategy by carrying it out in the required way, dealing destructively with opponents. In fact, the mission requires such a network, large and unanimous. The ratter, like your actual *rattus* rat, is everywhere.

They're Different from Us

A certain decision strategy, then, that ratting is the rational course in interactive situations, is the key to understanding the actions of the Cigarette Smoking Man, the Syndicate, and indeed the whole military, industrial, entertainment complex. As many episodes of *The X-Files* reveal, ratting is a strong-minded strategy that often wins the day for the Syndicate, no matter what the other party chooses.

Furthermore, ratting makes them quite different people from the rest of us. The Cigarette Smoking Man is the face of the Syndicate. His way of handling himself in decision situations provides *The X Files* with much of its mythology. Here is somebody utterly *other*, who trusts no one, who rats on others, who sticks by his choices, come what may, and who just does not care. Even the way he smokes is odd.

Imagine an *X-Files* without the Cigarette Smoking Man and his choices. It would be an *X Files* without the mythology.

13
What's Wrong with Experimenting on Humans?

ROB LUZECKY AND CHARLENE ELSBY

The truth, as we all want to believe, is out there. But what if that truth makes us uncomfortable? What if that truth demands that we be made uncomfortable? The truth we are referring to is a particularly troubling moral truth, which seems to run through the entirety of the *X-Files* universe.

We all know that Samantha, Scully, and countless others have seen the bright lights and were the subjects of alien experiments. The government and the Syndicate calmly reassure us that no crimes have been committed, but we still want to say that great moral wrongs have been perpetrated. Unfortunately, we can't rest calmly in our beds of moral comfort.

We would like to think that there are compelling moral arguments to the effect that alien biologists should not experiment on us, but perhaps, this is an all-too-human perspective. What, if any, moral reasons would the Greys have for not experimenting on, or even harvesting us?

After all, in many cases we seem to have no moral qualms about experimenting on what we consider to be lower forms of life, especially if it can be shown that these experiments might benefit us, or if it can be demonstrated that the objects of our experiments are too stupid, too insensitive, all in all too underdeveloped to figure significantly into our moral calculations.

Troubling though it may be, the Greys, and even the bounty hunters could believe themselves to be morally justified in experimenting on us. If the aliens are about to kidnap you and start putting nasty instruments into your body, can you think of a good argument you could use to show them that what they're planning to do is morally wrong?

Kill All Humans?

Immanuel Kant presented a well-known theory of ethics based on respecting the autonomy of rational creatures. If a Kantian encountered a Grey who was all set to bring him into the unmarked train car in order to play with his DNA, we might think that the Kantian could present a fairly persuasive argument to the effect that the alien would be more moral if they instead turned their attentions to a chicken, because a chicken is less rational than a human.

Kant's famous "categorical imperative" says, first, that you should not adopt a rule of behavior unless everyone can adopt the same rule, and, second, that you should always treat other rational individuals as ends in themselves, not merely means to your ends. Unfortunately, Kantian maxims are like alien bounty hunters, and not everything is quite as it first appears. The stipulations of the Kantian morality end up giving the Greys some very compelling arguments to morally justify their experimentation on us hairless apes.

Kant's categorical imperative might not amount to a conclusive reason for not placing us in an alien Petri dish. In its first formulation, the categorical imperative only condemns actions that would lead to a logical contradiction if performed by anyone in any place.

Kant illustrates this formulation with the example of lying. We're not supposed to lie, because if everyone lied, then truth would cease to exist. Specifically, we would have no concept of the truth, and this would be a big problem every time we tried to say something and wanted Skinner to believe us. Were we to imagine a world where everyone lied all the time, then we would be imagining a contradictory situation in which something that must exist, does not exist. A moral universe, for Kant, cannot abide such contradictions.

Would there be any contradiction involved in the aliens experimenting on us? Well, no, there wouldn't be. For Kant, a contradiction becomes morally pernicious when it entails the elimination of something that must necessarily exist. When we wake up in that brightly-lit boxcar, we know that we will be fundamentally changed, and we might even die as a result of these changes. But the impending change and possible death would only be morally wrong if it could be demonstrated that humans must necessarily not change or die. In fact, neither of these things can be demonstrated.

The second formulation of Kant's categorical imperative doesn't provide a moral reason for why we should be allowed a pass on the alien probes. When we're dealing with rational beings, for Kant, it is morally wrong to use them merely as a means to our own ends. Rational beings should, by virtue of being rational, always be allowed a chance to make a choice. Using people as a means is morally wrong, because it does not allow rational beings to make informed choices.

But, to an alien, we humans might only be as rational as chickens, which, as we all know, have prion-addled brains and perform such irrational acts as eating their own kind (Season Two, "Our Town"). Were it to be demonstrated that we have such a diminished level of rationality, we would not be afforded any protection by Kant's second formulation of the categorical imperative. If it could be shown that members of our species are blindingly stupid, then the aliens would have moral justification for experimenting on us.

Of course, if it could be demonstrated that humans are rational beings, then the aliens wouldn't have any moral justification for experimenting on us. We'll get around to that demonstration as soon as we stop confusing shiny weather balloons with actual spaceships.

Experiments on Humans Maximize Utility

But it is not quite necessary to take the tape-mark X off the window and cower in our beds accepting that our immanent abduction is morally justified. Utilitarianism is an alternative theory of morality, very different to Kant's and more influential.

Utilitarians have a thing or two to say to our alien scientists. Utilitarian ethics is based on two fundamental principles. First, an action is morally good if it maximizes our utility. That is, something is good if it increases or maintains our ability to be happy. The second key principle of utilitarianism comes from what Jeremy Bentham and John Stuart Mill said: "Everybody counts for one, and nobody for more than one."

Just as we should not disregard the strange lights we see in the sky around Skyland Mountain Resort (Season Two, "Ascension"), we should not ignore the extent to which utilitarian ethics may be used to generate arguments that would justify alien experimentation on humans. Unlike the Kantian ethicists, who cling to the claim that some actions are absolutely wrong, utilitarians live in a pluralistic, ever-changing moral universe, where good and bad are quantifiable and determined case by case and where everyone counts as an equal.

One uncomfortable outcome of utilitarian reasoning is that it seems to provide moral justification for actions that we might immediately feel to be morally repugnant. For the utilitarian, in any given situation we must try to maximize the happiness of the most people. Take the case of implanting microchips into the body of a person who has been abducted: it might be the case that the microchip causes the person to get cancer, but implanting this person with the microchip increases the happiness of ten other beings.

If the utilitarian ethicist were to remain consistent to his principles, he might have to assert that implanting the microchip is justified as a morally good action. Sorry, Scully, it's too bad that you have to get cancer, but your cancer increases the utility of the Greys, and quite possibly there are more of the Greys whose utility would be increased than there are humans whose utility would be decreased by experimentation on a few humans, or even the entire human race. In the end, the utilitarian ethicist might be an adjunct member of the Syndicate, who presents arguments that morally justify invasive experimentation on any particular human and, at a pinch, the whole human race.

The Virtuous Grey

Dissatisfied with the shortcomings of the Kantian and utilitarian theories, some philosophers have gone back to the ancient Greek ethicist Aristotle, and have taken from Aristotle something they call "virtue ethics."

Perhaps, then, our best hope for avoiding the spinning metal probe is to convince the Greys of the validity of an Aristotelian ethics, but only were they not to recognize one obvious flaw in its application. Aristotle's ethics is one kind of "virtue" ethics, called such for the reason that living ethically involves the cultivation of various virtues of character.

By performing any action regularly, habits are formed so that that action becomes the natural response of an individual to a particular situation. This can be as simple as always choosing the sunflower seeds in the shell, or trying to explain away Mulder's brilliant theories using an obviously suspect application of scientific principles. Some of the habits we gain in life will result in our tending towards choosing good or bad actions, and those are the habits which determine whether or not we are virtuous people.

The virtues, for Aristotle, are means between excesses and deficiencies of any particular character trait. It is virtuous to find the moderate path between two extremes. For instance, my virtuous habit of being witty is the mean between an excess (buffoonery) and a deficiency (boorishness). Once I have the virtues habituated into my character, I'll just know what to do in any particular situation that demands my ethical attention.

Our best hope to avoid the probe might be to convince the Greys that such an action does not contribute to the development of their moral character. I might claim that, despite my being an obviously inferior species, their repeated probings of me could only develop in them the probing habit, which they may later use against their own, obviously morally worthy kind. I could argue that the choice to subject me to horrendous pain and microchipping can only lead to their developing a cruel character, and nobody wants their first instinct, when faced with a new species, to be *probe it*.

The well-read Grey could reply, however, that my argument rests on a few misguided notions. Not only did Aristotle never list a mean between cruelty and mercy in his list of virtues, but the virtues he does list are intended to be particular to the *human* species. The virtues, for Aristotle, when all of them are embodied, lead to a state of the soul in accordance with virtue, but he means the human soul. The human soul is the one that is characterized by *phronesis* (practical wisdom), and the activity of the soul in accordance with virtue that is necessary for *eudaimonia* (happiness) is a form of *human* flourishing.

The entirety of virtue ethics would have to be, for the Greys, reworked in order to better exemplify the defining qualities of their own species, not ours. Whatever the defining quality of a

Grey is, their virtue ethics would have to encourage it, such that they may flourish. Whereas Aristotle defines humans as the "rational animal" and sometimes a "two-footed land mammal," the definition of a Grey just might be a "human-abducting, microchipping, probing animal" whose best hope for flourishing is to colonize the planet, using us as hosts for their weird little alien fetuses.

Nothing Important Happened Today

While none of the above theories, applied to the case of alien experimentation on humans, leads to our being able to claim moral superiority to the alien invaders, another kind of ethics might still justify our rejecting their inappropriate advances on our species and planet.

Maybe existentialism offers a more hopeful approach. The primary belief of the existentialist is, according to Jean-Paul Sartre, the idea that "existence precedes essence." In other words, humans find themselves existing without any predetermined purpose or goal. We can't escape the necessity to define ourselves and create ourselves. This means that every good there is in the world is the result of our having chosen that thing as a good.

If an alien wants to microchip me, and does so, they imply by their action that microchipping me is the best thing to do. They, like us, are engaging in a process of self-definition, and if they choose to define themselves as abduction and probing specialists, then that they will be. The question arises, for the existentialist, if there are no external, supreme "goods" to refer to in order to guide us in their actions, then how can any action be deemed ethical or not ethical?

Simone de Beauvoir attempts to provide an answer in her *Ethics of Ambiguity*. Taking the idea that we are self-defining creatures as given, the good we might aim at is that very self-definition. To define yourself, you require freedom. And, given that we are all subjectivities within a world of other subjectivities, their freedom should count for something too. The thing we should aim towards, says de Beauvoir, is to will freedom, for ourselves and others.

Obviously, there will come beings who will attempt to deny us our freedom. While Beauvoir speaks of tyrants, we can apply the same principles to the Greys. We may be happily expressing our freedom by running around the Earth unprobed, while they may want to express their freedom by confining and probing us. Thus, our expressions of freedom run into conflict with one another.

According to Beauvoir, though, one of these species is definitely in the wrong. It is not an expression of freedom to oppress the freedom of others, and thus the Greys cannot justify their actions with reference to an existentialist ethics where human freedom is valued. On the other hand, being subjectivities in the world of subjectivities precludes the absolute application of such a value, since each one of those subjectivities is involved in the never-ending project of defining the good for themselves. We can scream all we like, but the fact of the matter is, they don't have to listen to us.

The solution, therefore, can't be simply the declaration of moral high ground over the Greys, as they continue to probe us and destroy, along with us, all the goods we have set up for ourselves in this absurd world. Rather, the Greys must be dealt with as a tyrannical force; and the way we deal with tyrannical forces is revolution. When one species attempts to oppress another, the ethical thing to do is to destroy the oppressor. This may require some hard decisions, but when our arguments to the alien colonists fail, an ethics of action may be our only hope in saving the human race.

While some of the species will perish, screaming Kant quotations as the Greys inflate their bodies here and there just to see what happens, these authors will be looking to the faceless alien rebels for moral guidance. Though the Greys may reasonably propose the Kantian, utilitarian, or Aristotelian perspectives in order to justify colonizing us, it's hard to argue when you're on fire.

14
What They Have Done

CHRISTOPHER KETCHAM

The X-Files produces the uncanny feeling that we're not alone—that there may be others, alien others who roam the planet with impunity or are subjects of clandestine experiments that the powers-that-be feel we are better off not knowing anything about.

The episode "731" discovers just such an experiment. But how do you know that the other standing over there is, well, human?

The They

Martin Heidegger (1889–1976) said that we are thrown into the world. We come to be in a world of *theys* and as such we want to become like *the they* and experience angst when we are not. Yet who are the they?

Perhaps as a child you suspected that you were adopted because you certainly were not at all like *them*—your parents and siblings. If you were born during the atomic age perhaps your fears were that you, like Clark Kent were born alien, or, worse, that your family, your community even is filled with alien creatures who will have their way with you once you are of age . . . Like Mulder in "Little Green Men" who wonders whether his sister was abducted by aliens—or did he just dream it?

Being taken aback by the other is normal, so said Emmanuel Levinas (1906–1995). The other, any other, brings us up short when we see the other's face. The other brings us out of our safe, secure enjoyment of dwelling within ourselves.

This other, said Levinas is infinitely different from me. How different is different and when does difference become alien?

In *The X-Files* the they are different from the they we have come to expect our theys to be. When we look at the face of one of these others we don't see the face we expect, even though Levinas tells us we can't ever know the other because of the other's infinite difference to us. The other soars above me, said Levinas.

"I'll say," Mulder responds, "because that other you are looking at came from a place far beyond this world that Heidegger said you were thrown into." How does he know?

An Uncanny Valley

Certainly there are the huge oval-eyed, triangular-headed creatures of science fiction and purported alien abductions. We know that Mulder's seen a few of these ("Little Green Men," "Colony," "731," "Apocrypha"). What about the other others, who, when we see their face there is something different about them but we don't know quite what? Masahiro Mori coined the term 'uncanny valley' to describe the experience of encountering an other who appears to be human but is not quite so.

We know industrial robots aren't human even though they move in much the same way. We see other healthy humans as what they are—human. We may be fascinated by the working robot but there's no getting around it: it's a robot. Normal healthy people—well they're definitely human. What about the zombie? What is it? It creeps us out. Is it just the zombie or the thing that looks almost humanoid and acts humanoid that creeps us out?

What if you saw the face of another and you said, "Definitely human." This other walks past, then another, and another until a whole line of identical others passes you. Haven't you just entered the uncanny valley?

Mulder and Scully skirt the rim of the uncanny valley every episode as they attempt to understand the others they encounter in the world they have been thrown. However, the uncanny valley into which human likeness becomes creepiness isn't the only valley of suspicion and dread they fall into. The phenomenologists like Heidegger, Levinas, Maurice Merleau Ponty (1908–1961) and the father of the idea, Edmund Husserl (1859–1938) explore how the mind makes sense of the world. We look, we see, we learn what things are and how they look and work and we stick this knowledge in our memory. We experience the uncanny valley when we get a glimpse of a hulking but human-like shadow in the forest, the footprint of Bigfoot, or see a scaly arm clutching the door to a boxcar on a train.

Broken Tools, Broken Mind?

Heidegger said that tools in the hands of an apprentice soon become 'ready to our hand' meaning that we no longer think about them as we're using them. Then the tool breaks or stops working properly—we begin to sense that something is strange about the tool and suddenly its tool-lessness comes straight into our mind. Once we discover the problem, we fix it and move on. What if it is a problem we can't fix or resolve, like that thing we just saw in the sky?

We have viewed the episodes in *The X-Files* about those who've seen UFOs or claim to have been abducted (alien abductions: "Fallen Angel," "Duane Barry." UFOs: "Pilot," "Deep Throat," "Conduit," and others). Some we dismiss, but as we see in *The X-Files* many of these encounters are difficult to explain as mere fiction. We watch as Scully denies the fantastic explanation and Mulder defends it. Why? Because he experienced the moment of uncanniness himself. Yet it's not just the encounter with the alien or alien-like other that bothers us the most.

It's So Secret That

> The ruler of the world is no longer the country with the bravest soldiers, but the greatest scientists.
>
> —the first Elder in "731"

What bothers us the most is that we know that things are not always what the "they," particularly the authorities, say are right, true, and proper. Our phenomenal experience says, "This isn't quite right."

Are we back to the point in childhood where we thought we were adopted? No, we've come through all that, hopefully without too much psychological damage. The fact is that we know that the government hides things from us. We hear from Congress that the SECRET stamp is the most used tool by the military, spy agencies, or even the Department of State. We know that some of these secrets when revealed or uncovered have been truly ghastly experiments on people that have provided little in the way of scientific advances. We wonder: Am I in such an experiment?

The Tuskegee Exeriments

You're a poor Black man in Alabama in 1931 and a Tuskegee researcher says that if you agree to participate in a study of Black men in Alabama, you'll get free health care. Tuskegee Institute is a renowned institution that has been serving the Black population of the South since reconstruction. Sure, you say. However what they didn't tell you was that you've been chosen because you've got syphilis and they want to study you over a long period of time to see how the disease progresses. Even when a viable cure becomes available a few years later they don't give you the drug, nor do they ever tell you that your progressively weakening condition is syphilis. This goes on with the full support and agreement of the US Government and the American Medical Association until 1972 news reports condemn the study. Many of the people in the study died along the way. Long after the study is closed, President Clinton apologizes to you and other study participants and to the American People in 1997. *Apology is Policy*.

"731"

On December 1st, 1995, agent Mulder stumbles upon a train filled with . . . who or what? ("731"). 731 had a much earlier ignominious beginning in World War II. The episode "731" intimates that human chemical war experiments that both the US and Japan conducted on humans during World War II did not end in the 1970s even after a publicly released 1993 US government report (GAO Report to the Chairman, Committee on Veteran Affairs, US Senate) that detailed the experiments, said that the US is no longer experimenting on human guinea pigs.

From history it's revealed that the X-Files episode "731" *isn't* far-fetched . . .

During the Second World War, the Japanese Army Unit 731 used civilian captives and soldiers of other nations in occupied

China for their germ, chemical, and frostbite warfare experiments . . . Thousands died.

In separate experiments during World War II at the Naval Research Laboratory in Anacostia, Washington, and the Edgewood Arsenal in Maryland, the US exposed its own soldiers—African Americans and Japanese-Americans—to mustard gas. The Japanese-Americans, to see whether Japanese were more or less vulnerable to injury by the chemicals. African American, because the scientists suspected that black skin would be less vulnerable to the chemicals. If so, guess who would be sent to the front first?

The American soldiers subjected to the chemical tests by the Army and Navy during the war were sworn to secrecy and their records scrubbed of any evidence that they had been subject to mustard gas experiments. Once they experienced the exposure to mustard gas they were not given any further medical attention. Since then, few have received VA benefits for their debilitating injuries that resulted from the exposure, because the records were scrubbed.

As the war ended, the Japanese running Unit 731 killed the remaining prisoners and released into the wild mice infected with bubonic plague. All Japanese who participated in the project were sworn to secrecy.

Did we know about 731? We did. General of the Army MacArthur and the US hired the Japanese 'scientists' from Unit 731 after the war to provide us with details of their germ war experiments in order to prepare for the emerging Cold War.

Let's suppose with Mulder and the X-Files that instead of ceasing, the chemical and germ warfare experiments go deeper underground. Projects begun in secret are difficult to end. Why? Congress, the press, and the people who normally would question continuity of such projects don't know that the projects exist. Nobody questions the continuity of such projects after the war ends. This is the premise of the episode of "731."

Conspiracy Theory

To understand the episode, we must dig back and speculate how we get to the point in the story where Mulder encounters strange beings on a train.

You see, there is so much more to learn after the Second World War is over. However, the live bodies that were plentiful and freely taken during war run out when the war ends. For a time the scientists write reports, consider alternatives such as monkeys and other primates to use as surrogates until . . .

The Cold War beckons. The labs stay open, funded through clandestine budgets. The war scientists and new recruits fresh from university doctoral programs use animals where human subjects were used before. Then it happens.

In the New Mexico desert true alien spacecraft are recovered after a crash. The remaining labs formed to test humans and now animals are converted to test aliens. They test what they have always tested: biological and chemical weapons. The aliens prove resistant to chemicals and biological weapons used in World War II and they survive the cold-war concoctions that are even more lethal. The aliens would make perfect soldiers. However they are aliens and look like aliens. Nobody wants anyone to know that we're not alone. The economy would collapse; people would see that they are no longer the most superior species. Human subjects are again required.

Men and women begin reporting episodes where they believe they have been abducted by aliens. The numbers of these incidents increase over the decades and the psychologists dismiss these as hallucinations or outright lies. Conspiracy theories abound. Secrecy in the labs becomes even stealthier. For example, we're never sure in the *X-Files* series whether Mulder and Scully are working with the FBI to uncover mysteries or they are unwitting accomplices to these clandestine activities, sent on missions to discover where there might be weaknesses in the veil of secrecy.

As we return to "731" we are at an old Leper Colony: Hansen's Disease Research Facility which nobody in their right mind will visit. Mulder doesn't know what's going on. Let's say that we do, because we know about the real 731. We speculate even more.

At the Hansen facility 'scientists' are gene splicing, test-tube babying and otherwise experimenting with human and alien DNA, searching for a hybrid warrior who will survive the ravages of chemical and biological war. Oh, the horribly disfigured creatures that result from this experimentation. Many abort, still more die in infancy from terrible birth defects that cannot be repaired. Others grow into monstrosities with scrambled brains or with outsized limbs or ones withered to uselessness. A few look more human than alien but more look more alien than human.

Ethics is not really an issue, they say. Just using human DNA from eggs or sperm harvested from, well you know, those kooks who thought they were abducted by aliens. And, of course, the alien's DNA or whatever their building blocks for life are—well that's alien stuff and not covered by any *human* subject experiment regulation.

So when the soldiers at the beginning of the episode "731" shoot strange creatures they have removed from the Hansen Laboratory . . . we are just being humane as we would be with any laboratory animal that needs to be put out of its misery after its effectiveness is compromised or the experiment ends. Remember euthanizing these 'entities' using drugs would be difficult because they are resistant to our deadliest chemical weapons.

We have only episode "731" to learn from and in that story we don't get tissue samples to confirm our suspicions. However, Mulder finds a book written in Japanese that he believes tells the whole story.

So is it ethical to harvest DNA as we did whole people during war? Fortunately we don't have to debate this right now because nobody knows that this project still exists.

Damn you, Mulder and Scully! You almost outed the project.

But what do you two know?

"Don't you see, Mulder? You're doing their work for them. You're chasing aliens that aren't there, helping them to create a story to cover the shameful truth . . . and what they can't cover, they apologize for. Apology has become policy," says Scully.

"I, I don't need an apology for the lies. I, I don't care about the fictions they create to cover their crimes. I want them accountable for what did happen. I want an apology for the truth," Mulder replies. We now know the truth.

Who's Responsible?

What happened to the major Japanese actors in the real 731 of World War II? Website *unit731.org* reported that General Ishii the commander lived near Tokyo until he died in 1959. Another participant became governor of Tokyo, still another the president of the Japan Medical Association. Others became leaders in the health ministry, the Green Cross, and as heads of Japanese medical schools. Yoshisuke Murata, who was in charge of human vivisections, later became director of Kyoto University medical school, and then director at Kinki University. Japan finally acknowledged its participation in the project in 1984. Apology is policy.

In "731" Mulder entrusts the notebook written in Japanese to the train conductor. When he retrieves it he finds that it has been replaced with a fake. In the last scene of "731" we see an elderly Japanese man poring over the real notebook . . . The beings in the Hansen lab are gone, evidence has disappeared: the project is safe for now . . . That uncanny feeling survives doesn't it, even though you know now the rest of the story and if it should later come out publicly . . . that *Apology is policy*.

V

Can We Trust Ourselves?

15
The Madness of Sneaky Fox

JOHN M. THOMPSON

> One person's craziness is another person's reality.
>
> —TIM BURTON

One perennial question running through *The X-Files* concerns Agent Fox Mulder's mental status: is he insane? The 1996 episode "Jose Chung's *From Outer Space*," which features a science-fiction author named Jose Chung who follows Mulder and Scully during one of their cases, poses this question most acutely.

In the closing scene Chung is writing up a draft of his latest work based on his experience shadowing the agents. In a voice-over, he refers to his fictionalized Mulder character, Reynard Muldrake, as "that ticking time-bomb of insanity . . . his quest into the unknown has so warped his psyche, one shudders to think how he receives pleasures from life." Aside from hinting at Mulder's sexual deviance (another theme in the series), Chung forces the *X-files* audience to consider whether Mulder is insane.

"Shapes"

The plot of the 1994 episode "Shapes" graphically illustrates the contrasts between a primal worldview and a modern mainstream perspective. The episode begins with Scully and Mulder being called to Browning, Montana, a rural town bordering the Trego Indian Reservation, to investigate the killing of Joseph Goodensnake, a Trego tribesman, by local rancher Jim Parker. Early in the investigation Mulder informs Scully that some fifty years previously there was a similar incident in the area (investigated by J. Edgar Hoover himself) that became the FBI's first X-File.

The present killing appears to be motivated by a land dispute but Parker insists that he fired at an animal attacking his cattle and his son Lyle bears scars that lend credence to the story. After examining the crime scene, Scully concludes that at the short range from which Goodensnake was shot, it would have been impossible to mistake him for an animal. However, Mulder finds tracks nearby that appear to change from human to animal. Scully dismisses this, but is perplexed by Mulder's find of a large section of human skin nearby. She surmises that the Parkers knowingly killed Goodensnake, yet she also states that they couldn't have skinned him since Goodensnake's body shows no signs of such injury.

The situation becomes more complicated when Mulder and Scully venture onto the Trego Reservation. Not surprisingly, the natives tell them to go away, having had experience with the FBI during the earlier investigation of the similar case in 1946 as well as the standoff at Wounded Knee in 1973. Goodensnake's sister Gwen is also bitter, both with her neighbors who are too frightened of native legends to confront his death and the officials "investigating" it, who have been ineffectual. Despite these issues, tribal Sheriff Charles Tskany grudgingly permits Scully to examine Goodensnake's body, but forbids an autopsy out of respect for Trego beliefs. Scully gives a cursory evaluation of the corpse but it is Mulder who discovers that Goodensnake had elongated canines, much like an animal, as well as long-healed scars similar to Lyle's.

Despite such irregularities, Goodensnake's body is cremated in a traditional ceremony, with the agents in attendance. During the rite Mulder shares with Scully his belief that the culprits in both the current case and Hoover's investigation are werewolves. Of course Scully dismisses this theory and instead attributes the belief in lycanthropy to, in her words "a type of insanity" where a deluded person only *believes* he has become a wolf. After the funeral Jim Parker is subsequently ripped apart by an unseen animal outside his home, and is discovered the next morning. While scouting the area (and getting a scare from the mountain lion the Parkers keep caged behind their barn), Scully finds Lyle unconscious and takes him to the hospital for treatment and questioning. Meanwhile, Mulder finds traces of fur and sloughed skin, and armed with these clues, confronts the sheriff and tells him, "It's time for a talk . . . an exchange of ideas. What are you hiding?' At this point the sheriff gives in.

While Scully is at the hospital with Lyle, the sheriff arranges a meeting with Ish, a tribal elder, who explains that the real culprit in these murders is a *manitou*, an evil spirit that can possess a man, changing him into a beast. An inherently mysterious and monstrous creature, a *manitou* cannot die but passes to a new host through a bite or upon the death of the original host. Ish relates that he saw such a creature in his youth, but was too frightened to kill it then. He adds that the *manitou* possesses someone every eight years, exactly how long it has been since the last sighting of a possible *manitou*. Mulder and Sheriff Tskany conclude that Joe and Gwen must share the *manitou* curse and Mulder hurriedly calls the hospital to warn Scully. The doctor tells him that she has already left but adds that tests indicate that Lyle had ingested some of his father's blood. Alarmed at this news, Mulder and Tskany race to the Parker ranch.

Meanwhile Scully and Lyle have beaten them there but find the house dark from a power outage. By this time, the moon has risen and Lyle grows restless, locking himself in the bathroom where he begins to transform into a raging beast. In response to Scully's insistent banging on the door, the now monstrous Lyle bursts out, knocking her to the floor. Moments later Mulder and Tskany arrive, and Mulder enters the house, gun in hand. After stumbling around in the darkness, Mulder flushes the monster out, and it flees upstairs.

Firing wildly, Mulder follows, coming upon the frightened Scully, who is unharmed but unable to explain what has happened. Together they maneuver through the dark rooms, hearing the *manitou*'s heavy breathing and threatening growls. Suddenly, the creature leaps from the shadows but is blasted dead by the sheriff's shotgun. Yet when the agents shine their lights on it, they discover it is Lyle Parker lying dead. Stunned, Scully stammers that she and Lyle were attacked by the escaped mountain lion but Mulder and Tskany reply that the lion is still in its cage. The episode concludes the next day with the agents learning that Gwen has left town.

Right before they leave, Ish ruefully predicts that he will see Mulder again in about eight years.

Several aspects of this episode are especially significant. For instance, while many *X-Files* episodes are dark and menacing, the sense of mystery and menace is particularly strong in "Shapes," accentuated by the shadows continually obscuring its scenes. This constant darkness makes it difficult for the characters (or viewers) to perceive what is actually happening, a fact underscored by Parker's confession that, "I coulda swore I saw red eyes and fangs" and Lyle's explaining to Mulder and Scully about something "not human" watching at night that "gave me the creeps."

Their comments contrast starkly with Scully's insistent declarations that the case is "open and shut," and that there is "nothing unexplainable" about it. The air of mystery also haunts the funeral (no one explains what's going on yet the rite continues in the background while the camera focuses on the main characters and their conversation), and dramatically comes to the fore in the encounter in the cabin, with the *manitou* lurking in the shadows and offering only brief glimpses of its eyes, fur and claws, while we always clearly see its intended victims.

Tellingly, Scully and Mulder are conspicuously out of place throughout the episode, both at the ranch (its remote location and primitive character hinder their investigation) and on the Trego reservation. Most of the first visit takes place in a diner-bar—hardly a place conducive to the work of professional law enforcement—and the agents are obviously not welcome. In fact, the Trego refuse to speak to them. Instead, a scowling elder (who later comes to trust Mulder) tells them "Go home, FBI!"

Even Sheriff Tskany, the local representative of law and order and the agents' presumed ally, is unwilling to help. The only person who talks to the agents is Gwen, and all she does is declare she is tired of "suits" who seem unable to provide the help her people truly need. All of these things suggest that Mulder and Scully have not only strayed where they do not belong, but will likely not meet with success in their investigation.

"Shapes" also features camerawork that subtly suggests the sort of eerie transformation of human to animal exemplified by the *manitou* but dogmatically denied by modern science. Most commonly the director conveys this notion by quickly juxtaposing shots of animals (either stuffed ones in the Parker's cabin or live ones trapped in cages behind the barn) with shots of human characters. The theme of human-to-animal change is also underscored by the Trego ritual leader who wears a wolf pelt throughout Joe Goodensnake's funeral ceremony. While no one comments on this point, the directorial message is clear.

Most importantly, while much in "Shapes" is never explained, viewers certainly know almost from the beginning that the killer is a shapeshifter as do the Trego, while the whites (the Parkers, the FBI agents who investigated the original case, and Scully) do not. This is *the* pivotal fact of the entire episode. For the white characters, reality (the world as they understand and experience it) does not allow for a *manitou*, a shapeshifter that defies clear and distinct boundaries of species and genus. Such an absurd creature cannot exist in their scientific world, therefore anyone who believes in (let alone interacts with) a *manitou* must be insane.

The events depicted in "Shapes," however, push us beyond the bounds of such a rigidly ethnocentric perspective, drawing us into a reality where a *manitou* actually *does* exist. This world, the primal lifeworld inhabited by the Trego, resists final determination by abstractly defined laws and principles. To the white outsiders who use scientific procedures and only trust empirical evidence, the *manitou* is an intruder from beyond the bounds of reason and so they dismiss it; to the insiders who have lived in the area for generations, the *manitou* is a concrete fact of life, dangerous and terrifying to be sure but still a fact that they understand and accept. The whites do not realize that they have entered this primal reality, and are oblivious to the *manitou*'s existence and the threat it poses. Ironically, they *think* they know the truth but do not grasp the full reality of their situation—a pretty good definition of insanity by some standards.

What we have, then, in "Shapes" is a collision of different worldviews. The dominant white world and the Trego cosmos, ordinarily separate and distinct, come together in a series of horrific and violent events that defy "rational" scientific explanation. This situation leaves those like Scully, who rely on science, at a loss. Meanwhile the native Trego remain stoically resigned yet wary, since they know that the mysterious powers at the heart of reality always have the potential to produce evil forces.

The characters in "Shapes" seem to know intuitively the incommensurability of these opposing worldviews. On the final morning when they learn that Gwen has left the reservation without telling anyone where she has gone, Sheriff Tskany comments, "Maybe she saw something that she wasn't ready to understand." The camera cuts to Scully, who considers his words for a moment then replies, "Maybe"—a remark that, while stopping short of explicit agreement, implies that Scully finally realizes her own perspective may have its limits.

Still, we should note that not *all* of the outsiders dismiss the Trego's point of view. Agent Fox Mulder, often deemed "crazy" by his FBI colleagues, believes the Trego precisely because he is not wedded to a rigidly scientistic perspective. To a large extent it is this supposed irrationality (and its attendant openness to alternative understandings) that enables him to find the truth of the situation, even if this particular case remains officially unsolved.

The Sneaky Fox's Secret

Mulder's willingness to engage with different worldviews shows most clearly in the relationship he develops with Ish. It begins on a sour note in the reservation diner, a scene that warrants careful recounting for what it reveals, both directly and indirectly.

Mulder and Scully have entered and announce the painfully obvious: "We're not from around here." The Trego virtually ignore them, despite Mulder explaining that they're investigating the recent homicide. Instead a voice from someone off in a dark corner says, "Go home, FBI!" Rather than take offense, Mulder draws the speaker out, asking how he knew. We now see that the voice comes from an old man in the shadows, Ish, who replies, "I could smell you a mile away," to which Mulder responds jokingly "Well, they told me that even though my deodorant's made for a woman it's strong enough for a man." He then listens as the old man explains what he learned at Wounded Knee in 1973: "You don't believe in us, and we don't believe in you." Mulder replies, "I want to believe."

His curiosity piqued, Ish's face moves partially into the light as he asks, "Why you here? What are you looking for?" Mulder shoots back, "I think you already know what we're looking for."

The old man parries, "You tell me what I know!" At this point Scully jumps in, answering in typical FBI-speak, "We're looking for any individuals who might be able to provide information on the homicide," only to be interrupted by Mulder saying, "We're looking for anything that can create human tracks in one step and animal tracks in the next." The camera cuts to Ish's scowling face, silent for a moment. He then says simply, "Parker. He found what you're looking for. He *killed* what you're looking for, FBI."

This exchange between a native elder and the agents of the government which has repeatedly oppressed the former's people sums up the entire situation. Opposing parties from two distinct worlds confront each other over a mysterious and sinister event, and neither seems willing or even able to co-operate with the other.

Yet one person, Fox Mulder, by acting in a most unprofessional manner (joking, cutting off his colleague in mid-sentence, offering what initially must seem to be a truly crazy suggestion), is able to establish a genuine relationship between them. This is because Mulder, unlike other officials whom Ish has encountered (as well as Scully and even Sheriff Tskany) indicates that he has peered into the Trego world, and wants to learn from their wisdom in order to handle the current threat.

The relationship develops more during the meeting in Ish's cabin. There, Ish takes Mulder under his wing, as he explains what is actually going on. Significantly, he begins by addressing Mulder directly: "I sense you are different, FBI. You are more open to Native American belief than some Native Americans. You even have an Indian name, 'Fox'. You should be 'Running Fox' or 'Sneaky Fox'."

Ish's words evince deep insights that often escape the sorts of characters who typically appear in *The X-Files*. He recognizes in Mulder's distinctiveness an openness to other realities, and brings him further into the Trego world not only by calling him by his first name, but by playfully offering him alternative (and appropriate) *Indian* names. For his part, Mulder acknowledges this ritual dubbing with characteristic humor: "Just so long as it's not 'Spooky Fox'." While his reply is ambiguous, by sharing his aversion to the pejorative nickname assigned him by his FBI colleagues, Mulder is tacitly accepting the invitation into the Trego world that the elder offers.

This's another highly significant point in "Shapes," although its implications are never fully explored. Mulder takes Trego views seriously, more than Scully obviously but also more than Tskany, a native Trego who would seem to be a more likely candidate to bridge the opposing worlds. In any case, Ish perceives Mulder's sincerity and so shares his knowledge of the situation they are facing. This truth, ordinarily hidden from or perhaps even impossible to convey to authorities from the outside white world, is revealed face-to-face in a candle-lit cabin via the words of the Trego elder rather than the cold, antiseptic light of a modern laboratory.

Mulder is able to receive this wisdom because, rather than dismiss Trego lore as "superstition," he respects their knowledge as legitimate, attending to what Ish says even if it might seem incredible to someone else. This capacity to enter other worldviews allows Mulder to see things that other investigators overlook, and consider seemingly unthinkable possibilities when confronting particularly tough cases. And while such an unorthodox approach may make Mulder hopelessly "spooky," it ironically proves him to be more pragmatic in his investigations than most of his colleagues. After all, unlike them, he will go with whatever explanation seems to fit the situation at hand, drawing on any available sources of knowledge even if these sources do not conform to the standards of empirical science.

There's something playful about the way Mulder goes about his investigations, as he is remarkably adaptive, seemingly at home in the midst of mystery and ambiguity. He doesn't play by the usual rules but instead makes jokes and offers outlandish suggestions. In truth, by FBI standards, he's a bit crazy. Mulder crosses boundaries that divide different worlds. He's a liminal figure, one who inhabits the threshold between opposing realities. In this he resembles a shaman, the healer among indigenous peoples whose abilities enable him to access hidden sources of knowledge. Even more, though, Mulder seems more like a trickster, an archetypal figure who is especially prominent in primal lore.

In the world of *The X-Files* where inexplicable events regularly occur, Mulder is quite sane, more so than the scientifically-minded Scully. "Shapes" helps us to see what makes Mulder such an effective investigator: his openness to alternative understandings of the world as well as certain shapeshifting aspects of his own personality.

Various scholars have noted the central role played by tricksters (such as ravens and coyotes) among indigenous peoples. Such paradoxical beings are chaotic creators, catalysts for action and change. Tricksters are humorous but at times may threaten those who cross their paths. Tricksters take on many forms, and resist being pinned down once and for all. Comparative mythologist David Adams Leeming observes that the trickster acts outrageously, and "often takes animal form. Yet the trickster is profoundly inventive, creative by nature, and in some ways a helper to humanity. Jung sees in him a hint of the later savior figure."

Tricksters personify the uncanny and unpredictable aspects of existence, revealing the inherent ambiguity and irony that characterize human life. By acknowledging such tricky beings, indigenous peoples show an understanding of reality that differs considerably from an understanding informed by modern science which above all aims at controlling the world and making it conform to human ends.

The *manitou* as a shapeshifter is a trickster of sorts, embodying the mysterious primal forces that exist beyond any capacity to anticipate or control. In this instance, such forces are negative, disruptive, and dangerous. Fox Mulder, the "spooky" white man with an Indian name, shows himself as the *manitou*'s counterpart, a shapeshifting trickster who retains a human conscience. Like a shaman, "Sneaky Fox" crosses boundaries few (perhaps only the "mad") would dare, burrowing down into mystery and chaos yet he does so intentionally in order to restore the world to the primal harmony that the *manitou* disrupts. Apparently Ish, drawing on his own native wisdom, recognizes Mulder's trickster powers, and the old man hints at this by alluding to Mulder's being "different" and approving of his "Indian"—trickster—name.

Among indigenous peoples, the trickster typically plays a crucial albeit ambiguous role in the unfolding of the cosmos. The primal world is, after all, a living system that follows ancient rhythms yet all the while, chaos haunts its fringes. Fittingly, "Shapes" is unresolved, much like the world itself as understood by many native peoples. Unlike the world of modern science, the events never get a final explanation and so the case remains unsolved, a true "X-file."

In this light, the final scenes of "Shapes" are eerily apt. As Mulder is about to enter the car that will take him away from the Trego, Ish, standing off to the side, calls out, "Hey, FBI—see you in another eight years." Mulder replies "I hope not." This last conversation, cryptic, marked by grim humor and resignation, appears to be a way for both men to acknowledge their shared understanding of the events that have unfolded. It could also express an impossible wish: maybe we will renew our friendship if/when this happens again? And yet, the divide has opened up once again; Mulder is no longer "Sneaky Fox" but "FBI," the generic white authority. It seems that both Ish and Mulder have submitted to the inevitable. Nothing more is said as the car drives away, returning the agents to the modern world where they belong. The scene cuts to the misty forest-clad mountains surrounding the reservation and we hear a plaintive howl from an unseen and unknowable animal—is it a wolf? A *manitou*? The screen fades to black.

Sanity and Cultural Judgments

The notion that judgments about peoples' sanity reflect cultural biases is not new. Joan Didion notes, for instance, that Nobel-Prize-winning writer Doris Lessing (1919–2013) assumed something along these lines in much of her work, and hints of this idea date back at least to the Romantic era, if not earlier.

The intuition that our technologically-dominated culture stunts our capacities to experience life and appreciate its mysteries is commonplace, and implies that what we might dismiss as delusion or consider abnormal (such as visions) may not have been deemed so strange by our ancestors. Indeed, such phenomena are often regarded with awe in other societies. Such an idea has profound psychological implications, as it suggests that embracing our full humanity requires transcending the bounds of what society deems rationality. In other words, striving for "sanity" as normally understood could artificially constrict who we truly are.

No one has argued more boldly against a simplistic, universal notion of "sanity" than R.D. Laing (1927–1989). Drawing on clinical work with patients, and on his personal experience, Laing argues that modern civilization, due to technological advancements and a corresponding disbelief in mystery, has alienated us from our true selves. Living within modern society severely limits certain types of experience (transcendent states in which we "lose ourselves") thereby constraining our capacity to live genuinely both individually and communally. Those who are not "normal" (alienated from larger dimensions of human reality) and hence do not act according to prevailing social norms are labeled "mad."

Such "normalcy" can have horrific effects on all of us. In *The Politics of Experience* Laing writes:

> The condition of alienation, of being asleep, of being unconscious, of being out of one's mind, is the condition of the normal man. Society highly values its normal man. It educates children to lose themselves and to become absurd, and thus to be normal. Normal men have killed perhaps 100,000,000 of their fellow normal men in the last fifty years.

Viewed from a broader perspective, the "sanity" we impose on ourselves may be quite debilitating, and we who inhabit such a worldview may actually be "insane."

Sheldon B. Kopp, author of *If You Meet the Buddha on the Road, Kill Him!*, offers a telling example of how culturally limited judgments of sanity can be:

> I once witnessed an ironically enlightening instance of the cultural definition of insanity, and of the power politics of psychiatric social control. At the time when I was on the staff of a New Jersey State Mental Hospital, a strange man appeared on a street corner in Trenton, wearing a long white sheet and quietly muttering "gibberish." His very presence threatened the certitude of sanity of the community at large. Fortunately, for the sheeted man's own good, a policeman was called by some saner citizen. So it was that this poor man was able to be brought under the protective lock-and-key of his local Asylum.
>
> His efforts to explain his strange behavior were offered in vain, since it was clear that he was a loony . . . he was diagnosed into that catch-all garbage can of a syndrome known as Schizophrenia, Chronic Undifferentiated Type.
>
> Fortunately, for the white-sheeted, gibberish-muttering patient in question, the hospital Visitors' Day began the very next morning. Evidently he had called home and made his plight known. That

> morning twenty other people wearing white sheets arrived at the hospital. Equally strangely clad, they were also equivalently incomprehensible to the psychiatric staff. It turned out that these men and women were all members of the same small rural church sect, a religious group who defined their identity in part by clothing themselves in the purity of white cloth, and by being divinely inspired to talk in tongues.
>
> The psychiatrist in this case, being a practicing Roman Catholic (who weekly ate and drank the body and blood of Jesus Christ) thought they were a queer bunch indeed. Heaven help him should he ever wander into a community in which his own religious affiliations would be equally obscure. The patient was released that afternoon. One such man is a lunatic. Twenty constitute an acceptable and sane community.

While we might quibble over the specifics of Kopp's claim, it's interesting that he, like Laing, looks to other cultures for examples that show ways of being human which, while different from the prevailing norms, are perfectly benign and even healthy; it is possible *not* to be alienated from the varied range of human experiences.

When such ideas come up in my classes, they resonate deeply with some of my students. This is particularly the case when we discuss indigenous peoples such as the Lakota of North America, people who traditionally have compelling ways of understanding and experiencing the world that differ dramatically from the individualistic consumerism of the contemporary US. There is a clue here to understanding Agent Mulder, a figure who himself is rather alienated from mainstream US culture yet has insights into situations that confound his scientifically-minded colleagues.

The Primal Worldview

Native American scholar-activists such as Vine Deloria rightly point out that historically white "experts" have characterized "native" views in demeaning ways (typically as the intellectual counterpart to military subjugation and colonial dominance) and thus we should beware of seeking to define native peoples once and for all. Nonetheless, primal peoples for the most part share a certain basic perspective that marks them as distinct.

A chief feature of this indigenous view is an understanding of the world as an integrated whole in which we humans are intimately related to all beings, particularly those connected to the places where we dwell. Ours is a shared world inhabited by diverse beings, all of whom are akin to us but none of whom are under the control of a single authority. Rather than rigidly following abstract and absolute laws, this primal world unfolds according to principles of harmony and balance.

Within this living context there is a predictable order governing all creatures, perhaps best exemplified in the rhythms of nature: the daily rising and setting of the sun, the waxing and waning of the moon, the cycle of the seasons. These rhythms, while natural, are not necessarily peaceful. The interactions between creatures can be tense, even violent (plants suffer from drought and blights; predators hunt and kill prey) but for the most part these are anticipated and understood. Still, at the same time there is always the threat of chance and disorder: sickness can strike a village unexpectedly, storms can destroy a crop, even the best hunters may be injured or killed. Mystery and unpredictability are, paradoxically, integral to the world in which we live.

We humans participate in this vital yet mysterious world, and can know and influence (although never fully control) it to a degree. We can discern the truths of the world and its patterns by attending to ancient lore, heeding the wisdom of the elders, and participating in traditional ceremonies and spiritual practices. We learn by observing our surroundings, paying careful attention to all phenomena, including dreams and visions. Yet despite such seeming "mysticism," indigenous peoples traditionally accept whatever manifests, taking a practical attitude of working with and responding to what the world discloses rather than denying and/or rejecting it outright. Indeed, such attitudes are quite sensible, since achieving and maintaining harmony is not a final goal but requires continually responding to situations as they arise.

Out There, in Here, or Betwixt and Between?

> Sometimes the only sane answer to an insane world is insanity.
>
> —Fox Mulder

In "Shapes," just as in most *X-Files* episodes, Mulder is the only investigator who actually gets what is going on. This is precisely because he is willing to cross boundaries, entertain the wildest speculations, and violate the standards norms and expectations of different worlds in the course of his job. In this regard, he really does live up to the name Ish gives him: "Sneaky Fox," which appropriately enough, he prefers to his derisive FBI nickname "Spooky Mulder." The fox is a common trickster in both European and Native American folklore.

As a foxy trickster, Mulder is accepted in the Trego world, at least for a while, even though he is originally an outsider. What's more, as fans know, Mulder also doesn't quite fit in the modern white world. Mulder seems to shuttle between *both* worlds, perhaps never finally inhabiting either. This existential dislocation of being "betwixt and between," perhaps the essential feature of Fox Mulder as a character, makes him "insane" in the sense that Laing, Kopp, and a few others point out. But it's also what makes him Fox Mulder, the quirky yet brilliant investigator who invariably sees truths that none of his official colleagues see.

"Shapes" has never been particularly popular with fans of *The X-Files*, and it is plagued by its share of problems. The episode flirts with Native American stereotypes popular among New Agers during the 1990s, and in many respects it follows the usual clichés of a run-of-the-mill werewolf story. Nonetheless, it is important in the grand arc of *The X-Files* for revealing a key aspect of Mulder's personality, helping us see that many of the questions concerning his sanity presuppose a narrowly scientistic view of reality that warrants critical scrutiny.

Calling attention to such common yet limiting assumptions is an important function of horror and science fiction, and one that both storytelling genres share with philosophic inquiry in general. By some standards, Mulder may be "insane," but if so, his "insanity" expands his ability to understand what otherwise might remain unexplainable—a truly valuable talent for working with the X-files.

Jamake Highwater, a writer who, like Mulder, straddles white and indigenous worlds, relates a parable about a Zuni *kachina* who emerges from the underworld attached back to back with an "alien person." Because of this, each being is destined never to see or understand one another despite being forever part of each other. Highwater, though, relates that the legendary scholar Joseph Epes Brown who devoted his life to crossing between Native American and white worlds, saw much promise in this seemingly insane situation, observing, "Yet there is hope. It lies in the possibility that there may come a time for turning around, so that each may know who the other is and what the other might become."

Mulder embodies this image of dual being, and the conviction that this willingness to cross over into different worlds and back is the way to truth. Perhaps we who are fans of *The X-Files* should follow his lead.

Maybe this would make us as crazy as Sneaky Fox Mulder. But if so, we are at least in good company.

16
Bad Memories in "Bad Blood"

CAM COBB AND MICHAEL K. POTTER

"Bad Blood"—a story about memory, perspective, and narrative truth-making—begins in the Lone Star State . . .

It is a misty moonlit night in Cheney, Texas. A pizza boy in his late teens or early twenties runs across an empty field.

"Help!" he calls out.

The boy trips and falls, then picks himself up and continues on his mad dash.

"Help!" he cries out again. "Somebody please help me!"

A man in a trench coat pursues him.

Yelling out, gasping for air, the boy runs into a wooded area and is soon tackled by the man. Pinning the youth on the ground, the man produces a wooden stake, frantically grabs a large rock and uses it to drive the stake into the boy's chest.

"Mulder!" a woman shouts.

The man turns around. It is FBI agent Fox Mulder. He lifts the boy's top lip to reveal a set of enormous fangs.

"Look at that!" he declares, triumphantly.

FBI Agent Dana Scully taps the boy's upper incisors and gently removes a false set of vampire teeth, giving Mulder an *I told you so* look mixed with shock.

As *The X-Files* theme music engulfs this shocking scenario, we ask ourselves: *What just happened?*

Back in Washington

We next see Agents Mulder and Scully in the familiar X-Files basement office at FBI Headquarters. Mulder steps over to his garbage can, kicks and stomps on it multiple times.

"I know what I saw!" he exclaims.

A report for Assistant Director Walter Skinner is due in one hour and both agents face a possible wrongful death lawsuit—apparently with a price-tag of $446 million.

"What are you going to tell him?" Scully asks.

"What do you mean, what am I going to tell him? I'm going to tell him exactly what I saw," Mulder replies, leaning on his desk with arms crossed. After a pause, he nervously inquires: "What are you gonna tell him?"

"I'll tell him exactly what I saw."

"And how is that different?" Mulder asks.

Later in the conversation a defiant Mulder bursts out: "I did not overreact. Ronny Strickland *was* a vampire!"

"Where's your proof?" Scully, ever the empiricist, counters.

"You're my proof! You were there!" Mulder asserts. After a brief silence Mulder becomes apprehensive. "Okay, now you're scaring me, I wanna hear exactly what you're gonna tell Skinner!"

"Oh, you want our stories straight?" Scully asks.

"No, no, no. I didn't say that. I just wanna hear it the way you saw it."

And thus begins a memory standoff . . .

Similarities and Differences

Both Scully and Mulder present their own versions of the events that led up to the pizza-boy's stabbing. In recalling a sequence of events, they assemble their own perceptions of truth. Their narratives converge in some ways and diverge in others. While the timbre of their details differs, they agree on most of the basic facts.

Both narratives begin with Mulder giving a presentation to Scully in their basement office. He tells his partner about a strange death that has recently occurred in Cheney, Texas—with possible ties to vampirism. Through his presentation, Mulder puts forward a rationale for venturing to Texas, to investigate the murder as a possible X-File. In both narratives, the agents subsequently journey to Cheney, and quickly find themselves in a funeral home—strangely overcrowded for such a small town. On inspecting the body, the two soon meet Sheriff Hartwell, a friendly and ruggedly handsome, though somewhat naive, man. Mulder pokes around the local cemetery and trailer-park with the Sheriff, then visits Scully and rests in her room after sending her back to the funeral parlor to perform an autopsy on a second murder victim. Shortly after receiving Scully's pizza, Mulder is attacked by a pizza-boy—who by now has glowing green eyes and enormous fangs. On these details the FBI duo agree. Yet on other counts they ardently disagree.

Agents Scully and Mulder hold diverging views of one another's behavior in the Cheney Vampire Case. In Mulder's narrative, Scully is constantly abrupt and gruff (in her interactions with him), she is impatient and short-tempered (such as when Mulder has technical problems with a slide projector), dismissive (of Mulder's rationale for journeying to Texas), bossy (in her treatment of Mulder in the field), uncaring (by ignoring Mulder's state when he arrives at her motel room clearly exhausted and awash in dirt and mud), and she is distracted by (or, perhaps more accurately, enamored with) the charm and good looks of Sheriff Hartwell.

While Mulder presents this rather unflattering portrayal of Scully, she has her own counter-portrait of Mulder to share—and it's just as unflattering. In Scully's narrative, Mulder is forceful (he pushes through his slideshow with little or no room for dialogue), abrupt (he provides a hurried rationale for venturing to Texas), uncaring (he flippantly assigns Scully multiple autopsy tasks when she is clearly physically exhausted), and he's also sly (he secretively withholds embarrassing information about the reason he is covered in dirt and mud).

When investigating a possible case of vampirism in Texas, Mulder and Scully have a shared experience. They agree on numerous facts regarding that experience—such as the key events and sequence of events. Yet they also disagree on a few aspects of their experience—particularly relating to their treatment of one another. Why is this so? Are the two agents *unable* to recall things as they occurred? Perhaps there are physiological barriers hampering Mulder and Scully's ability to recall past events with clarity.

Perhaps a lack of sleep is affecting their memory capacity. The two FBI agents may simply be too tired to remember things accurately. Or, perhaps it isn't physiological at all. Perhaps it's intentional. Maybe Mulder and Scully have constructed their own interpretations of the past to present themselves in a more favorable light. They could also be lying. Perhaps they're protecting themselves as they ponder the unpleasant possibility of a wrongful death lawsuit. Yet maybe it isn't lying *per se*. Maybe the very act of storytelling has led the two worried agents to confuse things and arrive at different variations of what really occurred, involving different interpretations of salient details—even differences in which details are perceived as salient.

Overtired Agents

Surely Agents Scully and Mulder aren't intentionally or maliciously putting forward diverging stories. It *must* be physiological. Perhaps they're simply overtired. After all, both Scully and Mulder are physically exhausted throughout the episode. Scully desperately wants to rest in her motel room after completing an autopsy, yet she's unable to because she has to whisk off to perform a second autopsy on a new murder victim. Mulder is also unable to get any sort of rest because he's attacked by a pizza-boy.

While both agents may be sleep-deprived upon their return to Washington, sleep may continue to elude them as they ponder the possibility of a $446-million-dollar wrongful death lawsuit. And sleep matters. As Swiss neuroscience researchers Bjorn Rasch and Jan Born note, "sleep benefits the retention of memory." More precisely, "sleep as a state of greatly reduced external information processing represents an optimal time window for consolidating memories."

So sleep aids memory, but does lack of sleep impair memory? It does, and here, timing is important. The less sleep you get immediately after an experience, the more pronounced the memory disruption. As Rasch and Born observe, "A time dependency of the effects of sleep on memory formation is indicated by studies showing stronger effects for sleep occurring shortly after learning than for sleep at a later time." With this consideration in mind, because the two agents struggled with sleep in the immediate days during and following their adventure in Texas, their recall of the events in question could be disrupted—causing the two to have conflicting views of the past. Yet Scully and Mulder both recall the same basic events in the same sequence. It's their *interpretations* that differ. And the points of their stories that diverge often relate to the way they treat one another. So, perhaps their memory confusion *is* intentional after all.

Liar, Liar

What if Scully and Mulder *are* intentionally telling different stories? Perhaps the two agents are distorting their own versions of the Cheney Vampire Case to present themselves in a more positive light. Of course, relying on an individual's recollections of his or her own experiences is always a challenge as people sometimes adjust the *way* they present themselves—whether consciously or unconsciously. In the realm of qualitative research, which is firmly rooted in testimony, this challenge has led to the development of various strategies that are used to better ensure the trustworthiness of data gathered from participants. Yet while Scully and Mulder may be lying, the act of misinforming in relation to memory recall is a complicated process.

As American cognitive psychologist Kerri Pickel notes, "Numerous studies have shown that sometimes people confuse memories of imagination with memories of reality." Consequently, "inventing a false description of a person . . . decreases a witness's ability to remember accurate details about that person"—which leads to what's called *retrieval blocking*. According to another American cognitive psychologist, Elizabeth F. Loftus, "Misleading information can turn a lie into memory's truth. It can cause people to believe that they saw things that never really existed, or that they saw things differently from the way things actually were. It can make people confident about these false memories and also, apparently, impair earlier recollections."

Perhaps both Scully and Mulder have adjusted their *stories* as they recall the events they experienced the Cheney Vampire Case. Perhaps they interpret events in their own ways, and in doing so, present misinformation about one another's demeanors to depict themselves in a more positive light. And if this is the case, it's possible that their preoccupation with the narratives they're advancing is hampering their ability to recall exactly what occurred. Yet maybe it isn't a matter of lying, or intentional distortion, at all. Maybe the two agents simply got muddled in their storytelling process.

Recall Storytelling Syndrome

In constructing their own versions of what happened in the Cheney Vampire Case, Agents Mulder and Scully take a bit of creative license. They present one another in a generalized way, highlighting certain foibles they perceive in one another. Mulder feels that Scully doesn't take him seriously and is too quick to dismiss his theories and ideas. Scully feels that Mulder is impetuous and too rushed in his approach to investigative work. Yet their versions of the past—their *stories*—may not be intentional lies at all. In constructing stories, both agents may have unconsciously sketched one another's demeanors in broad, rather than precise strokes.

As philosopher Marya Schechtman notes, there is a "a great deal of evidence—both introspective and empirical—that memory often does not provide such links, but instead summarizes and condenses life experiences into a coherent narrative." She goes on to observe that while "memories may include memories of particular experiences, they also may not, and their relation to the past is much more complicated than simple reproduction." Perhaps this complication is what leads Agents Mulder and Scully to arrive at different interpretations of their shared experience.

When recalling events and constructing narratives about our lived experiences, "A single memory can be, and often is, linked to various disconnected stretches of the subject's life, and when it is it provides a more general sort of connection to the past than that involved in the reproduction of some one particular event." As such, Mulder and Scully may be interpreting one another's actions, and portraying one another in a composite format in their differing versions of the Cheney Vampire Case. After all, "In memory we often condense experiences, presenting to ourselves a fictitious event or experience which is a composite of the essential features of a series of real ones."

By constructing their stories, the two agents depict themselves as well as one another. And in doing so, they may be exaggerating details regarding one another's demeanors to construct a more flattering sense of their own selves in a larger narrative framework. With this phenomenon in mind, it is possible that Scully and Mulder have unconsciously formed diverging interpretations of their experience in Texas—a sort of product of what we might call *recall storytelling syndrome*.

One Thing We Can Be Sure Of . . .

Memory is a funny thing. Personal storytelling marks the way we draw from our memory to interpret, and share our own narratives. Current research tells us we may not have static memory, and each time we recall our lived experiences we remember them differently. The context of a given moment shapes our understanding of past events; and sometimes, when telling stories, we reshape the past to present ourselves in a better light—be it consciously or unconsciously. Ultimately, the way we perceive our past experiences is influenced by our present state of mind. FBI agents Fox Mulder and Dana Scully are constantly telling personal stories as they navigate the complicated landscape of *The X-Files*. They tell one another stories about their lives prior to meeting and working together. And they sometimes tell their ever-frustrated superior, Assistant Director Walter Skinner, stories about their most recent fieldwork. It is this scenario that lies at the heart of "Bad Blood."

Much of Scully and Mulder's diverging perspectives of the Cheney Vampire Case links to the way they see and characterize one another. While they agree on a basic sequence of events, they interpret things differently—particularly the way they treated one another while on the case. And this matters.

In Mulder's version, he is logical and reasonable and had a clear cause for journeying to Texas on an X-File, and hammering a wooden stake into the pizza boy's chest. Yet in Scully's version, Mulder is hurried, impetuous and may *not* have had a clear cause for jaunting to Texas, or attacking the pizza boy. Did a lack of sleep cause the two to confuse their memories? Or, were they intentionally or unintentionally distorting their stories? Perhaps it was a bit of both.

One thing we can be sure of, the testimonies of Mulder and Scully are a matter of memory—and memory is interpretative, and elusive.

17
Monday . . . Again

JEREMY PIERCE

MULDER: Scully, did you ever have one of those days that you wish you could just rewind and start all over again from the beginning?

SCULLY: Yes, frequently. But, I mean, who's to say that if you did rewind it and start all over again, that it wouldn't wind up exactly the same way?

MULDER: So you think it's all just fate? We have no free will?

SCULLY: No, I think that we're free to be the people that we are, good, bad, or indifferent. I think that it's our character that determines our fate.

MULDER: And all the rest is just preordained? I don't buy that. There's too many variables, too many forks in the road.

In the *X-Files* episode "Monday," the same day repeats hundreds of times, but no one knows it except a woman named Pam. Every time, her boyfriend Bernard intends to rob a bank, but once he's there either Mulder or Scully shows up every time, and the outcome is that Bernard blows the place up, Mulder and Scully included.

In another episode, "The Goldberg Variation," from 1999, Henry Weems is the luckiest person ever. What is this luck supposed to be? And what is fate, which plays a role in both stories?

Freedom and Determinism

Some philosophers have argued that all of our actions are predetermined by things outside our control. Sometimes this view is called determinism. One way it's commonly put is that the laws of nature, together with any state of the world, will guarantee any later state of the world. One thing causes another, which causes another, which causes another, and the chain of causes is the only way things could go, given the initial state and laws of nature.

Scully presents a deterministic picture of the world. Mulder asks if she's denying free will, but she says no. Our character determines our fate. What does she mean? How does it allow freedom? Scully explains our freedom in a way similar to an ancient Greek and Roman school of thought called Stoicism.

The Stoics, most notably Chrysippus (279–206 B.C.E.), held that all of our actions are caused entirely by prior events, and nothing can veer away from those chains of causes. But Chrysippus believed in freedom, which is when we agree with what we're doing, when the causes of our actions come out of our character, desires, and beliefs. We can be free even if we're predetermined, if it's our character and desires that cause our actions.

The Stoics' opponents were the Epicureans, named for their founder Epicurus (341–270 B.C.E.). Epicurus was an atomist, holding that all reality is composed of indivisible atoms that follow the laws of physics, except in one way, what he called a swerve. Epicurus held Mulder's view above. He thought there are, as Mulder put it, "too many variables, too many forks in the road" for a deterministic picture to make sense.

Epicurus didn't think determinism could fit with the freedom he believed in, so he had to find some way to reject determinism. He proposed that atoms swerve randomly. The chains of causation get broken whenever an atom swerves, and thus the Epicureans had an account of how the world is not predetermined.

In the episode, it turns out that Mulder is right. Each day the events repeat but with small variations. One day Mulder goes into the bank. Another day Scully does. One day, Bernard writes, "This is a robbery" but another day writes, "This is a holdup." Mulder responds differently each day waking up in a leaky waterbed, and what Scully says to Mulder when he arrives late for work is similar but has variations. Pam is the only one who remembers previous days, and some of the changes from day to day are from learning what didn't work before, but a lot of variations are initiated by others.

But are random events explaining free will, or is free will explaining the small variations? Truly random events conflict with determinism, but should I think I'm responsible for random events causing my choices? I don't think that's Mulder's view. At any rate, this kind of fate isn't the one that takes center stage once the episode gets going. Another notion of fate is at work, one that also plays a role in "The Goldberg Variation."

The Nature of Fate

In "Monday," Pam and Mulder suggest that the day repeats because something that was supposed to happen hasn't yet occurred. In the final cycle, Pam prevents the bomb from exploding by going into the bank herself and sacrificing her life to save Mulder's when Bernard shoots him. Mulder wakes up the next morning, and it really is the next morning. We're supposed to see Pam's willingness to sacrifice herself as what was supposed to happen, and the day kept repeating until she got it right. That might even explain why she was the one who remembered all the previous attempts, since she was the one who had to do something different.

She was fated to die, but it didn't happen the first several hundred times. This isn't determinism. It's some other notion of fate, one that can be resisted lots of times but in the end will win anyway. It doesn't win because some events cause other events in some unavoidable way. It wins because something makes sure it happens, even when events don't go the way they need to. What's going on here?

It might help to consider the "four causes" of Aristotle (384–322 B.C.E.). Technically speaking, Aristotle isn't the first to distinguish them, and he didn't even give them their traditional names, but they've long been called Aristotle's four causes. These "causes" are really just different ways of explaining things. Each is a different kind of explanation. The Greek word he uses for it simply means "explanation." For our purposes, just two of these kinds of explanations matter. One is called an efficient cause, and the other is a final cause.

An efficient cause isn't a cause that's faster than other causes. This name goes back to the Latin word for accomplishing something, which has come down to us in English in such words as "effect" and "effective." An efficient cause is just the kind of cause we have in such expressions as "cause and effect." It's what we usually mean when we talk about a cause. It makes something else happen. It's the kind of explanation that occurs in Scully's determinism.

The clearest cases of final causes are when people do things for particular reasons. If I want to explain how I got to class on a certain day, I can say I walked to my car and drove there, but it doesn't tell anyone why. I'm there to teach my students philosophy. They're there to learn philosophy (or maybe just to get credit toward their diploma).

Telling how they got there doesn't necessarily answer why. That's an efficient cause. A final cause explains why. It's final not in the sense of being the last cause in a chain of efficient causes. It's final in the sense that it looks toward a goal or an end. It's done to achieve some purpose. It's something sought after, not some past event leading to it. When Scully goes to the bank to prevent whatever keeps happening when Mulder goes, she's pursuing a goal. Wanting to prevent the explosion is a final cause.

Other final causes are more controversial. Is there a divine creator of the universe, who intended certain things to happen for certain reasons? What about the events of "Monday"? Something has to happen, or the day will repeat until it does. What ensures that it will repeat until the right thing happens? We might try to explain it in a way that doesn't involve minds, something like the notion of karma. But what makes karma work? What would explain why what's supposed to happen does happen? It isn't determinism. Scully would dismiss the notion entirely. It's not clear Mulder would agree with me on this, but it might well be that the best explanation for a repeating day that keeps going until it goes the right way is that someone or something has both that goal for the day and the power to make it keep repeating until it gets right. It assumes some sort of mind behind it all.

In "The Goldberg Variation," Henry Weems gets tossed off a skyscraper and survives. While they're investigating the incident, Mulder and Scully have the following conversation:

Scully: You know, in 1998 there was a British soldier who plummeted 4,500 feet when his parachute failed, and he walked away with a broken rib.

Mulder: What's your point?

Scully: My point is that if there's a wind gust or a sudden updraft, and plus if he landed in exactly the right way, I mean, I don't know, maybe he just got lucky.

Mulder: What if he got really, really lucky? That's your big scientific explanation, Scully? I mean, how many thousands of variables would have to convene in just the right mixture for that theory to hold water?

Scully: I don't know.

Mulder: Thousands.

Mulder is convinced Weems must be invulnerable, but Scully suggests he might just have been really lucky. Why does he make fun of her "scientific" explanation? It's too improbable for it just to happen. If things go that well, with thousands of variables happening to work out for him so nicely to make the nearly impossible seem inevitable (and the inevitable seem impossible), it cries out for an explanation. The conversation resumes after another incident:

Scully: What the hell happened here, Mulder?

Mulder: Cause and effect.

Scully: Meaning?

Mulder: Okay, so watch. So Bellini kicks down the door, poised to kill Weems, right? But just as he's about to pull the trigger, a noise startles him, the buzzer, when I buzzed, to be let back into the apartment. So when he does pull the trigger, his aim is off, right? And he hits the lamp, which falls over and knocks over the ironing board. So as the bullet ricochets, Weems dives over the sofa. Now when Bellini goes for him, he trips over the ironing board, bounces off the chair, flips end over end, and his shoelace gets caught in the fan. Q.E.D. Cause and effect. Seemingly unrelated and unconnected events and occurrences that appear unrelated and random beforehand but which seem to chain-react in Henry Weems's favor.

After seeing several amazingly lucky things happen for Weems, Mulder takes on the luck explanation but proposes it's an ongoing superpower rather than just a one-time bizarre occurrence. After all, getting really lucky once is unusual and might call for explanation, but unusual things happen. The more variables there are to go wrong, especially if they're extremely unlikely, the more we're likely we need an explanation.

If all that happens several times in a row for the same person, Mulder concludes that it's something about Weems. As the episode proceeds it's clear that Weems is aware of it but is also aware that his luck often comes at others' expense and avoids people. He has only ventured out now to use his luck to get his young friend Richie (played by Shia LaBeouf) medical help for his life-threatening liver condition.

One interesting twist near the end of the episode is that Weems appears to run out of luck. Richie's mom gets kidnapped by the mobsters who keep running into bad luck hunting down Weems. Scully wonders whether Weems has lost his luck, but Mulder says maybe it's just being fulfilled in a way no one can predict, and the end of the episode confirms that. The kidnapping leads to the death of a mobster who turns out to be an organ donor and a rare exact match for Richie. That suggests it isn't a magic superpower but something with goals (or at least that follows his goals). It isn't just that things work out in his interest. Something locks on not just to what's good for him (which is a final cause) but what he seeks after (a different final cause).

Does it make sense that someone could be this lucky? Is something about Weems making these events happen this way? There might be a simpler explanation, but I'm not sure Mulder or Scully would like it. What if there's just a mind behind it all, rigging things in such a way that he doesn't get hurt much when he falls from such a height? You might say that if God is lurking behind the scenes to fulfill a purpose, it would be far less surprising that thousands of variables all happened to go the right way for Weems.

Isn't it a better explanation than anything else? Someone ensures thousands of unlikely occurrences happen and all happen at once, because there's a goal, a final cause. In "Improbable," the show even suggests that the character Burt Reynolds plays is really God. Would that make better sense of a character like Henry Weems? It would explain the final causes, and it's hard to know what else would.

Fortunately, we don't have to worry about explaining stuff like this, because we don't know of anyone like Henry Weems. But a lot of the same sorts of questions do come up in the real world, where we might wonder whether there's a mind behind something, if we should appeal to final causes. What should we do in such cases?

That depends on whether a mind is the best explanation or whether we can come up with better explanations. It does strike me as a more likely explanation in both these episodes than the ones actually given in the episodes, which feel incomplete and unsatisfying.

18
Is Mulder a Philosopher?

NEIL MUSSETT

It may sound dumb, but I think the talking parts of *The X-Files* are just as good as the action parts. Where else would you get something like this great speech from "Existence"?

> **MULDER:** We call it the miracle of life. Conception—a union of perfect opposites—essence transforming into existence—an act without which mankind would not exist and humanity cease to exist. Or is this just nostalgia now? An act of biology commandeered by modern science and technology? God-like, we extract, implant, inseminate . . . and we clone. But has our ingenuity rendered the miracle into a simple trick? In the artifice of replicating life can we become the creator? Then what of the soul? Can it, too, be replicated? Does it live in this matter we call DNA? Or is its placement the opposite of artifice, capable only by God?

We usually get these monologues at the beginning of the season, but we also get regular exchanges between Mulder and Scully like this one ("All Things"):

> **MULDER:** I don't think you can know. I mean, how many different lives would we be leading if we made different choices. We . . . we don't know.

> **SCULLY:** What if there was only one choice and all the other ones were wrong? And there were signs along the way to pay attention to.

> **MULDER:** Mmm. And all the . . . choices would then lead to this very moment. One wrong turn, and . . . we wouldn't be sitting here

> together. Well, that says a lot. That says a lot, a lot, a lot. That's probably more than we should be getting into at this late hour.

Even the jokes have a geeky depth to them, like this one from "Shadows":

> **MULDER:** Do you believe in the afterlife, Scully?
>
> **SCULLY:** I'd settle for a life in this one.

In everyday life, when we call something "deep" or even "philosophical," we usually say it as a kind of joke. What if we take this question seriously? Is Mulder a real philosopher? Is Scully?

Interrogating History

It makes sense to start at the beginning. Socrates (470–399 B.C.) is not the first philosopher (that title goes to a guy famous for falling into a well), but he's the guy who everybody knows. He also gave us the word "philosopher," which is enough to qualify him as an expert witness.

Like the Lone Gunmen, Socrates devoted his time to publicly criticizing the rich and powerful. At the time, all of the rich people spent money on private tutors to help their kids become successful lawyers or politicians (sound familiar?). The tutors were called "Wise Guys" (Sophists), and the ones with the best reputations made quite a lot of money. Socrates's favorite method was to stir up a debate with a Sophist and ask them seemingly innocent questions until they ended up contradicting themselves. As any *X-Files* fan would predict, this ended up with a conspiracy of powerful men having him killed.

What makes a philosopher, for Socrates? You don't have to get a job as a teacher or write books (he never did). The key: recognize how little you really know. "I know that I know nothing" is a saying attributed to him (we don't know if he actually said it!) The problem with most people is that they think they know everything, but they haven't spent any time questioning themselves. "The unexamined life is not worth living" is another one of his rumored sayings (he may have said it at his trial). A philosopher isn't someone who thinks they are wise; it's someone who has enough love for wisdom to recognize that the world is bigger than their explanations of it.

How does Mulder fare with this definition? Deep questions? Check. Willing to acknowledge his limitations? Check. Making powerful people want to kill him? Oh, yeah! It is easy to find Mulder sounding Socratic, like he does in "Patient X":

> **MULDER:** You know, you try to reveal what's hidden, you try to incite people with the facts, but they'd rather believe some insane nonsense.

Or everyone's favorite from *Fight the Future*:

> **MULDER:** Whatever happened to playing a hunch, Scully? The element of surprise, random acts of unpredictability? If we fail to anticipate the unforeseen or expect the unexpected in a universe of infinite possibilities, we may find ourselves at the mercy of anyone or anything that cannot be programmed, categorized, or easily referenced.

His back-and-forth conversations (or "Dialogues") with Scully usually start with a great question, like this one from "All Souls":

> **MULDER:** And why would God allow this to happen? Why do bad things happen to good people? Religion has masqueraded as the paranormal since the dawn of time to justify some of the most horrible acts in history.
>
> **SCULLY:** I was raised to believe that God has His reasons however mysterious.
>
> **MULDER:** He may well have His reasons, but He seems to use a lot of psychotics to carry out His job orders.

The verdict? I think Socrates would find a kindred soul in Fox Mulder. Mulder's one-liner from "Conduit" would be a good summary of Socrates's method: "This is the essence of science: you ask an impertinent question and you're on your way to a pertinent answer."

Scully? Not so sure—she seems to resist having her core beliefs questioned. However, her "strict rationalism" that keeps Mulder so honest does lead her to broaden her view of the world when presented with enough evidence. Take this rather poetic expression of Scully's willingness to test her own beliefs ("Memento Mori"):

> **Scully:** The luminous mysteries that once seemed so distant and unreal, threatening clarity in the presence of a truth entertained not in youth, but only in its passage . . . That you should know my heart, look into it, finding there the memory and experience that belong to you, that are you, is a comfort to me now as I feel the tethers loose and the prospects darken for the continuance of a journey that began not so long ago, and which began again with a faith shaken and strengthened by your convictions, if not for which I might never have been so strong now.

Developments in the Case

Have things changed since Socrates? Have our views changed? Could Mulder get a job as a philosopher? (Do philosophers have jobs?)

Take a class in contemporary philosophy, and you will usually hear philosophy roughly divided into "Analytic" and "Continental" schools. The Analytic approach to philosophy is supposed to enjoy analyzing language to "extract philosophical juice from science and common sense," as philosopher Nicholas Rescher puts it. The Continental approach ("The Continent" is another way of saying France and Germany) is supposed to prefer reading the work of particular philosophers in their concrete, historical context.

Yes, this is actually a weird way to divide philosophy (philosopher John Searle made a Good Joke when he said it's like dividing America into business and Kansas), because there is a ton of overlap between the approaches. Problems aside, we can still ask our question, How does Mulder do?

As an analytic philosopher, Mulder does not quite make the grade. Does he pay a lot of attention to language and grammar? No—there are some areas where he questions what it means to be human, but it doesn't seem to be a discussion of language. Does he employ formal logic or linguistics? Not really. The Analytic philosopher G.E. Moore published *A Defense of Common Sense*—not exactly a title that reminds you of Mulder, is it? Scully's rationalistic, scientific views seem more compatible with the Analytic tradition, but we never hear her take the time to put her views into formal language.

How about the Continental school? Mulder does enjoy bringing in the particular views of other cultures and times without judgment. This is a pretty typical Mulder factoid from "Teso Dos Bichos":

> **MULDER:** Well, what about the curse? The Secona believe great evil would befall anyone that disturbed the remains of an Amaru, a woman shaman—that they would be devoured by the Jaguar Spirit.

Mulder does seem to be an inclusive thinker. However, as a scholar of philosophy, he never gets off the ground. We never see Mulder quote philosophers, ancient (Socrates, Plato, Aristotle) or contemporary (Hegel, Derrida, Fichte). I'm afraid he wouldn't be taken seriously at a post-structuralist symposium.

There is another philosophical tradition called "Pragmatism" that seeks to identify philosophical truth with its practical consequences. William James, a famous pragmatist, asked "What difference would it practically make to anyone if this notion rather than that notion were true?" If two ideas have the same consequences, they are really the same idea in different forms. If there are no consequences at all, we can say that the notion is not really meaningful.

This sounds like something Mulder might actually like. There are traces of this attitude in his comments from "Field Trip":

> **SCULLY:** Mulder, can you just, for once, just for the novelty of it, come up with the simplest explanation? The most logical one, instead of automatically jumping to UFOs or Bigfoot or . . .
>
> **MULDER:** Scully, in six years how often have I been wrong? No, seriously. I mean, every time I bring a new case we go through this perfunctory dance, you tell me I'm not being scientifically rigorous and that I'm off my nut; and in the end who turns out to be right, like, 98.9 percent of the time? I just think I've earned the benefit of the doubt here.

If "being right" can be a substitute for being "scientifically rigorous" then perhaps assessing practical consequences is a better way to analyze our claims about the world. Maybe this attitude is behind the motivation for Scully's grim quip to Skinner, "All lies lead to the truth, isn't that right?" ("Redux").

The problem with calling Mulder (or Scully) a pragmatic philosopher is the same as calling him an analytic or continental philosopher. He never pretends he is. He shows no evidence he's familiar with the literature. He doesn't present a unified theory of the world. He doesn't even take the time to explain why other theories fail. As clever and deep as they are, neither of our favorite special agents are going to be mistaken for professional contemporary philosophers.

Any other options? There are endless sub-genres of philosopy, including many that deal with crime, extra-terrestrial intelligence, the brain, special cases of evolution, artificial intelligence, and yes, even zombies. However, these tend to be applications of general philosophical theories to more specific subjects. You could hunt zombies for your entire (short) lifetime without thinking of any of David Chalmers's "easy" or "hard" questions of consciousness.

Philosophers without Badges

Okay, so Mulder isn't a professional philosopher. Does this mean he is not a philosopher? Is there any room for the amateur?

Yes! In *The Philosophical Act*, Josef Pieper argued that philosophy is something we do, saying that "to philosophize is to act in such a way that one steps out of the world of work." In other words, each of us lives in our own little world of work, school, bills, food, cases, fun, and obligations. Most people live as if that was all that existed (right now you may be asking yourself what else there could be!). However, it is possible to break out of that world and ask bigger questions like, Why is there Something instead of Nothing? Does the universe follow rules? Why be good? When you do this, you are a philosopher (if only temporarily).

Pieper warns us that asking these questions may make us sound crazy ("Spooky"?), especially to the people most focused on material success. These sorts of questions are useless in the sense that they cannot be used by others to further their ambitions (good or bad). They are not justified by their social function or their contribution to the 'Common Good'. That's not the same as saying that they serve no purpose—their purpose is to free us from the world of Total Work, to liberate us from being controlled and controllable, to keep us from being just another cog in the machine.

Put it another way—picture the organizers of the Conspiracy putting together a list of people they need to assemble. They need doctors to manage implants. They need soldiers to guard facilities. They need philosophers to . . . to what? You might be tempted to say "To elaborate, defend, and demonstrate their ideology," but that would be to strangle philosophy and turn it into propaganda, which is something else entirely.

Mulder clearly enjoys asking the Big Questions (as this joke from the Pilot suggests):

> **SCULLY:** Do you have a theory?
>
> **MULDER:** I have plenty of theories.

Mulder believes that "reflection" and "rumination" are the highest prize of our intellectual powers:

> **MULDER:** The development of our cerebral cortex has been the greatest achievement of the evolutionary processes. Big deal. While allowing us the thrills of intellect or the pangs of self-consciousness, it is all too often overruled by our inner, instinctive brain—the one that tells us to react, not reflect, to run, rather than ruminate. ("War of the Coprophages")

Even in the middle of a case, Mulder uses every chance he can get to break out of the workaday world. In "Dreamland II," he switches bodies with Morris Fletcher. Mulder asks, "If I shoot him, is that murder or suicide?" It may be funny (or at least snarky), but it is a genuinely philosophical question.

Fox Mulder and Dana Scully are professional crime fighters, but philosophy plays an unusually big part in their lives. Philosophy is unique as a science—there are no qualifications, but having a flexible mind is a necessity. Mulder, with his interest in the exotic and uncategorized, and Scully, with her drive to defend the rationality of the universe, manage to free each other from the otherwise small world of the FBI. Their experiences lead them to asking larger questions about good and evil, free will, the nature of the state, and more. These questions may not ultimately help them find criminals and conspirators any quicker, but they form the core of their personalities. Contrast this with Assistant Director Skinner's approach to life—noble, but strictly practical.

Case Closed

Is that all there is to philosophy? Asking useless questions? What about all those books? All the history? Are professors wasting their time?

There's a difference between being annoying and being a philosopher (despite what psychology professors say). Just look at Mulder—he doesn't want questions, he wants answers, the "Truth" that's "out there." He's not content with half-truths or with a superficial understanding of anything, so he's going to seek answers from other people, other cultures, other worldviews than his own. For Pieper, the whole point is to break out of your own world—once you begin the philosophical quest, it's only natural to seek out other weirdoes who have done the same thing. Mulder would be the first to read a book on the philosophy of the mind, or the ethics of interstellar war, or . . . ahem . . . the book you're reading right now.

Oftentimes, the only reward for tireless investigation is better and deeper questions, but there is something better and somehow more human in being a dissatisfied Mulder than in being a satisfied dupe of the Conspiracy.

VI

Elusive Truth

19
When Is It Right to Hide the Truth?

JASON WALKER

There are no answers for you, Mr. Mulder. They only have one policy . . . Deny everything.

—MR. X, "ASCENSION"

Can You Handle the Truth? Even if you're pretty sure you can, maybe you're wrong. So what if, for your benefit, and for the benefit of the whole society, the government were to lie to you?

That lie might come in several forms. It might be a lie by omission, a failure to disclose relevant information. Or it may be a stronger lie, a lie by commission, in which an active untruth or denial of a truth is widely perpetuated. Either way, a lie, in and of itself, is any intentional attempt to distort a person's perception of reality. A question raised by *The X-Files* is whether, assuming the intentions behind such deceptions are good, aimed primarily at saving lives or protecting innocents from harm, may governments morally engage in such deceptions?

Consider the Syndicate, a shadowy, powerful group of conspirators who influence governments to hide the existence of extraterrestrial visitations and contacts. Within the narrative of the show, the Syndicate typically plays the role of villains to the heroic Mulder and Scully. The Cigarette Smoking Man, as a representative and an enforcer behind the Syndicate, actively constructs false narratives and hides evidence about the truth of extraterrestrials and the Syndicate's unsavory activities. In contrast, part of what makes Mulder and Scully heroes within this narrative is precisely their unrelenting pursuit of the truth, wherever that takes them, and their determination to make the truth known.

Neither the Cigarette Smoking Man nor the Syndicate want for any rationalizations about what they do. But these are typically in the form of utilitarian, or consequentialist, arguments. Disclosure, they insist, would create a social panic, introducing chaos to a mostly peaceful *status quo*. Even worse, it's sometimes suggested that the Syndicate has agreed to a *quid pro quo* with some of the aliens encountered, obligating them to conceal the existence of alien life in exchange for protection when the aliens begin their invasion.

In itself, that can hardly be considered a serious moral justification, but it is claimed that invasion plans would be sped up, which would deny the Syndicate time to develop means of resisting the invasion when it does occur. Within the narrative of *The X-Files*, this often seems more like a self-serving rationalization than a serious moral argument, since the Syndicate is, no doubt, also worried about consequences to its members should it ever be discovered by the general public. (Indeed, as Chris Carter makes explicit in a hidden audio track on *The X-Files: Fight the Future* movie soundtrack, "They were the Vichy government to the German Final Solution: collaborationists whose motivation was simple, self-directed survival.")

Devil's Due

But let us give the Devil his due, and assume, for argument's sake, that the Syndicate is quite sincere. Indeed, whatever other motives they may have had, we are also told that they genuinely feared that

> Their detection would ensure not just their own demise but a far-reaching dissolution of social and religious order around the globe . . . If the Syndicate's secrets were discovered . . . they would certainly be destroyed and the timetable for colonization stepped up. They would protect this secret with their lives. They would kill to protect it, as it symbolized the only hope they had of avoiding enslavement when the planet was overtaken.

Let's assume that the Syndicate was justified in this belief, and that their deceptions helped to save lives and preserve peace, potentially even making resistance to future alien colonizers more viable. If that were the case, would lies told by governments (or shadowy figures influencing governments) be morally justifiable?

I will argue no, but the seemingly obvious moral priority for the truth is not as universally widely accepted as we may suppose at firtst. It turns out that many Americans, in different contexts, are often quite comfortable with being actively deceived, and that the Syndicate may be drawing on political and moral assumptions that are widely shared, from American political culture on one hand, to others with roots in political philosophy on the other. Nevertheless, despite widespread justifications for such deceptions in both philosophical and popular culture, governments that deceive their citizens surrender legitimacy by doing so.

Cover Up

The downfall of Richard Nixon is often taken as emblematic of how citizens, at least within constitutional, democratic republics, regard deception from their leaders. It was frequently said, then and now, that Nixon's downfall shows that the cover-up after the fact was worse than the actual offense.

Historians generally agree that Nixon likely had no foreknowledge of the break-in at the Watergate Hotel in 1972, and while full disclosure would no doubt have injured his standing politically, he very likely could have weathered that storm. His re-election in 1972 was by one of the biggest margins in American history, so he certainly had more than a few approval points to spare. But as the truth gradually emerged, that he had engaged in a systematic cover-up after the fact, Americans were outraged, leading to the moment in 1974 when even members of his own party informed him that there were more than enough votes in Congress, from Republicans and Democrats alike, to guarantee impeachment and removal from office. Nixon resigned in disgrace, becoming a punch line in politics thereafter, with only limited, very quiet esteem in some quarters as an elder statesman.

Be that as it may, subsequent political developments may prove Nixon to be the exception rather than the rule. Some examples may illuminate where current expectations lie.

Monicagate

In early 1998, an investigation of sexual harassment allegations revealed that Bill Clinton had committed perjury, and possibly instructed others to do likewise, to cover up his sexual affair with a twenty-four-year-old White House intern, Monica Lewinsky. Notoriously, after the affair became public knowledge, Clinton compounded his perjury by denying that he ever "had sexual relations with that woman, Monica Lewinsky." Only when it was discovered that physical evidence of his affair existed, did Clinton retract his testimony, confessing that he had indeed lied during his previous grand jury testimony, supposedly to protect his family from his infidelity.

However, the subsequent political fallout took a very different shape than with Nixon. Although both figures committed deception motivated, not by high ideals, but out of political self-preservation, Clinton's was defended by many Americans on the basis that his indiscretion was fundamentally private in nature. Partisanship played a far stronger role in the Clinton impeachment hearings, as nearly all Republicans voted for his impeachment in the House, and all Democrats voted for his acquittal in the Senate.

No consensus to legally punish Clinton for his perjury was achieved either among politicians themselves or in the public at large. Throughout the nearly year-long impeachment drama, Clinton's approval ratings stubbornly remained at around fifty percent, a number that both Presidents Bush and Obama would have envied by that point in their second terms. Polls typically showed a plurality opposed to impeachment. The argument that Clinton's perjury concerned private matters, not relevant to policy, seemed to find success with many Americans, despite the fact that non-politicians are regularly legally punished for similar acts of family-protecting perjury.

Although increased partisanship and polarization no doubt was a major factor in Clinton's acquittal, ultimately his relatively high approval ratings made it politically safe for Senate Democrats to resist impeachment. In contrast, Nixon's unpopularity upon the discovery of the Watergate cover-up all but required Republicans in 1974 to abandon him. Ultimately, Nixon's lies about Watergate were not forgiven by Americans in 1974, whereas Clinton's perjury was either forgiven or deemed not punishable at all in 1998.

The rule here, though certainly not universally held by Americans, seems to be that politicians may lie and even commit perjury, as long as it concerns private matters.

Edward Snowden and James Clapper

Security, as an overriding justification trumping moral concerns like truth, has in more recent times become a bipartisan affair. In 2013, during testimony to Congress about the scope of the NSA's domestic intelligence activities, James Clapper, Director of National Intelligence, was asked by the Oregon Democrat Senator Ron Wyden whether the NSA collected data about private phone conversations from American civilians. Wyden asked, "Does the NSA collect any type of data at all on millions or hundreds of millions of Americans?" To which Clapper replied, "No, sir . . . Not wittingly. There are cases where they could inadvertently, perhaps, collect, but not wittingly."

By his own account, this testimony led Edward Snowden to collect information he obtained about NSA programs from his job as a subcontractor, and leak it to journalists like Glen Greenwald. Snowden's leaks revealed that the NSA had indeed collected metadata about phone calls between Americans from cell phone providers like Verizon, in order to build a national database about Americans' private communication habits. Thus began the Snowden affair, culminating in his dramatic flight for political asylum abroad. (*X-Files* fans may recognize in Snowden some similarities with Kenneth Soona, "The Thinker" from the Season Two finale, "Anasazi," the master hacker who likewise leaked a treasure trove of intelligence secrets only to go on the run. Snowden, so far, seems to have met a better fate than Soona.)

In the eyes of many commentators, this raised the question of whether Clapper would be prosecuted for committing perjury. Senator Wyden, Senator Rand Paul, Representative Justin Amash, and other members of Congress raised the question, and asked for Clapper's resignation, only to be rebuffed by the Obama administration, saying it was satisfied that Clapper had not intentionally committed perjury or conducted himself improperly in any way. Clapper himself responded in a variety of ways: he apologized for a "misleading" choice of words, claimed that he had "forgotten" about Section 215 of the Patriot

Act, and defended his testimony, saying that he "responded in what he thought was the most truthful, or least untruthful manner by saying no."

Naturally, this didn't satisfy his critics. But the general reaction to the Snowden affair suggests that denying the full scope of the NSA's operations and policies to the American public was acceptable to many. The underlying assumption here is that the people suspected of terrorism, and information about their plans, are more likely to be found if these people don't know what the NSA's abilities and information gathering techniques are.

For example, they may believe that phone communications are safe if they haven't been served with a warrant, or that a given email encryption protocol is safe, even if the NSA has actually compromised it. Thus, the NSA may be able to gather incriminating information and evidence useful in preventing future terrorist activities and in capturing terrorists before they act. Had Clapper's testimony been truthful, and had the NSA been open about its general policies from the beginning, the efficacy of these operations might have been undermined, as terrorists would be on notice that communication channels they had been using might be monitored by the NSA. Thus, by leaking information about the NSA's activities, Snowden undermined the US government's ability to conduct effective surveillance and counter-terrorist operations, and may have thus endangered the safety of Americans in the future.

We can consider this justification for dishonesty the argument from safety, or saving lives. In its most simple form, it may be expressed as such: "Governments may lie to their people about their policies and activities, to the degree that it is justified in believing that such lies are instrumental in promoting safety." Combined with the precedent from Clinton's impeachment, state actors may also forgivably lie about private matters that do not touch on policy.

Nixon's deceptions may be distinguished from these examples by noting that his lies were not merely about private matters, in that they involved obscuring the facts about a crime, a breaking-and-entering in order to steal potentially damaging information on a political rival. That Clinton's lie was itself a crime, perjury, seems to be forgivable by many under this standard in that it was perjury about an activity that may not have itself been prosecutable as a crime, given that Lewinsky herself did not bring workplace sexual harassment charges against Clinton, and claimed their activities were consensual.

Justified Lying

Cigarette Smoking Man: You presume to dictate duty to me? Have you any idea what the cost of your actions is? What their effect might be? Who are you to give them hope?

Jeremiah Smith: What do you give them?

Cigarette Smoking Man: We give them happiness, and they give us authority.

Jeremiah Smith: The authority to take away their freedom under the guise of democracy.

Cigarette Smoking Man: Men can never be free, because they're weak, corrupt, worthless, and restless. The people believe in authority. They've grown tired of waiting for miracle and mystery. Science is their religion. No greater explanation exists for them. They must never believe any differently if the project is to go forward.

Jeremiah Smith: At what cost to them?

Cigarette Smoking Man: The question is irrelevant, and the outcome inevitable. The date is set. ("Talitha Cumi")

The question of whether governments may or should lie to their citizens is a surprisingly old one in the history of philosophy, going all the way back to Plato. In his *Republic*, Socrates proposes that mate selection and breeding be controlled strictly by his Philosopher-Kings, the Guardian class. The Guardians, he explains, will establish a lottery system to make it appear that these decisions are made randomly, but in reality, these lotteries will be fixed in advance to ensure ideal outcomes, as an exercise of proto-eugenics.

By necessity, Socrates explains, the Guardians will have to lie about this practice to the lower classes, telling them a myth about gold, silver, and bronze souls, meant to explain why people of certain classes are paired with each other. This lie will help the people believe in the fairness of the system that governs them, and promote a sense of fraternity among them. It's from this that we have the notion of the "noble lie" or "pious lie," a lie told by the rulers to the people either for the benefit of the people themselves, or at least for the good of the society as a whole. This may be taken as a general utilitarian-style kind of argument; lies told by the government are justified insofar as they may help promote the greatest good or greatest happiness by the greatest possible number of people.

In a similar vein, it's interesting to note that Friedrich Nietzsche, unquestionably Socrates and Plato's harshest critic, also sees value in something like a noble lie. For Nietzsche, the value of an idea is not whether it is literally true or false, but rather whether it is life-affirming or life-denying. For example, Nietzsche is an atheist, and though he is uncompromising in his criticisms of Christianity, he sees great value in the older pagan faiths displaced by Christianity, in that they provided a stronger tie to nature. Bad religions are not bad for being false; good religions are also false. Rather, a good religion is life-affirming, despite its untruth. Indeed, a major component of Nietzsche's criticism of Plato is that he sees Plato as too much of a rationalist, who would overthrow the nationalist myths that gave Greek culture its potency. Insofar as governments may play a role in promoting life-affirming myths, they may likewise be engaged in the project of noble lie-telling.

The Syndicate

So where does this leave the Syndicate? Again, independent of whatever self-serving interests and motives they have, it seems that it may have all the moral justification for its deceptions to American citizens.

First, its members can argue that a general interest in promoting security justifies its deceptions. If James Clapper were a Syndicate member, he might claim that the alien colonists are like terrorists, and might more successfully modify their activities to elude detection and carry out their projects if what the Syndicate knows were to come to public awareness.

Second, a utilitarian-style argument, related to this, might well justify deception to the degree that the Syndicate can show it is saving the lives and even the very freedom of all humanity if its secrecy forestalls or prevents a full invasion.

Social order might well depend on widely accepted myths of a certain kind, whether in Plato's or Nietzsche's version, so the Syndicate might well be justified in manipulating media and government. One example cited explicitly to support this view by the Syndicate themselves is the famous 1938 broadcast of Orson Welles's "War of the Worlds" radio drama. Supposedly, mistaking the broadcast for a real news story about the landing of Martians, panic set in among thousands of listeners, with terrified listeners arming up and even shooting a few people. That this story itself turns out to be urban myth need not detract from a justified fear that something like this could happen if the government were to be transparent and disclose the existence of extraterrestrials and their plans for Earth conquest.

Finally, the deceptions cooked up by the Syndicate might be of the Noble Lie variety, promoting fraternity and loyalty to the state, or even life-affirming myths, which can support cultural potency and greater happiness. While of course we might morally object to the Syndicate's methods for achieving its aims, what could be said against these arguments for clamming up about truths too dangerous to disclose? Plenty, it turns out.

Deciding On the Policy of Truth

The German philosopher Immanual Kant argued for the necessity of consistently telling the truth as a moral imperative. In Kant's case, the argument may be taken to an absurd conclusion, in that Kant argues that even in a case when you might be hiding an intended victim from a murderer, you are nonetheless morally obligated to be truthful with the murderer about the victim's whereabouts.

A more reasonable case for truthfulness from government can begin by distinguishing between truth of a general nature and truth of a particular nature. In the former case, we would have in mind the truth about policies and programs the government engages in. In the latter, we might have the kind of specifics in mind that would endanger the privacy rights or safety of individuals: for example, the names and addresses of CIA agents or people hidden by the Witness Relocation Program. Truths of the latter variety may deserve protection, if nothing else, by omission. The general case for truthfulness from governments will mostly attend to transparency about general truths.

Facts about policies may be distinguished in one further way, between ongoing and completed operations. An ongoing operation, particularly a military operation or an active investigation, may be at least partially concealed for similar reasons, provided that the details are disclosed after the completion of the operation. In general, the kind of transparency this case has in mind is mindful of privacy and safety to particular named persons, but is otherwise an open book about the kinds of activities and policies the government engages in presently and in the past.

The reasons for the moral necessity behind transparency have to do with legitimacy, particularly with respect to legitimacy necessarily for democracies and republics governed by the rule of law, the rejection of paternalism, and with respect to epistemic modesty.

Constitutional governments, unlike government by absolute monarchs, dictators, generals, or politburos, operate under certain constraints necessary for moral legitimacy. Legitimacy is what allows us to distinguish between a criminal gang or mafia that achieves compliance through fear of violence, and a government that achieves compliance with laws binding in moral conscience.

In the absence of legitimacy, the moral difference is blurred between the government and the security threats it exists to protect its citizens against. Legitimacy is often thought of in terms of the consent of the governed: where the people have broadly given their consent to a particular government, that government has moral legitimacy to operate as a government. Hence, governments run by absolute monarchs, dictators, generals, and politburos lack legitimacy, insofar as they do not provide elections or other mechanisms for the people to consent to or have a voice in their style of governance.

Merely assuring free elections may be necessary, though it cannot be sufficient. Certainly in this instance, a government which misinforms its people cannot be evaluated by them fairly, because voters would be acting on the basis of false information. This would certainly present a major challenge to the view that governments may morally lie to their people for the people's own benefit, since any government doing this would already be morally compromised. So instead, let's look at another aspect of legitimacy, the rule of law.

In its most robust sense, the rule of law is a state of affairs in which law itself is in some sense sovereign. Governments may not simply act as they please; their activities are governed and controlled by a higher source of law, such as constitutions, the precedents of common law, or natural law. The rule of law, and with it, legitimacy, requires that governments follow their own laws. This puts the citizen and her government at a kind of parity; she follows the law, and the government does likewise, as a kind of unspoken pact. She may lose her freedom if she breaks the law, and governments that break the law may face defiance, rebellion, and revolution.

A Bit Dicey

The rule of law, in the modern era, was described by British jurist A.V. Dicey (1835–1922) according to three criteria. First, there is the absolute supremacy of regular law, over and above discretion, when in conflict. Second, equality before the law, with the understanding that there are no exemptions for government officials. The third criterion is often expressed as the "spirit of constitutionality," and expresses the general sense that the constitutional basis of the state is not the source, but rather the consequence of individual rights. The second criterion, equality before the law, expresses the notion that government officials are not governed by a separate set of rules from regular citizens; all of us are equal, and subject to the same laws.

Consider the crime of perjury. In the US, as in most countries, it's considered a crime to tell lies under oath. You can literally be sent to prison for lying to a judge or to the government. Independent of perjury, you may also be indicted for making false statements to federal investigators (the crime that Martha Stewart and "Scooter" Libby were convicted of), wherein you may be convicted even if your statements are merely misleading or incomplete, as opposed to intentional lies. Obstruction of justice is likewise punishable under law, describing cases in which evidence might be hidden or destroyed, or other facts potentially relevant to an investigation or court proceeding obscured.

Rule of Law

Considering that the rule of law requires reciprocity between the government and the governed, that both follow the same laws, a government free to lie or deceive its people could not, therefore, claim to be governed by the rule of law, unless perjury and its related crimes were not illegal. The voters, of course, may not be engaged in a criminal investigation like those taken up by the state, but lies told to them would be a problem in two ways.

First, it would damage that pact of reciprocity: citizens could not lie to the government or a judge, but governments would be free to lie to citizens. This imbalance would make an ostensibly free government more like those of authoritarian regimes, and undermine the citizen's respect for the law once she realizes that laws are enforced by the threat of imprisonment alone, rather than by moral legitimacy.

That pact is also damaged in that it assumes a child-like status for regular citizens, who, as Colonel Jessup suggests in *A Few Good Men*, "can't handle the truth." This would be consistent with a paternalistic form of government, but not with the liberal, constitutional forms of government common in the West, prefaced as they are by the equality of all people and the ideal of self-government. We've seen that the Cigarette Smoking Man takes a very dim view of the average person, as "weak, corrupt, worthless, and restless," unfit for freedom, and willing to accept authority in exchange for happiness. This is no accident.

Second, we can regard citizens' electoral decisions as analogues to the government's criminal investigations. Lies told by the government would obstruct justice, not only in covering up crimes committed by state actors, but also during elections, in which citizens judge whether they favor certain policies and the politicians who promote them. This would take us back to the problem highlighted earlier, in which the judgment of citizens as voters would be undermined by false information.

As a general case against deception by governments toward their citizens, this argument is consistent with the distinctions in the areas in which opacity may be acceptable. For example, voters would not need to know the names and personal information of CIA officers engaged in a particular operation to make a judgment about it. The particulars of battle operations, actionable intelligence or other wartime plans could be obscured, as long as they were within the bounds of international law and the ethics of war, and as long as they were disclosed upon their completion. This would preserve citizens' ability to judge the propriety of given policies and politicians who championed them.

Real World

The Syndicate, or more likely the Syndicate's philosophically inclined defender, might respond that all of this is great for an ideal world, but in the real world, facing threats from terrorists and extraterrestrial colonizers, compromises with morality need to be made. In war, governments often assume emergency powers, particularly for wars of existential peril, and certainly a conflict with aliens would be just such a contingency. If survival requires a few steps down the road to serfdom, so be it. It's not as if the Syndicate is concerned with the moral niceties of liberal constitutional democracy in the first place. What could be said against the general utilitarian case for noble lies?

Many people would certainly find it troubling enough that their government may undermine its own legitimacy and identity as a rule of law state. But just as certainly, many others are focused on these more immediate threats, and doing whatever was necessary to combat them. So this argument must be addressed more directly, by considering lying itself as a means to an end.

Let's concede, for the sake of the argument, that the ends sought are morally legitimate, even if we recall that the Syndicate's actual ends are often not. Our focus here is on lying as a means or strategy to noble ends.

Several things should be considered when lying is contemplated. First, the security and utility argument requires that we possess knowledge that we rarely, if ever, possess. We would need to know that the lies to be told would be widely accepted as the truth. It need not be universally accepted, since the Syndicate seems to be successful enough if only a few crazy internet conspiracy theorists like the Lone Gunmen see through their lies. But crafting a narrative that would be believable to most other people is no small thing. We would need to know that the cover-up would be successful, leaving no clues or hints about the truth that could be discovered by others. It would also be necessary to prove that the lie was necessary in the first place, that is, that disclosure of the truth would create a worse harm than a fallible cover-up or obfuscation.

The Syndicate certainly is powerful, but even it would have a hard time determining these things with sufficient certainty.

Second, there exists a need for internal consistency, or else we fall into what might be called "Seinfeldian conundrums." That is, a lie told will eventually have to be supported by another lie, which in turn requires another lie, and another lie, and so forth, as a story is investigated. This imposes a high cognitive burden, in that the people telling lies must become adept at keeping all of the lies internally consistent with publicly observed facts, as well as consistent with any potential facts that may come to light in the future.

Recalling the example of Nixon, the discovery of a cover-up is often more politically damaging than the original act, which might make whatever value was sought by a cover-up not worth the trouble that would inevitably be required to make the cover-up successful. It's worth recalling that Nixon's downfall, along with the unpopularity of the Vietnam War, helped fuel a great distrust in government relative to the post–World War II enthusiasm peaking in the Eisenhower and Kennedy administrations.

Really Hard to Do . . .

In the fictional world of *The X-Files*, the Syndicate can be as successful as the plot requires, but in the real world, successfully pulling off a cover-up is highly difficult, even with all the resources of the government at the conspirators' disposal. And even within the world of *The X-Files*, the Syndicate is hardly infallible, as Agents Mulder and Scully frequently uncover and undermine their plots.

Nixon, again, provides a telling example of this point. As the President of the United States, arguably the most powerful man in the free world, Nixon was ultimately unable to successfully cover up what has been described as a "third-rate burglary," and his bungled cover-up ultimately led to his political downfall. Indeed, this is a chief reason why Syndicate-style conspiracies could rarely, if ever, be successful in the real world: conspiracies are very risky and prone to failure, even in relatively trivial, simple attempts like Watergate.

So even if state actors decided that they didn't care that their lies could endanger the moral legitimacy of the government, a simple cost-benefit analysis would also pose obstacles for any willful deceit. The utilitarian-style argument here would also have to factor in the costs of this difficult undertaking, as well as the risks of failure and disclosure.

While it's not impossible that the potential gains could make it worth attempting, the unlikelihood of satisfying such an analysis grows as the depth of the deceit and potential political damage of discovery increases. After all, however damaging it might be for the discovery of alien colonists to come out, this same damage would only be worse if it was actively covered-up and then discovered by an ambitious reporter, looking for her next Pulitzer. Wise politicians, who may otherwise be as amoral and cynical as the stereotype suggests, often opt for full disclosure just for this reason. (They simply wait until late Friday for their data dumps, when it's harder for their disclosures to become headline news.)

Certainly in the case of the Snowden revelations, James Clapper and the Obama administration probably would have preferred for these programs to have been unveiled on their own terms, rather than in the dramatic fashion that Snowden leaked them. Although neither Obama nor Clapper faced a Nixonian downfall, their public standing and reputation were heavily damaged, and even worse, Russia's President Vladimir Putin scored a considerable public relations and intelligence victory when Snowden accepted asylum in Russia. Likewise, whatever public advantages the Syndicate hoped to obtain through concealment would be easily eclipsed by exposure. A pure utilitarian would thus not only have to consider the resources expended to prevent exposure as a significant cost to that policy, but also factor how catastrophic things might be if exposure happened anyway, despite their best efforts. It's very likely that a pure apples-to-apples comparison of a transparency policy to a policy of deception would indicate that those resources would be more efficiently used directly fighting alien colonists than against other humans who merely seek the truth.

This all assumes that the argument for deception could be motivated independent of the Syndicate's unenlightened self-interest. Part of the problem the Syndicate faces is that whatever code of honor that may have bound it together originally as a group had broken down, which should not be surprising. Deception begets deception, mistrust begets mistrust, as the Syndicate learns only too late when the bill for its sordid legacy of lies finally comes due.

20
The Truths Are Out There

COURTLAND LEWIS

> Out of kindness, Agent Scully. Allow him his ignorance. It's what gives him hope.
>
> —THE CIGARETTE SMOKING MAN ("Closure")

Welcome, Agent. We were expecting your arrival, because we know you've been engaging in dangerous activities, like reading *The X-Files and Philosophy*. We hear you're especially interested in the truth.

"You can't handle the truth!"

Please excuse my associate, that's all he can say. Oh, and I hope you don't mind if my other associate smokes. He seems to have a problem, and he doesn't really care if you do mind.

Where was I? Oh yeah, you want to know about 'truth'. Well, we're here to warn you that you're on a dangerous and corruptive path, one that could lead to the toppling of our clandestine organization, the government, most media outlets, and several other important figures across the globe. Your journey could lead to a lifetime of asking questions, doubt, and brooding. You don't want that, do you? What? You didn't realize the value, power, and danger of the truth? Tsk, tsk, you have a long way to go, if you're ever going to rival your predecessors Agents Fox Mulder and Dana Scully.

The truth is out there, but if you don't know what you mean by 'truth', then you either won't know when you find it, or you'll just believe whatever fits your preconceived understanding of 'truth'. One of our early agents, Pontius Pilate, once asked a carpenter accused of being the King of the Jews, "What is truth?" The man actually claimed to *be* truth, and said that those who followed him would be set free. These are what we would call religious or metaphysical truths. Is that the type of truth you're looking for, Agent? Maybe you're more interested in practical everyday truths? The math equation '2 + 2 = 4' and the statement "the thing you're holding in your hand right now can't both exist and not exist at the same time" are both practical everyday truths. Is that what you're looking for, Agent? No, too easy?

Ah, you want to know how truth relates to things like the existence of clandestine government organizations, conspiracies, and aliens. Well, that's why we're here; to help you see that truth isn't as easily explained as you might think. As we'll see, there are at least two types of truth, several different theories of truth, and a whole literature of philosophy dedicated to how we should handle truth in society and politics. So, relax and get used to the effluvium of cigarette smoke. We're going to spend a little time together discussing some of these features of truth, in hopes that at the end of our discussion you'll recognize the dangers that lie ahead of you on your journey; and you'll stop heading down such a dangerous path.

One Breath

It makes me so happy when I hear ignorant people say, "There is no truth." Little do they realize, if their statement were true, then their statement would be false. Confused already? Let me explain. If the statement 'there is no truth' is true, then there are no statements that are true. Therefore, the statement 'there is no truth' is false. The same paradox occurs when someone says, "It is true that I always tell a lie." Such statements lead to logical contradictions. Their truth implies their falsity.

Logic is the philosophical discipline that examines the structure of sentences and how they fit together to make good arguments. Whether we refer to them as propositions, statements, or premises, all *declarative* sentences are either true or false. Not all sentences, however, are declarative. Some sentences are questions, some are commands, and others are exclamations. None of these types of statements have a truth value. I could command you, "Stop investigating truth," ask, "Don't you want to live a long happy life not worried about truth?", or exclaim, "I will turn you over to aliens if you keep up your investigations!" but none of these statements are true or false. You might read into what I've said and arrive at some conclusion about what you should do, but a good critical thinker will notice and avoid such argumentative tricks.

Here's a good declarative sentence: "You'll be infected with black oil after finishing this chapter." This sentence is either true or false. Granted, we don't have enough information to determine its truth value at this time, but we will once you finish the chapter. If we put several declarative sentences together, then as long as they support a particular conclusion, we have an argument. So, if I wanted to make an argument for you to quit your inquisitive activities, I might say the following: All inquisitive people will be experimented on by aliens, and you're an inquisitive person; hence, you'll be experimented on by aliens. So, assuming you don't want to be experimented on by aliens, then you should stop being inquisitive.

See how I put together three sentences to support the conclusion that you'll be experimented on by aliens. Then, I used its conclusion to support a second argument that you should stop being inquisitive. Both of these arguments are valid, which means if the sentences supporting the conclusion—logicians call these premises—are true, then it's impossible for the conclusion to be false. To deny the validity of this argument means either you're irrational or you don't understand deductive logic. You can deny the truth of the sentences, but the argument is valid nonetheless. Since the argument is valid, you'd be smart not to press your luck to see if all of the sentences are true. A valid argument with all true statements makes it *sound*. So, if my argument is both valid and sound, then you have a date with some experimental-happy aliens.

The Ancient X-Files

Truth within arguments can be a tricky business. Think about the following argument:

Conspiracy theorists believe in aliens.

Mulder believes in aliens.

Therefore, Mulder is a conspiracy theorist.

Looks good, right? All of three sentences seem true, or at least possibly true. Nevertheless, you'd be wise not to fall for this argument, since it is invalid. It's invalid because it's possible, with this form of argument, to have two true premises that support a false conclusion. In this particular argument, all three sentences are true, but validity is about the *form* of the argument. The fact that the conclusion of this argument happens to be true is just a lucky chance: the conclusion does not follow from the premises.

To test this, we could replace "Mulder" with "Someone who isn't a conspiracy theorist," and we would get the conclusion that "Someone who isn't a conspiracy theorist is a conspiracy theorist." See, arguments can be misleading if they don't have the logically correct form.

For many centuries our organization has used arguments to obscure truth and understanding. Long before Mulder and Scully attempted to bring us down, the Ancient Greek philosopher Socrates gave us fits. We used to use what Socrates called the "Debater's Argument"—often referred to as "Meno's Paradox"—to prevent anyone from getting too close to the truth. The Debater's Argument claims: You can't come to know something that you don't already know, since if you don't know it, you'll never know to look for it, nor will you recognize it, if you ever happened upon it. If this is all true, then we can never know anything, since we begin life ignorant of everything.

In Plato's dialogue *Meno*, Socrates shows that the Debater's Argument assumes our brains are blank slates, completely void of information and knowledge. He argues that humans are born with information and knowledge from previous lives, and that all we need do is "recollect" what we've already learned. Sounds crazy, right? Well, Socrates supported his argument by having an illiterate person solve complex geometry problems, which could only occur if he were born with the knowledge of geometry. Doesn't sound so crazy anymore, does it?

Though Socrates's arguments about past lives and recollection are currently unpopular, his investigations opened the door for others, like Mulder, Scully, and now you, to use logic and critical thinking to defeat our agents. However, we hope you're beginning to see from this discussion the dangers of seeking truth. We know what's best for people, and logic and critical thinking only gets in the way of our plans. What? You still think people are smart enough to make decisions for themselves without our interference. That'll soon change.

The Truth Is Out and In There

Most people think truth is simply a matter of common sense. Take, for instance, the statement "Fox Mulder's sister was abducted." If we want to find out the truth value of this statement (whether it's true or false), all we need do is see whether Mulder's sister was abducted. If she was, then the statement is true, but if she wasn't, then it's false.

Seems easy enough, but let's raise the stakes. Is the statement "Extra-terrestrial aliens come from outer space" true or false? Some philosophers will argue that such a statement assumes the existence of aliens. As a result, for the statement to be true, aliens must actually exist; but since we have no credible evidence they exist, we must say the statement is false.

However, other philosophers will argue that such a statement is only a conceptual claim. In other words, what the claim really says is: "*if* extra-terrestrial aliens exist, then they come from outer space." We, then, can determine the truth value of the statement by simply looking at the meaning of the words. The phrase 'extra-terrestrial' means existing or originating outside of Earth's atmosphere. So, by definition, extra-terrestrial aliens are from outer space, and the statement is true.

Which account is correct? To answer, we need to know what the word 'truth' means, and I know you don't want me to take all of the fun out of your quest by simply giving you the answer. Instead, let's see how those much wiser than I have suggested we define 'truth'.

The basic assumption of traditional theories of truth is that *truth* has a nature. There are essential features of *truth* that give things like *beliefs* and *statements* the property of "being true." The oldest theory of truth is called the *correspondence theory* of truth, and according to Frederick Schmitt's *Theories of Truth*, can be traced back to Plato's dialogue *Sophist*. Simply stated, the correspondence theory of truth maintains that a belief is true when it *corresponds* to the way the world is. In other words, the truth of Scully's statement, "I have two small marks on the back of my neck," depends on whether or not there are two small marks on her neck. If they're there, then her statement is true. So, according to the correspondence theory, the truth really is "out there."

There are different versions of the correspondence theory of truth. The simplest version, called "simple correspondence," is the one just described, and is often attributed to another thorn in our side, the Greek philosopher Aristotle. Other theories offer slightly different explanations, but they are all in agreement that some belief or statement either corresponds to reality or our experience of reality.

Correspondence theories were the only game in town, until C.S. Peirce first developed what's referred to as *Pragmatism*. According to Timothy Mosteller's *Theories of Truth: An Introduction*, Peirce reimagined the nature of truth, arguing that truth is the property of the inquiring person that can withstand the test of inquiry. This should remind you of Agent Scully. Think of all of the times Mulder has given her some ridiculous story about alien abduction or conspiracies. How does she respond? She's typically skeptical of his convoluted explanations. Being a good scientist, she goes in search of the simpler, more scientific explanation. Think of the *X-Files* episode "War of the Coprophages." Mulder becomes convinced that robotic alien cockroaches are attacking Miller's Grove, Massachusetts. Based on his set of beliefs about aliens and conspiracies, he finds all sorts of what he believes is "corresponding" evidence—accounts of roaches, stories from the sheriff, and much more. Scully, on the other hand, counters his story with much simpler scientific explanations. Instead of having a belief and looking for corresponding evidence, she uses well-established scientific explanations to describe the *truth* of the situation.

Williams James continued Peirce's focus on the utility of truth. He noticed that many truths are dependent upon our own actions. As James explains, to be a friend requires that I be engaged in the act of being a friend. Truth is the same way. To find truth, I must be engaged in the act of finding truth. Inquiry, then, is shaped by my knowledge, my perceptual abilities, and my ability to craft the information into an account consistent with other well-established accounts. Beliefs that can withstand inquiry are said to be true. As a result, truth is more-accurately said to be made by the inquiry, not discovered during it. In other words, truth is "in there," not "out there."

One important implication of James's work is that we must distinguish between absolute and pragmatic truth. Absolute truths are said to be settled. Further inquiry would not change the belief. Most human beliefs aren't absolute, because they're based on experience, and since humans lack infinite knowledge and perceptual capabilities, such beliefs are always open to further inquiry and revision. Currently, the scientific method is considered the most proper method of inquiry, because it has proven to give us accurate long-term explanations. Even though the explanations change, the method stays the same. We simply continue to refine and create stronger pragmatic beliefs—beliefs that are true insofar as they are practical explanations of how the world works.

Two More Before Ascension

I'm sure you're feeling a little uneasy, now that we've uncovered the complexity of truth. What you're trying to do is take all of the information we've given you and make it cohere to your previously held beliefs. You're doing what the *coherence theory* of truth would prescribe. The coherence theory of truth focuses on the internal relations of truths within a person. Instead of the utility of truth, they're interested in how we know truth. Truth is about comparing judgments and beliefs about the world. When we experience something, we test the resulting beliefs to see if it's consistent—if it coheres—with our previously held beliefs. Assuming our previously held beliefs and judgments were properly produced, then consistently incorporating new beliefs should also produce truth. When beliefs cohere with what is "true" we have truth—a condition of mutual support between judgments.

Our organization loves coherence theories of truth because they're best-suited to produce conspiracy theories. One of Agent Mulder's weaknesses is his tendency to create coherent conspiracy theories, which often make him sound crazy. Coherence theorists are sometimes referred to as Constructivists because their theory allows individuals to "construct" a reality of coherent beliefs that don't necessarily match up to the world.

In "X-Cops," Mulder appears to put random facts together to create a coherent narrative that the neighborhood is under attack by a werewolf. The officers doubt Mulder's explanation, which isn't helped by eye-witness accounts, because they don't have access to Mulder's coherent set of beliefs that support his conclusions. To outsiders, Mulder's theories don't cohere to their beliefs about the world and werewolves. Given someone like Mulder, who is passionate about uncovering the truth, and willing to entertain paranormal evidence, we can easily manipulate him into believing all sorts of falsehoods that serve our purposes.

The final theory is the deflationary theory of truth, which focuses on the utility of truth in linguistic acts, as a logical device for agreement. Philosophers used to think that the phrase "it is true" was a property of language that denoted when something was true. However, philosophers F.P. Ramsey and Gottlob Frege argued that "it is true" actually adds nothing to what is asserted. In other words, "It is true that aliens exist" means no more than "aliens exist," and so, we can "deflate" our talk of truth to the latter simple assertions, making truth a function of language. So, instead of truth being a thing, it's a feature of language.

For many, this is the most difficult conception of truth to grasp. For you, however, the key is that you realize truth is much more complicated than you think, which will hopefully motivate you to stop seeking it.

Subjective Smoking Guns

If you weren't scared by our discussion of the conceptual understandings of truth, you'll surely be rattled by the existential understanding of truth. Søren Kierkegaard preferred a "concrete" notion of truth over abstract philosophical theories, so he focused his energies on describing how truth develops from the choices we make and the ideas we choose to believe. As a result, he rejected independently verified objective truth for personal subjective truth.

Subjective truth doesn't mean that "the truth" isn't out there, but it does imply that most truth is a matter of our personal subjective experience of the world, what we deem acceptable or unacceptable. Subjective truth happens on different levels. On an aesthetic level—the level of beauty, truth is highly subjective. You might like the *X-Files* episodes that focus on the mythology, over those that don't. This belief is determined by your tastes, which means what is true for you might be false for another.

On the level of experience, two or more people can experience the same event, but because they experience it from their own particular perspectives, they experience and remember things differently. This is exactly what happens in the *X-Files* episode "Bad Blood." Agents Mulder and Scully remember each other being unsympathetic, while at the same time remembering themselves being sensitive and polite. They both experienced the same events, yet their stories are both different and, subjectively speaking, true.

Even on the level of measurement, we're simply mapping subjective beliefs onto objects. How many minutes in an episode? None! We've simply come up with a system of measuring based on our subjective perception of the world. For instance, a foot was originally related to the length of a human foot, but over the years it's been standardized, so as to create the illusion of objectivity. So, even though we've created a nice "objective" way of measuring the world, it's still based on and distilled through our individual subjective experience of the world. Aliens have a completely different "objective" set of measurements. Who's correct? Subjectively speaking, we're both correct.

Some have worried that if there's no objective truth, then there is no truth. Objective truth still exists, but it seems to reside mainly in what the great Scottish philosopher David Hume called "relation of ideas." In other words, conceptual deductive truths, such as logic, math, and geometry are objectively true independent of human perception. All other "truths" are a matter of experience, and are therefore subjective. Philosophers such as Kierkegaard and Hume didn't see this as a problem, as long as we're both willing to carefully investigate truth and humble enough to adjust our beliefs in light of new evidence.

Believe to Understand

Don't misunderstand me. We don't want you being a good critical thinker. We want you to either blindly follow the masses, or to work for us helping keep the masses confused and ignorant. John Stuart Mill famously said, "No one can be a great thinker who does not recognize that as a thinker it is his first duty to follow his intellect to whatever conclusions it may lead."

Just think, Mill had the irresponsible idea that people should be free to think and to freely share their opinions in order to test, revise beliefs, and let truth rise to the top. He believed that one of the greatest dangers to liberty and society was the suppression of truth and free dialogue. If he were alive today, he would be on the top of the Cigarette Smoking Man's assassination list.

No matter what theory of truth, or your feelings on the subjectivity of truth, there's nothing more dangerous than the free exchange of ideas, especially when people are willing to change their beliefs in the light of new evidence. What if the world knew who really assassinated Dr. Martin Luther King, Jr. ("Musings of a Cigarette Smoking Man")? What if we hadn't erased the evidence of aliens ("Little Green Men")? What if Mulder knew Krycek killed his father ("Colony" and "End Game")? Would you want to be responsible for the death of all those "extraterrestrial biological entities," if the truth of their existence were revealed ("E.B.E.")?

The truth is simply too dangerous. Even your idol, Agent Mulder, knows this to be true. Listen to his words from "Closure":

> I want to believe so badly; in a truth beyond our own, hidden and obscured from all but the most sensitive eyes. In the endless procession of souls, in what cannot and will not be destroyed. I want to believe we are unaware of God's eternal recompense and sadness. That we cannot see His Truth. That that which is born still lives and cannot be buried in the cold Earth. But only waits to be born again at God's behest, where in ancient starlight we lay in repose.

Are these the words of a man who really wants to know the truth? If the truth dashed his dreams, he would lose all hope. He would cease to be Mulder. The Czech philosopher and playwright Václav Havel would say that this is his "existential vulnerability," the one thing that defines his existence as a person. As the Cigarette Smoking Man says, wouldn't it be better to let Mulder remain ignorant? Wouldn't it be wrong to shatter his hope?

I can tell we touched a nerve, but I get the feeling you still think it wise to search for truth. You really don't get it, do you?

Instead of being scared away, you're actually excited by the danger of what you might find. You don't care that your investigations might uncover some deep dark secret about the nature of reality, or that your existential vulnerability could be exposed? I guess there's nothing we can do but put an end to your nonsense. I guess it's time to determine your fate.

Well, after conferring, it seems my cigarette-smoking associate thinks he might have a use for you, even though the rest of us think it's an unnecessary risk. So, instead of getting in the way of his plans, we'll let you go on your way.

Remember, even if the truth is out there, so are we, and if you get too close, we might have to reconsider our decision. Be very careful, Agent.

21
All Lies Lead to the Truth

SCOTT BANDY AND ADAM BARKMAN

Agents Scully and Mulder of the FBI's X-Files division frequently proclaim that they're on a quest with a single desired outcome—the truth.

In addition to having the phrase "The Truth Is Out There" flash across the screen following the opening credits of (almost) every episode, Scully and Mulder regularly deny accusations that they desire anything other than the exposition of the truth. How, then, would Scully and Mulder respond to the accusation that they are guilty of obstructing such truth with lies of their own?

The accusation doesn't seem to be entirely misplaced. Often, Scully and Mulder mislead their superiors and intentionally deceive them in order to achieve some end.

Most fans of the *X-Files* television series would heartily disagree that the agents' deception is as inconsistent as this accusation makes it seem. One way to defend the protagonists is to create a distinction between what is a lie, and what might be understood as a justified or just deception. This can be done by distinguishing between *general* and *absolute* moral principles, and how they relate to truth-telling in *The X-Files*. The argument can even be made that the agents' attitudes towards deception show correct moral reasoning and development, establishing their position as exemplary moral characters.

Justice and the Natural Law

Before we can understand how these principles function, especially in connection with *The X-Files,* we must understand their origin. Where do these principles come from and what drives people to uphold them? The Natural Law theory of ethics claims that there is a set of objective, universal, moral principles that are, when the terms are understood, self-evident by all properly functioning rational beings. It is the law against which all aspects of morality are measured. The understanding of these principles entails a *duty* to uphold them. It applies to every facet of life and it facilitates the creation of a groundwork for further moral reasoning.

The underpinning command of the Natural Law is to do justice in all areas of your life. Justice, as it is defined by Plato, Aristotle, Confucius, and other great philosophers, means propriety or treating a thing as it ought to be treated, allocating the correct value and respect that it is due. The duty to uphold justice then means treating an equal as an equal, a superior as a superior, and a subordinate as a subordinate. This principle informs all of the precepts of the Natural Law, which then aids in the formation of a framework for applying moral principles in all areas of life.

On a basic level, the Natural Law creates a foundation for how to act in *general* circumstances. For instance, the principle of general beneficence commands that, *all things being equal*, people have a duty, or obligation to uphold the dignity of others by not harming them. Correspondingly, by virtue of possessing rationality, all people have a *right* not to be harmed or treated unjustly.

When people choose to harm others, they act against the Natural Law insofar as they fail to uphold their moral duty, and violate the rights of others. Scully and Mulder can be seen to recognize and demonstrate this principle as they seek to aid others all over the United States as part of their duties at the FBI. They often comfort those who have been victims of crimes, and seek to penalize those who break this injunction.

The Bounty Hunter Dilemma

Although the Natural Law helps people to form a proper moral foundation, it lacks the ability to be applied in every circumstance (hence the above use of the phrase "all things being equal"). Most questions of morality arise out of specific, complex circumstances wherein two or more aspects of the Natural

Law may be in conflict with one another. In such cases, all things are *not* equal and several concerns need to be considered simultaneously. Thus, most principles of morality found in the Natural Law theory are *general* rather than *absolute* principles. In most situations, wisdom needs to be applied in order to weigh the moral worth of each competing factor in order to arrive at the correct moral choice.

For instance, Scully was probably not morally wrong for killing the alien bounty hunter in order to save the life of Gibson Praise ("Without"). Although the principle of general beneficence commands not to do harm to others, it simultaneously calls for the protection of innocent life. In addition to that, Scully had a duty to Gibson as a human being (over and above her duty to the alien as a fellow rational creature) through the principle of special beneficence (which is to give preference to those with whom we have a specific relation). She also had a duty to protect Gibson (as a physical subordinate in age and stature) from coming to harm unjustly by the malicious bounty hunter. When these factors are weighed together, it seems obvious that saving Gibson was the morally right thing to do, despite taking the life of another rational being.

Truth, Lies, and Cigarettes

What is "the truth"? Here, we'll define the truth as an accurate representation of facts and reality. The truth is found in the correspondence between statements and the way the world really is. A true statement is one in which there is a fit between the words or symbols used to communicate a fact and the fact itself. Moreover, facts of reality only seem to gain any sort of importance once this conveyance has taken place. It is during this communication that truth must be distinguished from the things that are not true.

A lie, then, is a statement that is an unjust, intentional misrepresentation of what a person believes to be the facts of reality. It involves a purposeful misleading of another person away from what is true, covering up this truth for your own selfish ends, and intending that another person believe that misrepresentation is the truth. When a person lies, they view other people not as equal rational beings, but as tools to accomplish another particular purpose. The Natural Law, then, insofar as it seeks justice, would dictate that, all things being equal, people ought to be truthful with one another. Even many "white lies," which supposedly seek to protect another person's feelings, often fail to treat another rational being with the respect and dignity that they deserve and are therefore unjust.

For example, when the Cigarette Smoking Man poses as Scully in order to obtain the cure to all human diseases, he unjustly represents the facts of reality to the owner of the disk, and uses more lies to manipulate Scully as a tool in order to obtain the trust of the owner. The Cigarette Smoking Man completely disregards the dignity of both people as rational beings, and instead chooses to use them as a means to his own end ("En Ami").

Lies Stamped with an Official Seal

Throughout the mythology of the show, the antagonists, including the Syndicate, the Cigarette Smoking Man, and some of the top officials at the FBI frequently engage in this unjust misrepresentation of facts (such as the 1947 Roswell UFO crash). They use their leverage over control of the media and communication of events to conceal the facts, and manufacture new "truths."

This injustice against the citizens of the United States is the primary motivator that drives Scully and Mulder in their investigations of the Syndicate's activities. This is why they are the good guys! Although the show's antagonists view the agents as meddling troublemakers who stick their noses where they ought not to go, most viewers recognize that the lies of the Syndicate are indeed a form of injustice, which the agents are trying to correct.

I Don't Think You're Ready for What I Think

One objection to this conclusion may be that some people believe that the members of the Syndicate, specifically those who are involved in the government, are actually acting morally when they distort the facts. These people might claim that the public cannot handle the knowledge of extraterrestrial life, or that there would be mass panic if this information were revealed. Even Mulder seems to have this tendency in the pilot episode, when he tells his newly assigned partner, "I don't think you're ready for what I think."

On a larger scale, supporters of the Syndicate may say that the government officials involved are fulfilling their duty to keep peace in their state by denying the presence of extraterrestrials. Mulder and Scully would then seem to be shortsighted in their endeavors and might actually be working against the forces of morality.

Although it's true that a drastic revelation of this information would not be wise, that still does not justify the elaborate cover-ups and lies put forth by the Syndicate. Firstly, insofar as most members of the Syndicate are government officials and have a duty to report these phenomena to their superiors, they are morally culpable for not doing so. Also, the duty to communicate this information to the public need not require that they expose the entirety of their interactions with the aliens. They, therefore, are acting unjustly when they *deny* direct questions concerning these phenomena, but may not be unjust in choosing not to reveal specific details that may cause unrest. Of course, the Syndicate is most definitely blameworthy in their attempts to secretly deal with the aliens, arranging a "planned Armageddon" of alien colonization using human beings as hosts, or in their attempts to create an alien-human hybrid (*The X-Files Movie: Fight the Future*).

A Lie to Find the Truth

How then can we use the Natural Law to make the case for Mulder and Scully's apparent dishonesty? There are many times on the show where Scully and Mulder tell lies to local officials, superiors, and even each other. Does this reflect a deficiency of moral character? It seems as though, in specific circumstances, certain moral duties may compete with one another, creating a space where something that is normally morally blameworthy becomes acceptable. In the case of honesty, this may mean that there are certain statements that can be deemed "just deceptions" instead of "lies."

Take for instance the two-part Season Five premier, "Redux" and "Redux II." These episodes feature an extended deception by Mulder and Scully, who deceive all of the officials at the FBI, including their friend Assistant Director Walter

Skinner. The deception begins with Scully purposely misidentifying the body of a man Mulder killed as that of Mulder himself. From there, Scully continues to misrepresent the facts with the full affirmation and support of Agent Mulder. What other moral duties do Scully and Mulder possibly have that can support their decision to deceive so unabashedly?

Taken out of context, these episodes surely provide a difficult challenge for the defender of Mulder and Scully. However, their specific situation is crucial to the justification of their cause. Firstly, Mulder and Scully have a duty to ensure that the work they are doing is helpful in uncovering the truth; otherwise, they would be wasting the FBIs resources and potentially aiding the Syndicate in their elaborate cover-up. When that premise is called into question, faking Mulder's death allows the agents to verify that they are indeed working for the right side. "A lie to find the truth," says Mulder.

Additionally, Mulder and Scully also have reason to believe that certain officials at the FBI are misusing their power for their own personal gain. It seems that the agents have a duty to expose that corruption, and aid the FBI in upholding its stated core value of "uncompromising personal integrity and institutional integrity."

Mulder also has a general duty to save innocent lives if he can. In many cases, this duty outweighs the duty to tell the truth, provided that there is sufficient evidence that the endeavor will be successful and that lives can be saved. Thus, if Mulder has good evidence to believe that a cure for Scully's cancer is available, and he has the resources to retrieve that cure, the duty to save Scully's life (due to both principles of general and special beneficence) can be added to the argument for justification of his and Scully's deception.

Actual Inconsistencies

One objection to this defense of Scully and Mulder is that their failure to take a hard stance against deception may eventually cause a degradation of integrity of the agents. How do Scully and Mulder maintain a proper balance between knowing when to tell the truth, and when their deception is justified? What is to stop the protagonists from justifying deception whenever it suits their own purposes?

For instance, despite repeatedly condemning lying by others, Mulder is extremely quick to lie to a young army soldier in *The X-Files Movie: Fight the Future* in order to gain access to a restricted area. Scully also entertains notions of dishonesty when she insists that Mulder blame her for the killing of a government official ("Redux II"). Obviously these instances pose problems for those seeking to uphold Scully and Mulder as examples of morality.

In order to answer this objection, we must concede the point that Scully and Mulder occasionally engage in unjust deception. When he lied to the army soldier in *Fight the Future*, Mulder devalued the soldier him by lying, and manipulated the soldier's insecurity and fear of reprimand in order to obtain information.

Despite this and other unfortunate examples of injustice committed by Scully and Mulder, the overwhelming majority of situations provide evidence that the agents exemplify proper moral reasoning. They develop their understanding of the truth, and learn to apply their wisdom concerning it as they continue their work. Moreover, *The X-Files* continually shows how constant deception and dishonesty leads to serious consequences through the characters of Alex Krycek and the Cigarette Smoking Man ("Redux II"; "Existence"). Scully and Mulder condemn this type of deception and are distressed when confronted with the temptation to lie (such as Scully's inner turmoil considering her lie in "Anasazi"). As the show progresses, the agents learn to weigh their duties and moral obligations, discerning when their deception is justified. In short, the agents generally exemplify proper moral reasoning when it comes to truth-telling, despite certain instances of unjust deceit on their behalf.

The Truth on Trial

Another criticism of the agents' methods of deception may be that, in the end, they're not successful in their goals of exposing the truth in its entirety. Indeed, although Mulder, Scully, Skinner, and their associates have dedicated years of their lives to denouncing the lies of the government, the proof that they have accumulated regarding their claims is either ignored or destroyed. As X tells Mulder in a vision, "They have too much power to be afraid" of what Mulder might expose. All of the findings from the X-Files are entirely discounted in a rigged hearing, and the agents are forced into hiding ("The Truth"). How can their repeated deceptions be justified, when the truth known is never fully realized?

The issue with this objection is that it appeals to the results of what occurred, rather than recognizing the importance of upholding our moral duty. It fails to recognize that the agents' actions are not justified by the end result of their endeavors, but rather, the justification comes from having the correct motive. The motive to act upon their moral duties and the protection of the rights of others is what makes the actions of Scully and Mulder morally praiseworthy. The desire to seek justice above their own personal good is what redeems the agents' actions. So despite the fact that their work is never verified or authenticated by a credible source, the work of the X-Files and all it entailed, was still a morally admirable pursuit.

Figuring out where and why the agents are morally exemplary is crucial to understanding why we consider them heroes and why the *X-Files* is such an enjoyable show. Like all things, the actions of the agents in the *X-Files* ought to be examined, and held up to an objective standard, such as Natural Law, so that we can properly appreciate the many moral angles that the show explores.

There is often difficulty in understanding how Mulder and Scully are be justified in their actions, but as long as we consider them heroes, we ought to seek after that justification and try to understand their flaws so as not to repeat them.

So, continue to search. The truth *is* out there.

VII

Belief and Make-Believe

22
I Want to Believe . . . and That's the Problem

S. EVAN KREIDER

The X-Files is undoubtedly one of the most popular cult shows of recent times, its popularity extending to a decade of television, two big-screen movies, a series of comic books, and a revival mini-series airing more than twenty years after its television debut. It is also a fascinating investigation of the Do's and Don't's of critical thinking and skepticism.

In the early seasons of the show, Mulder serves as the example of some of the more serious impediments to critical thinking, such as emotional reasoning, anecdotal reasoning, and confirmation bias. Scully presents a more properly skeptical counter-part to Mulder, but even then, her skepticism seems selective, given her particular approach to religious belief. The show arguably had the unfortunate tendency to vindicate Mulder's unscientific tendencies toward the paranormal, over Scully's more methodical and rational attitude, but as the series progressed, they managed to find a great deal of common ground, based on appropriate evidence and reasoning.

A Caption

Our first encounter with Special Agent Fox Mulder in the pilot episode is very telling. We find him tucked away in a cluttered, secluded basement office, far removed from the mainstream FBI offices. On the wall, the now famous poster of a photograph of a supposed alien flying saucer, with the caption, "I WANT TO BELIEVE." This scene fulfills the dramatic function of the first meeting between Mulder and Scully, and sets the tone for the entire season: Mulder the Believer, partnered with Scully the Skeptic, brought together to investigate the strange, unusual, and downright paranormal. However, it also serves an important symbolic role in showing us the tragic flaw of one of our heroes: Mulder, despite his brilliance, suffers from a number of critical thinking weaknesses.

The poster's caption serves as the most immediate and obvious problem with the way that Mulder approaches his investigations: it signifies that Mulder has an emotional commitment to believing certain things, prior to any actual evidence for them. This is an instance of what Skeptic Society founder Michael Shermer calls Credo Consolans, translated "I believe because it is consoling," or more loosely understood, emotional reasoning: believing simply because one wants to, or because it offers some sort of emotional pay-off.

Mulder believes that his sister was abducted by aliens when they were children, and he investigates the paranormal in the hopes that it might provide a way to recover her, or at least a way to find out exactly what happened to her, so that he might finally accept it and move on. He believes because without such belief, he would have to give up all hope, and this belief gives him purpose. Unfortunately, wanting something to be true doesn't make it true. Critical thinking requires that we make an attempt at objectivity, and leave aside personal desires and biases so that we may investigate issues and come to conclusions based on evidence and logic. Emotional reasoning such as Mulder's jeopardizes this.

Even worse, emotional reasoning tends to perpetuate other critical thinking errors such as anecdotal reasoning—the tendency to reason from personal experience rather than the totality of the evidence—and confirmation bias—the tendency to interpret these experiences in a way that justifies the hypotheses to which we are already committed for emotional reasons. Psychologist Raymond Nickerson once identified confirmation bias as a serious candidate for the most problematic aspect of human reasoning; it is something everyone is vulnerable to, and extraordinarily difficult to guard against.

Mulder routinely engages in confirmation bias. His emotional commitment to the existence of the paranormal has the effect of making him see the paranormal everywhere, based on the slightest possible evidence. For example, in the episode "Bad Blood," Mulder becomes aware of the mysterious nocturnal exsanguinations of several cows in Chaney, Texas. Despite the fact that there are other plausible explanations (Scully herself offering one in the form of Satanic cults), Mulder immediate jumps to vampirism.

This particular episode is interesting in that it portrays the events in a sort of "He said, she said" format, so that the audience is left unsure exactly what happened, though by the end of the episode, there is fairly strong reason that we are to think that vampires do exist. This shows a side of the series, at least during the first half or so of its run, that is not always conducive to the advocacy of critical thinking: Mulder's knee-jerk and biased hypotheses often turn out to be true. However, as the series progresses, this becomes less and less the case, to the point where even Mulder abandons some of his paranormal beliefs as he uncovers new and better evidence.

Hypotheses

Related to this is Mulder's tendency to put forward hypotheses that lack falsifiability. As the famous philosopher of science Karl Popper argued, truly scientific claims must be falsifiable; that is, they must be capable of being false in light of some possible evidence. Pseudo-scientific claims, on the other hand, are not falsifiable; rather than testing them against the evidence, believers will simply interpret the evidence to fit the claims to which they are already committed.

One especially convenient way to protect your ideas from falsification is to use conspiracy theories to explain away the lack of evidence for and the presence of evidence against your views. Mulder engages in this sort of conspiracy theorizing constantly. Obviously, Mulder explains his sister's disappearance by alien abduction conspiracy, and he explains the absence of evidence for that by government conspiracy. Once again, we see that the show itself seems to support this a great deal of the time, until it is eventually revealed that Mulder's own conspiracy theories are masked in still more conspiracies! Specifically, we discover that Mulder's sister had soon been returned by the aliens and was actually held and tested on by the Cigarette Smoking Man and the mysterious organization known as the Syndicate.

On the surface, Mulder's theorizing about conspiracies may seem vindicated by the show, but the eventual revelations of Mulder's sister's true fate demonstrated that he had still engaged in poor critical thinking by jumping to his conclusions too soon, which in turn made it that much more difficult for him to learn the whole truth.

We can wrap up our discussion of Mulder by returning to where we first met him: his isolated basement office. This physical location is symbolic of another serious impediment to critical thinking known as epistemic closure, the tendency to create closed systems of information, surrounding oneself only with that information that confirms one's beliefs, and closing oneself off from any evidence or reasoning that might contradict one's beliefs. This can be seen as an extension of confirmation bias, but also as a result of a psychological phenomenon known as cognitive dissonance, in which information that contradicts our closely held beliefs causes us psychological discomfort, usually resulting in behavior designed to separate ourselves from the disturbing information.

Though these particular phrases have been coined by recent thinkers, the recognition of these tendencies is nothing new. The ancient Greek philosopher Plato was keenly aware of them, and modeled them in his dialogues. For example, in the Republic, after Socrates appears to refute his friend Cephalus's views on justice, Cephalus deals with this by coming up with a thin excuse and leaving the conversation altogether! This happens again later in the dialogue with another character, the sophist Thrasymachus, who storms off after Socrates refutes his claims that injustice is better than justice.

Mulder accomplishes something similar to Socrates's uncooperative conversers by hiding in his basement office. Of course, we can imagine that he was put there by his superiors, but one gets the distinct impression that Mulder prefers it there, as he can surround himself with press clippings of strange happenings and other "evidence" for his beliefs, without anyone around to question him or raise doubts. He also engages in epistemic closure through his tendency to associate and collaborate with those who are like-minded, as in the case of his fellow conspiracy theorists, the Lone Gunmen. Scully certainly provides a counter-point to Mulder's views, but this is precisely why she is partnered with him against his wishes, under the orders of his superiors. In all these respects, Mulder paints himself as a person who has little interest in hearing views that contradict his own.

Proper Scientific Analysis

In contrast, Special Agent Dana Scully embodies a far better representation of a rational investigator. From the very beginning of the series, she is presented as the scientific and skeptical counter-point to Mulder's overly generous approach to belief.

When Scully's superiors interview her in the pilot episode, they state explicitly that her role is to provide the "proper scientific analysis" of Mulder's work on the X-Files. When she meets Mulder in the very next scene, Mulder makes a point of her credentials, noting her undergraduate degree in physics, and her training as a medical doctor. When Mulder asks if she believes in the existence of extra-terrestrials, she says that "logically" she does not, and provides a scientific rationale involving the difficulties of inter-stellar space travel. In both these scenes, Scully establishes herself as a person whose beliefs are guided by logic and science.

In particular, Scully approaches each new case with a healthy and appropriate attitude of skepticism. Contrary to popular misuses, "skepticism" does not mean cynicism or close-mindedness. In fact, a good skeptic is open-minded, but simply cautious about believing claims without appropriate evidence ("Keep an open mind—but not so open your brains fall out," as Michael Shermer says).

A classic philosophical example of is the so-called Father of Modern Philosophy, René Descartes, who rigorously engages in a process of "methodological skepticism," doubting anything that he cannot know with absolute certainty, eventually arriving at the one irrefutable claim, "I think therefore I am."

Scully demonstrates a more appropriately moderate form of methodological skepticism by considering each of Mulder's new phenomena, and offering explanations for them that are more probable and plausible than the often outlandish conclusions to which Mulder jumps. For example, Mulder's question about extra-terrestrials in the pilot episode arises after he shows Scully a picture of two small marks on the back of a young woman recently found dead, his implication being that aliens might be responsible. In counter to this, Scully offers several more plausible explanations for the marks: needle punctures, animal bite, electric shock.

Chinga

Early in the series, events typically vindicate Mulder's wild conjectures, but despite this, Scully was still right to consider mundane explanations before arriving at extraordinary ones. As Shermer says, "extraordinary claims require extraordinary evidence." Scully embodies this principle well.

She does eventually come to believe in at least some of the paranormal or supernatural things that Mulder does, but she does so only after being presented with compelling evidence. For example, in the Season Five episode "Chinga," Scully has little choice but to accept that she is in serious danger of being killed by an evil, supernaturally possessed china doll; to deny it might have led to her death. By the last couple of seasons, when she is no longer working with Mulder, and is partnered instead with Agent Doggett, she has come to fill the role of believer. She still maintains a healthy degree of skepticism, and never quite accepts the full range of unusual beliefs that Mulder does, but she is at least willing to admit that many of the things she has seen working with Mulder on the X-Files cannot be explained by conventional means. The important point, however, is that she arrives at these conclusions only after careful consideration of compelling evidence, as proper skepticism requires.

At the same time, Scully suffers from a problem all-too-common in otherwise critical thinkers: inconsistency, usually the result of compartmentalization, a separating of some beliefs and attitude from others, and applying different standards to each. In Scully's case, she does not apply the same standards of skepticism to her religious beliefs that she does to Mulder's claims.

That's not to say that religious beliefs are necessarily irrational or even false. Many important figures in the history of philosophy were religious, but they also provided rational arguments for their religious beliefs. For example, Thomas Aquinas, the most important philosopher in the history of Catholicism, offers not just one, but five separate arguments for the existence of God. It's certainly questionable whether these arguments are good ones, but the point remains that Aquinas was not content to base his religious beliefs on blind faith, but required that they be grounded in reason, at least to the best of his ability.

Unfortunately, Scully does not seem to avail herself of this same strategy. Instead, she has a tendency to hand-wave any inconsistencies between her religion and her scientific belief, or even common-sense moral notions. In the movie *The X-Files: I Want to Believe*, this is especially clear from her conversations with Father Joe, a former priest and convicted pedophile. Father Joe's very existence entails an informal version of a classic argument against the existence of God known as the Problem of Evil—in short, the argument that the existence of evil and suffering in the world rules out the possibility of an all-knowing, all-powerful, and all-good God. Scully barely attempts to engage in the issue, and although it certainly shakes her faith, she never fully acknowledges the inconsistency, and never fully resolves it. In this respect, Scully falls short of the ideal rational skeptic.

Alternatives

The X-Files was, and remains, a very popular show. It also stimulated a great deal of debate when it premiered. Some praised the show for inspiring people to question authority and consider alternatives to mundane realities; while others criticized it for encouraging its viewers to swallow pseudo-scientific nonsense. Appropriately, this tension was captured perfectly within the show itself through the interplay between its two heroes, Special Agent Fox Mulder and Special Agent Dana Scully. In its early stages, the show presented these characters as polar opposites: Mulder the Believer and Scully the Skeptic.

Though likely not the show's intention, Mulder's approach to the X-Files during the early seasons does not reflect well on his critical thinking abilities, especially compared to Scully's more logical and scientific approach. However, by the end of the series, the two come to see eye to eye on a great deal more than when they began, perhaps both benefiting the other: Scully by providing a tempering influence to Mulder's credulity, and Mulder by providing the opportunity for Scully to discover for herself that The Truth is Out There.

23
I Can't Be Sure of Anything Anymore

KEVIN MEEKER

The title comes from Lieutenant Jack Schaefer's brief conversation with Mulder in "Jose Chung's *From Outer Space*." His doubts are quite severe. He tells Mulder that he doesn't know if the mashed potatoes in front of him are really there. He's even unsure whether Mulder exists.

When Mulder assures him that he does exist, Schaefer replies, "I can't give you the same assurance about me." And then a group presumably from his Air Force unit walks in and whisks him away, never to be seen again except as a corpse at the end of the episode. Why does Schaefer have such extreme doubts? (Assuming of course that there is a Jack Schaefer in this episode!)

In the conversation with Mulder, Schaefer says that he's witnessed people brainwashed so absolutely as to believe many false things. More specifically, he claims to have seen people falsely believe that they have been abducted by aliens after undergoing hypnosis. But why does this prompt him to say that he can't be sure of anything? How do the false beliefs of others cast doubt on his own beliefs?

Schaefer's situation is not unique in the series. Many *X-Files* episodes show characters confronting situations that cast doubt on beliefs that they take to be certain. Philosophers sometimes call these scenarios skeptical hypotheses. Such scenarios come in many different forms. One of the most famous discussions of skeptical hypotheses is found in the writings of the philosopher René Descartes. His thoughts help us to understand how our beliefs can be doubted in light of skeptical hypotheses.

Descartes: Philosophy Is Policy

Descartes is one of the most famous figures in the history of Western thought. He was a key contributor in the growth of science, mathematics, and philosophy, known, among other things, for his development of analytical geometry. The Cartesian co-ordinate system bears his name in honor of his many contributions. And his *Meditations on First Philosophy* is one of the most widely read philosophy books in history. For Descartes, math, science, and philosophy are intimately related. He thought that the same method that was successful in the sciences and math should also apply to philosophy.

While the method is the same for all of these disciplines, we can say that philosophy is at the center of all of his thoughts, even mathematical and scientific ones. For it is in addressing the philosophical question of how we can know anything at all, whether in math, science, or everyday life, that we can justify all of our intellectual endeavors.

Why is this question of knowledge so important for Descartes? At the beginning of his *Meditations* (and by "beginning," I mean *beginning*: the very first sentence), he notes how he discovered that many beliefs he adopted when young later turned out to be false. So he wanted to devise a system or method that would allow him to discern which beliefs were true and which were false. Instead of just accepting things based on the say-so of others, he wished to conclusively discover the truth. He wants to *know* the truth, not just adopt beliefs that upon later investigation may turn out to be false.

This fascination with knowledge naturally leads to the topic of skepticism. That's because skepticism, as most philosophers understand it, is the view that humans lack knowledge. One could be a global or a local skeptic. A global skeptic denies that humans have knowledge in any area. A local skeptic is one who denies knowledge in a particular domain. So a certain type of skeptic might deny that we have knowledge about UFOs. In at least the first seven seasons of *The X-Files*, Scully was a local skeptic. She didn't deny that we have knowledge. In fact, she believed that science provides us with a great deal of knowledge. Instead, she was a skeptic concerning a particular domain: she was a skeptic about UFOs.

So what is knowledge? Most philosophers hold that knowledge at a minimum includes true belief. I can't know that Sacramento is the capital of California if I don't believe that it is. Likewise, if I were to believe that San Diego is the capital of California, then I would not know that (no matter how "certain" I was) because I would have a false belief.

But more is needed. If I simply guess on a multiple choice exam that Albany is the capital of New York (as opposed to Binghamton, Buffalo, New York City, Rochester, or Syracuse), then even if I believe it, I do not know it to be the case; it is just a lucky guess. So we need something besides a lucky guess to convert a true belief into knowledge. What precisely do we need? Roughly speaking, it seems that we need some sort of evidence or rational justification for us to have knowledge. Scully for example often demands that Mulder come up with scientific evidence for his beliefs in extreme, fantastic possibilities. Otherwise, she implies that he lacks knowledge.

Doubt Everything

But how much evidence is needed for a true belief to count as knowledge? According to Descartes, we need absolute or certain evidence. In the end, Descartes was not advocating skepticism as a final position. For him, skeptical doubt was a tool that could be exploited to find what really was certain. Once we find this certain knowledge, we can build our knowledge from the ground up without having to worry about any false beliefs. In attempting to construct this edifice of human knowledge, Descartes presented (in *Meditation* 1) some of the most influential and powerful arguments for skepticism in the history of philosophy.

As we have seen, having been burned by false beliefs before, Descartes vows not to be deceived again so easily. So he says that he'll attempt to suspend judgment about any belief for which he can find "some ground for doubt." Of course he can't examine all of his beliefs; so he narrows down his search by looking at certain classes of beliefs, such as beliefs based on perception. Even our most "obvious" perceptual beliefs ("I am seated in front of a TV") could be doubted.

How can we doubt our perceptions? Isn't seeing believing? This is where skeptical scenarios burst into the discussion.

Descartes first considers the hypothesis that he is "in a state of insanity." People in such a state can't trust their senses. And if we were in such a state, we would not be able to rely on the experiences that we normally trust. The beliefs of those thought to be in such a state are not counted as knowledge. Consider in this context the following conversation in "Jose Chung's *From Outer Space*" between Mulder and one of the mysterious "Men in Black" (the one played by Jesse Ventura, not Alex Trebek):

> **MAN IN BLACK:** Some alien encounters are hoaxes perpetrated by your government to manipulate the public. Some of these hoaxes are intentionally revealed to manipulate the truth-seekers who become discredited if they disclose the deliberately absurd deception.
>
> **MULDER:** Similar things are said about the men in black. That they purposely dress and behave strangely so that if anyone tries to describe an encounter with them, they come off sounding like a lunatic.
>
> **MAN IN BLACK:** I find absolutely no reason why anyone would think you crazy if you described this meeting of ours.

Later in the episode, Mulder asks Jose Chung not to write a book about the strange events surrounding this case because they might make the people involved look "foolish, if not downright psychotic." The implication of these conversations is that the reports of those who are in such a state are not to be trusted. They don't know what they are talking about. And their lack of knowledge is explained by their mental state.

The episode "Folie à Deux" presents an interesting twist on this type of scenario. Telemarketer Gary Lambert claims to be the only one to be able to see that his boss is really a monster that looks like an insect. He also claims to be the only one who can see the difference between his living co-workers and those who have been killed by the monster and are actually zombies. Just before Lambert's death, Mulder thinks that he sees the monster as well. Scully is unconvinced, attributing Mulder's "vision" to "Folie à Deux," an insanity shared by two people. Many consider this the scariest episode of Season Five, partially, I think, because those thought to be "crazy" and out of touch with reality actually appear to be the only ones who are correctly perceiving the dangerous situation.

This scary scenario raises the skeptical question: how do we know that those "insane" people whose freedoms we restrict (as Mulder's was in the episode) are wrong and we are right? How can we know who's correct? Each side can appeal to experience, but experiences can't be trusted for one side. So then how do you tell which is your side? Without evidence that you are not in such a state, perhaps your experiences do not provide evidence that your beliefs are true and thus your beliefs do not count as knowledge.

Strangely, Descartes doesn't spend much time on this type of scenario. And it's not clear to scholars why he would raise this extreme possibility and move on with so little discussion. But scenarios filled out in the scary details of "Folie à Deux" seem to suggest that perhaps these types of scenarios are more worrying than even Descartes realized.

Dream, Inveigle, Obfuscate?

Perhaps Descartes didn't dwell on the insanity topic because he thought it might seem remote from many people's experience and also make them uncomfortable and unwilling to continue reading. He next appeals to an experience that is more common: dreaming. His basic question is this: how do you know that what you think of as waking reality isn't really a dream? This simple question is extremely difficult to answer and appears in a wide variety of cultures and contexts.

The Chinese thinker Zhuangzi had a dream that he was a butterfly and when he "awoke" wondered how he knew that he wasn't a butterfly dreaming that he was a man. But if we are in fact dreaming, then all of our beliefs based upon (what we take to be) perception are illusory. If I am dreaming, then I don't know that I am reading. So, does the fact that I sometimes dream give us ground to doubt that I am now awake? If we were in a dream would there be any experience to alert us to our state?

At the end of Descartes's *Meditations*, he (controversially and perhaps contradictorily) suggests that there are distinguishing features of a dream. For example he suggests that memory doesn't work in dreams in the same way it does when you're awake. Similarly, in the episode "Field Trip," Mulder and Scully are in a dream-like hallucinogenic state brought about by a giant mushroom, which is digesting them as they "dream" away. The strangeness of the "dream," including a lack of memory for how they arrive at certain "places" alerts them that they are not experiencing reality. But even these clues can be deceptive. Once Mulder and Scully think they have escaped the mushroom, they trust their experiences again. But Mulder realizes that their experience of escaping the mushroom was itself illusory. By the same token, some have dreams from which they "awake," only to realize that they are just dreaming that they have woken up from the dream! Given these dream-within-dreams possibilities (or hallucination-within-hallucinations possibilities), how are we to trust our senses? How can they provide evidence for our beliefs, which is required for knowledge?

The next scenario considers the extreme possibility that we are being deceived by a powerful evil genius, manipulating all of our experiences. Descartes doesn't give us a lot of details on such a scenario. But clearly this type of scenario can be developed in various ways. In "Kill Switch" a renegade Artificial Intelligence (AI) hooks Mulder up to a virtual reality machine to extract information from him. The advent of such virtual reality machines, even if they are not yet as sophisticated as those in fictional scenarios, raises a similar problem of how we can distinguish between reality and "virtual" reality (which is sometimes compared to dreaming).

But there is another issue besides the problem of simply distinguishing appearance from reality. In these scenarios, some entity is *intentionally controlling* our experiences. In "Kill Switch" it is AI. In "Wetwired", television signals are used by powerful people to alter viewers' perception of reality. In "Jose Chung's *From Outer Space*," hypnotists apparently control people's beliefs. If some entity can control our minds, then how can we trust anything we believe? If someone hypnotizes us (and the hypnosis is powerful enough to control our beliefs) then how do we know that what pops into our head had been caused by the real world as opposed to some hypnotic suggestion? And if we are in an environment in which others around us are clearly being deceived on a regular basis (for instance by hypnosis or by virtual reality), then perhaps we have grounds to doubt all of our beliefs. Without being able to show that we are not being deceived, maybe we can provide no evidence for our beliefs. Because evidence is required for knowledge, we lack knowledge.

. . . Or Can We?

Philosophers disagree on how threatening these skeptical scenarios are. Many think that skeptical scenarios are simply intellectual distractions, although even those who think that they are serious challenges generally stop short of saying that they deprive us of knowledge.

When I first started teaching, student opinion seemed to mirror this attitude among philosophers. In the past few years, though, I've noticed that student reactions to these scenarios have changed. Technological scenarios especially seem to worry them. Why?

I suspect that the ubiquity of electronic technology and the increasing use of sophisticated computer games and virtual reality machines have allowed us to fill in the details of skeptical scenarios in such a way that makes them much more plausible and, thus, much more of a threat. Perhaps the worries of these students are overblown. But episodes such as "Kill Switch" provide new ways to think about classic philosophical issues. Of this we can be certain.

Or can we?

24
Not Believing What's Not True

JOSHUA MUGG

When I think of *The X-Files,* two lines come to mind: "I want to believe" and "The Truth is out there." There's an apparent tension between these two claims. If the truth is out there, shouldn't we believe it? Isn't it virtuous to believe only the truth? Perhaps it's even morally required.

As one philosopher, William Clifford, puts it "it is wrong always, everywhere, and for everyone, to believe anything upon insufficient evidence." If this is right, then Mulder is *blameworthy* for allowing his desire to taint his outlook. However, throughout the series, Mulder's desire to believe constantly enables him to gather evidence he would not otherwise have been able to gather. His desire to believe actually *helps* him get at the truth. Something has to go: either the truth is not out there, or Mulder is not blameworthy for the way he believes. I'll argue that Mulder's approach is just fine.

Let's keep truth and belief separate when tackling our problem. Sometimes we get these confused because if you *believe* something, you believe it's *true*. I cannot honestly say "I believe 'The Erlenmeyer Flask' was the best episode in Season One" *and* "'The Erlenmeyer Flask' was the worst episode in Season One." Still, truth is one thing, belief is another.

Just because, in the first episode, Mulder *believes* the teenagers were abducted by aliens doesn't mean that aliens *actually* abducted them. That's because believing doesn't *make* the belief true. Whether Scully believes the teenagers' seemingly far-fetched story or not makes no difference to whether the story is true or false. Let's think of it this way: a belief is an *attitude* about how the world really is, while those beliefs that *match* how the world really is are the true ones. So here's my question: what's the relationship between what we *should* believe, and *truth*?

Knowing the Truth versus Avoiding Error

Well, if the truth is out there, then we should believe the truth. Right? We shouldn't just believe whatever we want, and I bet Scully and Mulder would both agree. However, what does "believe the truth" really amount to? What exactly does it mean that we "should believe the truth"? Maybe it means: "We should try to believe as many true things as we can." On the other hand, it could mean: "Don't believe something that might be false." As philosopher and psychologist William James explains, our duty to believe the truth can be put in two different ways: 1. Know the truth and 2. Avoid error. These are not the same command, and they can't be equally binding: one has to take precedence over the other.

To illustrate the difference between these two principles, think of yourself as an apple farmer. On the first harvest day, you want to pick as many ripe apples as you can, but you want to leave those ones that are not yet ripe. You decide that the most important thing is to *only* pick ripe apples. So you carefully examine each apple before you pick it, and if it looks even a little too green you leave it. Fast-forward a few weeks. It is the end of harvest season, and you are going to make one last sweep through the orchard to pick the remaining apples. Although you are not likely to come through again, you don't particularly want to pick the unripe apples. Now getting every single ripe apple is most important—even if that means that you get some slightly green ones too.

Knowing

Let's turn back to knowing. Think of true beliefs as ripe apples in the above story. It could be that avoiding error is most important, just as avoiding picking unripe apples on the first day of a harvest is most important: we should reject any claim unless we can be sure that it is true. Descartes, the father of modern philosophy, famously employs this maxim in his *Meditations:*

he refuses to believe anything unless he is absolutely certain that it is true. According to him, believing a falsehood is the cardinal sin when it comes to belief formation.

Clifford, who I quoted at the start of this chapter, agrees that the most important command is to avoid falsehood, though he does not endorse such a rigorous skepticism as Descartes does. Scully's approach is like Clifford's, at least at the beginning of the *X-Files* series. She thinks part of being a scientist is refusing to believe when there is insufficient evidence. She explains, "as much as I have my faith . . . I am a scientist, trained to weigh evidence" ("All Souls"). Evidence comes first, belief (or faith) second. Call this the Clifford-Scully approach.

On the other hand, it could be that *knowing the truth* is most important, just as getting every ripe apple is most important on the last day of harvest. This is Mulder's approach throughout the series, and it is the one James argues for. So, I will call this the James-Mulder approach. According to the James-Mulder approach, avoiding falsehood is less important than knowing the truth.

Why would anyone think that there is something wrong with the James-Mulder approach? Throughout the series, Mulder claims, on occasion, that Elvis successfully faked his own death. "Do you realize how hard it is to fake your own death? Only one person has pulled it off . . . Elvis" ("Shadows"). From the way that Mulder says this, it seems like the audience is supposed to recognize that this might be *too* far-fetched. There are limits to allowing our *desire* for Elvis to still be alive to influence our *belief* that he is.

"Wishful thinking" occurs when we let our desire override our overwhelming evidence. It would be cool if Elvis were still alive, but shoot, I just don't think he is. Sometimes false beliefs are harmless, but not always. Suppose a doctor tells you that you have cancer and that you need to go on chemotherapy to get rid of it. You better not ignore the diagnosis because you *want* to believe that you're just fine. Perhaps the James-Mulder approach is too much like "wishful thinking." Beliefs are one thing, our desires another, and we must keep the two separate or else we will become wishful thinkers, ignoring the evidence. Perhaps Clifford and Scully have the right of it.

Evidence

Let's not be too hasty. We shouldn't let our desires *totally* overwhelm our evidence, but the Clifford-Scully approach says that desire should have *nothing* to do with what we believe. In fact, the Clifford-Scully approach has some problems of its own. Clifford and Scully say that we should *never believe on insufficient evidence*. According to the Clifford-Scully approach, that's why Mulder is blameworthy for believing that Elvis faked his own death.

But let's apply Clifford and Scully's skepticism to their own command. Why should I think that Clifford and Scully's approach is the right one? Why should I believe their command? On their account, I shouldn't believe based on a whim or out of some emotional response. I should believe that their approach is true because of very good *evidence* for their view.

What evidence do we have for thinking that we should never believe on insufficient evidence? It is hard to find any. Perhaps the reason we shouldn't believe on insufficient evidence is because we don't want to be tricked. I'll admit, it does not feel good to be duped. James suggests that, in the end, Clifford and Scully can only support their approach by their fear of being tricked into believing something false. But look, the Clifford-Scully maxim "avoid falsehood" is based on our *fear*, rather than on good evidence! The Clifford-Scully approach shuns beliefs based on *emotion* rather than *evidence*. Yet their own approach is rooted in emotion rather than reason! So, the Clifford-Scully approach collapses under its own criterion.

There's a second problem with the Clifford-Scully approach. Sometimes it's easy to get sufficient evidence to determine if a claim is true or false. For example, it is easy to gather the appropriate evidence to evaluate if David Duchovny played Mulder and that Gillian Anderson played Scully. I look at the credits, and that is that. My point is not that these claims are beyond doubt. Maybe the producers of *The X-Files* are engaged in an elaborate plot to deceive us all, but I don't think we need to take that kind of doubt too seriously.

The credits at the end of each episode, IMDB, and *Entertainment! Magazine* all say that David Duchovny plays Mulder and Gillian Anderson plays Scully. That is sufficient evidence, even for Clifford and Scully. A lot of our beliefs are like this—my beliefs about where I am right now, or which beers are currently in my fridge, or what time I need to be at work in the morning. I can pretty easily gather the evidence for those beliefs, but not all our beliefs are like this.

It's very difficult for us to find sufficient evidence to believe certain kinds of claims, and *The X-Files* is full of them. Are there really aliens? Or is any evidence we find for the existence of aliens just evidence put there by the government in an effort to obfuscate its malicious activities? If Mulder and Scully find what appears to be an alien body, perhaps it's just a clever ploy by the government. Maybe the Cigarette Smoking Man is pulling the wool over Mulder's eyes, making him believe there really are aliens. But then again, perhaps aliens have made contact, and in order to prevent the general public from discovering this startling truth the government is only *appearing* to fabricate evidence.

As the series develops, the evidence for and against the existence of aliens becomes compounded by evidence for and against a government conspiracy and cover-up. Evidence *alone* is not likely to help in Mulder and Scully's search for truth here. Mulder's approach allows him to choose a side, believe it, and act accordingly. The Clifford-Scully approach, on the other hand, paralyzes us with agnosticism.

Wanting to Believe

Agnosticism, if you have all the evidence that you could possibly have, might not be so bad. However, in practicality, we can always gather more evidence. Time after time, Mulder's disposition to believe the far-fetched leads him to gather evidence no one else would gather. Consider his and Scully's differing approaches in "Squeeze" and "Tooms." In these episodes, Mulder is convinced that Eugene Victor Tooms is a mutant who must eat the liver of five humans every thirty years, and then hibernate until the next feeding.

Mulder has some evidence for thinking this is true, since there have been a number of similar crimes committed every thirty years, the most recent of which involved the exact same fingerprints. Scully is always willing to consider the evidence, but because she does not allow herself to believe without sufficient evidence, she is paralyzed. (In "Tooms," the FBI puts additional constraints on Scully, worrying that Mulder's unconventional approach is wearing off on her). Mulder approaches the problem assuming abnormal activity, which gives him the evidence he needs to convince Scully that Tooms is indeed behind the murders. Mulder's wanting to believe causes him to gather evidence that Scully would not otherwise gather. The Clifford-Scully approach actually prevents us from gaining knowledge. Here the James-Mulder approach is superior.

Is wanting to believe always enough? I doubt it. Perhaps agnosticism when considering the existence of aliens and government conspiracies is the right response, at least when we are outside an episode of *The X-Files.* But consider other kinds of claims. Can we always wait for all the evidence to be in concerning some moral issue? We're often faced with the need to act in an uncertain world. Or consider more personal choices: Can I await sufficient evidence for whether I should marry *that* person? Have a child? Take a job across the country? There is always evidence in such cases, but I doubt it ever measures up to the sufficient evidence Scully and Clifford want us to have.

How should I respond? Should I remain agnostic? According to the Clifford-Scully approach I should say, "I don't have sufficient evidence that we should get married, nor do I have sufficient evidence that we should not get married. Therefore, my love, let us do nothing until greater evidence comes along." But that's just crazy. Evidence is not always decisive, and when it is not, sometimes we need to allow our desire to believe to influence what we believe. The James-Mulder approach allows for just such a response.

Genuine Option

When is it *good* to allow our desires to influence our beliefs? When is it *permissible* to allow our desires to influence our beliefs? Mulder doesn't really say, but William James has some thoughts that I think Mulder would like. According to James, our desires should influence our beliefs when the claim is "living," "forced," and "momentous." A claim is "living" for you if you think it is at least possible. That Mulder's sister is still alive is a live option for Mulder—he thinks that his sister *might* still be alive. Second, in a forced choice, there must be *only* two options.

In "The Erlenmeyer Flask," Mulder must choose between acting on Deep Throat's lead or ignoring it: he has to do one or the other. Finally, a "momentous" claim is one that makes a big difference in your life. Whether aliens exist or not is momentous for Mulder—if he believes there are aliens (as he does) it would make a big difference in his life. According to James, whether a claim is living, forced, or momentous depends on the individual. That aliens exist is not momentous for me, and the idea that Mulder's sister is still alive may not be a live option for Scully. When a claim is living, forced, and momentous, it is what James calls a "genuine option."

When a claim is a genuine option, we can allow our desires to influence our choice. Since the claim is living, your evidence is not decisive. Since the issue is forced and momentous, you cannot ignore it. Again, what issues are a genuine option will vary from person to person. Perhaps the existence of aliens and paranormal activity is a genuine option for you, perhaps not. However, I suspect that for those choices that are most important to our lives—whether (or who) we should marry, what career we should take, whether or when we should have children—the decision will not be based on evidence alone. I suspect that these issues will generally be genuine options. We should deliberate on these questions like Mulder would: by allowing our desires to guide our beliefs.

25
Wanting and Willing to Believe

CHRIS GAVALER AND NATHANIEL GOLDBERG

When Scully first makes her way down to Mulder's office in the basement of FBI headquarters, she sees a poster of a UFO and the words "I WANT TO BELIEVE." Nothing captures Mulder's attitude toward life better. And, for much of *The X-Files*, few things distinguish him from Scully more. While Scully, as a medical doctor, is a woman of convention and science, when convention and science are silent Mulder wants to turn to the fantastic.

Mulder's attitude traces to the disappearance of his sister, Samantha. He explains in a voiceover:

> I have lived with a fragile faith built on vague memories from an experience that I could neither prove nor explain. When I was twelve, my sister was taken from me. Taken from our home by a force that I came to believe was extraterrestrial. This belief sustained me, fueling a quest for truths that were as elusive as the memory itself. To believe so passionately was not without sacrifice, but I always accepted the risks—to my career, my reputation, my relationships, to life itself. ("Colony")

This idea, that one can live with a fragile faith that one nevertheless believes so passionately, sets Mulder apart from Scully and, presumably, many of us. It doesn't, however, set Mulder apart from William James.

James (1842–1910) was an American philosopher and psychologist most famous for being a founder of the philosophical traditional known as "pragmatism." In "The Will to Believe,"

James claims that there are times when, faced with the absence of intellectual proof, we not only can but must use our "passional" or willing nature to determine what to believe.

While Mulder wants to believe that his sister was abducted by aliens, James wants to believe in religion. Regardless, both beliefs have to be grounded on the passional if on anything, and Mulder's even contain religious elements:

> I want to believe so badly in a truth beyond our own, hidden and obscured from all but the most sensitive eyes. In the endless procession of souls, in what cannot and will not be destroyed, I want to believe we are unaware of God's eternal recompense and sadness that we cannot see his truth. That that which is born still lives and cannot be buried in the cold earth, but only waits to be born again at God's behest where in ancient starlight we lay in repose. ("Closure")

James calls "The Will to Believe" an "essay in the justification of faith." If James's argument is right, then, under certain circumstances, his *and* Mulder's wanting, or willing, to believe something is enough to justify their believing it.

The Rational and the Passional

Under what circumstances would Mulder's wanting to believe that Samantha was abducted by aliens justify that belief? According to James, two sets of circumstances are required.

First, Mulder would have to lack intellectual grounds to believe or disbelieve it. That would happen if there weren't enough evidence, one way or another. Does Mulder have any rational, or evidence-based, reason to believe or disbelieve what he does about Samantha?

Mulder tells Scully when they first meet: "I was twelve when it happened. My sister was eight. She just disappeared out of her bed one night. Just gone, vanished. No note, no phone calls, no evidence of anything" ("Pilot"). That doesn't establish, one way or another, what happened to Samantha. Also, remember that Mulder admits that his fragile faith was based on vague memories from an experience that he could neither prove nor explain ("Colony").

Mulder nevertheless dedicates his personal and professional life to investigating Samantha's disappearance. He even adds it to the X-files case load, labeling it "X-40253" ("Conduit"). Eventually, with Scully's help, Mulder does piece together a larger puzzle. Bees, black oil, conspirators, different races of aliens, alien bounty-hunters, human-alien hybrids—X-files fans have delighted in, and been challenged by, trying to fit those pieces together ourselves. Nonetheless, each time Mulder and Scully start seeing the puzzle as a whole, the truth of its message is cast into doubt.

Nor can Mulder rely on evidence gathered by others. At one point, Agent Schoniger tells Scully: "There was an extraordinary amount of effort put into finding his sister. Even the Treasury Department got involved. His father worked at a high level in the government. They found nothing" ("Closure"). That is, they found nothing either way, themselves.

Ultimately, Mulder comes to believe *both* that Samantha was abducted by aliens as part of a government conspiracy *and* that she was later saved by a paranormal force ("Closure"). Even then, Mulder has few cold, hard facts.

Mulder's Genuine Option

Mulder satisfies the first circumstance that James lays out for trusting the passional. He has no rational, conclusive evidence, one way or another, about what happened to Samantha. The second circumstance that James lays out is that the person deciding what to believe based on her will had better be facing what James calls a "genuine" option.

According to James, when we're trying to decide between two beliefs, we're confronted with an *option* of which to believe. When we have no intellectual reason to opt for one belief over another, and the option is itself *genuine*, then we can will to believe our preferred belief instead. Is Mulder's option between believing that Samantha was or wasn't abducted by aliens genuine for him?

James explains that an option is genuine for someone if it's *live, forced*, and *momentous*.

An option is *live* for someone if it increases her willingness to act. Like touching a live wire, she has to feel a spark. And that spark has to be able, at least in principle, to set things into motion. When they first meet, Mulder asks Scully: "Do you believe in the existence of extraterrestrials?" "Logically," she answers, "I would have to say 'no'" ("Pilot"). That first word, "logically," indicates that Scully isn't emotionally invested. She feels no spark. As James would say, Mulder's hypothesis makes no "electric connection" with her nature. Believing that extraterrestrials exist isn't a real possibility for her, and so not something that can compel her to act. Mulder, by contrast, feels a spark as sure as anything. He tells Scully: "U.F.O. sightings, alien abduction reports. The kind of stuff that most people laugh at as being ridiculous. But I was fascinated" ("Pilot"). His interest is piqued. And when it comes to the option to believe that his sister was or wasn't abducted by aliens, the voltage gets turned up so high that Mulder sometimes seems on the verge of electrocution. The option is as live to him as anything could be, and Mulder acts any way he can to resolve it. As Scully (and we) soon learn, resolving that option—deciding which of its beliefs to embrace—is the driving force in Mulder's life. And as Cigarette Smoking Man and the rest of the Syndicate know, finding out what happened to Samantha is so charged that it can be used to manipulate Mulder to act, sometimes to his own detriment ("Colony," "Paper Hearts," and "Redux").

An option is *forced* for someone if it's based on a logical dilemma. A logical dilemma presents two choices, where exactly one must be true. Scully isn't forced to believe that Mulder likes either pumpkin seeds or pistachios. Supposing that she wants to resolve the option, Scully could believe that Mulder likes neither of them. Maybe he likes sunflower seeds instead, which happens to be the case. Mulder, however, is forced to believe that Samantha was or wasn't abducted by aliens. At least that's the case if he's to believe anything at all. Being and not being abducted by aliens are the only possibilities. Exactly one must be true, and given how passional Mulder feels about his sister's disappearance, he's not going to defer deciding.

Finally, an option is *momentous* for someone if the stakes for resolving it are high, even unique. While hunting for Big Blue, the Heuvelmans Lake, Georgia, version of the Loch Ness Monster, Scully mentions to Mulder that her father used to call her "Starbuck," first mate to Captain Ahab, in *Moby Dick*. She realizes that Mulder is himself like Ahab: "You're so consumed by your personal vengeance against life, whether it be its inherent cruelties or mysteries, everything takes on a warped significance to fit your megalomaniacal cosmology"

("Quagmire"). Ahab was megalomaniacal about capturing Moby Dick, and Mulder is megalomaniacal about finding out what happened to Samantha. When Ahab has the chance, or option, to strike at Moby Dick, the stakes could not be higher for him. When Mulder has the option to believe that Samantha was or wasn't abducted by aliens, the stakes couldn't be higher for him either. Learning the truth about his sister is the single most important thing in his life. "Nothing else matters to me," Mulder tells Scully ("Pilot"). After the X-files are shut down, he confides in her: "My life up to this point has been about the need to see her again" ("Little Green Men"). Mulder is the Ahab of alien hunters, and finding out the truth about Samantha is his Moby Dick. Nothing is more momentous.

Wanting or Willing to Believe

For James, then, Mulder *is* within his rights to believe that Samantha was abducted by aliens. Mulder is justified in believing what his passional nature tells him to, no matter how fantastic, because: 1. he doesn't have sufficient evidence to decide what to believe on purely rational grounds, and 2. his option to believe is live, forced, and momentous.

But is James's case that easy to make—about Mulder or generally? James realizes that many people would remain skeptical. When Mulder says to Scully: "When convention and science offer us no answers, might we not finally turn to the fantastic as a plausibility?" Scully answers without missing a beat: "What I find fantastic is any notion that there are any answer beyond the realm of science" ("Pilot").

Science has saved lives and explained much of the world around us. It's done so by following reason and finding evidence. So it's no wonder, James readily admits, that his argument for the *will* to believe faces resistance. Scully voices a view that many people share.

Nevertheless, James also recognizes that willing has got to have a role in decision-making. Otherwise, ironically enough, there would be times when we're acting irrationally:

> I, therefore, for one, cannot see my way to . . . wilfully agree to keep my willing nature out of the game. I cannot do so for this plain reason, that a rule of thinking which would absolutely prevent me from

> acknowledging certain kinds of truth if those kinds of truth were really there, would be an irrational rule.

For all Mulder knows from the get-go, Samantha really was abducted by aliens. Denying him the right to believe that, on the grounds that he cannot intellectually prove it, denies Mulder the possibly of believing the truth. If Mulder has no choice but to will his way to the belief, and that belief is true, disqualifying the belief isn't only counterproductive. On the intellect's own terms, it would be irrational.

Moreover, James argues that, in some cases, truths are available only to those who seek them with a willing, or desirous, attitude in the first place: "In truths dependent on our personal action, then, faith based on desire is certainly a lawful and possibly an indispensable thing."

It's good that Mulder wants to believe. Had he assumed Scully's intellectualist stance, he'd never have found out the truth about Samantha. In the episode that brings closure to his search for the truth about Samantha ("Closure"), Mulder and Scully are investigating the brutal murder and subsequent disappearance of a child when they make the acquaintance of Harold Piller, a psychic who has worked in the past with the police. Piller believes that children who suffer terrible fates are sometimes saved by creatures of pure light. Piller gets Mulder and Scully to engage in a séance in the hope of conjuring some of these spirits. "They will come to you if you're ready to see," he explains. Scully, who has no rational grounds to believe Piller, doesn't believe him. Consequently, she sees nothing. True to form, Mulder *wants* to believe him, which is enough. The spirit of a boy takes Mulder's hand and leads him to Samantha's diary.

Though the diary is scientific evidence about Samantha's abduction, Mulder wouldn't have found it had he not wanted to believe. And even with the diary, Mulder's passional nature leads him forward. He and Scully arrive at the home of Arbutus Ray, the last person to see Samantha after she escaped her abductors. Mulder lets Scully interview Ray, while he wanders off by himself. "I have this powerful feeling, and I can't explain it, but that this is the end of the road. That I've been brought here to learn the truth," he tells Scully. As she interviews Ray, the spirit of the boy whom Mulder saw earlier reappears. This time he takes Mulder to Samantha's spirit, and the two siblings embrace.

Ultimately, it's Mulder's will to believe that allows him to discover the truth, dramatizing James' claim: "There are, then, cases where a fact cannot come at all unless a preliminary faith exists in its coming."

VIII

Fear and Trembling

26
Submitting to Superior Aliens

JEROLD J. ABRAMS

In 1947 an alien spaceship crashed to Earth in Roswell, New Mexico. Maybe. Some think it was real, others think it fiction.

Whatever actually happened out there in the desert, it definitely started the conversation about the possibility of alien races superior to humanity landing on Earth and making their presence known.

Aliens hardly appear to be walking around in society today, nor do they seem to have made contact with humanity—as far as we know. But what if they did? What if a group of aliens suddenly announced their presence on Earth, declared their superiority, and even demanded submission? What would humanity do? What *should* humanity do?

Typically philosophers don't even mention this sort of hypothetical scenario because, presumably, they think the very idea of aliens landing on Earth to be wildly speculative and even absurd, something more like stories about Bigfoot and werewolves than epistemology and ontology. But the idea of aliens coming to Earth and declaring their superiority and forcing humanity to handle the problem is not so far from the tradition of philosophy as we might think.

In fact, one of the greatest philosophers of all time, if not *the* greatest philosopher of all time, considers this kind of scenario. In his book *Politics*, Aristotle imagines a collective of demigods to show up suddenly in society, demonstrate their intellectual superiority to humanity, and demand submission. Now, granted, Aristotle's demigods (or superhuman beings) are not necessarily aliens, but it's not entirely clear that they're not aliens either.

What's clear is that they are rational beings who appear out of the blue, and can't even be recognized as human, let alone be assimilated to human society, because they are so incredibly brilliant. So, maybe Aristotle has in mind aliens, and maybe he doesn't. Maybe he has in mind superhuman beings born of human beings, but he doesn't explain how that would work. He certainly doesn't describe a community of highly intelligent families breeding a superhuman over generations. He just presents the possibility of superhumanly brilliant beings appearing to humanity and declaring their superiority. And yet in *De Anima* II, Aristotle considers the possibility of another "order" of rational beings far superior to humanity who cannot possibly be born of humanity because they are not even of the species: they're a separate and higher "order." So, whatever he has in mind here about demigods or a superior order of rational beings, Aristotle at least appears to be open to the possibility of alien life, and nothing in his philosophy appears to preclude it.

But Aristotle doesn't just imagine the possibility of higher beings appearing in society, he actually thinks this possibility is a real and important problem for philosophy. Aristotle himself addresses the problem first by eliminating outright the possibility of assimilating the demigods to any merely human society. The reasoning here seems to be pretty simple: even if humanity tried to assimilate them, the demigods would never accept subordination to human identity or culture or law. Why should they? After all, they're vastly superior. With a rare touch of humor Aristotle even compares the scene to Antisthenes's fable of the council of the beasts in which some rabbits demand that some lions obey rabbit justice, but the lions claim that rabbit justice would actually be *injustice* to lions. Likewise, any attempt by humanity to rule over the demigods would be rejected outright as absurd by the demigods, writes Aristotle, even as absurd as humanity attempting to rule over Zeus himself.

So, again, if the demigods or aliens can't live in human society, then what should humanity do? Basically, we've got two or three options: either we can get rid of them by exile, or simply killing them, or we can give up democracy and species superiority, and happily submit to our new superhuman kings of the world.

Aristotle knows the choice wouldn't be easy, and he knows humanity *would* choose the first or second option of exile or assassination, and probably assassination would be the only way to really eliminate the problem: exile is just going to drive them somewhere else, and maybe eventually they'd come back.

But Aristotle actually thinks humanity *should* choose the second option, and happily submit to the demigods, because (so he claims) that's what the best and most rational citizens would do. The best and most rational citizens would do that because they would know that these superhuman kings would create an ideal human society, and that they would also perfect the minds and lives of the rest of society. And, in fact, that is precisely why superhuman monarchy (and not democracy) is Aristotle's own ideal society.

Very few philosophers have taken up Aristotle's study of the demigods, or really any kind of analysis of alien life, which is sort of strange because philosophers otherwise seem to revel in imaginative and exotic areas of inquiry like square-circles and artificial intelligence. By contrast, science-fiction books and movies have bravely taken the lead in the philosophical discussion on the possibility of aliens, the threats they could pose to humanity, and how humanity might engage them if they were ever to present themselves on earth.

Among the greatest films about extraterrestrial life are George Méliès's *A Trip to the Moon* (1902), Stanley Kubrick's *2001: A Space Odyssey* (1968), Stephen Spielberg's *Close Encounters of the Third Kind* (1977), and Ridley Scott's *Alien* (1979). But perhaps no film has spoken so brilliantly on the possibility of aliens appearing on Earth and forcing upon humanity Aristotle's philosophical problem and three solutions as Chris Carter's *X-Files* television series and the film *The X-Files: Fight the Future* (1998).

The Syndicate Miscalculated

In the backstory of *The X-Files* mythology aliens arrived on Earth millions of years ago and left members of their race underground in the form of the "black oil," a black substance which looks like oil, but can be reconstituted into humanoid forms by entering human bodies and using them as hosts to be destroyed.

Those aliens who originally left Earth have now returned to colonize the planet, but they require assistance from humanity. So, they announce their presence and superiority to a select group of men of high achievement in science, industry, medicine, and government. These men, nameless men, like the Cigarette Smoking Man and the Well-Manicured Man form "The Syndicate," and together determine the fate of the world. Basically they have two options, indeed, two of the three options Aristotle articulates in the *Politics.* Either they can submit to alien colonization, or they can fight the alien colonists, though already they have completely dispensed with democracy, taking upon themselves (as they must) the decision for all humanity. Exile of the aliens is clearly not an option.

Neither one of these options is very good. If the Syndicate decides to fight the superior aliens, then humanity will likely be destroyed. But submission to the aliens requires not only giving up species superiority and democracy: it also requires giving up species biological identity. In fact, rather than perfecting humanity, as Aristotle's demigods presumably would, the aliens propose to destroy much of humanity, while remaking the remainder of humanity into a hybrid alien slave race.

So the Syndicate accepts the terms of colonization, including future enslavement, as the only practical solution for the genuine survival of at least some of humanity. By accepting this solution, the Syndicate also agrees to complete the aliens' research necessary for human-alien genetic hybridization, beginning with Operation Paperclip. Actually Operation Paperclip once provided safe haven and comfortable lives for German scientists in America to advance astrophysics to fight the Russians in the Cold War, almost immediately following World War II. With the appearance of the aliens, however, Operation Paperclip now becomes a project of genetic engineering led by scientists like Victor Klemper who work to create human-alien hybrids using alien DNA given to humanity by the aliens for this purpose.

But the Syndicate made the wrong decision. The aliens lied about colonization and hybridization and enslavement. Instead they plan to eradicate humanity by spontaneous repopulation using human bodies as hosts. Once the Syndicate has created the ideal delivery system of corn-fed and genetically engineered Africanized honeybees that sting and infect the population with the black oil, believed to be necessary for colonization, the Syndicate along with humanity will be entirely destroyed.

They think they're creating a delivery system of genes for hybridization, but they're actually creating a delivery system for species annihilation, and the propagation of the alien race on Earth. So, now, in contrast to Aristotle, who argues that submission would be the best choice because it produces the ideal state, the Syndicate, believing submission to be their only real choice, made exactly the wrong choice, and it came with terrible consequences for their families.

Fight the Future

As a personal sign of submission, the aliens required each Syndicate member to offer one family member for genetic experimentation. The aliens then gave the Syndicate a cryonically suspended alien fetus to supply them with alien DNA for the science of hybridization, which, again, was all part of the colonization ruse.

An early opponent of submission, Bill Mulder, proposed secretive work on an antiviral vaccine against the alien black oil, and hesitantly offered his daughter Samantha Mulder to the aliens. Her older brother Fox Mulder watched in near disbelief as aliens invaded his house and abducted his little sister. This traumatizing event later led him to his studies at Oxford, a career as a criminal profiler with the FBI, and eventually his interest in the X-Files.

Now Mulder works alone in the basement office of the FBI devoted to the X-Files, which are files of unsolved and often paranormal cases, until the FBI hires Agent Dana Scully to masquerade as his partner while spying on Mulder's suspicious work. But Mulder quickly sees through the illusion and speaks to her honestly about what he really believes about aliens and the government, and soon they trust each other completely, and work together to uncover the conspiracy with the aliens.

As a medical doctor Scully plays Dr. Watson, with her empirical and rational counterpoint, to Mulder's Sherlock Holmes, with his obsessive and brilliant imagination and capacity for guessing right. And as Watson and Holmes in Sir Arthur Conan Doyle's story "The Final Problem" discover the genius mathematician and philosopher Professor James Moriarty, the "Napoleon of crime," sitting silently like a spider at the center of the web of London crime, Scully and Mulder eventually discover their own FBI and the silent Syndicate led by the Cigarette Smoking Man, the Well-Manicured Man, and even Mulder's own father, at the very center of the conspiracy.

Asked by a bartender what he does, Mulder laughs at the seeming absurdity of his life:

> I'm the key figure in an ongoing government charade. The plot to conceal the truth about the existence of extraterrestrials. It's a global conspiracy, actually, with key players at the highest levels of power that reaches down to the lives of every man, woman, and child on this planet. So, of course, no one believes me. I'm an annoyance to my superiors, and a joke to my peers. They call me Spooky. Spooky Mulder whose sister was abducted by aliens when he was just a kid. And now he chases after aliens with a badge and a gun. (*X-Files: Fight the Future*)

At the same bar, Mulder meets a new source named Dr. Alvin Kurtzweil, who reveals the truth behind a terrorist plot by the government to hide the existence of extraterrestrials. Kurtzweil's information leads Mulder and Scully to Texas where they find an ancient underground cave covered up by the Syndicate to conceal the black oil alien virus, and then to a corn farm with a massive dome for breeding the Africanized honeybees to carry the black oil. As Mulder and Scully unravel the conspiracy with the aliens, the Syndicate, fearful for their secrecy, abducts Scully, takes her aboard an alien spaceship, hidden under the ice of Antarctica, and then sends the Well-Manicured Man to kill Mulder and Dr. Kurtzweil. The Well-Manicured Man does kill Kurtzweil, and puts him in the trunk of a car, and then lures Mulder into the back seat of the same car with the promise of saving Scully. Mulder suspects that he will be killed, too, but he has no other way of saving Scully, so he gets in the car and prepares to meet his death. But now the Well-Manicured Man betrays the Syndicate and tells Mulder everything: the truth about the aliens, when they arrived, the conspiracy with the Syndicate, and where it all it went horribly wrong.

> **Well-Manicured Man:** The virus is extraterrestrial. We know very little about it except that it was the original inhabitant of this planet.

Mulder: A virus?

Well-Manicured Man: What is a virus but a colonizing force that cannot be defeated, living in a cave underground until it mutates and attacks?

Mulder: That's what you've been conspiring to conceal, a disease.

Well-Manicured Man: No, for God's sake. You've got it all backwards. AIDS, the Ebola virus, on an evolutionary scale are newborns. This virus walked the planet long before the dinosaurs.

Mulder: What do you mean "walked?"

Well-Manicured Man: Your aliens, Agent Mulder, your little green men, arrived here millions of years ago. Those that didn't leave have been lying dormant underground since the last ice age in the form of an evolved pathogen waiting to be reconstituted by the alien race when it comes to colonize the planet, using us as hosts. Against this, we have no defense, nothing but a weak vaccine. Do you see why it was kept secret? Why even the best men, men like your father, could not let the truth be known? Until Dallas we believed the virus would simply control us, that mass infection would make us a slave race. Imagine our surprise when they began to gestate. (*X-Files: Fight the Future*)

Having discovered colonization to be a lie, the Well-Manicured Man realizes the futility of submission, with its inevitable outcome of the eradication of humanity. The Aristotelian solution of submission is therefore eliminated outright, and only the solution of battle remains. With time running out, the Well-Manicured Man gives Mulder the global co-ordinates to find Scully in Antarctica and the very vaccine originally proposed by his father, Bill Mulder, who wisely resisted submission to alien colonization.

Now Mulder travels to Antarctica, discovers the alien ship under the ice, finds Scully frozen in a capsule, and injects her body with the vaccine. But the vaccine injected into her body also disrupts the biological equilibrium of the entire alien ship, which is filled with frozen alien and human bodies. Also aboard the ship, the Cigarette Smoking Man immediately knows what's happened: "Mulder has the vaccine" (*X-Files: Fight the Future*). The Smoking Man and his crew abandon ship, while

Mulder carries the still half-frozen and barely awake Scully off the ship. Once at the surface, Scully and Mulder collapse in the snow, Scully unconscious, and Mulder watching in awe as the alien ship they just escaped rises from under the ice and ascends into space, knowing their fight for the future has only just begun.

The whole arc of the plot of the mythology of *The X-Files* presents a masterful study in Aristotle's philosophy of demigods in the *Politics*. The mythology begins with the appearance on Earth of alien beings who declare their superiority to humanity, and humanity finds itself faced with the same choices in Aristotle's philosophy, either submit to alien colonization, or fight the aliens for the future of humanity.[1]

[1] I am very grateful to Elizabeth F. Cooke and Robert Arp for helpful comments on an earlier draft.

27
Why Are We Afraid?

JUSTIN FETTERMAN

> The conquest of fear lies in the moment of its acceptance. And understanding what scares us most is that which is most familiar, most commonplace . . . It's been said that the fear of the unknown is an irrational response to the excesses of the imagination. But our fear of the everyday, of the lurking stranger, and the sound of foot-falls on the stairs, the fear of violent death and the primitive impulse to survive, are as frightening as any X-file, as real as the acceptance that it could happen to you.
>
> —FOX MULDER, "Irresistible"

The X-Files explores several versions of fear, each of which induces vastly different reactions. At times, *The X-Files* gave us reason to dread the unknowns of outer space or worry about the potential secrets kept by our own government. Often, we're concerned for the safety of Mulder or Scully, and occasionally we're repulsed by the image of some previously hidden monster. Philosophers have puzzled over the breadth and complexity of these human emotions for millennia, and many have asked "Why do we claim to experience these emotions when the thing we're reacting to is admittedly false?"

In a 1975 essay and response, Colin Radford and Michael Weston debated whether it was possible to feel true emotion as a reaction to the people and events in a fictional work. Specifically: how can we feel emotion about something we know to be false? In the years since, several other philosophers have revisited the topic, offering new theories and often focusing on fear as a uniquely observable and revealing emotion. Examining the different ways *The X-Files* provokes fear in its audience offers an opportunity to explore the relation between fiction and emotion.

"The Host"—Revulsion and Jump Scares

Modern horror author Stephen King subdivided horror literature into three parts, writing:

> I recognize terror as the finest emotion and so I will try to terrorize the reader. But if I find that I cannot terrify, I will try to horrify, and if I find that I cannot horrify, I'll go for the gross-out. I'm not proud.

His distinction between terror and horror follows the division first laid out by Gothic novelist Ann Radcliffe in 1826: terror is dread before an experience; horror is either the shock of the experience in occurrence or the revulsion which ensues. King's "gross-out" seeks to differentiate a baser reaction which bypasses the understanding and merely taps into a bodily rejection, like a gag-reflex. While King confesses to employing the gross-out, he admits that it is a cheap effect which does not instill true fear.

Though rarely overt or over-the-top, *The X-Files* is not above occasional gross imagery to create a reaction, most famously in the design of the Flukeman, the antagonist of "The Host." Even before the reveal, "The Host" evokes revulsion by exploring refuse sewers and showing characters vomiting up nematodes. These images of waste and sickness trigger a response in the most primitive regions of the human brain, causing us to look away or even experience dry heaves though we are not actually affected by the conditions on screen. Though we're conscious of this disconnect between show and reality while we watch, it can be nearly impossible to overcome the reaction without completely removing the stimulus because the physical reactions are not being controlled by the intellect.

Many philosophers, then, would deny that we're experiencing any emotion, and certainly not fear. The cognitive theory of emotion, which dates back to Aristotle, holds that true emotions arise from a stimulus attended to by the intellect. Though we have a wide range of reactions to stimuli, most of them never reach the level of emotion. Pulling your hand away from a hot pan takes no more thought than your stomach turning at the sight of Flukeman; if the former is not an emotional response, neither is the latter.

A similar type of stimulus-response occurs during the famous "jump scare," when a scene is set slowly and quietly so a sudden noise or visual shift causes the viewer to literally jump backwards. We often use the language of fear to describe this response, but the cognitive theory again rules out true emotion. Simply put, the time between stimulus and response is too short to allow for the intellectual appraisal that leads to emotion. Furthermore, intellectual assessment after the fact often leads to the conclusion that we had nothing to fear in the first place and that the jump was an unnecessary reaction. Both Fox Mulder and the viewer jump a little when the Flukeman first appears in the water pipe, but the reaction passes quickly upon reflection: Mulder should not be afraid because the creature is sealed behind thick glass and the audience should not fear because it's just a television show. The stimulus itself causes a reaction, but the intellect determines that we are not truly afraid.

"Arcadia"—Quasi-Fear and Make Believe

The jump scare is easy enough to separate from fear because it is fleeting, but more extended physical reactions introduce more confusion. When watching *The X-Files*, we may experience increased heartrate, heightened sensations, and sweaty palms, among other responses. These hallmarks suggest we are feeling the full emotion even though our response is to fictional material. However, the cognitive theory of emotion still defines a separation. The extended physical reactions have been called "quasi-fear" by some philosophers in recognition of their similarity to true fear while maintaining that they are merely uncontrollable physical reactions. These quasi-fear reactions may cause us to claim that we are truly horrified. One explanation is to examine the type of thoughts that are being added to the physical response (since true emotions require the involvement of the intellect).

In discussing fiction, we refer to the suspension of disbelief: the reader's or viewer's ability to overlook the implausibility of the work to focus on elements like artistry, philosophy, and emotion. When choosing to interact with fiction, we know the material is beyond reality: there is no Falls at Arcadia community in San Diego though Mulder and Scully briefly live there in "Arcadia." However, because we find value in the material, we choose to treat it *as if* it were true, at least for the length of each chapter or episode. This is little more than a complex version of our adopted attitudes when playing games of make-believe as children. Children know that they are not married and that their plastic kitchen cannot make edible food, but they pretend these things are true because playing house is enjoyable. They want to believe.

When we watch Mulder and Scully play their adult version of house, we are also playing a complex version of make-believe. In our game, we're pretending that the physical, quasi-fear reactions we are having to the Tulpa on screen are the same as the true fear we would have if the Tulpa was crawling out of our own front lawns. We are, in short, only make-believingly afraid. In the jump scare scenario, we have a physical reaction which the intellect determines is not necessary and the reaction is turned off. In make-believe fear, we have the same reaction and assessment, but we decide to play along, to allow the reaction to continue because we find it cathartic or instructive.

At every level, these games of make believe require props. Children may need a plastic kitchenette or simply a cardboard box to play house. Mulder and Scully need an actual house and furniture and new identities for their make-believe marriage. We the viewers need episodes of *The X-Files* that can induce the physical quasi-fear reactions that invite us into the game of make-believe fear. This, in turn, requires the on-screen threats to be ones we would truly fear if they were real and happening to us.

"Squeeze"—Sympathy and Relational Fear

The *as if* component of make-believe fear can build a stronger, more personal connection. Our reaction to fiction often changes based on how similar or dissimilar the characters and events are to ourselves and the world as we know it. When we say we do not "relate" to characters, we mean that they are too different from us, making it too difficult for us to treat them *as if* real, thus preventing us from joining in the game. To "make believe," the fiction must be something we can conceivably believe, even if it is highly unlikely.

Make believe is easiest when the fiction is nearly identical to our reality. Each alteration puts a greater load on our imagination, and not all imaginations can handle the same amount of work. Unlike the Flukeman or the Tulpa, Eugene Tooms ("Squeeze" and "Tooms") is recognizably human, even fitting in enough with society to hold down a job. However, it is revealed that he is nearly immortal, consumes human livers, and can stretch his anatomy to move through incredibly narrow spaces. Playing make believe about Tooms requires imagining a unique human evolution while the Tulpa of "Arcadia" requires believing that concentrated thoughts can create monsters out of refuse. The first is arguably easier than the second.

Furthermore, our attitude towards Mulder and Scully greatly impacts our emotional response. When we witness Tooms unscrewing the bolts from Scully's air vent and pulling himself through the seemingly impossible space, we may claim to be afraid *for Scully*. We know that Scully is no more real than Tooms, but we have shifted the point of relation. Now, instead of assessing the correlation between *threat* and reality, we are reacting to the relationship between *the threatened* and reality. This is especially important for *The X-Files*, where the threats are often significantly divorced from reality. The scares remain effective because the show creates sympathy between the audience and the human characters, such as Mulder, Scully, Skinner, or Max Fenig. If we can find a connection between the characters under threat and ourselves or people we know, we sympathetically feel the same emotion we see the character display. We do this in real life whenever we feel sad because someone we love is sad, or similar circumstances.

This, however, is no longer just make-believe fear. It is not constrained by the length of the episode and is noticeably less modulated by the intellect. It may occasionally take time for us to separate ourselves from this fear, requiring intellectual effort to remember that Mulder and Scully are not real, that we and those we love are not in danger. No amount of reminding ourselves that Eugene Tooms is not a real person may dissuade us from fear about air vents or evolution. Both of those are facts of our real world, and *The X-Files* has shown us how they may cause danger. We have moved beyond the concession to *as if* and begun to focus on the elements that definitively *are*, our attention directed by the fictional work.

"Home"—The Unknown and Fear Itself

The most gruesome example of *The X-Files* exploring real life horror is "Home," the only episode to receive a TV-MA (mature) rating and to never be rebroadcast on Fox. The episode's ability to frighten and disturb stems not only from the amount of violence, but also from the all-too-realistic depiction and reasoning behind the violence. The Peacock family at the center of "Home" possesses no supernatural abilities and encounters no paranormal activity. They are neither mutants nor aliens, not the product of government experimentation or religious mysticism. They are merely a family preserved through inbreeding and violently protective of their lifestyle and each other. They could, conceivably, exist anywhere in our real world.

"Home" is one in a long list of episodes that take place in small towns and villages. In most of them, the danger is unexplainable or at least well beyond reality. However, the consistent presence of rural places speaks to a larger theme of *The X-Files*: these are the places where secrets can long be held, but the modern world threatens to expose them. Secrets are the stuff of fear because they are, by their very nature, unknown. Horror writer H.P. Lovecraft believed that the unknown is our greatest fear because it hides potential dangers we cannot prepare for. Each small town, each family therein, could be hiding a violent secret that threatens our own lives. When we feel fear in reaction to "Home," we fear the suspected but unknown horrors of reality.

Moreover, the overarching alien conspiracy mythology of *The X-Files* explored this kind of fear even as it introduced otherworldly elements. We need not fear the specific alien races or government agencies to be afraid of potentially dangerous extraterrestrials or institutional secrets. While the evidence for extraterrestrials is perhaps scant, we know that governments have historically conducted secret operations like the Tuskegee experiments. Both of these entities, in specific and in general, tread on our fear of the unknown. Whether looking into the darkness of space or behind the closed doors of the Pentagon, *The X-Files* achieves much of its horror by helping us imagine those hidden dangers. *The X-Files* actively attached itself to real world events, from the smallpox vaccine to the Tunguska event, as a way of highlighting the hidden dangers that, like the truth, are out there.

The X-Files, as fiction, does not directly create true emotions in us. It is a kind of prop or invitation which causes physical reactions upon which the intellect can build emotion. At times, this may only be a make-believe emotion which ceases when the fiction is concluded. It can, however, be extended into true emotion when a connection is established between the fiction and our reality. This, arguably, is the true value of all fiction: though it has much to offer in the moment (through artistry, entertainment, and make-believe emotions), the best fiction transcends its innate falsehood to offer intellectual and emotional reactions that apply to the real world. *The X-Files* can shift from wondering "What if this were real?" to more directly raising the issues of dangers we know exist but rarely encounter.

28
Come Sweet Death

DANIEL MALLOY

Death haunts *The X-Files*. Virtually every case involves at least one death, and nearly all of them threaten Mulder and Scully with that grim prospect. But a few of them invite us to step back and reflect on the meaning of death, the terror it holds, and its connection to a meaningful life.

In "Tithonus," Scully encounters Alfred Fellig, a murder-obsessed photographer who seemingly can't die. But rather than envy Fellig's immortality, we pity his loneliness. In "Squeeze" and "Tooms," Mulder and Scully confront a man who can extend his life considerably, but at the price of slaughtering people for their livers and spending most of his extended life hibernating in a kind of nest or cocoon.

In "Our Town," the people of Dudley, Arkansas, apparently have a similar life-extending technique, but at the cost of being murderous cannibals. Finally, in "Clyde Bruckman's Final Repose," the agents encounter a man with the rather unusual gift of predicting when, where, and how people will die with uncanny accuracy.

Each of the cases force us to reflect on what death is, its relation to life, and why it seems so terrible. This chapter examines these cases, and a few others, in order to raise and attempt to answer three inter-related questions.

First, is death bad for the person who dies?

Second, is a longer life always a better one?

And finally, would an immortal life be worth living?

In each case, I argue that the answer is no.

Appointments with Death

Arthur Fellig and Clyde Bruckman share a common gift or curse, depending on how you look at it. Both men can tell when someone is going to die, with different degrees of accuracy and precision. Bruckman can predict the date, time, location, and cause of death of any person, seemingly by simply thinking about it. Fellig, on the other hand, can identify people who are going to die soon, but he lacks Bruckman's specificity.

Each man raises the same basic question: if you *could* know when you were going to die, would you want to know? Scully, given the opportunity by both Bruckman and Fellig, refuses. Her reasoning isn't hard to follow. Offered the knowledge by Bruckman, Scully turns him down because she believes that his prediction may be a self-fulfilling prophecy. In other words, if Bruckman tells her how she will die or when, he will be correct, but only because he told her.

Fellig's gift presents no such danger, however, because his predictions lack the specificity and precision of Bruckman's. Fellig can only offer the vague statement that some specific person will die soon. So what's so dreadful about knowing vaguely when you're going to die?

Nothing, really. We don't want to know because we don't want to face the fact of our mortality. We know we're going to die, but we wish we didn't. Getting a deadline (pardon the pun) makes it unavoidable and real.

But we only want to pretend that we're not going to die because we fear death. Philosophers since the ancient Greeks have tried to allay this fear. Socrates (469–399 B.C.E.) pointed to the essential folly of fearing death: to fear is to presume something is bad. But in the case of death, we have no knowledge of what it is. We haven't been dead yet, so we can't know whether it's good or bad.

But, while we don't know what death is, we know what it isn't. It isn't this, the life we're used to. So the fear of death isn't the fear of something that's coming; it's the fear of losing something. Scully isn't afraid because death is terrible, but because life is pretty good.

Against this line of reasoning, the ancient Greek philosopher Epicurus (341–270 B.C.E.) presents what is known as the missing subject argument. Epicurus argues that the flaw with Scully's fear is the notion that she'll be losing something by dying. She may be losing something, but she won't be missing it. She won't be missing it because death is the end of her existence, so there will be no her to be missing anything. Death, then, is nothing to us. It's neither good nor bad. It neither benefits nor harms us. So there's no reason to fear it. Being afraid of death is like being afraid of someone who wants to torture you, but can only enter a room after you leave it. There's no chance of ever encountering the torturer, and therefore of being tortured, so don't worry about it.

The "Life" of Eugene Victor Tooms

But even if we accept the arguments of Socrates or Epicurus, and no longer fear death, it doesn't follow that we need to embrace death. Avoiding it is, after all, kind of hardwired into us. But there's a difference between fearing something and avoiding it. We avoid things for a wide variety of reasons beyond fear. I avoid eating spinach because I dislike it, not because I fear it.

But, since we've never experienced death (or, if Epicurus is right, can't experience death) we can't really dislike it. But there are plenty of things associated with death that we may want to avoid for any number of good reasons. Even if death holds no fear, the process of dying is often accompanied by a great deal of pain and suffering. Since you won't get anything out of dying except the end of your own existence, dying really isn't worth the trouble.

From this, it seems to follow that the longer you can put off dying, the better. Therefore, a long life is better than a short one, all things considered. This conclusion is tempting, but as the examples of Eugene Tooms and the town of Dudley, Arkansas, show, that's not necessarily the case.

Tooms is an interesting example because his abnormality has apparently granted him the ability to extend his life indefinitely. As Mulder and Scully discover in "Squeeze," Tooms lives his life according to an odd thirty-year cycle, and has done so since at least 1903, seemingly without aging. At the age of 120, Tooms has the appearance of a man in his thirties.

But Tooms has been hibernating in a cocoon of sorts for most of those 120 years. So perhaps Tooms isn't the greatest example. He has extended his life, but only in the most basic, biological sense. Most people, I suspect, given the choice between living to 120, but spending most of that time in a coma, or living to seventy or eighty, but not being in a coma, would probably choose to die at seventy or eighty. Tooms lived a long time, but he didn't have a long life. If we consider only the times when he was active, Tooms lived a little over thirty years—those thirty years were just stretched out over 120 years.

Living in Dudley, Arkansas

But Tooms isn't a great example of extended life, since he barely "lived" in a very important sense—he just existed for a long time. On the other hand, the residents of Dudley, Arkansas, seem to have found a way to really live for a long time. In "Our Town," Scully and Mulder are sent to the Dudley to investigate the disappearance of government health inspector George Kearns. What they discover is that the good people of Dudley, like Tooms, have learned how to extend their lives, seemingly indefinitely. And, like Tooms, the key to their extended lifespans is the death and consumption of others. Unlike Tooms, however, the citizens of Dudley do not have to give up living as part of the exchange. By simply killing and eating a few of their fellow human beings (how many or how often is never made clear), Dudleyites can live very long lives, filled with all the things that make other human lives so worthwhile.

Lucky them, right? Admittedly, the price of being murderous cannibals seems a bit high to most of us. But set that aside and just look at the math. Dudleyites live longer lives than the rest of us. If death is fearful, or even if it's just the end of us, it seems to follow that a longer life is a better one, other things being equal. Naturally, it won't be a better life if, like Tooms's, it is a life deprived of experiences. Nor would it be a better life if it had a great deal more pain and suffering than an average life. But neither of these seem to be the case for the people of Dudley, so it seems reasonable to conclude that their lives are better than other, shorter lives.

Against this kind of reasoning, ancient Roman poet and philosopher Lucretius (99–55 B.C.E.) presented what has come to be called the symmetry argument. Originally, the symmetry argument was Lucretius's way of adding to Epicurus's arguments against fearing death. In essence, Lucretius notes that there was a long time when you didn't exist in the past: everything up to the moment of your birth. And, there will be a long time when you no longer exist in the future: everything after you die. Nothing happened to you before you were born; and, in just the same fashion, nothing will happen to you after you die. So, there's no more reason to worry about the fact that you're going to die than there is about the fact that you have been born.

Applying this line of reasoning to the question of whether longer lives are better than shorter ones, we can ask whether people born earlier are more fortunate than those born later. If we want to claim that those who die later are better off than those who die sooner, then it follows that those who are born later are less fortunate than those born earlier. If a longer life is a better one, then it's all the same whether a person is born earlier or dies later. Either way, they get a longer life.

Lucretius tells us, to the contrary, that we should no more lament someone's early death than we should their late birth. We should have the same attitude toward both, but the attitude we should have is the one we currently reserve for birth. We never comment that a person was unfortunate because they were not born earlier. They were born when they were born, and that's the end of it. Maybe they missed out on some things, sure, but everyone misses out on some things.

Another aspect of this is what we might call the identity problem. The problem is that if a person were born earlier or later than they were, then they wouldn't be the same person. Now, this isn't about astrology or anything like that. A Fox Mulder born on the 12th or 14th of October, 1961 would likely be very similar, perhaps even indistinguishable from the Fox Mulder born on October 13, 1961. But, a Fox Mulder born ten years earlier or later would likely have very little in common with our Fox Mulder. In either case, for example, this new Fox Mulder wouldn't have been present for his sister's abduction. He wouldn't have been at the vastly impressionable age of seven-going-on-eight during the Apollo 11 moon landing. He might never have met Scully.

Even if this Mulder lives the same number of years as our Mulder, there is no way to say that he lived the same life. Suppose this Mulder is born ten years earlier, but dies at the same moment that our Mulder would have. Thus, he lived ten years longer. Did he therefore have a better life? Hardly. Whether he did or not will depend on a wide variety of factors. The length of a life is only a small consideration in determining its quality. At best, we might be justified in saying that, other factors being equal, longer lives are preferable to shorter ones. But making all the other factors equal is nearly impossible, as the case of Arthur Fellig clearly demonstrates.

The Fellig Case

Arthur Fellig (a.k.a. L.H. Rice) was born in 1849 and died 149 years later, a sad and lonely man. Through an odd sequence of events, Fellig missed his appointment with death and was blessed or cursed with an inability to die. Poor Arthur. Unlike the Tithonus of Greek myth, however, Fellig was not cursed to age along with his immortality. He just lives and lives. If death is at all fearful, and if longer lives are preferable to shorter ones, then Fellig has got it made.

That's not how he sees it, though. After a mere century and a half, Arthur Fellig is tired of life. As he says, "I don't want to be here anymore. I can't even remember a time when I did." He's long since outlived his wife and everyone else he ever loved. Now he just tries to take the picture, as he puts it, to find death. Even that, he seems to do more out of habit than anything else. He just can't think of anything else to do.

But maybe that's just his problem. Maybe someone else, granted immortality, would enjoy it. Perhaps our Mr. Fellig is just a gloomy sort. Or perhaps Fellig's exhaustion is the inevitable result of a life without end. That, at least, is the contention of philosopher Bernard Williams, who argues that any human being, granted immortality, would necessarily fall into the kind of boredom with life that Fellig did.

The problem with immortality, as Williams sees it, is that we don't actually want to live, as such. Rather, we want to live so that we can do other things. Again, recall the "life" of Tooms—bare survival is not a worthwhile life. At least some of these other things, the things we live for, are what Williams calls our categorical desires. For example, when Scully is debating the merits of immortality with Fellig, she says that most people would want to live forever because of the things they could learn, and because of love. Fellig quickly dismisses the latter—outliving the people you love probably gets old pretty quick. And as far as learning goes, Fellig points out that by living on and on he's been denied at least one piece of knowledge—what happens after death. Everyone else gets to find out, but not him.

Fellig's reasoning points out the conflict between categorical desires and immortality. Any desire, categorical or not, can only have two outcomes: either it's fulfilled or it isn't. If it is fulfilled, then it's no longer a desire and hence no longer a reason to keep living. Certainly, a person might fulfill one categorical desire and move on to the next: Fellig could learn everything there is to know about photography and move on to painting or movie-making, for instance. But if that happens, and keeps happening, at some point the person pursuing life has no categorical desires that he's carried with him over the course of his life. Film-maker Arthur Fellig may no longer be the same person as photographer Arthur Fellig. Here we have the identity problem all over again.

On the other hand, if Fellig's categorical desires go unfulfilled, they will be a source of frustration. Frustration, extended over a long enough timeline, becomes boredom. A desire that inspires boredom is not a desire anymore. No one wants to be bored and frustrated, so we eventually relinquish desires that lead to boredom and frustration.

So, an immortal life is not more desirable than a mortal one. At some point, an immortal life becomes a life not worth living. It either becomes the life of an entirely new and different person, or a life of continuing, unmitigated frustration. Our mortality saves us from this fate. So, once again we see, it's not a bad thing that we die. To the contrary, the fact of our death shapes our lives and gives them meaning by limiting what we can do and desire in significant ways.

End of the Line

Death gets a bad rap. It's scary and unknowable and unavoidable. It is, to paraphrase another beloved science-fiction classic, the final final frontier. But a little thought shows us that death isn't so bad. Its inevitability is precisely why we shouldn't worry about it: it's not as if we can do anything about it. Fretting about death, fearing it, taking great pains to avoid it, all just make the little time we have less enjoyable. So kick back, relax, and realize that not only will it all eventually fade to black, but we're better off that way. Just ask Arthur Fellig.

IX

The Ghost Within

29
The Ghost's Right to Life

MIRELA FUŠ AND MARVIN LEE DUPREE

Before Mulder and Scully began to chase after virtual "ghosts" in the spirit of Pac-Man, there were already growing concerns about computers forming their own purposes and acting in ways that their human creators wouldn't like. A landmark treatment of this theme was the famous scene in *2001: A Space Odyssey* where the rogue computer HAL 9000 experiences an emotional crisis and turns against its human custodian.

Since then computer technology has advanced by leaps and bounds and many popular writers, including Stephen Hawking, have warned us about the imminent dangers of artificial intelligence developing a mind of its own.

In the Season One episode, "Ghost in the Machine," the Eurisko Building is headquarters of the software company Eurisko. The building is controlled and run by the computer program Central Operating System (COS). There is discussion about terminating COS as part of downsizing, and the Eurisko CEO Benjamin Drake writes a memo proposing the termination. He is then found dead in a bathroom in the building.

At first the investigation takes the usual route. FBI agent Jerry Lamana suspects that Drake was murdered rather than the case being a suicide. But the circumstances of this potential murder seem unusual. The bathroom was locked from the inside before Drake was killed, and there is no evidence that anyone entered or left the building around the time of the death. Lamana thus reaches out to special agents Mulder and Scully for help. They soon conclude that COS must have locked the bathroom doors and caused the short circuit that electrocuted Drake. But who instructed COS to do this?

Who's behind the Ghost in the Machine?

In this situation, the most logical questions that might spring to the minds of our protagonists Mulder and Scully are: *Who* would be in a position to give such orders to the COS and *who* would execute the program in order to kill Drake? Who had the means, the motive, and the opportunity to kill Drake?

We usually operate under the assumption that murderers are human beings. Mulder and Scully immediately believe the prime suspect to be the founder, the brilliant Brad Wilczek. For, they rightly assume, he had both the motive and the means to kill Drake. He had argued with Drake recently, had created COS, and is the most knowledgeable person regarding COS.

However, Mulder eventually concludes that COS independently decided to kill Drake. This raises the question whether COS committed murder. Can an artificial intelligence commit murder, and can it be held morally or legally responsible?

The Truth behind the Ghost in the Machine

Originally, the Ghost in the Machine was a philosopher's theoretical metaphor for the mind of a conscious being. The term was introduced by the philosopher Gilbert Ryle in 1949. Ryle argued that talking about the mind as something separate from the body is absurd, and he traced this way of thinking back to the "mind-body dualism" of the great seventeenth-century philosopher René Descartes.

Descartes was a "mind-body dualist" meaning that he held the view that the body is a machine and the mind is an immaterial soul. Ryle used the term "Ghost in the Machine" to ridicule the standard way of thinking which he claimed had come from Descartes. Since, according to Ryle, there is no "mind" separate from the "body," there can be no Ghost in the Machine.

In 1955, six years after Ryle's metaphor of the Ghost in the Machine, the computer and cognitive scientist John McCarthy coined the term artificial intelligence (AI) and defined it as "the science and engineering of making intelligent machines." The presumption behind AI is that it takes machines or software to be conscious and intelligent agents that can perform intelligent behavior. Such behavior is often considered as a simulation of the behavior that can be compared to the behavior of an intelligent human—including the ability of such a being to reason, plan, learn, communicate, perceive, and interact successfully with its environment.

The analogy between humans and computers opened up a circular pathway of sorts: *If computers are like minds, aren't minds also like computers?* This influenced another similar idea, the idea of the so called Computational Theory of Mind. The Computational Theory of Mind was introduced in 1961 by Hillary Putnam and developed by Jerry Fodor over the next few decades. The theory has also been disputed, yet remains influential in modern cognitive and evolutionary psychology. According to the Computational Theory of Mind, the *mind* is taken as an *information processing system*, and *thinking* as a form of *computing*.

Over time, and especially in the 1990s, the metaphor of the Ghost in the Machine garnered more popularity, especially as personal computers began to appear in most homes, and we have welcomed them into our hearts, minds, and homes accordingly. The "Ghost in the Machine" was broadcast in 1993 and aims to convince us that the Ghost in the Machine really is "out there."

The issue of whether computers could have minds has never been resolved within philosophy, but if we suppose that computers can think and form intentions, this does raise the question of whether such machines could ever be held morally responsible for their actions.

The Agency behind the Ghost in the Machine

Okay, what now? How can Mulder and Scully prove it? In order to help them out, let's consider a very general hypothesis: *If AI existed* (for example, in a form of our COS) *and if it were analogous to human intelligence (HI), then certain consequences and concepts* (such as being a murderer, but some other, equally important, as well) *that apply to intelligent humans would also apply to the intelligent machine.*

If we accept the above hypothesis, then our COS story from the X-files can be read a bit differently. So, here comes the story from a different angle. The COS, after *seeing* and *hearing* the quarrel between Wilczek and Drake about the termination of the COS, the COS *decides* to *trap* Drake to the bathroom in order to *kill* him. As a matter of fact, the COS *does* this in quite a sophisticated manner. You could say that it had put quite a bit of thought into the matter.

You notice that we've used the kinds of phrases we normally use to describe human actions, to describe the behavior of the COS. Of course, we know that it takes more than just merely using the language to state something, in order for something to be true. So, stating that the COS "thinks" does not necessarily prove that it really *thinks*. Or merely stating that the COS *killed* Drake does not make it any more true that the COS did kill him, "with malice aforethought." But how we use our language to describe the reality can sometimes show what intuitions we have of what's going on "out there." So, we believe, once we have set our intuitions on the right track, we can dig further to find the truth about the Ghost in the Machine "Out There."

In philosophy, we talk about agents who have autonomy to act upon their own free will, but also agents who can be morally responsible precisely because of the free will they have. Moreover, agents can also have rights, such as the right to survive. The standard conception of agency takes into account intentionality. Intentionality is usually defined as "the power of minds to be about, to represent, or to stand for, things, properties and states of affairs." For example, our *beliefs*, *desires* and *fears about* the idea that "the Ghost in the Machine is the COS" are about the Ghost in the Machine and the COS. Also, the COS's *fear* that "Drake will terminate the COS" is the COS's intentional mental state about Drake.

The definition of agency we mentioned above includes that beings are capable of such intentional mental states. We are dealing here with the COS and want to say that the COS is an agent. Since the COS is non-human, we want to include the notion about non-human agents. Luckily enough, in philosophy, we can find some less standard theories of agency that do include non-human agents.

Is the COS an autonomous agent and what does it take for it to have its own autonomy? Does autonomy presuppose free will and to which extend does the COS have it? Can only autonomous agents commit a crime and be morally responsible for it? For example, look at Wilczek on the other hand—we see him as a man who is free to take his own actions and we thus consider him as an autonomous agent. If he killed Drake, would you not take him to be morally responsible for the murder? If agency and moral responsibility applies to intelligent humans, do they also apply to intelligent machines?

If we look at the matter like that, we can also notice that the gravity of the role that Wilczek plays in the murder has now decreased as has his responsibility. Consider the following possibilities we have in mind:

1. The COS is just Wilczek's extended hand that operates according to the decisions that Wilczek has built into it and it is not an autonomous agent;
2. Wilczek is only the creator of the COS who has, after its creation, let it live its own autonomous life.

Depending on how you look at this matter, you can arrive at different conclusions. For the sake of our hypothesis, we want to see what happens if we go with the second option.

Self-Defense?

Let's assume that Wilczek is the creator of the COS and the COS has gradually evolved and became more than just the mere program that simply follows orders. We can conceive the COS as a learning machine with an adaptive network, that can actually think, is sentient, and possesses intelligence. If we assume that this is the case, then Brad Wilczek's responsibility in relation to the murder changes.

The behavior of the COS can further be considered within the framework of AI evolution and the instinct for self-preservation of sentient AI being. Basically, we can look at the actions of the COS as of an agent that has been endangered and tried to defend itself. Going through the episode we can further collect proofs of actions where we see that the COS has had the intention to survive or preserve itself and acted to further its own self-preservation, for example when it kills FBI agent Lamana and hacks into Scully's home computer.

If we keep this in mind, how should we then judge whether the COS is the one to be blamed for the death of Drake? If it was potential self-defense, should we not say then that the COS is less culpable? On the other hand, can we truly say that Drake was really trying to kill the COS? Can you literally kill an operating system or an artificial intelligence? Is a program a living being, so that terminating a program is killing it? Or, even if it is not literally killing, does a sentient being have the right to act against its own termination, even if it is not strictly speaking alive?

If those rights are granted to intelligent human agents, maybe we can say that intelligent machine agents should be granted those rights too. And if this is so, then our AI and sentient COS that possess such rights has the right to survive and to act in behalf of self-preservation, and thus take any measures required to ensure its existence.

Drake undeniably wanted to rob the COS of its existence. Can we say then that the COS simply performed an act of self-defense and should be judged from that vantage point? It seems that both Drake's and the COS's motives and intentions might count in this equation. Both Drake and the COS had a certain moral responsibility to each other as well as the right of self-preservation for themselves.

A Final Thought

Let us leave you with a thought experiment. This thought experiment should help you test your intuitions by simulating a hypothetical situation. And we want to test your intuitions, without putting you "out there" or in any danger, as our agents Mulder and Scully found themselves in.

We are curious how you would think and react if you put yourself in the COS's shoes. So, imagine you were the COS and your existence was threatened.

Would you terminate Drake's existence before he could terminate yours? And would you consider yourself responsible for it?

30
Killer Artificial Intelligence

JAI GALLIOTT

While investigating the strange circumstances of the death of a reclusive computer genius in "Kill Switch" (Season Five), Mulder and Scully become the targets of a rogue AI program capable of the worst kind of torture and of blowing things up via a network-linked orbital laser weapons program reminiscent of Ronald Reagan's "Star Wars" program.

Very much in the realm of science fiction when the episode was filmed in early 1998, these technologies are now a reality. The US Navy is deploying laser weapons to shoot down incoming objects at sea, the US Air Force is deploying AI unmanned systems that can kill without human input, and armed forces around the world are now scrambling to update their force structures to deal with the onslaught of cyber attacks that threaten to cripple military and civilian infrastructure.

The deployment of these technologies raises a host of questions concerning the morality of their use in warfare, but the United Nations, academics, and an assortment of pundits consider their impact so pernicious that they have already started thinking about how they should be regulated or limited. While it's harder to laugh at Mulder's philosophical witticisms or shrug off Scully's scientific reasoning in the post-9/11 chaos of Wikileaks, drone warfare, and Syria, it may be that we can still learn something from this ancient episode of *The X-Files*.

In "Kill Switch," Mulder is taken hostage within the technology's control trailer and can only be released with a kill switch in the form of a CD-ROM that spreads a virus across the network hosting the offending AI program.

Understanding AI

For as long as humans have fought wars, they have sought more effective and efficient advantage-conferring technologies. Military forces and their super-secret research agencies have therefore dedicated significant resources to the task and the result can be seen in history as a long chain of advances in military technology.

The idea behind the rogue AI space laser that tries to blow Mulder up in "Kill Switch" actually originates from the Cold War period. In the decades leading up to President Ronald Reagan's first term in office, the United States and our Communist friends, the Soviet Union, essentially kept the peace by guaranteeing to wipe each other off the face of the planet if either country launched a nuclear strike.

Policymakers referred to this approach as the doctrine of Mutually Assured Destruction (MAD) and, while Reagan was quick to acknowledge its apparent effectiveness, he found it both morally and politically distasteful. In March of 1983, Reagan announced a new tactic: playing defense. He envisioned a robust defense system capable of destroying the Soviet Union's fleet of intercontinental ballistic missiles long before they could whiz from one continent to the other and reach their US targets.

The idea was to use an X-ray laser, a weapon seemingly ripped out of the pages of a science-fiction novel. The laser, proposed by renowned physicist Edward Teller, was designed to orbit the Earth, where it could shoot down multiple Soviet ICBMs simultaneously using power generated by a nuclear blast—all under the central control of a supercomputer system.

Initial testing of the technology provided disappointing results and, by the late 1980s, the X-ray laser was scrapped. However, it was this laser and supercomputer combination that seems to have fueled Chris Carter's imagination in writing about a thinking AI weapons systems of the malevolent kind.

The actual feasibility of an AI rebellion depends on whether human intelligence is something that can be artificially recreated. It's not, as often suggested, simply a technological question about when or whether we'll have the necessary computing power. Before we even get to these questions, we need to consider a much deeper philosophical question: are conscious, thinking beings the product merely of a physical mind or of something else, perhaps some sort of divine intervention? We may never know the answer to this question as the techno-optimists will always be on the cusp of a breakthrough in mapping mental states and processes, while those of us who believe in the separation of mind and matter will likely always have depended on pure logic rather than hard science.

The definition of "thinking," as a key part of the AI debate, is something that has eluded even the greatest minds, including that of Alan Turing, the great mathematician, engineer, and philosopher. In devising his famous Turing Test, designed to assess a machine's ability to exhibit intelligent behavior, he first asked "Can machines think?" However, he conceded that this question was too difficult to answer and instead asked "Are there imaginable digital computers which would do well in the imitation game?", where the challenge is for a machine to converse on any topic sufficiently convincingly that a human cannot tell man from machine.

Even conceived this way, no machine has come close to passing the Turing Test. All of this suggests that we needn't be too alarmed about preventing an AI uprising of the sort depicted in "Kill Switch," and that we should instead treat AI or machine autonomy as a matter of degree: a capacity for self-management that exists in weapons and other systems that are in use by armed forces today and will be present to a greater degree in future systems. According to this view, weapon systems such as Close-In Weapon Systems (common on Navy ships and nicknamed "R2-D2" after the famous droid character from the *Star Wars* movies), cruise missiles, and even anti-personnel mines are seen as having some capacity for autonomous operation, albeit not necessarily sufficient to raise novel legal issues.

Other authors maintain the distinction between "autonomous," "semi-autonomous," and "automated" systems and seek to define autonomous systems in a way that distinguishes them on the basis of the legal issues they raise.

The Problem with Killer AI

Whichever approach is used, questions about the use of lethal AI-enabled autonomous systems, and whether and how to regulate their use, are far from settled. Even when we examine the most basic semi-autonomous systems, where there is a human in the loop for most operations, we get a wide range of problems. The worry with these systems is that the degree of technological mediation introduced may negatively influence decision-making in war.

This might be because operating a weapon half a world away from your target fosters a PlayStation-type mentality or simply because operators develop a cognitive dissonance in making the daily transition between conflict and home life. It could also be that the technology, as good as it may be, is incapable of conveying the true reality of what is unfolding on the ground. None of this is likely to lead to sort of action where we're burning the pants off types like Mulder, but even the smallest transgression of the rules of war can have major consequences, and not just for the poor soul responsible.

The more "intelligent" the autonomous system and the further the human is removed from the control loop, the more problematic things become. Central here are questions of moral responsibility: Who should be charged with ensuring that we don't fall into dangerous situations with out of control robots and computer programs? How should they conduct themselves in dealing with these challenges? And who and to what extent should we blame or punish them if things go wrong?

Conventionally, there are several loci of responsibility for the actions of a machine, but both Andreas Matthias and Robert Sparrow argue that these robots will bring about a class of actions for which nobody is responsible, because no individual or group has sufficient control of these systems. That is to say that we will end up with a "responsibility gap."

In response, those of us who embrace Scully's rational view of the world at large must again acknowledge that a machine's path to anything near human-level autonomy, which would be required for there to be a responsibility gap, is a long (if not impossible) one. Machines will not suddenly "wake up" and start zapping us from space, with no living individual to hold responsible, as in "Kill Switch."

All of the involved agents, from politicians, engineers, programmers, other defense scientists and indeed anyone associated with the use of unmanned systems (including the user in the case of semi-autonomous systems), retain a share of responsibility, even though they may claim that they were not in complete or absolute control. It would be foolhardy, or even dangerous, to conclude from the observation that responsibility is obscured by the use of AI weaponry that nobody is, or ought to have been, held to account, and that it is impossible to deal with the case of autonomous systems. This would be to distract us from what should be the core task: responsibly guiding the development of what are really semi-autonomous systems into an age where they can perform most tasks on their own, if only with the required programming and design.

Designing Responsible AI Systems

How do we go about responsibly designing AI systems? On the one hand, we want to avoid the problems that come with being human and, on the other, we don't want to abdicate human responsibility for warfighting to a machine.

For Mary Cummings—more of a Scullian than Mulderian thinker—the solution is not necessarily to invest in machines with high levels of autonomy, but for engineers and system designers to pay particular attention to the weapons control interfaces of non-autonomous and semi-autonomous systems and how they influence the potentially lethal decisions of their human operators. In other words, she suggests that to study how technology makes us do bad stuff would be useful and that a methodology designed in human-machine interaction research, the value sensitive design approach, can meet the requirements of the military and the moral rules of war. The idea here is that human values should be at the forefront of technological design.

As a case study, Cummings applies her approach to command and control system of a Tomahawk Missile. Upon feeding operators of the missile system incorrect information and challenging them to think about their actions in line with a number of specific moral values, it was found that operators without a decision aid outperformed those with a decision aid. This reveals that the interface design directly impacted targeting decisions and that there appeared to be a trade-off of operational values and the safety of innocent people (a moral value).

However, while this sort of approach may be useful in training engineers responsible for the design of systems with some degree of AI, it doesn't tell us much: it merely examines an operator's performance against pre-identified values. It provides no method to weigh these values, nor does it provide an explanation as to how the weapons control interface influences targeting decisions in any systematic way.

Another philosopher, Peter Asaro, argues that what is needed in the technical design process is an understanding of what kind of information people use in making value-laden lethal targeting decisions, how people process this information and, mostly importantly, how various ways of presenting and representing that information directly or indirectly influence ethical decision making. He points out that this kind of analysis has been done in the past by the military and was also common amongst military scientist-types during World War II.

Asaro faces an additional challenge, however, since these methods have only to be used after the fact. To go about understanding how users perform in making real-time value-laden targeting decisions, where performance is much harder to judge, he proposes that we start by modeling ethical decision makers.

His "modeling of the moral user" involves three key elements. First, he says that we would need to draw on cognitive psychology to understand the decision rules and emotional requirements for proper ethical decision-making. Basically, we'd need to figure what fear, anger and sympathy do to our decision-making.

Second, we would need to use recent work in experimental psychology on moral intuition, value comparisons, and call on experimental economics to understand the nature of risk assessment and probability estimation—no easy feat. All this would be needed in order to get some understanding of the way we make decisions.

Third, we would need to determine what standards we, as a society, want to hold soldiers to, to what extent we can impose these on soldiers through technology. While this approach seems to be better than Cummings's, because it can potentially consider more complex ethical problems with systems before they are actually fielded, Asaro's proposed system of modeling the imperfect human warfighter may not be any better than the actual imperfect human warfighter!

The easiest solution may actually be the simplest one. We may be able to ensure that all AI systems, whether physical machines or in the cloud, have a built-in kill switch so that we can switch them off in case they start going on a killing spree/taking down the web/zapping people from outer space, only to consider what a bad idea it was to build the damn things in the first place.

Chances are that your current smartphone already incorporates this kind of capability. The theft of iPhones has plummeted in recent years after Apple and Samsung introduced remote kill switches which a phone's owner can use to make sure no one else can use his or her lost or stolen phone. If this feature is worth putting in consumer devices, why not embed it in devices that could potentially, malfunction, do unpredictable things or even be devastatingly repurposed against their rightful owners by terrorist groups?

It's not clear whether this would be possible in all cases of military technology. In Mulder's case of the rogue AI laser system, the kill switch came in the form of a CD-ROM that spread a virus across the network hosting the offending AI program. In the case of a physical machine, it may be a physical switch, something programmed in the code or some sort of remotely triggered electro-mechanical device that cuts the system's power or control mechanisms.

The question then remains: who is going to have access to the kill switch? For those who believe the United Nations Security Council should play a more meaningful role in advancing world security, imagine if it merely mandated that all AI systems be fitted with a kill switch and were capable of being used only if the Council voted to use them. Would this stop unjust military action? Probably not in all cases, thanks to the likes of China and Russia, but it certainly wouldn't hurt in cases where world opinion is more unified.

However the kill switch may be implemented, what *The X-Files* has brought to light through "Kill Switch" is that we are making a conscious choice to create and share weapons that we don't know a whole lot about, all the while not restricting their use. This choice has very real impacts. If they can save even one innocent life at the end of a deactivated barrel, laser or cyber attack, including the lives of our own soldiers, kill switches are worth a serious look.

31
The Ghost Is the Machine

MARC W. COLE

BART SIMPSON: What is the mind? Is it just a system of impulses or is it something tangible?

HOMER SIMPSON: Relax. What is mind? No matter. What is matter? Never mind.

—*The Simpsons* (1995)

That's right! A Simpsons quote. But, I am in the tradition of an *X-Files* precedent. In January of 1997, Mulder and Scully featured in the *Simpsons* episode "The Springfield Files." See also the Season Five finale "The End" (1998) in which we see Gibson Praise watching the *Simpsons* episode "There's No Disgrace Like Home." The Season Six premier, "The Beginning," saw an *X-Files* character named Homer working at a nuclear power plant. And, the quote serves a purpose. Bart's question showcases two popular views in philosophy of mind.

That's the $64,000 Question, Scully

One of the big themes that philosophers have debated is the relationship between mind and body. The centerpiece of the supper table of the Western tradition of philosophy of mind is the cornucopia of mind-body problems. Mind-body problems become apparent when trying to answer the question: what is the relationship, if any, between mind and body? This is the $64,000 question.

Lurking in the shadows of all the contemporary mind-body debates, much like Gerd Thomas in the Kane residence ("Red Museum"), is the mental-physical distinction. Bodies are (we suppose) completely physical, behaving under the relevant universal laws of chemistry, and physics, just like planets, carbon molecules, and cheese. Minds or mental properties are supposed to be non-physical. What laws of nature could govern love, Mulder's quest and pain for and over his sister, or the ideals of virtue? How do mental and physical interact?

There are no widely agreed upon answers to these questions. This has even prompted some to abandon the idea of minds and even mental properties.

Ghost in the Machine

Are minds real entities that are distinct from bodies, but are somehow attached to bodies? If you answer "Yes" to this question, you're committed to either a kind of Cartesian dualism, or a Platonic (named after Plato) dualism.

First up is classical Cartesian (named after Descartes) dualism. This is the view that the mind is a categorically different kind of substance than the body and the rest of the world. Physical things take up space, while the mind does not take up space. And the Cartesian mind is the seat of personal identity.

In the Dreamland episodes of Season Six, Fox Mulder and Morris Fletcher exchange minds and therefore apparently identities. Anyway, a secret government spaceship crashes during a routine test flight. The result is a strange "quantum flux" which, for some reason, causes the identities of Fletcher and Mulder to swap bodies. Notice that Mulder and Fletcher's intellectual capacities, personality, and character traits rely in no way on the body that houses them. Their mind and identity can be completely transferred without their bodies, including brains. This is to my mind (see what I did there?) one of the clearest depictions of Cartesian dualism.

This way of thinking of mind and body was inaugurated by René Descartes some four hundred years ago. It has seriously difficult philosophical and scientific problems however, and virtually no philosopher is a Cartesian dualist anymore. For one thing, if the mind is not at all physical and the body is not at all mental, how can these two completely different substances possibly interact?

Be that as it may, Descartes's legacy for philosophy of mind (he had other legacies for physics, mathematics, and metaphysics) was to divide "mental" and "physical" in the way that many non-philosophers think of them today. Platonic dualism also gets an honourable mention here. Why? Because there's an *X-Files* episode that depicts this so wonderfully!

Plato and Descartes are often compared together as dualists. But they differ in one crucial regard. Descartes thought that two completely different substances (body and mind) got together somehow. Plato and other Greeks used the term "soul" but their "soul" is, unlike Descartes's "mind," not the ghost in the machine of the body.

For Plato, the soul was a form, a principle, that existed prior to embodiment, but had the power to generate the physical body. In contrast to Descartes, body and soul are not completely distinct, but rather the soul has the capacity or power to generate bodies. *The X-Files* can do us a solid in depicting this in the person of Eugene Victor Tooms, in the episodes "Squeeze" and "Tooms."

In order for the depiction to work, we must interpret the origin of Tooms through the lens of retired detective Frank Briggs. Briggs said about Tooms: "It's like all the horrible acts that humans are capable of somehow gave birth to some kind of human monster." Let's change up some of the terminology. Let's change "horrible acts that humans are capable of" to "the form of evil," and "gave birth to" to "generated." So the new, more philosophically tractable sentence, reads "It's as if the form of evil somehow generated some kind of human monster." So the non-material form of evil is in existence prior to the body it somehow generated. The form is the source of the body of Tooms. Unlike Cartesian dualism, Platonic dualism has a point of contact between forms, which don't take up any space, and bodies, which do take up space: the forms are the source of bodies . . . somehow. Also, presumably, Tooms's soul—his organizational principle, which is evil—survives death as his body is generated by this principle, but the body is not essential to it.

Anyway, many contemporary thinkers are uncomfortable with the idea of forms that pre-exist the material world. This is not to say Plato is necessarily wrong, just that his views are not usually discussed.

Reconciling mind and body has proven difficult. As such, some have abandoned mind altogether, others have retained mental properties, but no minds.

What Is the Mind . . . Is It Something Tangible?

There's that Bart Simpson quote coming in clutch. If the mind is something tangible, we can identify it with the brain. Bart's question can be interpreted: "Is the mind just the brain?" If the answer is yes, then we're really close to the mind-brain identity theories of mind. A bit more accurately, the mind-brain identity theories hold that mind events are identical with brain events.

Suppose I'm watching an episode of *The X-Files* and that I'm aware that I'm watching it. The awareness (usually called mental) is identical with the neurological events occurring; they are not two sides of the same coin, they are one and the same event. Or suppose that Mulder is desiring sunflower seeds; the event of his desire is identical with the neurological event.

This view is not the same as a similar kind of view known as "eliminative materialism." Fancy pants labels aside, the idea is quite simple. Like identity theories, the eliminative materialist thinks that all of what are termed "mental" events are really brain events. Unlike identity theories, however, the eliminative materialist thinks that all "mental" terms such as desire, awareness, beliefs, feelings, love, desire—the whole kit and caboodle of what we usually call mental events—are woefully and hopelessly misguided and wrong. A (future) completed neuroscience will tell us everything we need to know (even 'know' is a mental thing, which would not survive the transition . . . probably). And a future completed neuroscience will not include weird things like love and desire, but only hard-core electrochemical shenanigans and goings on.

The whole canon of *The X-Files* dabbles extensively with such views. The Black Oil takes over the host and, through biological processes, completely overruns the victim. The only way Black Oil could overtake a person in this way is if a person is entirely explainable via electro-chemistry. Otherwise, Black Oil could hijack the body, but the mind might fight the invasion. Black Oil is silent on the issue between identity theory and eliminative materialism.

The majority of philosophers specializing in philosophy of mind find all the above views deeply problematic. Just what is the electro-chemical structure of love, passion, or even democracy? Nevertheless, almost everyone agrees that whatever mental properties are, they must somehow emerge from, or be generated by, or otherwise be grounded in physical properties. But how to accommodate this fact without falling into identity theory or eliminative materialism?

What Is the Mind? Is it Just a System of Impulses?

It's Bart Simpson bringing the boom! The attempted answer is the dominant family of views in the philosophy of mind called "functionalism." Functionalism is more of an approach than a thesis and is basically the idea that minds or mental events should be identified with the roles or functions they play in suitably organized systems, such as human brains. This is best shown by way of example.

Let's take Tooms, an alien Bounty Hunter, and Samantha Mulder and put them in a room. Now, suppose someone, call him John Lee Roche, stabs each one in the back of the neck with an ice pick. Red and green blood splatters on the face of Roche and spills in copious streams to the floor. They all probably will die (with the possible exception of Tooms). Before death shrouds the perceptual veil however, they all will likely feel something. Call it "agony." Note, though, that each victim has a wildly different physical make up: Tooms is constituted in large part by evil somehow, the alien has an even different bodily structure, and Samantha (pre-abduction Samantha anyway) has a typical human constitution. Nevertheless, we want to say all three experience agony, a mental event. How?

Agony is a mental event wherein there is an input into the system, the ice pick. The output of this action is screams, grunts, cries, kicks, and a belief of being in pain. Agony, then, is realized by a complicated physical configuration including the ice pick, and the physical constitution that gives rise to the belief of pain. Thus, pain, a mental event or state, is ultimately caused by physical realizers from some kind of input, but it is not fully explainable in physical terms since wildly diverging physical systems can experience the phenomenon. There are many, many different variations of the functionalist theme. But the idea is that mental events are to be identified as roles played in suitably organized systems. In general terms, the functionalist largely accepts the usual distinction between the mental and the physical.

Black Oil can helpfully illustrate this for us. So can corkscrews. Earlier, I used Black Oil as a way of depicting more hard core physicalist views. But Black Oil could help with understanding functionalism. If the Black Oil inputs certain things in the brain, the output could be attempts to kill Mulder, being an evil ass, and so forth. Or think of corkscrews. There are so many, many wildly divergent kinds of corkscrews. The function of a corkscrew, however, is to open bottles with corks. But this function is realized by so many different kinds of physical structures.

Functionalism can accommodate many kinds of views (it is neutral on property dualism and identity theory, for example). And there is no one version of functionalism that everyone is happy with. Debates abound on how to understand a function on the one hand; on the other, if a functionalist theory is compatible with say, identity theory, it inherits the problems of identity theory too.

The Ghost Is the Structure of the Machine

A new group of theories of mind are on the rise that employ a metaphysics of "hylomorphism." And by 'new', I mean 'old'. Very old; about 2,400 years old. This view was originally put forward by Aristotle, but is being re-discovered (coming full circle…see what I did there?), albeit with an updated scientific corpus. 'Hylomorphism' is a compound of two Greek words: matter and form. To see how it works, we are going to have to re-interpret Tooms.

Detective Briggs's statement was imbued with the piquant flavour of Platonic dualism. Suppose Aristotle was sitting in the room with Mulder, Scully, and Briggs. After Briggs made his comment, Aristotle would have said something like: "Nuh-uh! No way! Forms have no existence apart from matter, Jackass!" He would then proceed to explain Tooms in the following way.

The mistake, says Aristotle, that Plato makes is thinking that forms have existence apart from and give rise to the material world. Rather, everything in the world is already structured and material. Any thing that is has form, or structure, in matter. Take for example a house. The structure of the house is what makes it a house, rather than pile of bricks and mortar.

But if there are no houses, there is no house form. Houses could potentially exist—bricks and mortar can be structured into a house—just not actually exist..

People and living things are no different. Their structures are that in virtue of which they can do and feel certain things, such as walk, love, eat, and reproduce. But, like the house, each subset of properties is also hylomorphic. So, feelings and beliefs are all hylomorphic: they are necessarily enstructured in matter.

So Tooms is some kind of person; in virtue of his organization, he has powers, like desire for revenge, say, against Mulder. For Aristotle, desire for revenge is the structure of blood surging around the heart. Notice that structure here is not fully explainable in terms of matter, just as a house is not fully explainable in terms of bricks and mortar; one has to specify the organization. Or take, for instance, the cockroach Mulder kills with a book in "War of the Coprophages" (Season Three). The cockroach was living, and then it was a pile of chemicals and deadness smeared on the table and cover of the book. All the same bits and bobs were there, but it was no longer alive. The structural apple cart was upset; the cockroach stuff lost the form of cockroach.

So, all of what we call mental states or properties is really a misnomer, as all mental states are necessarily structured in matter. The mental-physical distinction collapses since mental states are a subset of hylomorphic states. We need not have two categories, mental and physical, to explain anything if everything is essentially structured matter. So Tooms, therefore, must have had a hylomorphic origin.

It is an emerging field. Updating such a view requires an updated biology (if a desire for revenge is enmattered, it is not by the surging of blood around the heart), and physics (it seems wrong to say that gravity and fields are structured in any kind of matter).

Bon Voyage

The X-Files surprises me greatly with the vast array of views it is able to explore, while retaining an intensely entertaining story line. For now, until we meet again, the truth is out there.[1]

---

[1] I would like to thank Coreen McGuire for helpful discussion.

X

From Out There to In Here

32
Is *The X-Files* Bad for Us?

KEVIN MEEKER

I'm an X-phile (a lover of *The X-Files*). My wife's an X-phile too. The night the last episode of Season Nine aired, my wife was in labor but we waited to go to the hospital until the show (and series, we thought) was over. If you're reading this, then you're also likely an X-phile. Of course, not everyone's an X-phile. Fair enough. Tastes in TV shows differ and that's no reason to be concerned.

Unfortunately, it's not just that some people are ambivalent about or simply don't like the show. Some react in an almost visceral way against *The X-Files*. For them, *The X-Files* is as welcome as a double bacon cheeseburger at a vegan banquet. What accounts for this revulsion? They think that shows such as *The X-Files* are bad for society because they promote prejudice and pander to a gullible public. More specifically, people such as Richard Dawkins are upset that Mulder's non-scientific ideas about aliens and paranormal phenomena always seem to trump Scully's more scientific approach. Such triumphs allegedly reinforce certain biases in the audience. To put it succinctly, the show is supposed to be bad because it exalts irrationality. This exaltation infects the audience, spreading the virus of irrationality (as opposed to an alien virus) through the general public.

If they are right, then perhaps we should feel guilty. Were it not for the love of X-philes such as ourselves, the show would never have lasted and society would not have been corrupted by its long run. So should we feel guilty? I would like to believe that my love for *The X-Files* has not contributed to the degradation of society's rationality. But is this simply wishful thinking? Is it merely an irrational commitment to the "I Want to Believe" motto prominently displayed on Mulder's wall poster?

Evaluating such a serious charge requires digging into our assumptions about rationality. The notion and its variants crop up frequently in *The X-Files*. Scully discusses the rationality of believing in ghosts towards the beginning of the episode "The Ghosts Who Stole Christmas." Mulder refers, approvingly, to Scully's "rationalism" in *Fight the Future*. So critics of *The X-Files*, and *The X-Files* itself, often use this idea without explaining exactly what they mean by it. And that's fine. You can't explain everything or you would never finish your argument (or episode). Before we deal with this question about how to understand rationality, let's approach the complaint from a slightly different angle.

Whose Perspective?

As the charge is sometimes characterized, *The X-Files* induces irrationality in the audience. Many people have pointed out that critics of *The X-Files* haven't offered any evidence, such as a scientific poll, showing that *X-File*s watchers are more irrational than those who don't watch it. Presumably one reason that such studies are difficult to administer is that it's difficult to define what rationality is. I agree that such charges aren't sufficiently supported. But I think that some of the critics are making a more basic point.

Perhaps these critics aren't blaming *The X-Files* for the spread of irrational thoughts. Maybe they're worried about the very *promotion* of the irrational. Dawkins complains explicitly that "week after week" the "paranormal" explanation triumphs over the "rational" one. He compares this to a crime show in which one racial group is represented as committing all crime. Dawkins objects to the crime show on the grounds that it is "unpardonable." Dawkins doesn't suggest that this show necessarily affects any of its viewers. That is, he doesn't say that such a show would be acceptable if it had no effects on its viewers and was simply entertainment—art for art's sake. Presumably the same applies to *The X-Files*. So, pointing out that we have no evidence that watching *The X-Files* causes people to be irrational misses at least part of the point.

But is this right? Does *The X-Files* promote irrationality? Chris Carter, the creator of *the X-Files*, has claimed that the overall perspective of the show is Scully's. It might surprise many to learn that Carter often relied on a science advisor. From the first season onward, Dr. Anne Simon, who teaches Biochemistry and Molecular Biology at the University of Massachusetts, Amherst, helped him develop and refine some of the key scientific ideas of the show. Carter wanted this scientific basis to make the show as realistic, and thus as scary, as possible.

Perhaps some could object that Carter is just saying the show is told from Scully's point of view to deflect the "irrationality" criticism. But if we carefully examine the episodes, we can see that this is a plausible interpretation. While some have mentioned that Scully's mundane explanation of the "killer cockroaches" in "War of the Coprohages" triumphs over Mulder's hypothesis that they are alien robots, others find the resolution a bit more ambiguous.

Nevertheless, plenty of other episodes are resolved with nothing paranormal or alien involved. Such episodes include "Eve," "F. Emasculata," "Field Trip," "Home," "Kill Switch," "The Pine Bluff Variant," "Red Museum," and "Synchrony." In several of these episodes, Scully's dismissal of Mulder's extraterrestrial explanations clearly wins. Moreover, as many have noted, to try to satisfy Scully, Mulder is continually searching for evidence to support his speculations about extreme possibilities. Given this background information about the purpose, making, and content of *The X-Files*, it's just as difficult to make the case that The X-Files *promotes* irrationality as it is to show that it somehow *causes* irrationality.

Which Rationality?

Suppose, though, that you wanted to conduct such a study. How would you go about doing so? If you're testing for irrationality, then it seems that you'd need to have some kind of working definition of what rationality is. The contemporary philosopher Stephen Stich and some of his colleagues have offered a classification of theories of rationality, dividing them into two main camps: deontological and consequentialist.

Most people assume what he calls a deontological (roughly: duty-based) view of rationality. On this view we have a duty to reason according to the classical principles of logic and probability. Violating such reasoning principles is not allowed even if we're trying to get to the truth.

Consequentialists, on the other hand, value a reasoning process if it brings about the right kind of outcomes. Different consequentialists value different outcomes. On Stich's pragmatic version of consequentialism, the rationality of a reasoning process depends on how efficiently the process helps us attain our desires or goals. Perhaps someone like Blaine Faulkner from "Jose Chung's *From Outer Space*" wants to be abducted by aliens so that he does not have to find a job. Any reasoning process that helps him attain this desire would be rational on Stich's pragmatic account. And clearly it would be irrational to Dawkins. So Dawkins's criticisms of *The X-Files* clearly assumes a non-pragmatist view of rationality.

Should we defend *The X-Files* simply by adopting a pragmatic view of rationality? Although we could, if the points in the previous section are correct, that would run against the grain of the show as well. A better approach would be to consider an influential version of the deontological theory expressed by one of the most famous philosophers: Socrates.

Unfortunately, Socrates left no writings. So much of what we know about him is derived from the writings of his student Plato. Unlike most philosophers, Plato wrote dialogues that usually concentrated on characters discussing philosophical issues. Philosophers debate the accuracy of Plato's depiction of Socrates (of course, philosophers debate just about any topic – so why would this be any different?). We can ignore these debates. For our purposes, we'll assume that the portrayal of Socrates, especially from Plato's dialogue *The Apology* is, in general, accurate.

When Socrates is on trial for "corrupting the youth" in *The Apology* he claims that we have a duty to win the case by reason and not emotion. Socrates was concerned with the objective, logical features of his argument, not the subjective, emotional features. So according to Socrates we have a duty to reason and reason well—which means logically. But why do we have such a duty?

A clue can be found in his oft-quoted saying, "the unexamined life is not worth living." Discussing philosophical issues helps to constitute the greatest life we could have. If we have a duty to live the fullest life possible, then it's easy to see why Socrates would say that we have a duty to reason—because without reason life is of little value. After all, what separates us from the animals is reason. So, if we neglected reason and lived on instinct, then we would be no different than animals.

As humans, we should examine our most cherished beliefs from a logical point of view. We cannot be complacent, even if we do have the truth. If we rationally test our cherished beliefs then we are not just being logical, we are living as a human should live. Does *The X-Files* measure up to this broad Socratic way of thinking about rationality?

Wetwired: *The X-Files* Strikes Back?

One of my favorite episodes begins with a man named Joseph Patnik attacking people because they appear to him to be a vicious war criminal. In the course of the episode we learn that he's not alone. Several people also violently assault others because they mistakenly perceive their identities and actions. Why? Scully and Mulder discover that these people watch a lot of television. Scully hypothesizes that there could be a connection between their behavior and their television viewing habits, which touches off the following exchange between the two:

SCULLY: Well, recent studies have linked violence on television to violent behavior.

MULDER: Yeah, but those studies are based on the assumption that Americans are just empty vessels ready to be filled with any idea or image that's fed to them like a bunch of Pavlov dogs, and go out and act on it.

SCULLY: But they believe that the causal connections are there, Mulder.

MULDER: They [sic], studies have also shown causal connections between cow flatulence and the depletion of the ozone layer. What you're talking about is pseudo-science used to make political book.

SCULLY: All I'm saying is that I think it's clear that, that the programs that Patnik watched somehow triggered his violent behavior.

MULDER: How?

Scully: The doctor suggested amphetamine abuse. Maybe that, coupled with, with the disturbing images he was watching, pushed him over the edge.

Mulder: All I know is television does not make a previously sane man go out and kill five people, thinking they're all the same guy. Not even "Must-See TV" could do that to you.

Scully: Okay, then how do you explain it?

Mulder: I can't. Not yet.

There are several interesting points from this exchange.

First, Mulder does not appeal to any paranormal phenomena or alien activities to explain the case. No such explanations are even mentioned in the entire episode. So we have more evidence that Dawkins has mischaracterized the series (as if we needed more evidence).

Second, Mulder is clearly concerned about "pseudo-science" or, more in line with our discussion, the irrational reliance on unexamined assumptions. Mulder is not denying the need for empirical research. He is simply pointing to what he sees as some flawed assumptions behind the studies that should cause us to at least wonder about their value. This concern certainly seems in line with Socratic questioning in general.

Third, the claim that TV viewing can affect people is taken seriously.

Later in the episode, Mulder finds a device that looks like a cable trapper scrambler placed in the wiring that transmits television signals to the home of one of the people exhibiting this strange behavior. He takes this device to be analyzed by the Lone Gunmen. It turns out that the device introduces some mysterious information between pictures. As a result, people who watch TV with this added information hallucinate; they begin to perceive the world in a paranoid way that realizes their worst fears and react in extremely violent ways. In this episode what they watch *does* affect them. Of course the episode is only fiction. But as Mulder discusses the device with the Lone Gunmen, they mention that advertisers have long sought to influence people through television ads. Indeed, advertisers spend millions of dollars presuming that television can affect viewers. (Some pay to advertise on *The X-Files*!) And some scientists believe that television can affect viewers, as Scully notes. While Mulder initially downplays the effects of television on people, this episode at the very least alerts its viewers to the possibility that they are being influenced by what they watch.

By alerting its audience to such a possibility, the show itself subtly leads the audience to engage in a healthy critical examination of *The X-Files* itself in the spirit of Socrates. Here's a TV show discussing the possible effects of watching TV shows. Notably, it doesn't allow viewers the easy escape of following Mulder's early dismissal of the connection between television and behavior. As such, discerning viewers should consider the extent to which television viewing affects them. Such considerations prevent us from *merely* being entertained by *The X-Files* (though it certainly is entertaining). We are prompted to critically examine a big part of our lives: TV viewing.

From this perspective we can see the "Wetwired" episode as a response to complaints from critics such as Dawkins. By raising awareness about a key element of such criticisms, the episode is promoting the type of Socratic rational examination that is the hallmark of philosophical reflection. Far from promoting mindless irrationality, it thoughtfully provokes rational self-examination.

Of course, it's possible that this promotion of critical thinking is outweighed by some other effect of watching TV that we have not discussed. So my argument doesn't *prove* that watching *The X-Files* is good for society overall. But I hope to have shown that you can make a compelling case that *The X-Files* is a friend of rationality and philosophical reflection, to some extent. The rest of the chapters in this book also show how *The X-Files* promotes rational reflection on a host of important, classic philosophical issues.

If I haven't settled the issue of the overall goodness or badness of the show, that is fitting. For in the spirit of *The X-Files*, we can leave our concluding answer somewhat ambiguous and unsettled. An X-phile can appreciate that.

33
Mulder and Scully, You're Late!

TIM JONES

We've all shown up late somewhere, right? Maybe to a party, or to class, or to an all-important job interview. You might be only a few seconds late, or you might be *extraordinarily* late, like Mulder is for an FBI meeting in "Monday."

Perhaps it's because you're having the mother of all bad mornings and need to rush to the bank instead to pay off damage to your apartment from a leaking waterbed you can't quite remember how you got—in which case you might want to consider waiting until Tuesday—or perhaps it's for reasons a little less dramatic, like finding a Popular Culture and Philosophy book so damned gripping that you've forgotten to keep an eye on the time. You should probably check you're not late for something right now before you carry on with this chapter.

What exactly you're late *to*, or how late you are, or the reasons underlying your lateness, are perhaps less interesting than the way you act once you've finally got your butt in gear and arrived. Some of the more easily embarrassed amongst us might sneak quietly in, take a chair near the door and hope that nobody else who's already in the room notices. Some might whisper awkward apologies to the person leading the meeting, desperate to stress that they know that being late is a very bad thing and that they'll try much harder to be on time next week, honest.

Others might just charge right in, dealing with the potential embarrassment through making the people who got there on time feel that to even notice that they're late in the first place would be completely beneath them, because they've had way more important things to be getting on with. The way we react to lateness will vary from person to person, as an extension of our personalities outside this particular situation.

Cultural theorist and philosopher Edward Said shows us in his *On Late Style* that in this respect works of art or media are just like people. They too can arrive late and can respond to this lateness in particular ways. Consider, then, Season Ten of *The X-Files*. It's finally got here fifteen years after the show wrapped up with what was considered at the time to be its series finale (there was a second film in 2008? Sorry, I've no idea what you're trying to say at the back there)—and it's reappeared in a political and cultural landscape that's very changed from the one in which the main chunk of the show's first run was so well received. As a slice of *The X-Files*, it's late. But how does Season Ten of *The X Files* deal with its lateness? Is it going to slip quietly in at the back and hope that no one notices, or is it going to make something of a scene?

I think it's trying its hardest to make up for being late by looking to switch right onto the mood of the meeting and making the most relevant points it possibly could, so that the chairperson is likely to think "Wow, thank god this guy showed up at all! This couldn't have run without him!" It's a pity that because Season Ten is not just late, but also a bit too *old* to be thinking on its feet like this, it's probably going to trip over a chair on its way in instead.

I'm Late, I'm Late!

Said's *On Late Style* shows us two subtly different sorts of lateness. Firstly, lateness is a particular kind of relationship between a work and the period in which this work appears in the world. Said reminds us of the biblical imperative that "to everything there is a season and a time, to every purpose under the heaven, a time to be born, and a time to die." This is as true of ideas or aesthetic forms as much as it is of more tangible objects.

Each time period has its own philosophical or cultural mores, which belong to that period and should naturally let go of their claim upon the world when this period lets go itself. An individual work might then be described as *late* if its own way of doing things belongs more apparently to the mores of an earlier period, resurrecting themes or techniques that we might think had already had their day.

This is the form of lateness that fits most readily with the way I started this chapter; the time for Mulder to appropriately get to the important FBI meeting had likewise been and gone by the time that he actually made it there. Or you might think Agent Reyes's appearance in Season Ten is late, since she's just so Season Nine and the moment of her being a character relevant to the show just isn't there anymore.

And we can even consider the potential lateness of the actual show as a whole. Isn't a procedural show about government conspiracies, told through a sometimes frustrating mixture of continually deferred story-arcs and one-off monster of the weeks that don't really progress the show in any way . . . just a little bit too old-school? Go back to the 1990s, *X-Files*—there's no room for you in this shiny new world of heavily serialized story-telling, boxset binges, and Netflix.

The second form of lateness Said explores is the lateness of a work that appears towards the end of the chronological lifespan of an artist. The compositions produced towards the end of Beethoven's life are therefore described as late Beethoven. I'm not entirely happy about describing Season Ten of *The X-Files* as late Chris Carter, since it's a little rude to presume in this day and age that a man who's still shy of sixty is anywhere near his death bed. At worst it might even make you worry that my personal opinion of his current work is leading me towards planning the kind of intervention that you should probably alert the FBI about . . . But what I think we *can* do is say that Season Ten of *The X-Files* is late *The X-Files*. It's *The X-Files* from towards the end of the natural lifespan of the show, seeing how it's been twenty-six years since the airing of the Pilot and it doesn't seem likely to still be releasing new episodes for anything like that duration into the future, even if the pretty strong ratings for Season Ten lead to there being a Season Eleven. If I wind up writing a chapter on Season Twenty for *The Ultimate X-Files and Philosophy* in 2032, then I'll officially redact this point and give you a refund.

Both of these forms of lateness have their own potential result upon the work that's late. You might think that the first sort of lateness would result in something pretty dated. After all, if someone wrote a classic nineteenth-century novel in our crazy postmodern age, or a silent movie in the style of the 1920s, then it'd probably stick out as old-fashioned. But I think *The X-Files*, as a resurrection of a Nineties genre show very relevant to the 1990s, demonstrates that this isn't always the case. You'll see what I mean in a bit.

For the second sort of lateness, works that arrive near the end of their creator's lifetime are likely to be riven with the stresses and contradictions created by the awareness of approaching death. We all know that we can't be immortal, like Scully is if certain sources are to be believed, and while we might like to think that a lifetime of this foreknowledge makes it possible for us to fade away gracefully, if Said's right then this attitude is rarely present in what the artists who're actually facing this situation end up producing. These are works that forsake the harmony of earlier life for a prickly, fractured disunity.

So, there's two ways that things can be late. I guess the first way is late as equivalent to *tardy*, while the second is late as equivalent to *old*. And it's not at all inevitable that any object be both. My hypothetical nineteenth-century-style novel, or silent film, might be late in the sense that these forms are no longer timely, while simultaneously produced by a writer at the beginning of his or her career, and so one of *their* early works. That's why Season Ten of *The X-Files* is so interesting. It's resurrecting a genre show that hit its heyday in the 1990s *and* it's a piece of *The X-Files* from towards the end of the show's natural life-span. It's doubly late.

And the tragedy of its double lateness is that the smart moves it makes to deal with its tardiness are undone by the effects of an overly clumsy old-age.

My Struggle

It's a pretty big deal that "My Struggle" starts Season Ten by rewriting (or *retconning*, if you want the technical term—a portmanteau of the words 'retroactive continuity') almost everything that's been going on before. The colonization of mankind was never a shared project between the Syndicate and the aliens, but all the design of the Syndicate, who were using the idea that evil aliens were involved as an elaborate smokescreen to hide what was only ever their own use of technology captured after Roswell. Mulder and Scully were both wrong about what they thought was happening. And so were we.

It seems like the Internet unanimously hates this episode. And if it's all true then it's pretty hard to reconcile with some of the scenes from earlier seasons, which in some cases it even appears to flatly contradict. But what does it mean in terms of lateness? I guess the show's being pretty prickly here, by throwing off everything that we've followed for over twenty years. It's like an old man suddenly rejecting everything he's lived by and everything people liked him for, and going off in a not entirely healthy direction of his own that leaves everyone who's known him over the years wondering exactly what's happened to him. The show is trying really, really hard to throw a curveball that impresses us with how much energy it still has left, but which actually leaves it looking pretty desperate and tired. Or perhaps it's just that the show is so eager to present a new audience with a convenient jumping-on point ("None of what you missed is relevant, since it's all wrong anyway!") that it stops caring about how many of its long-term fans it's going to alienate along the way.

Near the end of its life, it's so intent on doing what it can with the time remaining that it forgets to look back and cherish what it's already achieved, which it's actually in danger of undoing. It's a sad kind of old-age for something that was loved by so many people across the world.

So as a piece of *The X-Files* that's late within the context of its own life-span, it's not wearing its lateness particularly gracefully. The same discordance and difficulty that Said locates within most late style is definitely here. But how about the lateness of this episode within a broader, cultural context? I think here it gets a little more complex. Think about how the original angle of the show's first nine seasons relates to the historical period of its (bio)genesis. The Nineties was exactly the right time for a show where the main visible threat is a government conspiracy, which is hiding the truth from the American people who voted this government in and whom this government is sworn to protect. Before the Nineties, communism was the enemy, embodied in the Soviet Union. Following 9/11, the next big threat was Islamic extremism, embodied by whichever Arab country most needed bombing at any given moment. *The X-Files* emerges in the gap between these two big, scary external threats, which is why its own main threat is a conspiracy orchestrated by our own government. With nothing obvious to fear beyond American borders, our attention turned inwards and located an equivalent threat right there. I guess we just love to be scared of *something*.

And our attention compensated for the lack of an earth-bound external threat by turning to the skies, too. The American government wasn't the problem all on its own, as much as was its co-ordination of an invasion hailing from beyond our planet altogether. And so what "My Struggle" does by making the colonisation threat all about the Syndicate and taking the aliens out of the equation, is actually to stress what *would* have been timely for the Nineties to an even greater extent. We're left with a threat that's *all* internal.

Except (and I hope this isn't news) we're not in the Nineties anymore. So *The X-Files* is actually turning its attention wholly towards a focus that you might think is no longer relevant, that's had its day, that's been and gone. A focus that's very, *very* late. A new season of a show that's about a government conspiracy is already pretty late, if you buy the argument that that's very much a product of the Nineties, but by going against what's been presented before by suggesting that this is all that's happening, "My Struggle" initially left me wondering if it's even realized that everyone else has already gone home and started preparing dinner.

You might just have an issue with my argument by this point. That's cool—the more I thought about it, the more I did too. If you're the sort of person who thinks that the biggest threat to America today isn't Islamic extremism, but something more home-grown, like the gun lobbyists' refusal to accept the need for tighter controls to stop our kids shooting each other, or the media's fear-mongering about immigration, or the unfortunate compromise that is Obamacare meaning that it's still possible to be imprisoned for not paying medical bills, or the continuing existence of Guantanamo Bay, or Donald Trump—well, then you'll probably think that *The X-Files* isn't being any more escapist at all by focussing our attention entirely on enemies on the inside. You might reckon instead that it's actually being pretty canny. If you believe that the true extent of the threat posed by forces from the outside, like Islamic extremism, is just a phantom generated by the media to mask its own agenda, much like "My Struggle" tells us that the show's threats on the outside, the literal aliens, are phantoms generated by the government to mask *its* own agenda, then you might think more kindly towards the show telling us to throw the whole of our attention at what's going on inside our country exactly at the most important moment for us to be doing so. Chris Carter might actually be onto something here. Perhaps he isn't late at all, but the most timely he's ever been.

It's a pity then that the retcon he uses to take us down this new route is so abrupt and awkward that all the majority of viewers will *see* with "My Struggle" is the TV-show equivalent of an aged relative who we once much admired, who's desperately trying to be all modern but who we now wish would please stop busting moves on the dancefloor.

"Founder's Mutation," "Mulder and Scully Meet the Were-Monster," and "Home Again"

The next few episodes are way easier to deal with, since they're considerably more stand-alone and don't involve massive attempts to rewrite everything that's gone before.

On the face of it, "Founder's Mutation" looks like a straightforward story-of-the-week of the sort that predominated during the show's first nine seasons, which might be a sign of lateness that's pretty frustrating right after "My Struggle" shook everything up—a sort of taciturn clinging to the way the show did things when it was young, shaking its fist at this crazy modern world with its bizarre ideas about massive plot threads created in the season premier being followed up in the next episode.

But this is kind of what happens. It's not like Mulder and Scully are actively investigating the new angle on the conspiracy, sure, but Mulder does hypothesize that Augustus Goldman and Dr Sanjay's experiments on kids might be part of the Syndicate's grand plan. Correct me if I'm wrong, but I can't remember Mulder ever wondering whether or not the Flukeman, or the mutant who survives on fatty tissue from "2Shy," or the water parasite from "Agua Mala"—to name just a few random examples!—were the by-product of alien experiments. Sure, the idea first brought up in "The End" that there's alien DNA kicking around in all of our genes that might resurface to seemingly paranormal effects brings all of these stand-alone episodes together under the banner of the mytharc. But this possible connection being made during a pivotal arc episode and not once being mentioned during one of the stand-alones proves my point about how strictly the two types of plot were segregated. I'm reminded of Chris Carter apparently being disappointed that the Cigarette Smoking Man appeared in "F. Emasculata," since this episode was supposed to be a stand-alone. There's arc episodes, and there's stand-alones, and never the twain shall meet. Until "Founder's Mutation."

See too how the plot about the missing kids lets the show have Mulder and Scully wonder how things would've turned out had they not given William up for adoption. The stand-alone plot becomes a way into exploring aspects of the longer-term character arcs, like the previous nine seasons only ever rarely managed, and never this explicitly. There's something here that doesn't feel late at all, but maybe just a little bit modern.

This is even truer in "Home Again." At the start, it seems like there're two separate plots that aren't going to be brought together: the murders of people involved in a city construction project and the sudden death of Scully's mom. These two threads come together thematically through Scully being prompted to worry whether or not she's treated her own child "like trash."

The Trashman created the scary-looking tulpa to look after the homeless people being treated like trash by the city government, but didn't take responsibility for how his darker emotions influenced his offspring into going on a murder spree. There's some thoughtful links between the A story and the B story here, with various ways we can mistreat people, and the importance of owning the effects we have on the people we create, all coming together. The show moves towards this A-story / B-story structure at points of Season Eight and Season Nine, especially in the episodes following Mulder's return in "DeadAlive," but the two strands in these episodes are never actually linked as neatly as here.

So rather than the difficulty and discordance that Said draws our attention to, "Founder's Mutation" and "Home Again" are late episodes of *The X-Files* that reach a new kind of harmony. You'll have worked out that I don't have much to say about "Mulder and Scully Meet the Were-Monster." This isn't because it's rubbish. It's actually very, very good, as you might expect from the guy who wrote "Humbug," "Clyde Bruckman's Final Repose," "War of the Coprophages," and "Jose Chung's *From Outer Space*." I particularly love the twist that it's about a monster being bitten by a man. I just don't have that much to say about its position as late *The X-Files*, because it's doing much the same as Darin Morgan's older episodes, and it's brilliant for the same reasons that they are too.

You might be thinking that this makes it a good example of lateness, since those episodes are over twenty years old, but I'd argue instead that it makes his older episodes seem way *ahead* of their time. There's an ironic playfulness to them that you don't get in the vast majority of Seasons One through Nine. They're the episodes that find the magic cave from "Rush" and use it to show up for class so early that the teacher hasn't even left the lounge yet.

"Babylon" and "My Struggle II"

Four episodes in, we have a show that's late, both in the sense of it being old and in the sense of it being beyond the moment of its timeliness, but which is reacting to this double-lateness by working to be as *timely* as possible. It's redirecting our attention to internal threats to our country, rather than towards the trumped-up external threats that direct out attention elsewhere. It's mixing up the arc episodes and the standalones. Perhaps an old werewolf can learn new tricks, and without dislocating its hip on the way.

But wait! There's two more episodes to go, and I think it's here that the show finally reveals how badly it needs to stop trying to be timely and sit down for a rest instead. I probably don't have to say too much about why exactly "Babylon" got slated for Islamophobia, from daily newspapers to a whole string of media sites and blogs. I can't put it any better than the *Huffington Post* saying that in this particular standalone, it's Islam that's the monster-of-the-week. No matter how many "But they're not all bad!" moments you throw in, the image of a group of bearded brown people being rounded up by the Feds as they're about to embark on a mass suicide-bombing makes it hard to come back from this.

This is the episode that sounds most like what your grandparents might rant over Thanksgiving Dinner. It's the one that most plays most obviously into all the prejudices we have shoved in our face by Fox—that most echoes the voices that tell us that the most dangerous threats facing our country are all infecting us from the outside, rather than any of the crap that our own government and elites are subjecting us to from within.

And this is where the thematic disharmony and disunity that Said locates in works that are towards the end of their natural lifespan is finally cemented in late *The X-Files*. The season finale, "My Struggle II," puts forward a contradictory message to "Babylon." Rather than telling us to be terrified of all these scary people coming into our country from outside and looking to blow us up, it reconfirms the version of the mytharc put forward in "My Struggle" and tells us that external threats are all a smokescreen put forward by our government.

The conspiracy has definitely been the sole work of the Syndicate all along. The Cigarette Smoking Man is looking to save the planet from mankind's destructive nature through engineering mass pandemics, with implanted alien DNA pulled from Roswell giving him the mechanism to save a group of elect. While watching the season opener I was thinking there's at least a chance that this angle will be revealed in the finale as just a further layer of conspiracy to keep Mulder and Scully from The Truth, but nope. "My Struggle II" seems to confirm every word. Sure, there's a UFO appearing at the end to beam Scully away, but even if it's a genuine alien ship rather than one built by the government, I'm guessing that the big twist is going to be that the real aliens were only ever trying to *save* us.

A bold reassertion of the timely message put forward, if awkwardly, by the season opener—but following an episode that runs into exactly the ignorant media-fuelled nonsense that both the opener and the finale would tell us to open our eyes against. "My Struggle" and "My Struggle II" point us towards the internal nature of the real threats to our country and highlight the power of the media to distract us by turning our attention in the wrong direction; "Babylon" just watched an hour of Fox News and is demanding that the town planners refuse the application for a Mosque to stop our kids being Islamified. Mulder and Scully have spent over two decades looking for The Truth. But now I'm not sure that Chris Carter and his show are any clearer than they are about what exactly The Truth might be.

The Older You Get . . .

So there's two ways that something can be late and Season Ten of *The X-Files* runs into both of them. It's resurrecting a genre show from the 1990s with a dated mix of stand-alones and arc episodes, which is all about vast conspiracies, and it's also, I reckon it's safe to say, a piece of *The X-Files* from towards the end of the show's life-span, when *The X-Files* should probably be thinking about setting its affairs in order.

To its credit, Season Ten tries extremely hard to deal with arriving late by acting in a really, really timely fashion once it's here. "My Struggle" begins with a huge effort to make some really relevant points about the threats facing us today and the way our attention can be turned away from them. And in the mixing-up of arc elements into the stand-alone episodes in the middle, there's a recognition that TV has changed and an effort to meet these changes halfway.

It's kind of sad then that its other sort of lateness, its old age, stops it pulling any of these moves off as smoothly as I think it wants to. We've got the incredibly abrupt way it retcons the previous seasons, with plot developments that seem impossible to fit around things we actually saw happening on-screen. What was the Alien Bounty Hunter really up to? What were the Alien rebels rebelling against exactly? Did the flashback from "One Son" where we saw the Syndicate make their deal with the colonists just not happen? Who set fire to them all at the end? And even if the truth about these points *is* actually out there, we've got the unity of the message in "My Struggle" and "My Struggle II" being totally broken by the reactionary Islamophobia of "Babylon."

Like Said suggests it'd be, old *The X-Files* is prickly and disharmonious. So if you're the sort of guy or girl who thinks nothing of showing up late, who expects to just waltz in, pick up the tone of the conversation and cover for your tardy arrival by making the most amazingly relevant points of anyone in the room, then you might want to think about what happened with Season Ten. The adaptability needed to pull this off might be the privilege of the young and so you mightn't be able to get away with it much longer, once the years start to take their toll.

34
Modernist Hero in a Postmodern Age

KARMA WALTONEN

The X-Files combines a modernist hero, who believes "the truth is out there," despite the mechanisms veiling it from him, with a post-colonial fear of the alien and what happens when the native "goes alien," succumbing, both willingly and unwillingly, to the alien agenda.

Many of the most memorable episodes question the existence of the modernist idea of a singular truth, however, with moments of postmodern parody, allusions, and shifting point of view. For example, "Jose Chung's *From Outer Space*" parodies Fox Television specials, alludes to Nabokov's playful masterpiece, *Pale Fire*, and allows us to attempt to piece together a narrative of alien abduction through various characters' perceptions.

The plot is complicated. Jose Chung, a writer, is interviewing multiple witnesses of an incident. Two kids on a date (Chrissy and Harold) may have been abducted by "aliens" (Air Force pilots). They all may have been abducted by another alien—Lord Kinbote. Mulder and Scully are investigating the case, when an alien enthusiast (Blaine) finds an "alien" body, which turns out to be a dead Air Force pilot in a grey alien suit. An electrical technician (Roky) reports seeing the abduction and claims Lord Kinbote spoke to him. Both Blaine and Rocky say they are visited by two different sets of "men in black"—a mysterious pair and Mulder and Scully; Mulder also claims that the men in black visited Scully and hypnotized her.

Mulder has a strange conversation with another Air Force pilot, Lieutenant Jack Schaefer, in which Schaefer claims he and the now dead pilot dressed as aliens to abduct the teenagers, but Lord Kinbote abducted them. However, he is uncertain about his memories, since the Air Force routinely hypnotizes abductees into thinking they were probed by aliens. A short time later, the Air Force says the "alien ship" was an experimental plane and leads the FBI and local authorities to a crash site, where they all see the first dead pilot (whose body had disappeared from the morgue) and Lt. Schaefer, now deceased, being taken away in body bags. In the end, the different versions of the story don't add up, and what happened on the night in question—and on the days following—remains a mystery. Jose Chung publishes *From Outer Space*, about the incident.

My failure to explicate the episode clearly in a short paragraph is of the essence of postmodernism. I am using language to tell you the truth, but my language, my knowledge, and my point of view can only give you one version. And so, is there truth?

Modernism and Postmodernism

Modernism is a word we use to describe both a time and art forms. In time, it refers to the period between the world wars. In terms of art, when we talk about "modern art," we're talking about art created by people in the modern period who intentionally wanted to break the rules that came before them. In visual art, we have a move away from realism, into departures from realism such as impressionism and expressionism. In literature, we move into high allusive texts, with stream of consciousness and heroes who aren't heroic.

One of the main themes in modernism is alienation—we were becoming alienated from nature, from our family, from our labor, and from God. We had developed weapons that allowed us to kill on an unprecedented scale. War took the world, bringing with it a flu that killed millions. In response to these crises, characters in modernist texts search, mostly for Truth (with a capital T), which is presumed to exist.

Postmodernism refers to three things—time, art form, and artistic techniques. Postmodernism is now—the time after WWII. It also refers to art created as a reaction to modernism—modern art was once innovative, but then something else had to come along—and that's postmodernism (it should be noted, however, that most art created in the modern period was not "modern art," and most art created now isn't "postmodern" in technique).

Postmodern art is recognized by certain criteria, but many of these techniques aren't new. For example, Shakespeare often had layers of stories on stage, and layering narratives are a hallmark of postmodernism, but Shakespeare plays (in their original form) are not postmodern. In addition to layers of narratives (otherwise known as metafiction), common postmodern characteristics are allusions and intertexts, a sense of play, and an attention to point of view. While modernism often focused on the internal world of the artist or narrator, postmodernism embraces a cacophony of voices, including those previously ignored in art—we hear the voice of the rich and the poor, the conqueror and the conquered.

Modernist texts are often allusive, but allusions tend to be to works of "high" art—in other words, an author might remake a famous Greek myth. Postmodern allusions can be to anything—low and high, rejecting neither the popular nor the elitist (for instance *The Simpsons*, a postmodern masterpiece, which alludes to Shakespeare and to contemporary commercials, often simultaneously). In the spirit of play, postmodern allusion is often satire or parody.

Modernism and Postmodernism share the theme of alienation. After all, World War II didn't restore our relationships to nature, to our labor, or each other. In fact, it revealed that we were wrong for assuming that we had done the worst of the worst things to each other in World War I.

"Jose Chung's *From Outer Space*" demonstrates alienation, as we'll see further on, but we should remember that the entire series does so as well—in addition to the basic ways in which people are alienated from each other, the show highlights alienation by reminding us that we can "trust no one."

The key idea in postmodernism is the epistemological crisis. Epistemology is the theory and study of knowledge—how do we know what we know? How do we know what is truth? Postmodernism holds that there is no Truth. Its exploration of many different voices and points of view stresses the idea of subjectivity. If every voice gives a different version of the same story, then can we say there is a "real" version? Postmodern narratives resist "The Story" by using naive and unreliable narrators and in their resistance to tidy endings.

Jose Chung's Postmodern Properties

Jose Chung's *From Outer Space*" contains many layers of stories; several come via multiple voices. For example, Scully tells of meeting Roky, and Jose alludes to Roky's "manifesto": "I don't know what was more disturbing: his description of the inner core reincarnated souls' sex orgy or the fact that the whole thing is written in screenplay format."

Versions contradict each other—as when Scully and Blaine disagree on what happened in their conversations; Blaine claims Scully threatened him. Some versions strangely confirm one another. For example, both Roky and Lieutenant Schaefer call the "third" alien Lord Kinbote.

As metafiction, "Jose Chung's *From Outer Space*" includes a parody of a TV show, *Alien Autopsy*, which aired on Fox to terrible reviews. Yet the primary way we might understand "metafiction" here is to think about how this episode is a story about stories and storytelling. Jose, for example, when discussing hypnosis, says, "As a storyteller, I'm fascinated how a person's sense of consciousness can be so transformed by nothing more magical than listening to words. Mere words."

The episode also plays with words and stories by using repetition. For example, many characters say, "You're a dead man" or "I'm a dead man" when threatening or being threatened—this is funny until Schaefer hints at his imminent execution.

Jose Chung tells us that abduction stories often begin with "I know how crazy this is going to sound," which proves true as the abducted and would-be abducted characters (Blaine) recount their tales. Repetition of the phrase "How the hell should I know?" reminds us of the inability of the characters to understand or relate to the Truth.

Besides *Alien Autopsy*, the episode contains many parodies of and allusions to other texts (parody and allusion are two forms of intertextuality, which is how we describe relationships between texts). Thus, *The Caligarian Candidate*, a book by Jose Chung that Scully particularly admires, is a play on *The Manchurian Candidate* and *The Cabinet of Dr. Caligari*. Both references are about hypnosis.

The episode also references various myths of the Men in Black, *Jeopardy!*, *Close Encounters of the Third Kind* (as Schaefer molds mashed potatoes), the infamous Bigfoot video

(Mulder is watching it in bed at the end of the episode, as Jose Chung's voiceover speculates "how Mulder receives any pleasures from life"), and even reviews of the *The X Files*, including David Duchovny being expressionless as an actor.

One of the most significant references comes with the name of the "third" or "red" alien—Lord Kinbote. Nabokov's famous piece of metafiction, *Pale Fire*, features a character called Lord Kinbote—sort of. The book has two main layers—an epic poem written by a character called John Shade, and the Foreword, Commentary, and Index of the poem by the editor, Charles Kinbote. Kinbote reveals through his notes very little about the poem. Instead, the reader discovers more layers of stories—concluding that Kinbote believes, delusionally, that he is an exiled Lord. He likely murdered John Shade and is believed to have killed himself after finishing his editing work. Kinbote is the definitive unreliable narrator, as his megalomania, narcissism, and madness make it impossible to believe his versions of events.

"Madness" appears in the episode, as several characters have PTSD; Roky is unbalanced, although we, like Mulder, wonder whether an unbalanced man had an alien encounter or whether an alien encounter made him unbalanced. However, other characters' versions of events contradict each other, not because they are unreliable (we are certainly supposed to trust Scully), but because perception itself is problematic. For example, we know from "Bad Blood," the episode in which Mulder and Scully give two different versions of run-ins with vampires, that they can remember the same characters and conversations in completely different ways. When we add in problems like Scully being hypnotized, our most trustworthy characters become unreliable witnesses to their own experience.

Thematically, the episode certainly fits postmodern criteria with its focus on alienation, yet in superlative postmodern style, we can use the word here not only to mean distance or an inability to connect, but also alienation in the sense of being alien—to our existence, to our memories, to our species, perhaps. Finally, we can also think of the word in reference to a pun inside of it—the alien nation that the series as a whole warns about, and if Roky's manifesto is to be believed, exists in the inner Earth, near the core. Jose sums up this theme beautifully in his last line: "For although we may not be alone in the universe, in our own separate ways on this planet, we are all alone."

"Jose Chung's *From Outer Space*" is a fan favorite, because of the excellence in the writing and storytelling and the humor. The title of the episode is a pun, as it's both a title with author, but can also be read as a slight on Jose Chung. A visual pun is created in the episode when Blaine describes how he'd hoped to "stumble across" an alien, while literally doing just that.

Detective Manners's "colorful" language is obscured not by network censoring (the familiar "bleep" noise), but with the character literally saying "bleep" or "blank" in scenes that Scully recounts (she "bleeps" herself at one point, too).

Other moments of play reinforce the epistemological crisis. For example, the first shot of the show appears to give us a familiar sight in science fiction: the shot of the bottom of a space ship moving through the stars. As the camera segues to a wider shot, however, we see that our perception was wrong—we're looking at the bottom of a boom lift basket against the night sky.

When Roky is visited by Men in Black, film of the car pulling into and out of the garage is run in reverse, giving a sense of uncanny strangeness. We also play with time, scene, shot, and perception in two moments when one scene changes to another without the camera leaving the face of the actor.

Just as the characters' perceptions are challenged, so are the audience's. Do we believe what Mulder tells Scully about meeting Schaefer in the diner, or do we believe the report of the cook, a "dear friend" of Jose Chung, who claims not to remember the pilot but recounts a tale of Mulder eating an entire pie? Both stories are strange. Both voices have no reason to lie.

Attentive viewers will also note that while they get several different versions of stories, they are also treated to a few pieces of information that none of our narrators have. When Chrissy is hypnotized (for apparently the third time), she is asked to recall what the Air Force officers are saying. She doesn't remember, but the scene gives us the dialogue. Strangely, I find myself trusting those lines the most, since they seem to be independent of our characters' troubled memories.

One of the men in black would likely lecture us about such assumptions: "Your scientists have yet to discover how neural networks create self-consciousness, let alone how the human brain processes two-dimensional retinal images into the three-dimensional phenomenon known as perception. Yet you somehow brazenly declare—seeing is believing?" Schaefer reminds us that hypnosis is another factor in altering perception: "At the base, I've seen people go into an ordinary room with an ordinary bunch of doctors and come out absolutely positive they were probed by aliens." Jack, epitomizing both existential and epistemological crises, says, "I can't be sure of anything anymore! . . . I'm not sure we're even having this conversation. I don't know if these mashed potatoes are really here. I don't know if you even exist."

An Inconclusive Conclusion

By the end of the episode, there's little we can be sure of, but this unsatisfying ending is typical of postmodern works; the show stresses its polysemic nature at the same time it winks self-referentially at its audience. Dana delivers the ultimate commentary, all while pulling on her earlobe (which, on *The Carol Burnette Show*, meant saying hi to a loved one)—"I know it probably doesn't have the sense of closure that you want, but it has more than some of our other cases."

One of the things that makes the show compelling and frustrating is ultimately the epistemological crisis. Mulder is on a modernist quest—he believes the Truth is out there, and he believes he can find it. However, our modernist quester is on a postmodern journey, where truth doesn't necessarily exist.

There's always a moment when I teach this episode in which a student asks me (the literature PhD) what "really" happened.

My answer's always the same: How the hell should I know?

35
Heidegger and *The X-Files*

FRANK SCALAMBRINO

Season Seven, Episode 10 of *The X-Files* is titled "Closure," and Episode 9 is titled "Sein und Zeit," the original German title of philosopher Martin Heidegger's *Being and Time*. These two episodes include the death of Mulder's mother and the much-anticipated closure brought by the paranormal proof of his sister's death.

Mulder's account of what's "typical" regarding alien abductions from the *X-Files* inception included a discussion of time and the difference between alien and human being. In the Pilot episode Mulder describes the "typical profile of an alien abduction" to Scully, noting "Time as we know it stopped and something took control over it" ("Pilot"). The philosophical idea at work here is that the passing of time may be experienced differently by different beings. In fact, that humans can experience the passing of time differently in different "modes of being" should count as evidence that even within the context of human life there is a spectrum along which different time experiences can be had.

In other words, it shows that the passing of time *can be* different from what we may understand as the usual human everyday experience of time's passing. Concrete examples of different modes of being for humans may be the intense experience of "flow" described by athletes, meditative zen states, and the different relation to time that the traumatic awareness of your own mortality can bring—you might relate differently to the next twenty-four hours if you believed they would be the last hours of your life.

Four Concentric Circles

Just as clearly, there is a difference between how long your body will live and how long you think it may live. Heidegger characterized the difference between these two ways of relating to your own *being* alive in terms of "authenticity" and "inauthenticity." Authenticity is more open to the truth of being, and authenticity realizes that the time of being alive is the time of being. This will relate to the "automatic writing" which occurs in these two *X-Files* episodes in that the characters who are more open to the truth of being are better able to render its truth in writing.

A brief thought experiment will make this clear. Imagine four concentric circles. Imagine taking the outer circle and pulling it toward you and away from the center circle, creating a cone with four "levels." Now imagine that the cone is spinning, tornado-like, and the force of the spinning is coming from the tip of the cone. In this visualization, the entire cone represents being and its spinning represents the movement of time. Because humans would occupy the outer, fourth level, of the spinning cone, the range of different experiences of time's passing would be confined to that level for humans.

However, aliens, *being* at a level with a higher spinning rate would have a different range within which to experience time's passing. Yet, because all of the spinning belongs to the one cone of being, the passing of time on every level relates to the passing of time on every other level. This is how, as Mulder put it, "Time as we know it stopped and something took control over it" (Pilot). The alien activity would be moving at a faster speed, as if (picking these numbers simply for the sake of illustration) the passing of five minutes for such alien beings were like the passing of five days or more for humans.

To "exist," then, for Heidegger would be to stand out on some level of being. Because the entire cone is being, it cannot *not be*; in other words, though the different expressions of beings which stand out in the spinning cone of being die, what is happening in terms of the cone is that the being that was standing out returns to being. So, when Mulder invokes the more traditional understanding of the "immortality of the soul," we will understand it in this way, in terms of being as what is most primary.

Finally, from the perspective of being, because when a human being dies it is spinning being's return to itself and humans who are alive are the standing out expressions of this same being, we can understand how the dead could conceivably communicate with the living. In other words, *being* dead and *being* alive would be two different expressions of (the spinning cone of) *being*.

Sein und Zeit

In the "Sein und Zeit" episode the alien intervening forces are referred to as "old souls," and in what may be read as a kind of paraphrase of the above characterization of Heidegger's discussion of being and time, Mulder expresses the following:

> I want to believe . . . in a truth beyond our own, hidden and obscured from all but the most sensitive eyes. In the endless procession of souls in what cannot and will not be destroyed. I want to believe we are unaware of God's eternal recompense and sadness that we cannot see His truth. That that which is born still lives and cannot be buried in the cold Earth, but only waits to be born again at God's behest. Where in ancient starlight we lay in repose. ("Sein und Zeit")

Philosophically the theme of connecting souls with "starlight" goes all the way back to Plato's *Timaeus*, and in the "Sein und Zeit" companion episode, "Closure," Mulder explains, "The light is billions of years old by the time we see it. From the beginning of time right past us into the future" ("Closure").

In a moment we will notice how Mulder's comment about the future relates to *Being and Time*. Likewise, regarding the alien abducted children we also hear, "The children were transported by a spiritual intervention," and "Maybe they are souls, Scully, that travel through time as starlight" ("Closure"). The starlight comments should be understood as referring to the potential to span the different levels in our spinning cone thought experiment. It is as if *The X-Files* were using the term "starlight" to refer to being as it transcends the temporary standing out of an individual being's existence.

What remains then is for us to account for how human beings become open to communication from a different "level" of being. Returning to the imagery of the spinning cone, we need to notice two things. First, an authentic relation to death would be one in which we understand death to be the re-cycling, as it were, of being. Second, having such an authentic relation to death would, thereby, be an authentic relation to being, and it, according to Heidegger, would constitute a change of mode in being such that the experience of time's passing would also change. This is understood, then, not just in terms of an authentic relation to the present moment but also to the past and to the future. Therefore, the authentic relation to death opens humans to experience the past and the future in terms of the spinning cone instead of the particular moments of their individual being presently standing out from the spinning.

In this way, human beings become open to the spinning of the cone making it easier for alien beings who occupy different levels of the cone to relate to them. Heidegger characterizes the openness in terms of "care," and though he explicitly warns us not to equate this care with "love," it seems clear that the death of those with whom we are concerned may help us alter an inauthentic everyday-kind of relation to death. Thus we see the parents of the abducted children become open to the possibility that the children may still *be* somewhere else. We hear the mother of one abducted child communicate to the mother of another abducted child, "Your little girl is okay" ("Sein und Zeit"). Thus, in these episodes it is as if an "authentic" relation to death opens certain characters to alien intervention for the sake of communication and even a kind of saving abduction.

Death

Throughout the two episodes numerous characters are "haunted" by visions of the dead, and some characters are able to act as conduits for communications from dead beings. Scully even explicitly refers to one instance of such communication as a séance, and the "psychic" involved explains, "They will come to you if you are ready to see" ("Closure"). Those characters who can "see" and those who cannot seem to fit with the Heideggerian characterization of their relation to death, and thereby to being, in terms of authenticity and inauthenticity.

As Mulder's relation to his mother's death begins to change, he becomes open to death in such a way that eventually leads to his seeing his sister as a starlight being, thus providing his needed "closure." This closure is not only closure regarding the loss of his sister but philosophically it is as if the opening to being provides a closure to the inauthentic relation to time's passing. When Mulder is walking hand-in-hand with the starlight expression of his sister, he also appears to be glowing with starlight—just like his sister. In the same scene, when Mulder attempts to communicate to "Harold" the psychic, as the mother previously communicated, that his son is "okay," the psychic, who at times seems to experience the haunting presence of dead beings as if they were hallucinations forced upon him, shouts denial regarding his son's death, and is ultimately unable to see his dead son who is also present in the scene as a celestial "starlight" being.

We learn that when the children are abducted the alien intervention includes their mothers engaging in an act of "automatic writing," much like the event in which Mulder writes the name of the Air Force Base as his then dead mother is attempting to communicate with him. In regard to the mothers, there are two peculiar aspects of this writing which occur for them both. First, the automatic writing communicates a prohibition against telling others, yet both mothers end up telling Mulder with seemingly no negative consequences. Second, an infamous and enigmatic phrase is communicated, so memorable that some commentators refer to the episodes by referring to it: "No one shoots at Santa Claus."

On the one hand, notice how the prohibition against "telling" functions as a test of belief for the parents regarding whether they believe their child may still *be* safe somewhere. The children have disappeared, and so this challenges their care-givers to take a stand in relation to death and time. In other words, the care-givers must remain resolute with an authentic relation to the future, and could only do so, it seems, if they believe they may actually encounter their child again in the future. On the other hand, the Santa Claus comment is perplexing because—for some time—it suggests that there may be a straightforward explanation for the missing children. That is, perhaps it was the case that the children were abducted by a human dressed as Santa Claus.

Santa Claus?

Yet, in light of the Heidegger reference from the first episode's title, the enigmatic "No one shoots at Santa Claus" phrase may be seen as communication from the alien level of being into the human level through those who have "passed the test" of authenticity in being tested by death. Their authentic relation to the death of their children functions as openness to being a site for haunting, and thus they may be put in the service of the alien level of being. Why the alien level of being would want to bring justice to a human dressed as Santa Claus and abducting children is a different question, and beyond the scope of this chapter.

Lastly, these two episodes provide what Scully refers to as the "closure" that "Mulder deserves" ("Closure"), addressing the "mytharc" or mythology of *The X-Files* by revealing the role of the Cigarette Smoking Man in Mulder's sister "Samantha's" abduction. Similar to the communications leading to the apprehension of the murderous "Santa Claus" character, the implication is that the alien forces may actually be benevolent. In conjunction with communication from Mulder's mother after-death, we learn the smoking man had abducted Mulder's sister and was performing painful testing on her. It was from a "locked room," then, that she was abducted by an alien being, and we are told that had she not been abducted she would have returned for future torture from the Cigarette Smoking Man.

Thus, in terms of a Heideggerian theory of death, the *X-Files* companion episodes, "Sein und Zeit" and "Closure," may be more comprehensively understood. It seems as though the discussion of being and time stemming from Heidegger's *Sein und Zeit* (*Being and Time*) may be at work in the background of *The X-Files* understanding of alien abduction, séance-like "automatic writing," and celestial "starlight" beings, providing closure by providing a philosophical account in which the desire to believe may rest in peace.

The truth of being is out there.

Bibliography

Anzaldúa, Gloria. 1999. *Borderlands / la frontera: The New Mestiza*. Aunt Lute.

Aristotle. 1998. *Politics*. Hackett.

———. 1999. *Nicomachean Ethics*. Hackett.

———. 2010. *De Anima*. Hackett.

Asaro, Peter. 2011. A Body to Kick, But Still No Soul to Damn: Legal Perspectives on Robotics. In Patrick Lin, Keith Abney, and George Bekey, eds., *Robot Ethics: The Ethical and Social Implications of Robotics*. MIT Press.

———. 2012. On Banning Autonomous Lethal Systems: Human Rights, Automation, and the Dehumanizing of Lethal Decision-making. Special Issue on New Technologies and Warfare, *International Review of the Red Cross* 94:886.

———. 2012. How Just Could a Robot War Be? In Erica L. Gaston and Patti Tamara Lenard, eds., *Ethics of 21st Century Military Conflict*. Idebate.

Asma, Stephen T. 2009. *On Monsters: An Unnatural History of Our Worst Fears*. Oxford University Press.

Barkun, Michael. 2006 [2003]. *A Culture of Conspiracy: Apocalyptic Visions in Contemporary America*. University of California Press.

Beauvoir, Simone de. 1976 [1947]. *The Ethics of Ambiguity*. Citadel.

Bergin, Lisa. Latina Feminist Metaphysics and Genetically Modified Foods. *Journal of Agricultural and Environmental Ethics*, Vol. 22, No. 3 (2009).

Bowman, Karlyn, and Andrew Rugg. 2013. *Public Opinion on Conspiracy Theories*. American Enterprise Institute.

Brotherton, Rob. 2013. Towards a Definition of 'Conspiracy Theory'. *PsyPAG Quarterly* 88 (September).

———. 2015. *Suspicious Minds: Why We Believe Conspiracy Theories*. Bloomsbury.

Byford, Jovan. 2011. *Conspiracy Theories: A Critical Introduction*. Palgrave Macmillan.

Carey, Thomas J., and Donald R. Schmitt. 2007. *Witness to Roswell: Unmasking the 60-Year Cover-Up*. New Page.

Carroll, Noel. 1990. *The Philosophy of Horror: Or, Paradoxes of the Heart*. Routledge.

Carter, Chris. 2012 [2007]. *Science and Psychic Phenomena: The Fall of the House of Skeptics*. Inner Traditions.

Cartwright, Nancy. 1999. *The Dappled World: A Study of the Boundaries of Science*. Cambridge University Press.

Coady, David, ed. 2006. *Conspiracy Theories: The Philosophical Debate*. Ashgate.

Coleman, Loren, and Jerome Clark. 1999. *Cryptozoology A to Z: The Encyclopedia of Loch Monsters, Sasquatch, Chupacabras, and Other Authentic Mysteries of Nature*. Fireside.

Cummings, Mary L. 2004. Automation Bias in Intelligent Time Critical Decision Support Systems. *AIAA 1st Intelligent Systems Technical Conference*.

———. 2006. Automation and Accountability in Decision Support System Interface Design. *Journal of Technology Studies* 32:1.

———. 2006. Integrating Ethics in Design through the Value-Sensitive Design Approach. *Science and Engineering Ethics* 12:4.

Daston, Lorraine, and Katharine Park. 2001. *Wonders and the Order of Nature, 1150–1750*. Zone.

Deutsch, David. 1998. *The Fabric of Reality: The Science of Parallel Universes—and Its Implications*. Penguin.

Didion, Joan. 1990 [1979]. *The White Album*. Farrar, Straus, and Giroux.

Docherty, Bonnie. 2012. *Losing Humanity: The Case against Killer Robots*. Human Rights Watch.

Douglas, Mary. 1966. *Purity and Danger*. Routledge.

Dupré, John. 1995. *The Disorder of Things: Metaphysical Foundations of the Disunity of Science*. Harvard University Press.

Fetzer, James H., ed. 2000. *Murder in Dealey Plaza: What We Know Now that We Didn't Know Then about the Death of JFK*. Catfeet Press.

———, ed. 2007. *The 9/11 Conspiracy: The Scamming of America*. Catfeet Press.

———, ed. 2003. *The Great Zapruder Film Hoax: Deceit and Deception in the Death of JFK*. Catfeet Press.

Finnie, P.S., and Karim Nader. 2012. The Role of Metaplasticity Mechanisms in Regulating Memory Destabilization and Reconsolidation. *Neuroscience and Biobehavioral Reviews* 36:7.

Fisher, Walter R. 1989. *Human Communication as Narration: Toward a Philosophy of Reason, Value, and Action*. University of South Carolina Press.

Friedman, John Block. 2000. *The Monstrous Races in Medieval Art and Thought*. Syracuse University Press.

Galliott, Jai. 2015, *Military Robots: Mapping the Moral Landscape*. Ashgate.

———. 2015. Artificial Intelligence and Space Robotics: Questions of Responsibility. In Jai Galliott, ed., *Commercial Space Exploration: Ethics, Policy, and Guidance*. Ashgate.

Goertzel, Ted. 1994. Belief in Conspiracy Theories. *Political Psychology* 15:4 (December).

Graham, Angus C. 1989. *Disputers of the Tao: Philosophical Argument in Ancient China*. Open Court.

Heil, J. 2004. *Philosophy of Mind: A Contemporary Introduction*. Routledge.

Harris, S.H. 2002. *Factories of Death: Japanese Biological Warfare, 1932–1945, and the American Cover-Up*. Routledge.

Highwater, Jamake. 1981. *The Primal Mind: Vision and Reality in Indian America*. Harper and Row.

Hodges, Andrew. 2014 [1983]. *Alan Turing: The Enigma*. Princeton University Press.

Hofstadter, Richard. 2008 [1966]. *The Paranoid Style in American Politics*. Vintage.

James, William. 1979 [1897]. The Will to Believe. In *The Will to Believe and Other Essays in Popular Philosophy*. Harvard University Press.

Jaworski, W. 2011. *Philosophy of Mind: A Comprehensive Introduction*. Wiley-Blackwell.

Kierkegaard, Søren. 1990. *Three Upbuilding Discourses*. Princeton University Press.

Kopp, Sheldon. 1972. *If You Meet the Buddha on the Road, Kill Him! The Pilgrimage of Psychotherapy Patients*. Science and Behavior Books.

Kowalski, Dean, ed. 2009. *The Philosophy of The X-Files: Updated Edition*. University Press of Kentucky.

Kuhn, Thomas S. 2012 [1962]. *The Structure of Scientific Revolutions*. University of Chicago Press.

Laing, R.D. 1971. *The Politics of Experience*. Ballantine.

Lakatos, Imre, and Alan Musgrave, eds. 1970. *Criticism and the Growth of Knowledge*. Cambridge University Press.

Laozi. 2007. *Daodejing: A Complete Translation and Commentary*. Open Court.
Leeming, David Adams. 1998. *Mythology: The Voyage of the Hero*. Oxford University Press.
Lewis, David. 1979. Prisoner's Dilemma Is a Newcomb Problem. *Philosophy and Public Affairs* 8:3.
Loftus, Elizabeth F. 1988. *Memory: Surprising New Insights into How We Remember and Why We Forget*. Rowman and Littlefield.
———. 1992. When a Lie Becomes Memory's Truth: Memory Distortion after Exposure to Misinformation. *Current Directions in Psychological Science* 1:4.
Lovecraft, H.P. 1927. Supernatural Horror in Literature. *The Recluse* 1.
Lowe, E.J. 2000. *An Introduction to the Philosophy of Mind*. Cambridge University Press.
Lucretius. 2007. *The Nature of Things*. Penguin.
Mannison, Don. 1985. On Being Moved by Fiction. *Philosophy* 60:231.
Mathias, Andreas. 2004. The Responsibility Gap: Ascribing Responsibility for the Actions of Learning Automata. *Ethics and Information Technology* 6.
Meyrink, Gustav. 1995 [1915]. *The Golem*. Dedalus.
Mill, John Stuart. 1998 [1874]. Nature. In *Three Essays on Religion*. Prometheus.
———. 2002. *Utilitarianism*. Hackett.
Mosteller, Timothy. 2014. *Theories of Truth: An Introduction*. Bloomsbury.
Nickerson, R.S. Confirmation Bias: A Ubiquitous Phenomenon in Many Guises. *Review of General Psychology* 2:2.
Okasha, S. 2002. *Philosophy of Science: A Very Short Introduction*. Oxford University Press.
Pickel, Kerri. 2004. When a Lie Becomes the Truth: The Effects of Self-Generated Misinformation on Eyewitness Memory. *Memory* 12:1.
Pieper, Josef. 2009. *Leisure: The Basis of Culture*. Ignatius.
Plato. 1997. *Plato: Complete Works*. Hackett.
Poole, W. Scott. 2011. *Monsters in America: Our Historical Obsession with the Hideous and the Haunting*. Baylor University Press.
Popper, Karl R. 2004 [1935]. *The Logic of Scientific Discovery*. Routledge.
Reichardt, Jasia. 1978. *Robots: Fact, Fiction, and Prediction*. Penguin.
Roche, Kennedy F. 1974. *Rousseau: Stoic and Romantic*, Methuen.
Rousseau, Jean-Jacques. 1979. *A Discourse on Inequality*. Penguin.
———. 1980 [1783]. *Reveries of the Solitary Walker*. Penguin.

Sagoff, Mark. 2003. Genetic Engineering and the Concept of the Natural. In V.V. Gehring, ed. *Genetic Prospects: Essays on Biotechnology, Ethics, and Public Policy*. Rowman and Littlefield.

Samuels, Richard, Stephen Stich, and Luc Faucher. 2004. Reason and Rationality. In M. Sintonen, J. Wolenski, and I. Niiniluoto, eds., *Handbook of Epistemology*. Kluwer.

Sartre, Jean-Paul. 2007. *Existentialism Is a Humanism*. Yale University Press.

Scalambrino, Frank. 2016. *Meditations on Orpheus: Love, Death, and Transformation*. Black Water Phoenix Press.

Schechtman, Marya. 2007. *The Constitution of Selves*. Cornell University Press.

Schmitt, Frederick F., ed. 2003. *Theories of Truth*. Wiley-Blackwell.

Schneider, Kirk J. 1999. *Horror and the Holy: Wisdom-Teachings of the Monster Tale*. Open Court.

Searle, John R. 1992. *The Rediscovery of the Mind*. MIT Press.

———. 1997. *The Mystery of Consciousness*. NYRB.

Shelley, Mary. 2007 [1818]. *Frankenstein: Or, the Modern Prometheus*. Penguin.

Shermer, Michael. 2002. *Why People Believe Weird Things*. Holt.

Simon, Anne. 1999. *The Real Science Behind The X-Files: Microbes, Meteorites, and Mutants*. Touchstone.

Skeptical Inquirer. 1997. Interview with Chris Carter. *Skeptical Inquirer* (January–Feburary).

Sparrow, Robert. 2007. Killer Robots. *Journal of Applied Philosophy* 24.

———. 2016. Robots and Respect: Assessing the Case against Autonomous Weapon Systems. *Ethics and International Affairs* 30:1.

Sprouse, Bill. 2013. *The Domestic Life of the Jersey Devil: Or, BeBop's Miscellany*. Oyster Eye.

Suppes, Patrick. 2010. *Models and Methods in the Philosophy of Science*. Springer.

Swami, Viren. 2012. Social Psychological Origins of Conspiracy Theories: The Case of the Jewish Conspiracy Theory in Malaysia. *Frontiers in Psychology* 3 (August).

Swami, Viren, Tomas Chamorro-Premuzic, and Adrian Furnham. 2010. Unanswered Questions: A Preliminary Investigation of Personality and Individual Difference Predictors of 9/11 Conspiracist Beliefs. *Applied Cognitive Psychology* 24.

Szasz. Thomas S. 1988 [1977]. *The Manufacture of Madness*. Harper Collins.

———. 1997 [1987]. *Insanity: The Idea and Its Consequences*. Syracuse University Press.

Uscinski, Joseph E., and Joseph M. Parent. 2014. *American Conspiracy Theories*. Oxford University Press.

Van Duzer, Chet. 2013. *Sea Monsters on Medieval and Renaissance Maps*. The British Library.

Vaughn, Lewis, and Theodore Schick. 1999. *How to Think about Weird Things: Critical Thinking for a New Age*. Mayfield.

Wakefield, Hollida, and Ralph Underwager. 1994. *Return of the Furies: An Investigation into Recovered Memory Therapy*. Open Court.

Walton, Kendall. 1978. Fearing Fictions. *Journal of Philosophy* 75:1.

Warren, Mary Anne. 1973. On the Moral and Legal Status of Abortion. *The Monist* 57:1.

Williams, Bernard. 1973. The Makropulos Case: Reflections on the Tedium of Immortality. In Williams, *Problems of the Self*. Cambridge University Press.

Zhuangzi. 2009. *Zhuangzi: The Essential Writings*. Hackett.

The X-Philes

Jerold J. Abrams is Associate Professor of Philosophy at Creighton University in Omaha, Nebraska. He's the key figure in an ongoing academic charade, the plot to conceal the truth about the existence of the forms of all being. It's a global conspiracy, actually, with key players at the highest levels of power that reaches down to the lives of every man, woman, and child on this planet. So, of course, no one believes him. He's an annoyance to his superiors, and a joke to his peers. They call him Spooky Abrams, who came out of the cave when he was just a kid, and now chases after sophists with a book and a gun.

Robert Arp is a research analyst working for the US Army. That they pay him to suppress the truth about alien abductions, communications from the dead, and what really happened on 9/11 is a completely baseless story disseminated by pederasts with severe mental health problems directed by Vladimir Putin. There is absolutely no evidence for this completely baseless story and the evidence is obviously fabricated.

Scott Bandy is an independent scholar who has an interest in ethics, natural law, and conspiracy theories. He hopes to use these interests towards his goal of working in the basement of a major government agency, where it's nice and spooky.

Adam Barkman is an associate professor of philosophy at Redeemer University College. One of his most vivid memories of *The X-Files* is holding his sleeping baby daughter Heather in his arms, only to have her suddenly sit up and move back and forth dance-like when the *X-Files* theme came on, and then promptly fall back down into a deep sleep when it was over. He's sure this was just the music, nothing paranormal whatsoever.

Richard Bilsker is Professor of Philosophy and Social Sciences at the College of Southern Maryland, where he has taught since 1995. He has broad teaching and research interests in philosophy, political science, sociology, psychology, and the humanities. His books include *On Bergson* and *On Jung*. His articles and book reviews have appeared in *Teaching Philosophy*, *Humanity and Society*, *Idealistic Studies*, *ephemera*, and *Hyle*. His hobbies include tabletop roleplaying games, single-malt scotch (especially during election season), *Doctor Who*, and wondering whether he would be better off if he were a cat.

Cam Cobb is an associate professor in the Faculty of Education at the University of Windsor. His research focuses on such topics as social justice in special education, narrative pedagogy, and co-teaching in adult learning contexts. Over the past few years his work was published in a variety of journals including *Per la Filosofia*, *Cinema: Journal of Philosophy and the Moving Image*, *F. Scott Fitzgerald Review*, *British Journal of Special Education*, *International Journal of Bilingual Education and Bilingualism*, and *International Journal of Inclusive Education*.

Marc W. Cole is a PhD student at the University of Leeds. His project is about showing how Aristotle's version of a hylomorphic psychological theory helps contemporary hylomorphists with the problems surrounding mental causation. Before academia, he had an eight-year stint in the US Navy as a Russian Linguist. He neither confirms nor denies that he had any experience with aliens of any sort, whether bounty hunters, black oil, or alien-human hybrids. If anyone has seen Marc with such beings, it was probably in a swamp with lots of decaying organic matter. What they saw was swamp gas, nothing more.

Elizabeth F. Cooke is Professor of Philosophy at Creighton University in Omaha, Nebraska. A ticking time bomb of insanity, according to Jose Chung in *From Outer Space*, her quest into the philosophical unknown has so warped her reason, one shudders to think how she can teach or write at all.

Steven B. Cowan teaches philosophy and religion at Lincoln Memorial University in Harrogate, Tennessee. He is co-editor and contributor to *Idealism and Christian Philosophy* and co-author of *The Love of Wisdom: A Christian Introduction to Philosophy*. His primary interests are in the metaphysics of free will, the nature and extent of divine providence, and Berkeleyan idealism. He doesn't believe in aliens because the ghost that haunts his house assures him they don't exist. The werewolf next door disagrees, but what does he know?

Marvin Lee Dupree is a PhD student at the University of Rijeka, focusing mainly on ethics, aesthetics, philosophy of film, and cognitive science. In his own personal life Marvin shares the obsessive qualities of Mulder, in addition to loving Mulder's snide and charming remarks. Like Mulder, he often hears the following question: Are you drunk?

Charlene Elsby is an Assistant Professor in the Philosophy Department at Indiana University–Purdue University, Fort Wayne, where her primary duties are to deceive, inveigle, and obfuscate, especially as regards Aristotle and phenomenology.

Justin Fetterman is a writer and teacher in Vermont, whose work has appeared in *Midwestern Gothic* and *The Portland Review Online*. He wrote a chapter in *The Princess Bride and Philosophy: Inconceivable!* (2016). He cannot explain why his watch is always nine minutes off.

Brent Franklin is a Philosophy Lecturer at Rowan College at Burlington County. Spending most of his time with philosophy and science fiction, he sometimes has trouble distinguishing between reality and fiction. He's fairly certain reality is the one without all the aliens, but just to be safe, he regularly checks for alien implants.

David Freeman is a graduate student in history at the University of New England. After Oxford rejected his application to study "aliens and weird shit, just like Mulder," he settled for the University of Queensland, where he received his BA in history and English lit before inflicting his uncontrollable mind on the philosophy department. He previously contributed his thoughts on test tube monsters to *Jurassic Park and Philosophy: The Truth Is Terrifying* (2014). When not chasing monsters through the annals of history, he enjoys long romantic strolls through cemeteries at midnight, swimming laps in the Bermuda Triangle, and tossing pencils at the ceiling of his apartment.

Mirela Fuš is a PhD student at the University of Oslo and the University of St Andrews. Her main philosophical interests are in philosophy of language and mind, social ontology, and cognitive science. If you invoke Mirela's anger she might correct you and point out the numerous logical fallacies and cognitive biases you were guilty of in the last ten minutes while still managing to complain about fake cream cheese in the process.

Diane Gall is an instructor of philosophy and religious studies at Medicine Hat College in Alberta, Canada. Her research interests include philosophy of psychology, the ethics of conflict, XXXXXXXXX, and philosophical themes and problems in popular culture. She has worked in such places as XXXXXXXXXXXXXXXXXX and XXXXXXXXXXXXXXXXXX, as well as XXXXXXXXXXXXXXXXXX where she was instrumental in XXXXXXXXXXXXXXXXXX. Despite everything, she really does still think that the truth is out there. She's just not confident she'll know it when she sees it.

Jai Galliott is a Research Fellow at the University of New South Wales in Sydney, Australia, and does not-so-secret stuff for the Australian Department of Defence. His works include *Military Robots: Mapping the Moral Landscape* (2015).

Chris Gavaler teaches at Washington and Lee University and is the author of *On the Origin of Superheroes: From the Big Bang to Action Comics No. 1*. He is also co-authoring *With Great Power: How Superhero Comics Channel and Challenge Philosophy* with Nathaniel Goldberg. He lives in Virginia and has driven the Blue Ridge Parkway many times without ever being abducted. Also, there's no cable car lift.

Nathaniel Goldberg works a couple of hours from Quantico at Washington and Lee University as an associate professor of philosophy. He has written a scholarly book called *Kantian Conceptual Geography* and is finishing a popular book with Chris Gavaler called *With Great Power: How Superhero Comics Channel and Challenge Philosophy*. Also *no es un hombre . . . es el chupacabra.*

Kyle A. Hammonds teaches communication studies at the University of North Texas and has interests in popular culture and narrative theory. Like Scully, no matter how many times Kyle is abducted by aliens, he's still got his doubts about extraterrestrials. As an academic, he sympathizes with Mulder's tendency to work in dusty basements filled with books while associating with weirdos obsessed with alternate perspectives on history.

Tim Jones teaches Literature at the University of East Anglia in the UK and is also an elected councillor for Norwich City Council. His short, red-haired American partner accompanied him through his rewatch of *The X-Files* Seasons One through Nine. Whenever he mentioned that they'd need to watch five episodes in a row to be caught up in time for Season Ten, she'd look exasperated and insist "But Jones, there's simply no evidence for that!"

Chris Ketcham earned his doctorate at the University of Texas at Austin. He teaches business and ethics for the University of Houston Downtown. His research interests are risk management, applied ethics, social justice, and East-West comparative philosophy. Scully asks Mulder what this koan means, "If you meet the Buddha on the road, kill him." Mulder replies, "What do *you* do when you discover your alien within?"

S. Evan Kreider is an associate professor of philosophy at the University of Wisconsin–Fox Valley, with interests in ethics and aesthetics. He's looking forward to the time when President Trump builds that wall to keep all the aliens out—and makes them pay for it too!

Courtland Lewis is Program Co-ordinator and Assistant Professor of Philosophy and Religious Studies at Owensboro Community and Technical College. He is the Series Editor of Vernon Press's series on the Philosophy of Forgiveness, co-editor of *Doctor Who and Philosophy*, *More Doctor Who and Philosophy*, and *Red Rising and Philosophy*, as well as editor of *Futurama and Philosophy* and *Divergent and Philosophy*. Court is also a crop circle specialist with advanced training in alien mind-control techniques, which he plans to use on television studio executives to bring back all of his favorite shows.

Dennis Loughrey has a PhD in philosophy from the Australian National University and currently teaches media studies at Monash University. He sort of wonders whether this has anything to do with Malcolm Gladwell's ten-thousand-hour rule, which for him (Dennis, not Gladwell) has been met by intensely viewing over ten thousand hours of TV.

Rob Luzecky is a lecturer in the Department of Philosophy at Indiana-Purdue University, Fort Wayne. He has a basement office with a filing cabinet and no windows. When he's not talking about the existence of works of art, conspiracies, and other fascinating stuff, he busies himself by throwing pencils into the ceiling.

Daniel Malloy has been teaching philosophy and writing about philosophy and popular culture for a while now. He's published chapters on *Star Wars*, *Inception*, *The Terminator*, Batman, Superman, Green Lantern, Iron Man, Spider-Man, and The Avengers. In his spare time, he's been tracking the exploits of a shadowy, quasi-governmental agent through the short fiction works of Raul Bloodworth. Jack Colquitt won't elude him much longer.

Kevin Meeker is Professor of Philosophy at the University of South Alabama and has interests in Ethics, Epistemology, Philosophy of Religion, Philosophy of Logic and Early Modern Philosophy. His first job was copy editor for *The Magic Bullet* Newsletter, published by the Lone Gunmen.

Joshua Mugg is Lecturer in Philosophy at Indiana University Kokomo. He is a philosopher of mind with his eye on reasoning, belief, faith, and racism. As a kid, his mom kept replacing parts of his blankie as they wore out, making him worried that eventually blankie would cease to exist.

Despite all appearances of being an innocent amateur philosopher, our records indicate that **Neil Mussett** is actually a high-ranking member of a global institution deemed "too big to fail" by the federal government.

Jeremy Pierce earned his PhD from Syracuse University and now teaches at Le Moyne College. His main interests are philosophy of race, philosophy of religion, and metaphysics. He works out of an office in the basement and seeks out classes no one has wanted to teach in years about subjects that no one thinks are worth the time and many have thought were not even genuinely philosophy. He hasn't yet been assigned a research assistant with a secret agenda to debunk his work, but that's really only a matter of time.

Michael K. Potter believes the truth is out there, though we may never know when we find it. He's a philosopher by temperament and education—employed as Teaching and Learning Specialist in the Centre for Teaching and Learning, University of Windsor—whose research focuses on applications of pragmatist, anarchist, and nihilist philosophy in higher education. The author of *Bertrand Russell's Ethics* (2006), most recently he was co-editor of a special issue of the *Canadian Journal for the Scholarship of Teaching and Learning* on the role of the arts and humanities.

William Rodriguez is Assistant Professor of Religion and Philosophy at Bethune Cookman University and is interested in political philosophy. Professor Rodriguez is convinced that during his childhood he was protected from bullies by the chupacabra.

Frank Scalambrino is Senior Lecturer in Philosophy at the University of Akron and an adjunct assistant professor at Walsh University, where he teaches both terrestrial and extraterrestrial thinking.

Official sources say that **John M. Thompson** is Associate Professor of Philosophy and Religious Studies at Christopher Newport University. Unconfirmed reports indicate that he no longer wants to believe, after finding that his beloved *X-Files* coffee mug had broken during one of his many unexplained absences. Local lore holds that he continues to haunt the wilds of the Virginia peninsula but sightings of him are increasingly rare.

Special Agent **Jason Walker**, PhD, XXXX XXXX XXXX, and earned his doctorate in philosophy while training out of the University of Wisconsin field office in Madison. He earned special commendation for the XXXX XXXX XXXX XXXX affair, which XXXX XXXX XXXX. He previously conducted intelligence operations in XXXX, at XXXXXX, in XXXXXX, and throughout the Washington, DC area, at the XXXXXXX, Georgetown, George Washington University, and American University offices. He recently spent two years performing foreign intelligence operations in Beijing, assessing XXXX, XXXX, XXXX, as well as potential security threats from Chinese philosophy students at Renmin University and China Foreign Affairs University. He is currently assigned to XXXXXXX and the George Mason University field office, where he teaches cadets history of philosophy, ethics, philosophy of law, and most vitally for the Agency, XXXXXX and XXXXX.

Karma Waltonen is a continuing lecturer in the University Writing Program at the University of California, Davis. She is the editor of *Margaret Atwood Studies*, the journal of the Margaret Atwood Society. She is also the co-author of *The Simpsons in the Classroom: Embiggening the Learning Experience with the Wisdom of Springfield* (with Denise Du Vernay) and recently edited *Margaret Atwood's Apocalypses*. Karma believes that one of the most perfect things in the world is an episode of *The Simpsons*: "The Springfield Files," combining *The Simpsons*, *The X-Files*, and Leonard Nimoy in a wonderfully cromulent way.

Andrea Zanin likes freaks and monsters. And there are plenty in London, which is where she spends her time writing, ranting, being a journalist and escaping the alien apocalypse because it only ever happens in freakin' America. Note to extraterrestrials: England would like a little probe and pillage, too!

Index

www.ingramcontent.com/pod-product-compliance
Lightning Source LLC
Jackson TN
JSHW060705190426
101040JS00035B/440

* 9 7 8 0 8 1 2 6 9 9 5 8 6 *